Haya Safari

by

H.J. Popowski

authorHOUSE®

AuthorHouse™
1663 Liberty Drive, Suite 200
Bloomington, IN 47403
www.authorhouse.com
Phone: 1-800-839-8640

This book is a work of fiction. People, places, events, and situations are the
product of the author's imagination. Any resemblance to actual persons,
living or dead, or historical events, is purely coincidental.

First published by AuthorHouse   7/21/2008

ISBN: 978-1-4343-9066-0 (e)
ISBN: 978-1-4343-9065-3 (sc)

Library of Congress Control Number: 9781434390653

Printed in the United States of America
Bloomington, Indiana

This book is printed on acid-free paper.

INTRODUCTION

Sunday, August 16, 1953
German Lloyd Liner SS Danzig
The Indian Ocean

A s I sit here in my cabin, I am reflecting on having managed to come full-circle in the second half of my life. If the beginning of this narrative seems to be a bit disjointed and taken out of its proper sequence in time, I would ask the gentle reader to indulge an old man for his use of this style to suddenly regain some thirty five years of what he thought was permanently lost. It is only in the last few days I have been reunited with these journals thought lost since 1917. They essentially tell the story, Henry Feller's story, of the years immediately preceding what is now called the First World War, and how I came to be there, and further, on how I came to be here, now, in the same place, nearly thirty six years later.

Briefly, let me explain. I had started out my writing career as a stringer for two newpapers. I came into that position through sheer dumb luck after have been hired on as a beast of burden for James (Jimmy) Hare, a professional photographer employed by the Eastman Company as a field tester of a new type of photographic film Eastman was developing to produce color images. The field test was to take place under abysmal conditions, mainly in tropical environs, Cuba and the Philippines—the thinking at the time being, if the stuff could work under those conditions, it could work anywhere. In addition to my job of carting Jimmy Hare's equipment around, I was also given the task of making certain the slug-work—that is, the captions and explanations going back to Eastman—was decipherable, Jimmy Hare having little or no grasp of any portion of the English language and its usages beyond profanity.

As it turned out, while in the Philippines at the turn of the century, Jimmy Hare and I spent time photographing the activities of Major General Arthur MacArthur's division on the island of Luzon. One of MacArthur's brigades was commanded by Brigadier General Harrison

1

Otis, who also happened to be the owner of the *Los Angeles Times* and the *Emporia Kansas Enquirer*. General Otis—who I should explain further, bore the same surname as the Military Commander of the Philippines, Major General Ewell Otis—happened to read some of my slug work on Jimmy Hare's photos and, to make a long story short, hired me as a stringer and set me up with the necessary credentials.

Jimmy Hare and I compiled all of the photos we had taken into a book, *Our Newest Territory, the Philippines* which was published shortly after I had been sent to China, and Jimmy had returned to the United States.

My experiences in China led to my next book, *To the Gates of the Forbidden City*, which was published in 1902. It was in China where I first met Paul Von Lettow-Vorbeck, at the time an artillery lieutenant in the German portion of the International Relief Force. From China I returned to the Philippines where I ended up working on my third book *The Little Colonel Who Could*, about Fred Funston's capture of the insurrection leader Emilio Aguinaldo. It was during this period I became acquainted with Douglas MacArthur, a newly minted Second Lieutenant fresh out of West Point, and with Frederick Dent Grant, the son the President Ulysses S. Grant, who had, on his first assignment after West Point, worked for my grandfather on the Union Pacific Railroad.

It was also during this time I learned I was far better off wealth-wise than I had ever dreamed of being, thanks mostly to the largesse of my grandparents and especially of my Dutch uncle, David Welsh, who had served in the Union army with both my grandfathers—had, more accurately, been their commanding officer. I discovered this happy fact through the auspices of the young man, Stefen Wilhelm, who became my lifelong friend as well as my financial advisor—just as his father and grandfather had been to my family.

In any case, I returned to the United States in 1904 to complete *The Little Colonel Who Could*, and was then sent by my publisher to observe and report on the Russo-Japanese War, resulting in another book, *Marching Thru Manchuria*. Following its completion, I took a Sabbatical of sorts to indulge myself with a steady dose of my first loves, hunting and target shooting. I allowed my best friend, and later partner, to think he had talked me into joining the South Dakota National Guard. While involved with the local company, I formed a company shooting team and we managed to win the state rifle championship, and to get soundly beaten in the national matches shortly thereafter. However, before I could only begin to prepare them for the next years' rounds of competition, my editor, Frank Harris, informed me, on extremely short notice, I had been selected to accompany the Smithsonian Safari, organized by former President Theodore Roosevelt.

I spent more than a year in East Africa and then accompanying the Roosevelts, father and son, on a tour of England and Europe. I returned home in 1910 determined to live a life of leisure and managed to do so for nearly three years, writing nothing under my own name except a short eulogy when I learned of the passing of General Arthur MacArthur. I regret to say I would not have done even *that* except for the fact General MacArthur and my Dutch Uncle, David Welsh, had both died on the same day in 1912. I wrote the MacArthur eulogy on a whim and it is written as much or more in memory of David Welsh as of the other. Unfortunately, my publisher used the little piece of writing as a pretext to cajole me back into the saddle. The dangled carrot was that this was to be the only assignment they had ever offered me wherein it was unlikely someone would take a shot at me.

It was also my typical luck this safest of all assignments ultimately put me into the middle of one of the little remembered corners of the Great War. And then, full circle nearly forty years later. With everything explained, then, I'll begin this story with the happenings suckering me out of retirement. We'll jump to what brought me back here, and then pretty-much tell the rest of it in a straight line, finishing back where we began. On a ship, in the Indian Ocean, off the coast of East Africa.

I miraculously found a copy of the first part of the eulogy in an old clippings file as I was putting the final draft of this book together and decided to include it. Mostly it had to do with David Welsh, but I'm sorry to say I haven't been able to find anything other than this excerpt. Regrettably, the rest remains lost.

From: Feller, Henry A. *Passing of an Era: The Death of Lieutenant General Arthur MacArthur*. Ryan's Magazine, March 1913. pp 23-passim.

On September 5th of last year, Lieutenant-General Arthur MacArthur, Retired, was back in Milwaukee, the city where he had joined the volunteer army fifty years before as a 17-year-old boy. Before him sat ninety aging men, the remnant of his comrades from the 24th Wisconsin Volunteers, and it was time for him to once more speak to the soldiers he had so valiantly led decades before.

Despite his illness and the oppressively humid heat, to walk to the podium, he summoned from within the same fortitude that had sustained him at Missionary Ridge. He glanced quickly again at the tattered flag on the wall behind him, a flag he dearly loved.

"Your indomitable regiment," he began in a weak but steady voice. Then suddenly added, "Boys, I don't feel very well..."

And then a hush fell over the room as Arthur MacArthur collapsed to the floor. Dr. William J. Cronyn, who had been a surgeon for the 24th Wisconsin, was the first to reach MacArthur's prostrate form. Quickly he examined the man they had all come to love and admire, then he turned to what remained of the heroes of Missionary Ridge and said, "Comrades, the general is dying."

Solemnly ninety aged veterans gathered around the frail body on the floor, reciting in unison the Lord's Prayer. When they had finished, Lieutenant-General Arthur MacArthur was dead. Captain Edwin Parsons rose to his feet and, as is recorded in the minutes of that emotional meeting, "took from the wall the battle-torn flag MacArthur had so gallantly carried, and wrapped it around the general's body..."

September 5, 1912
Office of the Vice President for Operations
The Great Northern Railroad
Minneapolis, Minnesota

David Welsh, The Colonel, sat in his large, comfortable leather chair turned toward the window of his office on the top floor of the Great Northern Building and gazed southeast out across the yards and the Mississippi River. His mind was not on any of the usual things normally occupying his day. Of course it was years since he had to worry about the day-to-day stuff of railroad operations. He now hired people who hired people to worry about those things.

Today—he had checked the calendar hanging on his office wall when he came in this morning at his usual 7:15 AM on the dot—was an important anniversary in his private life, one he had never discussed with anyone in his present circle save possibly Kevin Mahoney before he had died, and who had been there. It was the fiftieth anniversary of the little ceremony that meant more to David Welsh than any other, with the exception of the day he married Theresa Dorner.

On September 5, 1862, in a little nameless fort outside of Washington City, the men of Company H, of the 132nd Pennsylvania Volunteer Infantry had surprised their Lieutenants—probably at the instigation of the First Sergeant, Patrick Reardon—with engraved Model 1851 Foot Officer swords and scabbards. David's had been engraved with his name and rank and the Company designation and *"Herr* Boss," which was what he had been called by his workers on the Pennsylvania & Eastern, the first railroad he had ever worked for. It had been a surprise ceremony, and he and John Taylor, the other Lieutenant, had been touched and very nearly unable to speak.

The sword was his most treasured keepsake of a war long passed. *Thank God I didn't take it with me to the 190th.* When he and Mahoney had gone back to the army late in 1863, he had bought another, less ornate sword, leaving the presentation one in the dresser drawer. The plain sword had been taken from him when the 190th had been led into an ambush by a drunken staff idiot out seeking his daily share of glory. David had never bothered to try to get it back, had never even asked about it.

He rested his fringe of silver hair on the soft leather back of his chair. A little nap wouldn't be bad. He allowed himself to almost doze. *So far...So far...fifty years...more than many men's lifetimes...*way more than many of those who had stood in ranks, grinning at his and Taylor's discomfiture...*God help me, not half of them lived to the end of the nine months...not half...*

A tear ran down David's cheek. *Dear God I tried...I tried to do right by them.*

"It's alright David," John Taylor said, "you did what you could."

"Yes Sir," Pat Reardon added. "It was for the best of causes ye know...we don't mind one bit."

"You were a good man, *Herr* Boss," Rudy Seebaum chimed in. "We all knew it..."

I tried, boys, really I did...

"Yes, oh yes, my love," Theresa said sweetly. "You always did your best by all of us...Now, come. It's time to go. The others are waiting..."

"But I have so much to do...so much..."

"Leave it, my love...you've done all you can." Tess held out her hand to him, beckoning. "Come, my love...Steven is waiting."

David Welsh swung his sword onto his shoulder, carrying it the way he had for so many times a half century ago, and hurried after his wife, Theresa, the single great love of his life, and his youngest brother. They turned to him, their arms spread wide to welcome him into their embrace. They smiled at him.

Gerald Kenner, David Welsh's assistant, knocked quietly on the office door and when Mister Welsh didn't answer—he was, after all, older even than Mister Hill, the President of the Great Northern, and he was also a little hard of hearing—Kenner opened the door a crack and called softly, "Mister Welsh, Sir. It's Mister Hill on line one for you..."

David Welsh was looking out of his office window. His chair was turned away from the desk, and only the very top of his head was visible from the door. *Probably asleep,* thought Kenner, who now cleared his throat. There was still no movement as Kenner walked around the side of Mister Welsh's desk and lightly touched his arm.

David Welsh's unseeing eyes were open. He was smiling. He looked very happy.

Gerald Kenner quickly walked out of the office, closing the door behind him. When he reached his telephone, he quickly informed Mister Hill of what he had discovered, and then he followed Mister Hill's instructions, immediately calling the Company Doctor.

PROLOGUE

FROM: Henry A Feller. *HAYA SAFARI*. Anderson Publishing, Hartford 12 Conn., 1955. 1ˢᵗ Edition.

One of the best known and most commonly misquoted lines from the poet Robert Burns is the one usually cited as "The best laid plans of mice and men oft go astray." *To add further insult to injury on poor old Robby, not one person in a thousand can give the correct title of the poem the famous misquote is gleaned from:*

The actual lines go "...*The best-laid schemes o' mice an 'men / Gang aft agley, / An'lea'e us nought but grief an' pain, / For promis'd joy!*"

The lines were one of the first things I thought of when I discovered I had taken, instead of retirement, merely a short sabbatical from a career as a writer/correspondent. Even now, as I write this, some forty years after the fact—thirty-five years of which were spent in the belief writing about it at all was a forlorn hope—Robert Burns' words still bring a good deal of grief and pain, at least some of which could have been avoided if I had only allowed my editors to continue thinking I had been swallowed up by the earth. But then, there would be no one to tell the story.

If I might digress for a further moment: In 1884, when I was barely two years old, events half a world away commenced moving toward an inevitable confluence with my life and the characters in it—some of whom I had not met and others who renewed acquaintance—to become part of my life as inexorably and inevitably as the plot of some Greek tragedy. Looking back these forty years removed, I can verify this was the time, the period, and the places having the greatest impact on my life—much more so than the events so far covered in the books I had managed to have published.

Looking back with the intense focus provided by age, I now understand everything before this time and these events was mere prologue—a training program of sorts—which, though interesting in the details, prepared me for my little place in my time and indelibly marked my life.

And, oh yes—the title of the poem is *"To A Mouse, On Turning Her Up In Her Nest With The Plough,"* by Robert Burns, 1785.

So to begin.

In 1884, *Doktor* Carl Peters presented Otto von Bismarck, Chancellor of Germany, with an unwanted *fait accompli.* The portion of the eastern coast of the African continent between the great Horn of Africa and the Portuguese and French colonies—what is now Mozambique and Madagascar, and what is still called the "Swahili Coast" by most of those who live and work there—was under the nominal control of the Sultan of Zanzibar, an island some twenty-five miles to the east in the Indian Ocean. It is an area of several hundred thousand square miles of scrub thorn coastal plain, with several mountainous inland ridges dividing the territory into parcels of upland plateau stretching several hundred more miles until reaching the shores of great lakes—really inland seas—Nyasa, Tanganyika, and Victoria, dividing the continent in two.

The good *Doktor* Peters had spent many of the past months stalking through this territory, seeking out local chiefs and coming away with a myriad of treaties signed with the marks of innumerable of those tribal chiefs now swearing true allegiance to the Kaiser. These treaties Peters presented to Bismarck, who, though a sworn enemy of imperialism in general and German Imperialism in particular, saw them as an opportunity to twist the nose of the English Lion in the game of *Realpolitik* as played by the great powers in the last half of the Nineteenth Century. Through the work of *Doktor* Peters, Germany, literally overnight, and without cost, controlled an empire more than twice the size of the *Vaterland,* an empire which became known as German East Africa, or "German East" for short.

The next quarter century saw German East pass through three phases. The first decade was in the domain of the German East Africa Company, a poor German copy of the British East India Company, with the same, inevitable result. With no infrastructure and with no knowledge of place or people—other than the fact now Director Peters had once trekked through it—German East languished until it was put under the direct control of the German government. Unfortunately, however, Peters remained.

It is often used as an excuse, by way of comparison, German rule in East Africa, compared to, say, Portuguese or Belgian rule in their respective African Empires, was downright benign and benevolent. Still, Peters' administration ultimately led to the first of the great tribal revolts. In 1894, the Wahehe, who dominated the central region of the Colony, rose under their tribal leader, Mkwana. It took the German Army several years to subdue the Wahehe and several other tribes, each of which revolted against their colonial rulers in succession, culminating in the worst uprising of all, the Maji-Maji Revolt, which sprang up in the summer of 1905. The suppression of the revolt literally devastated the southern third of the Colony, both sides using scorched-earth as a practical and tactical method of holding territory. By the time the revolt was over, German East had a much smaller population and millions of acres of ruined land, and the German government had been forced to make a massive revision of its colonial policies.

Following the end of the Maji-Maji revolt, new governors were sent out by Bernhard Dernberg, the head of the newly created Colonial Office. They brought strange, idealistic reforms with them and enforced those reforms on the white and Arab populations as well as on the natives. One such idea was the colonial government was to run the Colony for benefit of the natives. Everything else gravitated from there. The natives were to be educated, paid for their labor, allowed to farm for cash crops. All of the reforms and reformers met wholesale resistance by the white settlers, who were quite used to free pressed labor, and by the Arabs, who used the natives as a bottomless pool for the slave trade flowing through Zanzibar to the Arabian Peninsula, as it had for centuries. When both Dernberg and the first of the reform governors, Albrecht von Rechenberg, were finally removed—following long and loud complaints by the white settlers—they were replaced by other, even more idealistic Progressives: *Doktor* Solf in the Colonial Office, and an anthropologist, *Doktor* Heinrich Schnee, who brought with him to the Colony an even more formidable force, his wife, *Frau* Ada Schnee.

CHAPTER ONE

Saturday, May 16, 1953
On board the NLG Liner *Bremen V*
Bound for Dar es Salaam, Tanganyika
The Red Sea

T he grand, white, 50,000-ton ship had the distinction of being the first
of the post-war passenger vessels to bear the name Bremen—although
it was actually the fifth vessel to bear the name. Completed in 1938 by the
French as the SS Pasteur, and though a bit smaller and a little less luxurious
than the competition, the British Cunard Line ships (the Queens—Mary
and Elizabeth, and soon the Elizabeth II—and the new USS America) now
plying the trans-oceanic luxury tourist trade, it was leased after the war by
the North German Lloyd (NGL) line. It was nonetheless sumptuous even
by pre-war standards set in the 1920s and 30s. The First Class passengers
occupied the upper three decks: the promenade, just below and around the
two large orange-painted funnels; the amenities deck with its pool, clay
target area, and the usual shuffle-board and dance-floor; and the First Class
Staterooms, which were actually suites.

It was unfortunate the weather had been so nasty since the vessel
boarded its last group of passengers in Naples, because everyone admitted
the Naples-to-Suez leg of the cruise was usually the most pleasant. In
this case, however, the usually placid Mediterranean had been churned
by successive storms, causing the ship to wallow along at reduced speed
and leaving a great deal of stored food unprepared and uneaten, or in the
worst cases, spewed up in fits of *mal de mer*. Even the Suez Canal had
been a problem. There had been an announcement by the Captain, due
to the unforeseen weather in the Med, the speed for vessels traversing
the canal had been reduced to just slightly higher than steerageway in
order to keep the banks of the canal from washing out.

Even once the *Bremen* steamed into the Red Sea, the weather,
though no longer stormy, was still operating against the passengers.
Now the African coastal climate kicked in and the decks were hot and

quite steamy for most of the day. Few of the First Class passengers cared to come out of their air-conditioned suites even to bask in the shade of the promenade. Those passengers who did were mostly the older tourists who didn't seem to mind the heat or the humidity. A few would even admit the warmth felt good on the old bones. So mostly the promenade deck was empty during all the sunlit hours, save for the odd septo- or octogenarians bringing their blood up to temperature on deck chairs widely spaced along both sides of the deck.

Such was the case with a pair of older German gentlemen, one obviously in his declining years and the other old enough to be approaching retirement from his obviously successful career. One didn't book First Class on NGL unless one was successful, or at least, as in the case of the numerous *Afrikaner* of one bureaucratic stripe or another, one had an upper class, heavily successful expense account commensurate with the number of words in one's job title. The German pair generally avoided contact with these bureaucrats, and the two were, if not shunned, at least left alone after they made it readily apparent they did not wish polite conversation with someone on a world-class mission—with its world-class expense vouchers—for the United Nations.

The elder of the two was probably approaching or in his eighties, and was, by all appearances, frail. His white hair was cropped close, and his tailored suit still couldn't manage to hide the fact it covered a withered frame. Walking with the aid of a cane, he nonetheless needed the younger man's assistance in getting around, sitting, rising, that sort of thing. He probably even needed the younger man to help him dress—at least that was the consensus among the UN clerks.

Every day the pair would hobble slowly to a set of deck chairs where the older man would be aided in taking a seat. The chairs were low to the deck, and the old man was in a good deal of pain as he forced his joints to bend onto the canvas. The younger man would then pull another deck chair close by and take his place. They had been doing thus since the weather had abated and the *Bremen* had entered the Suez Canal, nearly eleven days before. If any of the UN clerks had bothered to listen, he would have heard the younger man always refer to his elder as *Herr General*.

Today, however, their routine was broken by one of the Naples-boarded passengers. He was an American—you could always tell an *Amerikaner* by his shoes—and he walked down the deck, also using a cane, and then pulled up a chair directly behind *Herr General*, in spite of the frigid look given him by the younger German. The American was in his early seventies, just a shade under six feet in height, trim at about what the younger German judged as around 75 kilos—roughly 160 pounds—and impeccably groomed and dressed, except of course for the shoes. His white hair was neatly trimmed, and though it could hardly be called a mane, he was far from being bald. He lowered himself into his chair, grunting a little as he did, and gave the younger German a slightly lunatic grin in answer to his frostiness. He pulled out a copy of the Michelin Guide to Kenya-Tanganyika, and raptly studied the maps. *Ach, Mein Gott,* thought the younger German, *he's going to be with us all the way to Dar, unless we are lucky and he gets off at Mombasa.* As the American turned the pages, he began to half-whistle, very annoying, but when the younger man started to turn to tell the American intruder to please cease and desist, the older man held up his hand to stop him. In fact, *Herr General* was smiling. The younger man had never seen him smile before, and God knows, he had had very little to smile about in the last twenty years. Perhaps the smile had something to do with the tune being whistled. The American began to sing quietly, in a surprisingly strong voice:

> *Wie oft sind wir geschritten,*
> *Auf schmalem Negerpfad,*
> *Wohl durch der Wüste mitten,*
> *Wenn früh der Morgen naht...*

"Let him finish, Dieter," *Herr General* said. "I want to see if he knows all of it, or if he has forgotten more than he thinks he has."

The American knew the rest of the tune. The younger German did not, though it was obviously a march of some kind and probably German in origin. When the American came to the part that *had* to be the chorus, the American was suddenly joined by *Herr General*:

Wie lauschten wir dem Klange,
Dem altvertrauten Sange,
Der Trägen und Askari:
Haya, haya, Safari.

The words seemed to have some sort of tonic effect on *Herr General*, both soothing and animating him.

Then the American started in again, at the beginning of the tune, but now the words were definitely NOT German:
Tunakwenda, tunashinda,
Tunafuata Bwana Obersti.

And here *Herr General* again joined in:
Askari wanaendesha, Askari wanaendesha,
Tunakwenda, tunashinda,
Haya, Haya, Safari.

Then both men fell silent. There was a tear rolling down *Herr General's* cheek. He wiped his eyes with a handkerchief and put his arm on the younger German's arm, a fatherly touch for a lost son no longer there.

"He does that just to irritate me, you know," *Herr General* said to Dieter Sietman. "He was a horrible soldier, never followed orders, and never took advice. I should have had him shot when I found out he was an enemy spy." Then turning painfully in his chair, *Generalmajor* Paul Emil Von Lettow -Vorbeck extended his hand. "How are you, Heinrich? It has been a long time." To his assistant he said, "Dieter, this is *Herr* Heinrich Feller. Heinrich, this is my able assistant, Dieter Sietman, former *Leutnant Oberst* Dieter Sietman, now with the *Bundesbanc*."

Feller shook Sietman's hand and nodded to him before turning back to *Generalmajor* Von Lettow -Vorbeck. "It is a very long time, *Mein Obersti*," agreed Henry Feller, author, and independently wealthy retired publisher. He grasped Paul's hand in both of his. "A very long time indeed." Henry Feller turned to the younger German. "I fear *Mein*

Obersti is losing his memory. He forgets I was never a soldier at all—just a poor old country-boy writer, plying my trade."

If Dieter Sietman was anything at all, it was not stupid. He knew full well when he took this assignment he would be traveling with a genuine German hero, a hero who just happened to be a folk legend as well. He was on special assignment directly from the President of the *Deutsches Bundesbanc*, the German State Bank, who was under instructions directly from the Chancellor of the Federal Republic of Germany. And to hear this American, Feller, refer to *Generalmajor* Von Lettow as *Mein Oberst*—no, not German, in some other language very nearly the same—but *Mein Oberst*, meant their relationship, whatever it might be, but in any case one of true affection, went back all the way to *Herr General's* career in *Die Einer Weltkrieg*, the First World War.

In the briefing he had received from the Chancellor's staff, Dieter had learned many things about *Generalmajor* Von Lettow-Vorbeck . The *only* German army commander from the First War who had never been defeated; had, in fact, not surrendered, but had been ordered to lay down his arms by the government *after* the Armistice had been signed; the *only* German general to be given a victory parade down *Unter den Linden* upon his return to Germany; the National Hero who had commanded a *Friekorps* during the Communist troubles and had kept Hamburg from falling to the *Gottverdammt* Communists.

He had also learned *Herr General* had lost both of his sons in the last war; he had been in house arrest from 1938 until nearly the end; he had never been implicated in the 1944 von Stauffenberg bomb plot; he had openly, if quietly, loathed the Austrian Corporal, Hitler; and he had successfully opposed the Austrian Corporal in the 1920s while a member of the *Reichsstag*. All these things Dieter had been told. But he had never heard of this man Henry Feller. Of course, not much could shock Dieter Sietman after what he had seen and been a part of since 1939, and then afterward, after early 1945, in the hands of his Russian captors at various nameless places within the Workers Paradise, the Union of Soviet Socialist Republics.

Sietman had served loyally in the *Wehrmacht*, entering service in 1938 as a *Leutnant*. By 1944 he considered himself 1) damn lucky to be alive after nearly three years on the Eastern Front, and 2) damned unlucky not to be on the Western Front against the *Amis*, the Americans. He had not had a considerable amount of time to contemplate his fate, given the daily need to attempt to keep the Red Army at bay. That hadn't worked at all, and by April, 1945, close on the Oder River, and after several thousand *Katyusas*—rocket artillery projectiles—had landed on his position, then *Leutnant Oberst* Sietman found himself being pulled out of a collapsed trench-cum-bunker by a bunch of Cucumbers[1] with strange slanted eyes. At the time *Leutnant Oberst* Sietman thought his life was about to come to an abrupt end. Siberian soldiers generally didn't take prisoners.

The first Russian Soviet he had actually spoken to—that is to say, had received an understandable verbal order from—had told him, in not very good German, to hand over his paybook and climb aboard the American-built GMC six-wheel-drive truck. The Red Army officer had been wearing the red-striped shoulder boards and star of a junior lieutenant, and more ominously, the hammer, sickle and red star of the commissariat[2]. *Well,* thought Dieter, *maybe they'll wait until tonight to shoot me.*

The prisoners were all officers above the rank of major—everyone else had apparently been summarily executed. Every fourth day they were given a ration of either thin potato soup or equally thin cabbage soup. It would be nearly two years before Seitman tasted any form of meat, and on that occasion it was a very unfortunate cat that had wandered into the work camp, was dismembered and eaten raw, the bones then buried to conceal them from the guards since eating anything other than the rations generously offered by the great Workers Paradise was a capital offense.

Late in 1948 Dieter was transferred from the wherever-the-hell-it-was work camp to the infamous Lubianka Hospital[3] in Moscow. There he underwent intensive—read "painful"—interrogation for what must have been three or four months. Then he was given a cheaply made suit of clothing—a gift of the munificent Workers Paradise—put on a train, and sent back to Germany. 21 March 1949. Every imprisoned man always remembers the date of his release. It was the first time since

April 1945, Dieter Sietman could be fairly certain he would definitely be alive the following day.

In a Germany still half rubble-strewn, he was out of synchronization with time. Four years had evaporated. Where the Americans had been the enemy, now they were at the same time, both occupiers and allies. The United States Army was headquartered in the Farben Chemical Building in Frankfurt. The capitol of the Federal Republic was Bonn. Berlin was a divided city, and the Americans had kept it an open city by flying in tons of food and coal day after day after day for more than two years. Slowly, Germany—at least the western half, the half not fortunate enough to be part of the Worker's Paradise—was rebuilding and coming back to life. But the scars, physical, cultural and emotional, were going to take generations to heal, if ever.

Dieter, after regaining some of the weight lost from the enforced starvation diet, and after having extensive dental work done to repair the damage of the same diet—and a bit more damage from the interrogation—found a position with the rebuilding *Bundesbanc*, which suited his pre-war, pre-Wehrmacht credentials as a degreed and able business administrator alumnus of Wittenberg University, class of 1933. Three years into what he hoped was his lifelong career, he had risen to be the special assistant to *Herr Doktor* Friedrich Kaufman, the *Bundesbanc* President. Dieter did odd jobs for *Herr Doktor* Kaufman, jobs no one else could be trusted to do or had the hope of success of doing. Jobs like escorting the national hero Paul Von Lettow -Vorbeck back to Africa to attempt to find his old soldiers—black native soldiers, *Askaris*—from the First War, and to right an injustice. The injustice being the collapse of the Kaiser's government at the end of the first war, more than thirty years before, had precluded those soldiers of the Kaiser from being paid off. Until now.

The Chancellor was determined to go back and right all of the wrongs of the past—actual and perceived. And who better to locate those old soldiers than their old commander. The mission had been given to Dieter Sietman by the *Herr Doktor* Kaufman, who had also given him a letter of introduction explaining the purpose of the mission. And yet another letter, an extraordinary letter from a British citizen with a very German name, Meinertzhagen, urged Von Lettow-Vorbeck to go along with the scheme. After a certain amount of wheedling, Sietman managed to learn from *Herr General* Meinertzhagen had been head of British intelligence in East Africa for part of the campaign and they had become close friends after the war.

All of this ran through Dieter Sietman's mind as he patiently waited for *Herr General* to add information beyond his brief introduction of this American. What he was not expecting, and what shocked him, was to have the American address him.

"*Vie gehts, Herr Sietman*—how goes it, Mister Sietman—I believe we have some mutual friends."

The befuddled look on Dieter's face caused Paul Von Lettow-Vorbeck to tip his head back and roar out a deep, resonant laugh. "Watch out for this man, Dieter," he laughed, "he is much, much brighter than he lets on."

"I'm at a loss," Dieter stammered.

Feller sported the lunatic grin again. "You know of *Herr Doktor* Kaufman's friend, Stefen Wilhelm of the Morgan Bank?"

"Of course. But I've never had the pleasure…"

"Well, I was in Coral Gables at Slim's place—that's Stefen's nickname, by the way, 'Slim'—just before I flew to Naples, and he told me about this affair, this mission, whatever you wish to call it. He thought I might like to tag along, being as how I'm pretty much on the political shit-list at home, since I, that is, since my money backed the wrong horse before the election last year. He figured it would behoove me to take an extended vacation—something about making the sycophants around Eisenhower and the loony lefties around Stevenson breathe a little easier when they didn't have to be looking over their shoulders all the time to make sure my magazines weren't getting ready to kick them in the ass for doing something stupider, or more venal, than usual."

"You know about the mission?"

"Of course I do. And I agree with it wholeheartedly. That's why I'm riding on this damned slow-ass boat, when I could've flown into Tanganyika three weeks ago. That's something you can take back to Doctor Kaufman, Dieter, is it? Or do you prefer *Herr* Sietman?"

Dieter waved his hand, signifying either address would be fine with him, and Feller continued. "Tell him to get his money out of the passenger boat business and into airlines. It's where the growth is going to be for the foreseeable future. Lufthansa looks good, but so does Sabena, and El Al is going to be right in there. Or if he prefers, Boeing—they're going to have an operational *jet* airliner in a couple of years, in the test phase right now..."

Paul Von Lettow-Vorbeck's laugh stopped Feller in mid discourse. "I'd listen to him, Dieter," Von Lettow-Vorbeck said. "It's how he made his money."

"Bullshit, *Mein Obersti*, I made my money the easy way—I inherited it. Then I used *that* money to make me a hell of a lot more money by letting the Wilhelm family, *pere et fils*, handle it, as they have for damned near a hundred years. And very well, I'll have you know."

"A hundred years?" Dieter put in, sounding skeptical.

"Yes, since before the Civil War, starting with my Grandfathers— both of them, the Irish one and the German one."

"Ah," Von Lettow-Vorbeck said, "I remember your telling, the *Feldwebel*—the Senior Sergeant."

"Actually, one ended up as a Sergeant Major, *Unterofficier*, I think you'd call it. And the other, the Irish one, was commissioned and ended up as a *Hauptman*—Captain."

"And I seem to recall you also did very well in publishing for a number of years," Von Lettow-Vorbeck said.

"You know I did. I published at least the North American editions of two of your books, plus most of the Division histories of the A.E.F. after the First War."

"And you still publish?" Von Lettow-Vorbeck asked, before Sietman could.

"I started in again after the last war and did a few." Feller sighed deeply. "To tell the truth, when I started to do the *History of the 35th (Santa Fe) Infantry Division* I just lost interest. I sold my half of the business—except for the magazines, of course—to my partner and retired." Henry Feller shrugged absently, as though he were shifting a heavy weight on his shoulders.

"Was the 35th your son's division?" Von Lettow-Vorbeck asked softly.

"Yes. It was."

"Henry lost his son in the war." Von Lettow-Vorbeck explained to Sietman.

Feller exhaled a long breath. "He was an Infantry Captain, had a company in the 320th Infantry. He was killed in Normandy in August of '44."

"I am so sorry," Von Lettow-Vorbeck said.

"And I too" Sietman added.

"Meinhartzhagen lost his son too." Feller said. "Took it pretty hard."

"Well in any case you did very well by me. Thank you very much." Paul Von Lettow-Vorbeck was obviously trying to change the subject to something more pleasant. He most certainly did not want to talk of his own dead sons—one on the Eastern Front and the other in North Africa. And he knew Sietman did not wish to speak of the three brothers he had lost—a U-boat *Kapitan Leutnant*, a Me-110 pilot, and a *Panzer Jaeger*. Everyone in Germany had lost someone, and one just didn't wish to dredge up the painful memories. *Mein Gott in Himmel*, ten percent of the population had been killed in the war. One person in ten. Men, women, children. Gone.

It was Feller's turn to force a laugh. "You sound just like a New York cab driver right after he gets a tip smaller than he thought he earned. You're lucky I was smart enough not to send you all of your royalties. I held enough back so when old Adolph Hitler, your most gracious *Fuehrer*—Mister Schnickelgruber to us—tried to starve you to death, I could claim you had earned those American dollars prior to his ban on foreign currency, and Mister Schnickelgruber didn't care to contest it."

Dieter Sietman looked askance at Feller.

"Don't look so bemused, Sietman. While you were off fighting *fur Vaterland und Erbe*—Fatherland and Honor—against the Godless Communists, the Oberst here was in house arrest. Even Mister Schnickelgruber couldn't take the chance of throwing him into a concentration camp. He was a National Hero, for God sake—

systematically..." Feller was visibly searching for the right words, "proscribed, in the old *Junker* meaning of the term, by your *kleine Ostreichische Gefreiter*—little Austrian Corporal. The only reason he wasn't successfully starved to death was two of his First War friends got together and found a way to indirectly send him the funds to stay alive."

"You mean Mister Meinertzhagen?"

"Indeed. Colonel Sir Richard Meinertzhagen OBE, writer, raconteur, helluva good ornithologist...or all of the above at once, depending on his mood."

"You've seen Richard?" Von Lettow-Vorbeck asked.

"Not since '50," Henry thought for a moment, August of '50. We met in New York at some bullshit writer's conference."

Paul Von Lettow-Vorbeck again chuckled. "You've always had a way with words, Henry."

"*Mein Oberst!*, as I've grown older, my tolerance for fools and idiots has diminished proportionately, to the point where I now don't tolerate them at all. Like my Grandpa taught me, I don't even bother to telegraph them a warning any more. I just kick them in the ass. With the spoken and written word mostly, but occasionally with a well-placed size-eleven brogan."

Von Lettow-Vorbeck chortled.

"Fascinating," said Dieter Sietman.

"So, how do you plan to find your *Askaris?*" Feller asked, turning the page on their conversation.

Von Lettow-Vorbeck and Sietman looked at each other, and then both looked at Feller. "We were just discussing it. Do you have any ideas?" Sietman asked.

Feller again took time to think about his answer, nodded to himself and then said, "A couple. Let me think it through some more and maybe we can talk about it over dinner."

CHAPTER TWO

Sunday, May 17, 1953
On board the NGL Liner *Bremen V*
Bound for Dar es Salaam, Tanganyika
The Red Sea

Another day further south, the temperature was perceptibly warmer and the humidity higher as the three elders gathered their deck chairs in the shade of the promenade deck awning keeping the painfully bright early afternoon sun at bay. They had passed a pleasant two-hour, seven-course midday meal at the Captain's table, chatting with the Officers of the Bremen, most of whom had served during the war with the Kriegsmarine—the naval branch of the Wehrmacht, the German Armed Forces. Feller noted there were no U-boat veterans in the group, but understanding why, he chose to remain silent. His youngest son, Otis, now a newly frocked Methodist-Episcopal minister—Tufts 1952—had been a sonarman on the USS Amick (DE-168) doing anti-submarine duty during the war. This is why he held his tongue and nodded knowingly as the former enemies told their war stories.

Feller was surprised when Sietman, the Bundesbanc's man, asked after his other sons before they were seated at the Captain's table. It meant Sietman had access to and had spent time on the ship's radio-telephone talking to the Chancellery.

Dieter had, in fact, been on the radio for over two hours, and now knew far more about Mister Henry August Feller—his background, his politics, his money, and his family than he really cared to know, but nonetheless found "interesting." Once he had been briefed on the fundamentals, it had not surprised him Henry Feller, if not considered immensely wealthy—as in Rothschild or Du Pont wealthy—was, as they say, "comfortable." His two surviving sons were doing well in careers of their own, one a minister of one of the *evangelische*—Protestant—sects; the other a college professor at a small school with a strange name no one in the chancellery had ever heard of, Shimer College, somewhere in the Midwest. They were going to look it up.

And neither had Feller been completely honest about selling out his business and retiring. Yes, he had, in fact, sold the publishing company he had founded along with a partner, "Dodger" Anderson—what a prosaic name—who, it was noted, was of late often confined to a wheel-chair, reason unknown. Again, they would look into it. He had also nearly told the truth about inheriting his money. Almost. It had originally been a gift of some sort, mostly in stocks and other equities, before the turn of the last century, held in trust for him in several accounts by the Wilhelm family, who were now associated with the Morgan Bank of New York. His money had amounted to a healthy share of three major American railroads, even before he used some to capitalize the publishing business.

The publishing company had amplified his wealth greatly when he had published one after another photographic histories of all of the American Divisions serving in the First War. He had gone on to publish the North American editions of other works, including *Herr* General Von Lettow-Vorbeck's books, and also the bird books authored by this British Meinertzhagen fellow. And strangely enough, he was now known to be involved in a search for an extant copy of *Herr* General Von Lettow-Vorbeck's father's six-volume study of the Austro-Prussian War of 1866, perhaps only because when you have the money, you can do whatever damned well pleases you.

In addition, *Herr* Feller still owned and published a core of various magazines covering several subjects in different genres, hunting and shooting, baseball, and science fiction and fantasy (which was growing increasingly popular) and politics. Politically, Feller was staunchly conservative. He had been the primary money behind former General of the Army Douglas MacArthur's failed bid for the Republican nomination for President of the United States in 1952. When Sietman heard this he thought *Ah, that is what he meant about being on the shit list and having to lay low for a while.*

The MacArthur link interested Sietman most of all, and so he had waited, tying up the ship's radio-telephone an additional half-hour to get an answer of sorts. Feller and MacArthur had both served for a time in the same Division in the First War. This didn't seem like much of a reason to Dieter Sietman, however, at least not enough of a reason to gladly hand over several million American dollars—the report estimated 16.8 millions of dollars—on the odd chance it could buy a political opportunity to lose an election. But, he confessed to himself, stranger things had happened. He would try to find out more without being too overt.

Or at least not too obviously covert, remembering, as he had been told by *Herr General*, Feller was far brighter than he let on. In fact, Feller's affectation of a country-bumpkin manner was just a well-thought-out, and well directed affectation, planned to put one at ease and open. Von Lettow-Vorbeck knew it, and it was possibly why he had warned Sietman? Or he didn't want Sietman to make an ass of himself in front of a person for whom *Herr General* felt a great deal of affection. In any case, all of Sietman's machinations were immediately dashed as they took their seats.

"Dieter spent most of last night on the radio to Bonn finding out what *Der Konrad's* Intelligence Service had in your file," Von Lettow-Vorbeck said. *Der Konrad* was the commonly used nickname for Konrad Adenauer, the Chancellor of the Federal German Republic, then just beginning to be called "West" Germany.

Feller blinked, but his face didn't change expression as he looked at Sietman. "I'm honored the Chancellor's people would have a file on me at all," he said, casting a benign, though intense, stare at Dieter. "Anything in it worth knowing about? Color of my underwear, sexual peccadilloes, number of white parents—that sort of thing?"

So much for subtlety, thought Sietman. *What the hell, as the Americans say, when in doubt tell the truth.* "Mostly you haven't been completely honest, probably for your own reasons." Dieter answered. "What I found most interesting was your link to General MacArthur."

"Now *that* I, too, find interesting," Von Lettow-Vorbeck added. "I didn't know you ran in those circles, Henry."

"I try not to run in circles at all, *Mein Obersti*," Feller said. "I try to be one direct son of a bitch."

"Like now, correct?" Dieter asked.

Feller snorted, thinking *Sietman's not lacking in the brains department either. Then again, I wouldn't think Adenauer or Kaufman would suffer a fool any quicker than I would.* "I've known Douglas… General… MacArthur since in the Philippines when he was a fresh-out-of-West-Point Second John—American Army shorthand for Lieutenant, and I was a wide-eyed and bushy-tailed war correspondent for *Ryan's Magazine* and stringing for a couple of newspapers on my second assignment. Hells bells, I knew his father, General Arthur MacArthur, from the first time I was there, in the Philippines, right before I went off—was sent off—to China. My first independent assignment." He looked quickly at Sietman. "You might make a note for my file, Dieter, China is also where I met *Mein Obersti*, here, for the first time. We were both in the International Relief Force. But where the hell was I? Oh yeah, the Philippines, for the second time. And Douglas and I crossed tracks on occasion. We struck it off right away, especially after we found out we were both pursuing the same sloe-eyed, raven-haired Filipina opera singer."

"Who won?" Von Lettow-Vorbeck laughed.

"Why, I did, of course, *Mein Obersti*. Otherwise, I wouldn't bring it up. Even young, innocent correspondents have more money to burn on pretty ladies than new Second Lieutenants. Then we met again in Manchuria, right at the end of *that* war, and again a few years later when he was doing some engineering around Minneapolis. Not a very happy occasion then. I was in town to visit a grave and he had just lost his father."

"I thought you and General MacArthur served in the army together?" Sietman said.

"Oh, we did, later, in the First War, after I left the company of *Mein Obersti* here, and under less than usual circumstances, I might add. I managed to not get shot or eaten by two legged or four legged carnivores, and was bundled off by recently former enemies to "jolly old Blighty," as Dick Meinertzhagen always calls it. Made it all the way to London, as a matter of fact, where I was immediately put under arrest by the American Expeditionary Force's Military Police and escorted forthwith to France, to explain to one of General Pershing's minions, as well as Colonel MacArthur and others, why I hadn't reported as ordered when my National Guard unit had been called up. And well, evidently Douglas believed me when all the others thought I was just some babbling lunatic ranting about some unknown campaign in far off darkest Africa."

Von Lettow-Vorbeck cocked his head. "You've never once mentioned any of this, Henry. Not once, in all those years."

"I never thought it was germane to the issue, *Mein Obersti*. It was a different war than the one we were together in."

"So you and MacArthur were together until the Armistice?" Sietman asked.

"No. I took a little gas and a machinegun slug through the rib-cage on the first day of the St Miheil fight. Nothing overly serious, but enough to get me sent to the hospital long enough to miss the rest of the war. Then we were together for a couple of months on Occupation duty, chasing *Fräuleins*—young ladies who we weren't supposed to fraternize with. And then we were on the same boat going home, Douglas going on to West Point. Of course we didn't associate much in public because he was a Brigadier General and I was a lowly First Lieutenant. The rest, as they say, is history."

CHAPTER THREE

May 19, 1953
On board the NLG Liner *Bremen V*
Bound for Dar es Salaam, Tanganyika
The Red Sea

Feller couldn't remember exactly how the day and its challenge had started, but he surmised Paul Von Lettow-Vorbeck was probably trying to prove something to Dieter Sietman. *Just what remained obscure, though Feller figured if he went along with the program, eventually he would understand Paul's game. So far as he remembered, the challenge had begun at the noon luncheon. Evidently someone had talked privately to the ship's officers, and so they were now avoiding telling their usual war stories. They had either gotten the word the talk was bringing back unpleasant memories for Paul—and parenthetically, for Henry—or they did not like being reminded they had lost, and badly. And every time they looked at Feller they had to instantly rethink a decade and a half of master race bullshit by realizing this old, inoffensive-looking American represented the people who had literally kicked their ass, twice. So talk turned to other things warriors liked to talk about. And on this particular day the subject had been hunting and shooting in general. This was soon followed by an offer to use the fantail facilities, the clay pigeon traps, which in quick order amounted to some seventy-year-old little boys essentially saying "I can shoot better than you can." Now it was time to put up or shut up.*

Not surprisingly, Von Lettow-Vorbeck, Feller and Sietman had all brought shotguns along. After all, Von Lettow-Vorbeck and Feller had survived by way of their ability to take game in Africa—in Feller's case, twice. Sietman had been a shooter since the early 1930s, beginning with air rifles and rimfires while still under the restrictions of the Versailles Treaty, and finally with full-power rifles and shotguns.

Von Lettow-Vorbeck unsnapped the leather case, revealing an absolutely superb Austrian-made skeet set with two differently sized breeches and stocks of marvelously figured walnut and multiple barrels,

28

"I'm too old to take the recoil anymore. I think I'll shoot the 28-gauge today."

Feller gestured grandly and said, "Your option," as he pulled his Winchester Model 12 pump 12-gauge out of his case.

Von Lettow-Vorbeck looked at Feller over his shooting glasses. "Henry, you're not using your double 12 bore?"

"I don't have it any more. I traded it for a *Gewehr* 98. I'm surprised you've forgotten. And of course my Winchester 95 .405, the one I gave as a wedding present to one of our mutual friends is also somewhere in darkest Africa. If it still exists."

Von Lettow-Vorbeck said nothing, simply raising an eyebrow, questioning. Sietman, overhearing the conversation, was only slightly at a loss.

"You kept your pistol though?" Paul asked.

Henry nodded. "It's in my trunk. I hope Tanganyika isn't as fussy about pistols as England—or at least they can be bribed more easily."

"There shouldn't be any problem," Sietman said.

"Good. It wouldn't do to have a representative of *Der Konrad* arrested for possession of illegal arms." Von Lettow-Vorbeck added.

"Is that what I am now? A representative of the Chancellor of West Germany?"

"But, of course."

"Hmmf. Well, better that than a member of the Democratic National Committee."

Feller's remark left both Von Lettow-Vorbeck and Sietman looking vaguely uncomfortable for their ignorance of what they assumed were the intricacies of American politics.

Following the old principle the junior man goes first, each of them took a pair of test birds. Feller was surprised when he saw Sietman heft what looked very much like a Browning. Seeing Feller looking, Sietman stepped to him and showed him the shotgun saying "It's made in Belgium on a Browning license. I think you would call it an Auto-5."

Feller nodded as Von Lettow-Vorbeck broke his test birds. Then, before Feller stepped to the line, he looked back over his shoulder and asked Von Lettow-Vorbeck, "International Rules?" Von Lettow-Vorbeck in turn looked to Sietman, who nodded. And Feller spoke loudly to the sailors manning the traps, "International Rules, *bitte*," and a moment later, "Pull" the butt of his Winchester resting lightly on his side at his belt-line. Two clay birds suddenly emerged from the traps traveling in diverging directions. In a hard to follow blur, Feller shouldered his gun and fired, breaking the first bird as he jacked the slide to chamber a second shell, all the while swinging the muzzle through the arc of the second bird and firing as he pulled slightly ahead. The second bird shattered with a gratifying puff of dust.

"Yeah, that'll work," he said as he worked the slide to open the action. Turning back to his companions, he said, "OK, Sietman. You're up first. Want to make it interesting?" Feller asked benignly.

"How so?" Von Lettow-Vorbeck asked back.

"Dollar a bird?"

Again the look to Sietman. Again the nod as Sietman took his position and called "Pull." Feller swore he could hear the Browning, or FN, or whatever it was now called, go kerchuncketa-kerchunketa as it cycled through its shots. And he refrained from saying, back home they had always called the Browning the corn-sheller, because both made similar sounds when they were at work.

After finally missing the thirty-second thrown clay pigeon, Sietman recased his Browning. Feller and Von Lettow-Vorbeck continued until Von Lettow-Vorbeck finally missed the second bird of the thirty-fourth pair and after Feller cleaned his shots. Feller collected his one-hundred and twenty-eight dollars from Von Lettow-Vorbeck and Sietman and put the folded money in his trouser pocket. Then he checked his Winchester to make certain it was unloaded before putting it back in the case.

"Quite good shooting, *Herr* Feller" Sietman said. "Wherever did you learn to shoot like that?"

"Promise you won't tell?"

"But of course."

Feller looked around very theatrically, and then in a low whisper only Sietman and Von Lettow-Vorbeck could hear, said, "My mother."

"Who?" Von Lettow-Vorbeck blurted.

"My mother. She was the best wing shot I've ever seen in my life. In all the years I was growing up, I never saw her miss a shot on a flying bird of any kind. She bought herself a little side-by-side exposed-hammer sixteen-gauge with her egg money when I was about five years old 'cause she said she didn't like to be hammered by the recoil from my dad's ten bore. She was absolutely deadly with her little sixteen. And she taught me how to shoot it when I was about seven or eight. And it stuck."

"Well, in any case," Sietman said, "very fine shooting."

"You really mean 'good shooting for an old fart who hasn't shot much in the last few years," Feller grinned, snapping his shotgun case shut.

Von Lettow-Vorbeck laughed. "And how many 'few years' is that Heinrich?"

"Last time I shot at the Grand National—in the thriving metropolis of Vandalia, Ohio, by the way—was in '48. I didn't win, place, or show. I only managed to clean 92 birds, but those were with American Rules, one at a time, gun shouldered. I think the winner went something on the order of two-hundred or two-twenty, something like that. That's when I figured I was getting too long in the tooth for competition and gave it up. Same thing had happened in the '30s for pistol and rifle— couldn't even see the damned thousand yard target anymore. Eyes just got too bad, so I quit that too. But it was lots of fun while it lasted. And occasionally I can still string a few together." Feller grinned, again.

They sauntered back to their regular places on the promenade deck and, after giving their gun cases to a steward to take to their staterooms, Feller ordered a bottle of Islay whiskey and appurtenances to be brought them. He poured each of them a portion and added a single ice cube. "Absent comrades" he said raising his glass to them as they touched their glasses to his. "Thank you for the excellent whiskey, Paul, Dieter."

After settling himself onto one of the cushioned armchairs, Feller said, "Now, let me tell you a story of some *real* shooting I was witness to, back when I could still see to shoot. In fact, it was right before Mary Evelyn and I got married. Sort of a last bachelor fling. Anyway, we went to the National Matches at Camp Perry. I'd been going there off and on since aught-eight or –nine. I was hanging out with a couple of shooters from the Marine Rifle team—they won the United Service Trophy as I recall—so, I was standing around with Mike Edson and a kid named Culver, watching as some of the individual shooters were checking in. Sort of as an aside, and for your general fund of information, Sietman, Mike Edson commanded one of the Marine Raider Battalions in the Pacific and retired as a Major-General in '47. I got to know him even better when he worked on editing the Marine Brigade part of the book I published about the 2nd Division in the First War—1926, '27, somewhere in there.

"Where the hell was I? Oh, yeah, we're standing there and this guy checks in. Six feet tall, long in the tooth, he's wearing a khaki shirt and dungarees and a black slouch hat. He was sixty-two years old and everyone immediately began calling him 'Old Dad.'" Feller chuckled. "His name was George Farr. He said he was from Washington, the state, not the city, and had been sent by the Washington Rifle and Revolver Club team. He hadn't even brought a rifle, so Ordnance issued him one of the National Match Springfield '03s, and since he hadn't brought any ammunition either, they issued him some National Match Ball ammo from Frankford Arsenal. He was so late signing in he got put on the last relay, so he never even started to shoot until about 4:30 in the afternoon. His scope was one side of a pair of opera glasses he had cut down... A real hick from the sticks...

"Now before 1922 all the matches were of the 'shoot until you miss' variety. Everyone in a relay was issued 22 rounds by the scorer behind their position on the firing line—two sighting shots and twenty for record. Old Dad goes out to his place, and digs a pair of reading glasses out of his shirt pocket, gets down on the ground, and scrounges around until he finds his record book from back in Washington and an O'Hare Sight Micrometer, probably about thirty years old. Old Dad's first sighter shot goes into the 3-ring—in the black but not dead center; dead-center being a twenty-inch circle in the thirty-six inch black. The center of the bullseye, at 1,000 yards is the 5-ring. But that seemed to suit him 'cause he squirmed around some and then he loads a whole clip of five rounds, instead of shooting one at a time. One sighting shot was all he ever took.

The next twenty-one were in the five ring. Up he gets and goes to leave the line and the scorer asks him where the hell he's going and he says he'd fired all the cartridges he'd been given so he figured he was done. The scorer hands him twenty more and tells him he's supposed to shoot until he misses. So Old Dad gets back down and squirms around some more and loads another five round clip, and another, and another, and another. By this time he has quite a crowd gathered around him, and the scorer keeps feeding him ammunition and he keeps plunking them in the bullseye.

"Oh, yeah…he used up all the Match ammunition on the line after about fifty shots. It took them a while to scrounge up some more and by then it was nearly too dark to see the target. He'd been shooting for damned near two hours steady. He finally had to quit because nobody could see any more. He had put *seventy-one* consecutive bullets in the 5-ring, with an issue rifle and issue ammunition and iron sights. So far as I know, *no one* has ever managed to do it again.

"The real pisser is he didn't win the match. A Marine Sergeant named Johnny Adkins—one of Mike Edson's shooters—had 76 bullseyes but he'd used commercial match ammunition and a scope-sighted Springfield to do it. And Old Dad would have probably beaten him if Old Dad hadn't run out of light."

"Whatever happened to him?" Von Lettow-Vorbeck asked.

"Don't know—we took up a collection for him and bought him his rifle, and I went around to the other state teams and we kicked in enough money to have an engraved plate put on the butt. And the next year the NRA started giving out the Farr Trophy to the highest score with an iron-sighted service rifle. I think Old Dad died sometime in the thirties. He'd have been seventy-something by then. All in all it was just an oddity, something I was lucky enough to have been around for."

Von Lettow-Vorbeck nodded, understanding.

"Now you can answer a question I've had," Feller said.

"And what would that be, my friend?"

"Why did we just play out this little contest?"

Von Lettow-Vorbeck looked at Feller for several seconds, trying to decide on his next words. "Mostly to show Dieter, who I sometimes feel doubts my complete veracity but is too much a proper gentleman to say he thinks I am, how do you say it, 'full of shit.' That's one of the reasons."

Feller glanced at Sietman whose face was showing half a wry grin while trying to conceal he was aghast at *Herr General's* crudity.

"And another?" Henry asked.

"I think Dieter will agree. When you were telling your little parenthetical story, it was as though I were reading one of your books. You are your style. You write as you think. And now, I think Dieter finally realizes your memory is quite remarkable, provided the subject interests you."

"My memory, memories, are not what they used to be."

"Nevertheless, I could not hope to choose anyone better to tell the story of what happened here..." Von Lettow-Vorbeck motioned to the south, toward Tanganyika, "so many years ago."

"Unfortunately, the hard evidence, my journals, are probably fertilizing a very nice crop of corn or somesuch, in the middle of nowhere."

"Possibly..."

"Why, *Mein Obersti*, do you know something about my journals I do not?"

"Only that you gave them to one of the few men who might actually have been able to save them."

"Jabari?"

"Yes. Jabari."

"Who is this Jabari?" Dieter asked, interrupting.

"He was my orderly," Paul Von Lettow-Vorbeck said.

"He was my friend." Henry Feller added quietly

"And why would he do that?" Sietman continued.

"Because Henry asked him to," Von Lettow-Vorbeck answered. "And because he was Heinrich's brother-in-law," Paul added before holding up his hand to cut off further interruption.

"I repeat, *Mein Obersti*, do you know something I do not? Because the last I saw him, or them, they were in a cloth bag carried by a *ruga-ruga* as he helped Jabari stagger off into the Bundu," Henry said.

"I know only that Jabari survived—at least until 1919."

"You saw him after the surrender?"

Paul Von Lettow-Vorbeck stiffened. "*We never surrendered.* No, he came back to duty after his wound healed. After we lay down our arms, in Rhodesia, the British sent us up the lakes to the western end of the Lunatic Line, and from there to Mombasa and a ship to Germany. We never went back into German East. They sent the *Askaris* overland. I never saw Jabari again. But as you told him to keep your journals safe, he would have died trying, and so would his family. Of that you can be sure. You should know that. They are, or were, Wahehe."

"And are you?" Feller asked.

"Which, my friend? Certain of Jabari, the Wahehe, his family? Or 'full of shit'? No, I think even Doubting Dieter here is now sure you have proved you are everything I've told him you were."

Feller snorted at the oblique answer. "Well, on that pleasant note, I think I'll be off to bed. Before Doubting Dieter—I like it, it has a Biblical ring to it—wants to see me walk on water and I drown." Feller rose and walked to the companionway door, where he turned back to face them. "See you in the morning, Dieter, *Mein Obersti.*"

"*Gute Nacht, Heinrich.*" Von Lettow-Vorbeck and Sietman answered.

CHAPTER FOUR

May 20, 1953
On board the Union Castle Liner *Rhodesia Castle*
Bound for Dar es Salaam, Tanganyika

They were a day out of Dar es Salaam, having spent the day before at Mombasa, Kenya, trading passengers and cargo into the Union Castle liner that would take them on the last leg of their journey. Now it was just a matter of hours until they arrived and could then begin to try to find the equally aging survivors of a war nearly forty years past.

The evening meal at the Captain's table, brought another long, sad retelling of more war stories—made all the more bittersweet because the British officers couldn't care less whether the Germans and Americans were offended by the fact it was England, after all, who had really won the bloody war. The three sat around a small table on the promenade deck. The sunset was less than spectacular, blotched with clouds and obscured by haze. They were dressed casually, Henry wearing a zippered jacket because the evening was chilling—at least compared to the afternoons—while Paul and Dieter wore sports jackets, the pockets bearing embroidered crests Henry assumed were of their respective universities. On a closer look, however, he realized Paul's pocket patch was, as far as he could remember, the insignia of the *Schutztruppen. We all have our little keepsakes*, he thought, remembering the small pieces of wool felt in the jewelry box at home. There, nestled amid the various outdated tie-clasps, cufflinks, collar stays, and shirt studs, were his Lieutenant's bars, two sets, one gold and one silver, and his crossed rifles and national eagles. There too were his ribbons, the Victory Medal, the Army of Occupation, the Distinguished Service Cross, and the Purple Heart. And under it all the curved red, blue, and yellow patch of the Rainbow, the 42d Division. Like Paul Von Lettow-Vorbeck, he had never been able to bring himself to throw the stuff away. And he knew Dodger still had his, too.

As they sat, smoking their cigars and sipping at snifters of after-dinner brandy, Henry felt a palpable reluctance to talk about the last war emanating from Paul and Dieter. They had come to know one another very well indeed in the days of this voyage, and, with Henry and Paul's renewed friendship through close contact, there was very little they could not say, especially through the pain of their experiences and losses.

Henry settled back in his chair and put his snifter down on the table. He was about to speak, thought better of it, but then considered the time and place and decided there would be no better time than now. "You know, the very saddest part of it all, is it could have been completely avoided."

"What's that? Paul asked.

"The last forty years. One small change—well, not small if you think it through—and it could have all been avoided."

"And what would the change have been?" asked Dieter.

Henry grinned ruefully,

"America should have sided with Germany in the First War."

"You make it sound very easy," Dieter said.

"Oh, it would *not* have been easy, but it *would* have been *possible*. Remember what a large percentage of our population at the time was German or Irish and thereby profoundly anti-English. Until about the middle of the war, that is. And it would have spared the world two massive cataclysms, Communism and its handmaiden, Nazism."

Dieter and Paul both gave Henry looks of great skepticism.

"I am not drunk, regardless of what you might think," Henry continued. "That's why I stopped and thought about it before I even brought this up. I realized at dinner the greatest thing all of us share from the last war is the loss. My son, Paul's sons, your family, Dieter, Richard's son. Their deaths were all unnecessary. They could all still be alive and vital and productive, if only America had taken the right course, the *other* course. Instead, they were all led down a primrose path. It *sounded* oh so very good, but in the long run it proved to be both morally and mentally arid.

"How so?" Paul asked.

"If the United States would have sided with Germany," Henry answered. "To hell with Austro-Hungary, they were essentially a non-entity in any case, the war wouldn't have lasted through 1916. Germany wouldn't have been blockaded and starved, for one, because the British Navy would have had to fight the second largest modern navy on one side of the island and the third largest on the other. So in all probability Germany wouldn't have *needed* to conduct the U-Boat war. And Germany would have had an ally producing ten times the raw materials as the Central Powers and Allies *combined*. There would have been no shortages of steel, coal, iron ore, production capacity or manpower. Germany would have won the war in 1916, as they damned-near did anyway. The Allies only held on by the skin of their teeth until the Americans arrived—and only just. Hell, the French army *mutinied* in 1917 for Chrissake. It was the best kept secret of the war."

Both Paul and Dieter looked at one another. It was the first time they had ever heard of the French mutinies spoken of openly. There had been rumors of course, but the records were simply not made available by the Allies post-war. "You are certain of this, Heinrich?" Paul asked. When Henry nodded, Paul and Dieter exchanged glances.

Henry noticed the looks and the eye contact between his companions and forged ahead before they could sidetrack his discourse. "And Germany wouldn't have had to send Mr. Lenin back to Russia to try to knock it out of the war by a revolution," he continued. There would probably have been one, 'cause the Czar was just too damn dumb to prevent it, but it would not have been taken over by the Bolsheviks. In other words, no Lenin, no Stalin, no Iron Curtain, no purges, no Berlin Air Lift, no Korean Police Action still going on.

"And take it still further—if Germany had won the war, there would have been no Versailles or Lucarno treaties. There would have been no need for *Friekorps*, because there would have been no communist uprising in 1919-1920. And there would have been no oppressive indemnities, no trade restrictions, no military occupation, no Weimar Republic, no Polish Corridor. In other words, my friends, no reason for someone as evil as Hitler to try to take power. *Ergo* no Hitler and Stalin. *Ergo*, no World War Two.

"Accept the basic premise, and because Germany and the United States both had considerable interest in the Pacific, they would have presented a solid front against Japan—and China. Without a war to fight the Japanese invaders to make him famous, Mao Tse Tung—or as we call him, Mousey Dung—would have never amounted to more than another half-assed Chinese bandit. Because the Germans and the Americans would probably have sided with Chiang or someone like him through sheer self-interest. And a good little one can't beat a good big one most times."

"You make a good case," Paul said soberly.

"So where did America go wrong?" Dieter asked.

"You mean other than reacting to the unconditional U-Boat war?" Henry asked.

"Yes," Dieter said. "I believe I recall way back at the beginning of this rhetorical study, you said it would not have been necessary."

"Since this is all hypothetical anyway," Paul added, "Let's assume there had not been a U-Boat war. So, then, Heinrich, given that, where, as Dieter asked, did America go wrong?"

"It took the easy way out. It was told flowery lies over and over until they were thought to be true. Your *Doktor* Goebbels did the same thing less than twenty years later with the same result. Hell, it started ten years and more before the war. Fella' named William Jennings Bryan ran for President in 1896 on a single plank platform that had already been flummoxed when he presented it. He was one of those 'Progressive' types, Henry put it, nearly spitting the word, a Progressive who wanted to do away with the gold standard. They wanted silver to take the place of gold—as I recall the ratio was sixteen to one, something like that— silver as the backing for the national currency! The whole thing was based on the perception not enough gold was being produced to have any sort of growth in the currency. In other words, the perception Bryan and the Democrats wanted promulgated to show gold production had declined for a quarter-century—which it had, relative to the growth in the population in America.

Paul looked askance at Dieter and found at eye contact that the younger man seemed to actually understand what Henry was talking about.

"So, if gold production was in decline," Dieter asked, "what happened to change everyone's thinking. I mean, you didn't vote against Bryan, is that right, Bryan, because he had the wrong hair color or wore a shabby suit."

"What actually happened," Henry went on, "was there were two Scotsmen living in South Africa, MacArthur and Forest, working in the mining industry. They developed the Cyanide Process which started to be used in the Rand, in, I think, 1890. Got most of this from Slim Wilhelm. Anyway, with the cyanide process, a company could extract far more gold from ore than before, and the perceived shortage simply didn't exist. And everybody who worked for a living knew it. They could see it in their earnings. They knew it was a lie. But since Bryan was a 'Progressive' Democrat and a newspaperman, and a lawyer to boot... Of course, the Progressive newspapers conveniently forgot to mention any of it. But the voters saw through that too.

"Well, Bryan hitched his horse to the silver-standard cart and went down to defeat. McKinley beat him badly in 1896. But it gave the 'Progressives' their first good practice at twisting things to appear to be what they weren't, and they've become damned good at it since.

"So your William McKinley became President and America fought the Spanish and won and became owners and operators of an empire." Paul said, adding, "Overnight."

"That's a pretty fair country one-sentence summary," Henry agreed. "But not very many people remember that, even more important than the Spanish War was that Bill McKinley was the last President from the Civil War generation. He was shot by a lunatic office seeker, and so Theodore Roosevelt, who had been shunted into the Vice-Presidency as a way to get him out of politics by the New York Republican boss, ended up as our President. Senator Hanna was supposed to have said, 'Now, that damned Cowboy is President.' Well, Roosevelt was a hell of a lot more Progressive than he was Republican. Once I got to know him personally..."

Paul saw the skeptical look on Dieter's face and interrupted again at a point he found where he could get in a word edgeways. "Henry was on President Roosevelt's safari for a year, in case you didn't know, Dieter,"

"Actually, I ran around with his son, Kermit—his middle son—more than I did with TR," Henry corrected. "Kermit and Tod Loring and I were the three youngest members on the Roosevelt Safari, so we chummed around. That's where I also first met Fred Selous, by the way. He was along on the ship going back to Africa on his own safari. Anyway, once I got to know Roosevelt personally…This is some years after I got to know William Howard Taft in the Philippines."

Taft had been sent to the Philippines by Roosevelt right after old TR had become President. They had been buddies for quite a while, started when both were junior clerks or somesuch. Anyhow, Taft was one hell of a Governor General. He did more to pacify the Philippines in six months than the army had managed in three years. Started schools and brought the Flips into the government, starting at the local level. He literally took the whole damned population in his hands and led them into citizenship."

"Ah yes," Paul said ruefully, "and everyone in the Philippines lived happily every after. I seem to recall some of the stories you told way-back-when of the things you'd seen in the islands."

"It was no paradise," Henry answered. "But neither was German East at first. Yeah, I remember the Flips and the Moros, but I remember the *kiboko*, too. And so do you.

"And since you know all of that, remember of all the colonial populations of the entire world, the Filipinos were the only ones to actively participate with their parent government against the enemy in the last war. Just like the *Askaris* in the *Schutztruppen* in German East did in the First War. The Indians, the Indonesians, Indo-Chinese were all sending reinforcements to the Japs, to fight against the Colonial Governments. The Flips, Bless their Little-Brown-Brother hearts, organized local forces against the Japs on damned near every island of the several thousand in the archipelago. And regardless of how brutal the Japs were in their retaliation, the Flips continued to resist." Henry raised his hand to cut off Dieter who was about to say something. "And, let me remind the both of you, of all the Colonial powers, the English in India and Burma and Malaya; the French in Indo-China; the Dutch in Indonesia, *only* the United States made good on its promise, a promise first made by Big Bill Taft in 1906, the Philippines would be given their independence after forty-years. On July 4th, 1946, the Philippines were granted their independence. *That's* what Big Bill Taft did. And he's *never* been given credit for it."

"And why do you say that is so?" Paul said, also holding up his hand to restrain Dieter.

"Taft has never been given credit for most of what he did before, during, and after his term as President because the Progressive types vilified him. He actually accomplished most of the things TR wanted to take credit for. And when he wouldn't be a good boy and let Teddy lead him around on a leash, Teddy went from being his best friend to being his greatest detractor in four years flat."

"How so?" Dieter finally managed to wedge in, disregarding Paul's raised fingers.

"Well, you see TR was already thinking of running for President again when he got himself out of sight—but not out of the press—by going to Africa. Then when he didn't get the nomination, he broke the Republican Party in half and formed his own party—the one the press called the Bull Moose Party—to run against both Wilson and Taft, but mostly Taft. And by doing that, he gave the country to that goddamned lily-livered Progressive buffoon, Woodrow Wilson."

Paul Von Lettow-Vorbeck chuckled at Henry's vehemence. Henry glowered. "You may think it's funny forty years after the fact," he snapped, "but if you compare what your Mister Hitler and his bunch did, and what that hatchet-faced sonofabitch Wilson did, I think you'd be more shocked than amused." Henry let that sink in before continuing.

"I don't suppose you've ever heard of George Creel, have you?"

Paul and Dieter both shrugged.

"He was the Chairman of the Committee on Public Information. He was a Wilson appointee—never had to worry about being elected or re-elected. A little, unknown Progressive bureaucrat of the finest stripe. His duty was to—and I'm quoting Newton Baker, here—'*mobilize the mind of the world. To make it a fight for the minds of men, for the conquest of their convictions…'* Now, you tell me if that doesn't sound like the same sort of bullshit that came out of your *Doktor* Goebbels."

By the looks on Paul and Dieter's faces, Henry could see he had struck a nerve. Perhaps too close to the core. Dieter managed only to ask who Newton Baker was.

"Got to know Newt when we were publishing all of the histories in the '20s, he was Wilson's Secretary of War," Henry explained before re-launching into his discourse.

"George Creel was essentially the United States Minister of Propaganda and Censorship, but he always managed to make it sound as though everything was voluntary. The newspapers wouldn't be censored because they would *voluntarily* not print things detrimental to the war effort. After, of course, Creel told them what sort of things those might be.

"I, personally, ran afoul of some of the little weasel's work when I was shanghaied back into the Army after I had left the company of *Mein Obersti*, here." Henry nodded to Paul. "My best friend just about had a shit-hemorrhage when I openly mentioned some of the things I really didn't like about Mister Wilson's administration. He literally put his hand over my mouth and told me to shut up, because what I was saying might be overheard and I could be sent to a Federal prison for a long time for uttering the truth as I saw it."

"Oh really." Paul said. Henry's statement sounded too familiar to him. Some of his experiences with the Gestapo lurked just on the edge of his mind, barely held in the shadows during his waking hours, to lurk in his dreams.

"Creel and Wilson had rammed through a law called the Espionage Act in June of '17," Henry stated flatly, "and a year later added a companion law called the Sedition Act. So my friend was absolutely correct when he shut me up. It was against the law to speak, print or otherwise express contempt for the government or the Constitution, or the flag, or the uniform, using language calculated to aid the enemy's cause, using words to favor any country to which the United States was at war, or saying anything restricting the sale of war bonds.

"But what about your famous Bill of Rights?" Dieter asked, barely able to suppress an I-told-you-so smirk.

"Dieter," Henry said furiously, "The Bill of Rights got flushed down the shitter by Mister Wilson and some of his minions. The Espionage and Sedition Acts were so fundamentally unconstitutional, they were overturned by the Supreme Court as soon as the war ended. . .in 1919. And George Creel slunk back into well-deserved obscurity, hopefully under a rock. But while it was in force, it was the law that allowed federal agents to arrest and jail thousands of citizens, among them Eugene V. Debbs, the socialist candidate for President; Big Bill Haywood of the Wobblies—the Industrial Workers of the World, or the I.W.W., or the 'I Won't Work, depending on your point of view. There were even provisions in the goddamned laws to make it a capital offense to disagree with that sonuvabitch Wilson. To be honest, just talking about it still pisses me off, after nearly forty years."

"To be honest," Paul said, "they sound like the same sort of social dregs we fought in the *Freikorps.*"

"Pretty much," Henry agreed. For example, there was the famous case of Missus Rose Stokes who was unfortunately both immorally rich and immoderately socialistic. She was a Russian Jew who emigrated to New York by way of London, where she was a factory worker, and Cleveland, Ohio. She joined the Socialists in New York and married James Phelps Stokes, who had been one of the idle, academic, spoiled rich kids who formed the Intercollegiate Socialist Society—he and Upton Sinclair and Clarence Darrow. She never did any hard time, but she was sentenced to thirty years. Typically, she divorced her hubby after he bailed her out and hired a good lawyer for her. Married some Greenwich Village socialist teacher…and died in Germany, of all places, in '32 or '33."

"I somehow feel you know more about her, a good deal more about her—and bout these other obscure people—than you are letting on," Dieter said.

"I believe in the old adage you should know everything you can about your enemies," Henry answered. "I've made it a general rule of life since… since the war, I guess. That and the fact she tried to have me publish some of her socialist bullshit in '23 or '24." Henry snorted. "I threw her out of my office, then I spent about the next twenty years making sure her ex never had much success in most of his enterprises. It's amazing what a bastard you can be and what you can do when you own a big block of stock and show up at the shareholders' meetings as a hostile shareholder." Henry smiled a large insincere smile—then laughed. "I hope I gave him an ulcer."

Henry took the bottle of Islay scotch and poured each of them another drink, again going through the ritual of clinking glasses and toasting "Absent comrades."

"Anyway, back to my main harangue...Creel and rest of the Wilson administration silenced opposition in the quickest and most direct way possible—a fact conveniently overlooked and thereby forgotten. Hell, if it ain't in the *New York Times* it never happened. And the fact the way the Department of Justice enforced the law was called to task by a panel of judges after the war...well, that's conveniently forgotten, too. Of course the Progressive press spent so much time with their collective noses up Wilson's ass they would not suggest he might in some way be wrong about something, regardless of how small. And compared to the way they fawned after Emporer Franklin the First, though, they could *claim* to have been highly critical. But I suppose the whatever *Tagblat* could do the same about Messers Hitler and Goebbels. Sound familiar?"

"Very..." Paul and Dieter said at once.

"I'd never heard of him being called anything other than FDR," Paul added, grinning.

"He was called a lot of things—'Prince Machiavelli' being about the kindest. Even the Democrats admit he was something of a socialist, but they apologize by saying if he hadn't have pushed through his loony lefty programs, the country would have fallen to the communists. Of course, they never actually explain *how* it could happen. They never will admit his programs to end the Depression were all stolen from Herb Hoover and renamed. In fact, anything the sonofabitch came up with on his own only made the Depression worse. If we had followed his sage economic advice, the United States would have been a third world power on the same level as Mexico or Peru by 1936."

Henry took a long sip of his Scotch and waited for the tingling to warm the back of his throat and smiled at the memory of David Welsh's 'whiskey drinking instruction.' *The Colonel had always said, the better the whiskey, the farther back in your throat the after-burn. good whiskey, really good whiskey, will be felt at the very back. Bad whiskey at the tip of the tongue...*

"Where the hell was I?"

Paul waved his hand for Henry to continue. He knew it was not going to be within the realm of possibility to change the subject until Henry was finished with his 'American History lesson.'

Henry waded back in. "I don't suppose it would be considered a breech of security to tell you in 1941, when Emperor Franklin the First finally managed to do something about the state of affairs of the country, *vis-à-vis* the war in Europe, the United States only had 1,200 aircraft of all kinds—and 2,100 pilots to fly them. They had to schedule their flight time in advance. Our army was the *fourteenth* in size in the world. Our navy had not fought a major engagement against a modern enemy since 1898—the anti-submarine war of 1917-18 included."

Henry took another long sip. "Pity of it...in 1950, less than *five years* after the successful end of a two-front world war, we were right back to the same starting position, thanks to the Progressives, who now call themselves Liberals. Same animal, different paint-job. When the government tried to recall my second son, Skeeter, to the colors in 1950...Wait a second, this is too good not to go into detail..." Henry refilled all of their glasses and settled back in his padded chair.

"When they tried to recall my second son, Skeeter, who you'll probably find listed as 'Kevin', Dieter—and they called recalling 'retreading,' as in a re-treaded truck tire—anyway, Skeeter showed up for his pre-induction physical *sans* his artificial leg and with his trouser leg pinned up to his uniform coat. Then he *demanded* he be given the same level of rank he had had in 1945, not less than Captain, and in command of a battalion of Marines, on Iwo Jima. It pretty much got him out of service in the Korean Police Action. The point is, though, when they tried to recall him, the First Marine Division, which in 1945 had something on the order of twenty-thousand-plus men, could muster about *seven thousand* give or take. Mister Truman's wunnerful secretary of war had managed to put the United States back into third or fourth world status, where we had been in 1940. Bad enough so we were horribly outnumbered by a country like North-freaking-Korea, a country that less than five years before, we could have turned into a smoldering ruin. *That's* what we owe the Progressives."

Paul and Dieter exchanged glances. Henry was preaching to the choir. They had both walked along the parallel road and looked at the guard towers and the barbed wire and the mine-fields now dividing Germany. Built there, of course, to keep the eastern zone from being over-run by the masses of West Germans who wanted to reap the benefits of the great Workers Paradise. Neither of them said anything.

Henry ploughed on. "The problem is the Progressives—no matter what they call themselves *du jour*, Liberals, Democrats, or whatever— by and large have quietly insinuated themselves into the institutions controling the way we think: the universities, the press, radio, and the new television. So now they control the use of the language, and the way we can use it to describe the way we see things. I'm sure they'll eventually come up with an appropriate term for it." Henry took another sip of his drink before going on. "But so far they have done one hell of a job of turning the truth around, especially when it comes to your former 'Fearless Leader, Mister Hitler'. Oh they don't claim what he was responsible for wasn't hideous in all dimensions. What I mean to say is they have turned him into a right-wing lunatic, rather than what he was, namely a left winger, on the same level as Uncle Joe Stalin.

"Tell me if I'm wrong, but I seem to recall N.A.S.D.A.P.—which that clown Churchill called NAZI—stood for National *Socialist* German *Worker's Party*. Now, if that isn't a left-wing organization, what the hell is?" Henry drank deeply again and looked at each of his companions in turn. Neither of them told him he was wrong.

"Anyway, the good American Progressives have had ten years or so—because don't you ever for one minute think they waited for the end of the war—to teach Hitler wasn't a German Progressive, like Stalin wasn't a Russian Progressive—but Hitler was a lunatic Franco. And Joe Stalin, that murdering sonofabitch, is one of their heroes, now. Of course, they never mention Franco had enough brains to stay the hell out of the war."

Henry caught Dieter and Paul rolling their eyes as he finished speaking, and Henry suddenly said, "I'm nowhere near as drunk as you think I am. Did either of you hear or see anything of the McCarthy hearings?" Paul nodded, and Henry continued. "Parenthetically, I happen to be an acquaintance of one of Dwight Eisenhower's inner circle, a man named Kevin McCann. He was a light Colonel on Ike's staff during the war and was one of Ike's speech writers during the campaign last year." Henry waved his hand in a gesture of dismissal, before Paul could tell him to get on with his story. "Anyway, his job in the White House Staff is to keep Eisenhower the hell away from Tail Gunner Joe McCarthy, and vice-versa, because the man had been targeted by the Progressives in the television and print media, and Eisenhower was smart enough to not want to get splattered with the shit that would surely hit the fan. And McCann's job is to make sure that it doesn't happen.

"Edward R. Murrow, who made a name for himself pretending to be reporting on the London Blitz in 1941 called Joe McCarthy's bluff and shamed him into oblivion on nation-wide television shortly thereafter. Trouble was, what television showed was Joe McCarthy was an absolute asshole. A typical politician, playing to the camera to get a vote…just like all the rest of the bastards in Washington."

Henry paused to look at Dieter. "Just for your store of information, Dieter—I expect you'll be smart enough to know not to pass this on, but to store it away—it is something of an American tradition to *not* send our best to the government, regardless of who happens to be in power— because of what is known in the rest of the country as the Washington Rot. Washington Rot is addiction to political power pervading the District of Columbia, which began as an abysmal swamp and hasn't changed a helluva lot since. We gauge a man's worth by the time it takes him to become addicted to power…Where the hell was I…Oh yes…"

"Murrow and the other networks pilloried Joe McCarthy because he dared to say the Progressives in the State Department and in the movie industry were a bunch of card carrying Communists. They showed he was exaggerating. *Not*, mind you, he was *wrong*, but only that he was *exaggerating*. They took delight in pointing out the people in the industry like Ron Reagan and Charlton Heston were definitely *not* left wing loonies, and it diverted the whole thing from what McCarthy *said* to what McCarthy appeared to do. And they are past masters at it. They made 99.9 percent of the people in the country forget what Joe McCarthy *said* was abso-frigging-lutley true. And it doomed him and his cause…and left the leftwing Communist bastards secure in their places in the State Department and the motion picture industry and—even more important—television and radio in place to continue to skew what is seen and shown to get only their point of view across. Coupled with the teaching in the universities or the left-wing point of view since Dewey and LaFollette and Wilson, and you now have four generations spoon-fed the Progressive doctrine. Three more and it'll equal the seven generations that grew up on the McGuffey system. They're catching up—the difference is they're patient. They don't care if it takes two-hundred years. They know it will last beyond their lifetimes." Henry finished his drink and set the empty glass on the table between them.

Dieter looked first to Paul, then to Henry. Dieter had just sat through a lengthy, if somewhat naïve and disjointed, discourse on the last fifty years of American politics, only a portion of which he would remember in the morning. "All right, America has problems. So, tell me, Henry, how does that affect Germany or, for that matter, me?"

Henry looked at Dieter and shook his head sadly. "Because, Dieter, who the hell do you think are the American representatives teaching you how to be civilized following your 'crushing defeat'? Who the hell do you think are the Americans in, say, NATO, or the IMF or any number of other programs established by the Marshall Plan?"

Dieter said nothing but made a mental note to get the backgrounds of the Americans in, especially, the International Monetary Fund, which struck too close to home to be amusing.

Henry looked to Paul. "Don't expect help from the United States, *Mein Obersti*, they have conveniently forgotten the First War. You, my friend, are an aberration. If your name ever comes up, it will be in relation to what you did after the First War—as a footnote. But, I think you already know that…"

Paul nodded, acknowledging the truth in what Henry had just said.

"I'm tired," Henry said. "I'm going to bed. I'll see you two tomorrow." Henry moved deliberately toward the companionway door. He didn't turn back or acknowledge their *"wiedersehen."*

After Henry had gone through the companionway door, Paul and Dieter sat in silence, sipping the Scotch their lack of shooting skill had purchased. Finally, Dieter broke the silence, "How much of discourse did you understand?"

Paul Von Lettow-Vorbeck remained silent as he looked to his companion, his raised eyebrows saying more than the words that followed. "About half I think. I don't pretend to be well-grounded in Contemporary American Political Thought, but I know *Herr* Feller well enough to know he was passing on to us both a warning of the situation and a means to make a path through the minefields planted by our new allies—at least as far as he interprets it."

"He is obviously pro-German," Dieter said, stopping when he saw the look on *Herr General's* face.

"He is obviously pro-American, but, yes, he likes the German people, and always has, more than he does the other present allies of the Americans—especially the British. Which I find odd. You would think it would be the French. Or are you asking me whether he would be the sort who could be used as a conduit for information?"

"Could he be?"

"I think, Dieter, if anyone tried, they would find out just how strong a patriotic American he was. If, I think, you were so foolish as to try to milk him for his sources, say, it would be the very last time either of us would ever hear anything from him of any use. Do I make myself plain enough?"

"*Jawohl, mein General…*"

"*Sehr gutte.* I would return your question with this one: How much of *Herr* Feller's little soliloquy did *you* comprehend? And further, how do you interpret it?"

"It is my impression *Herr* Feller was passing on to us his impression of the present internal power struggle within the United States, where it began and what it means to Germany. It was concisely devious. It is *his* interpretation, after all, and it has, therefore a built-in point of view which he is quite ready to admit is not the prevailing view. He is, however, a past master of allowing us to find out only those facts about him he wishes us to. Even you, *Mein General,* were not aware of his close personal ties to Douglas MacArthur or his apparent open line to the White House. My first, and greatest impression is we, that is, Germany, should be very careful in dealing with anyone from the American Department of State, or NATO."

"And the IMF?"

"Even more so, the IMF and the World Bank. NATO, because it is military, is by its very nature, transitory—usually two-year terms in most of the positions. But the bureaucratic positions in the others might last for most of a lifetime."

Paul's eyebrows raised. It was something he had not considered.

"I would say," Dieter went on, "based on *Herr* Feller's assessment and background of the American internal power struggle, my first duty is to have the Chancellor's people do a thorough background check on all of the American appointees to those positions, with a view as to whether they are aligned with the, for lack of a better way to put it, FDR/Truman side of the spectrum; or the Hoover/Eisenhower side; or some point in between."

"Yes, my young friend, but never forget bureaucrats seldom work for anyone except themselves—theirs *or* ours." Paul rose from his chair. "I think I will follow *Herr* Feller's advice and go to bed. It has been a long, but interesting day. *Kommen bitte.*"

CHAPTER FIVE

May 21, 1953
Dar es Salaam, Tanganyika
Union Castle Liner *Rhodesia Castle*

T*he Rhodesia Castle dropped anchor inside the bar of Dar es Salaam
harbor on a clear, crisp, cloudless morning. Lettow-Vorbeck, Sietman,
and Feller had been at the rail as the ship followed the channel, Paul making
comments to Sietman about its erratic movement. "They still have to steer
around the hulk of the sunken floating dock, Dieter," he explained. The
obstruction had blocked the entrance to the harbor since the harbormaster
had panicked and scuttled it prematurely when he heard British cruisers were
on the way to shell the town a mere thirty-nine years before. What he had
done of course was to exclude Dar, and its shipyard, from being used by SMS
Königsberg as a base, thereby exiling the cruiser to the pestilential Rufiji
delta.*

Because the *Rhodesia Castle* was only making a short stop to
discharge passengers on her usual run between Mombasa and
Capetown, she anchored in the middle of the inner harbor and dropped
the accommodation ladder. Within minutes, a lighter tied up to the
platform and another nudged into the hull at the luggage hatch. While
the debarking passengers' luggage was being handed out through the
hatchway, the passengers began their way down the ladder to be helped
aboard the lighter, which would then carry them into the dock at the
harbor's edge. The whole affair took no more than fifteen minutes
before they untied and began to make their way through the throng of
large Arab dhows and the smaller lateen rigged *jahazis* servicing them,
bringing out cargoes of mangrove poles and *simsim*—sesame seeds—as
they had for hundreds of years.

As they chugged sedately toward the shore, Lettow-Vorbeck pointed
out the spire of the Lutheran Church and the Governor's Palace, now
called the Government House, still looking as he and Feller remembered
them nearly forty years before. Along the shore, the coconut palms

stirred in the pleasant breeze off the Indian Ocean, and even several hundred feet out on the water, the fragrance of the casuarinas scented the air. What Feller stared at intently were the several hundred old Africans standing near the dock where the lighter would discharge its passengers. It was unusual to see so many old men in one place, and Feller began to suspect all of them were on the shore for a single purpose. When the lighter bumped against the dock pilings, Henry Feller put his hand on Dieter Sietman's arm and nodded for him to lag behind Paul Von Lettow-Vorbeck who stepped spryly up onto the dock despite his years.

Before he could turn to find out where Henry and Dieter had gotten to, Paul was surrounded by twenty or so Africans as old as he was or older. Toward the edge of the crowd, a white fellow, obviously a government official of some kind, was attempting to press through the throng. As Dieter Sietman had explained it, they were supposed to be met by someone from the British Colonial Service and be escorted about to various and sundry events. Henry Feller nodded and then motioned with his head toward where Paul Von Lettow-Vorbeck was standing in a growing circle of old black faces, most of them chattering away in Swahili. Finally, one who appeared to be the oldest of the old-timers, limped up to within inches of Paul and looked intently into his face.

"*Na wewe, Bwana? Jina lako nani?*"—Who are you, Sir? What is your name?

Paul brought his hawkish nose to within an inch of the man's face. "*Pumbavu!*—Idiot!" he roared. "*Usifanye wewe kutanbua? Yako mzee Obersti*"—Don't you recognize me? Your old Colonel?

The old man stepped back. His chin began to tremble. With shaking hands he gave the old imperial salute and said, "*Mimi ni Askari Mdaichi*"—I am a German soldier. Then he fell to his knees and wrapped his arms around Paul Von Lettow-Vorbeck's legs. "*Yangu Obersti, yangu Obersti, yangu Obersti*"—my Colonel—he repeated over and over as the rest of the grandfathers and great-grandfathers crowded around Paul Von Lettow-Vorbeck, clapping him on the shoulders and back, or simply touching his clothing, as Henry and Dieter watched from the edge of the crowd. The white colonial official finally made his way over to them and introduced himself, in a rather Etonesque accent, as the Deputy Governor. He explained he was supposed to escort Mister Lettow-Vorbeck, pointedly leaving off the "von."

Henry turned to the Deputy Governor and chuckled. "Tell *that* to his old *Askaris*. But I don't think it will do much good. I think they've managed to change your schedule for you."

The old *Askaris* had lifted *Generalmajor* Paul Von Lettow-Vorbeck onto their shoulders and were carrying him toward what had once been called the Kaiser Hotel. As they carried him they began to chant:

Askari wanaendesha,
Askari wanaendesha,
Tunakwenda,
Tunashinda,
Haya,
Haya, Safari.

The Deputy Governor gave a wry smile, and the three white men followed behind the old Africans carrying their Colonel to his hotel.

CHAPTER SIX

Wednesday, October 1, 1913
Editorial Offices, Ryan's Publishing
37th Street and Third Avenue
New York, New York

Karl Hostetler had finished moving his few personal possessions into his new office and had arranged his desk so he would not have to look out of the eighth-story window into the wall of the adjoining building hour after hour. Though the office was far from roomy, it was still better than the near-closet-sized space he had occupied for the last two years as an assistant copy editor, which was a polite way of saying senior proof-reader. Karl had wondered slightly who might have been his patron in this advancement up the chain at Ryan's, considering he had never met the owner, Everett Dolson Ryan, and had only a passing acquaintance with the Senior Editor, Harold Knox. His move to replace the departing Frank Harris may simply have been due to the fact he was next in line and hadn't screwed anything up badly.

Hauling the last box-load of supplies into his new office, he was surprised to find both Harris and Knox waiting for him as he pushed his way backwards through the door. Both men grinned at him when he turned and discovered them.

"Come on, Karl," Harris joked, "this office isn't *that* small you have to wedge into it ass-end-first."

Harris was a short, well-proportioned man in his mid-forties, in other words, about ten years older than Hostetler. A natty dresser, Harris also had a reputation for being quite the swordsman with the ladies, though Karl wasn't sure whether Harris either knew or cared about it. Harris had been a full editor with Ryan's since before the turn of the century—fifteen or sixteen years—and had established a reputation as someone who could smell a good story and coax the writing of it out of any number of the Ryan's stable of recalcitrant writers. It was part of his reputation, his skill and expertise as an editor and a prodder of the unwilling *artistes*, that had brought about Harris's departure—though on the best of terms with the senior editor and publisher. Frank Harris had managed to land one of those opportunity-of-a-lifetime positions, an editorship at the *New York Times*. And Harold Knox's being here with his butt planted on the edge of Karl's desk—as it happened, right where Karl wanted to set down his box of pens and pads and typewriter ribbons—more or less proved the truth of that.

Karl ignored Harris's joke and put his box down on the floor—he'd distribute the office supplies later—and asked, "What can I do for you gentlemen?"

"Well, if you can," Knox said, "I'd like to start off by finding out if you have any particularly pertinent plans or ideas you'd like to start working on. It doesn't matter whether they are long- or short-range. Just give me a general idea of something you'd like to do. Got anything at all you've given any thought to as yet?"

Karl looked directly into Harold Knox's eyes, and without a moment's hesitation said, "Africa."

Knox blinked. "Yes…it's a continent—large, hot, filled with natives of various kinds…black, white, brown. And God knows what all. Got jungles, and deserts, and lakes, and things—lots of animals, that sort of thing. Could you expand on your idea a little?"

Karl slid his box of office supplies around the end of his desk with his foot and bent to grasp a handful of tablets, which he put into one of the lower desk drawers without rising so as to give himself enough time to ponder his next words. "Which serial, and later book, has made the most money for Ryan's in the last five years?" he asked.

Knox shrugged and looked at Harris, who grinned at his former boss's discomfiture, finally answering for him. "*Alone in Africa*," he said, using the in-house title for the chronicle of events on the periphery of former President Theodore Roosevelt's African safari. He chuckled, remembering the old Mr. Dooley joke that had caused the author to call it that—privately, of course. "You did most of the copy editing on it, didn't you?" he said to Karl.

Hostetler nodded and answered "Only because the goddamned author didn't want to—in fact, refused to read the galleys."

"Because the goddamned author knows he didn't *have* to read the galleys. He had three other top sellers on his hands, another still in print, and he could have peddled it to anybody—MacMillan would have grabbed it in a second and so would Century since they had already taken the other best seller about the damned safari away from us. Every publisher in the country would have gotten in line to pay him for the manuscript, and he knew it. And besides, he doesn't need the money. The sumbitch could have told us to pack it in our ass—and would have. It's his fifth book, you know, each one of which has made us—that is you and Ryan's—quite a bit of money, 'cause he's as good at smelling out a story as I am. But that's neither here nor there. Go on and expand on Africa."

"Yes, please do," Knox added. "It might be interesting."

Karl Hostetler plopped into his chair and pulled out a bottom drawer to use as a foot prop. "Within a year," he began, "depending on when the Central Railroad is finished—but I don't think it'll matter all that much—within a year, there is going to be one helluva trade fair or exposition thrown by the Kaiser's government in German East Africa. For any number of reasons, I think it would be worthwhile for Ryan's to have someone on hand to, first, report on it, and then write a book-length serial, which we could double-up on later and put out as a single volume. I've been reading up on what I could find about it, and it looks like there are enough different aspects to the story it would be no problem to get a book-length piece out of it—with the usual embellishments, photographs, mini-biographies, that sort of thing." Karl paused, waiting for Harris or Knox to say something, anything.

Knox nodded. "Interesting," was all he said.

Karl looked to Harris, who held out a thick manila folder. "Sounds like you'll need this sooner than I thought you would," he said. The tab of the folder had "FELLER, HENRY A." written on it in heavy pencil. "He belongs to you now, anyway. And yes—he's the sumbitch that had you do all the proof reading. He's also the one writer in the stable who knows what the hell Africa looks like. And like I say, if you sweeten the pie enough, he'll probably do it for you—without costing Ryan's a fortune—because he'll pay his own bills for anything he thinks is beyond the normal expenses. But don't dare try to bullshit him. He travels because he likes to, and he writes because he's damn good at it. He owns a big enough chunk of a couple of railroads and some other stuff so there isn't enough money in the world to make him do what he don't want to do. So you've got to pique his curiosity or challenge his abilities in some way. With that said, I'm on my way over to the *Times* to move into *my* new office." Harris shook Karl's hand and walked out of the door to what had formerly been his office.

Karl Hostetler turned to Harold Knox. "Now what?" he asked.

Knox harrumphed. "Frank said you'd have some off-the-wall ideas when he recommended you for this job. I'd say the first thing to do is get Feller in here and see if he can be piqued or challenged. Then we go from there. When's this big shindig supposed to start, anyway? Don't tell me it starts next month."

"Next spring—April, May, thereabouts. It would be nice to have someone in German East by then. That way, when the railroad is completed in June or July, he'll have been there, and been familiar with the place, and it won't sound as if he just blew in for the show, like most of the other hacks."

"All right—get hold of Feller and get him in here as quick as you can." Having said all he cared to say on the subject, Harold Knox walked out of Karl Hostetler's office and closed the door behind him.

Well, now at least I know who my patron was, Karl thought, reaching for his Western Union telegram pad and pulled across the Feller file on his desk. He scanned the top page of information to find the address for Feller, Henry A.'s home in—*Oh, for Chrissake—Mitchell, South-By-God-Dakota.*

CHAPTER SEVEN

Monday, November 3, 1913
Editorial Offices, Ryan's Publishing
37th Street and Third Avenue
New York, New York

Henry Feller shook the snowflakes still clinging to his fedora and overcoat onto Karl Hostetler's office carpet and then tossed his overcoat and hat onto the coat rack. He pulled an armchair in front of Karl's desk and seated himself heavily.

"I have been summoned. I am here," he said, not pleasantly, adding, "This had better be good, because, one, I *hate* New York, and two, I could be deer hunting. And I don't know which is worse, having to come to this God-forsaken hell-hole or missing deer hunting."

"That's redundant," Karl said. "If it's a hell-hole, it only follows it's God-forsaken. And you used two references to each objection twice in the same sentence. Christ, I hope you don't write as wordy as you talk. Besides, what have you been doing that's so hell-fired important you haven't written anything significant for nearly two years? Or don't you call yourself a writer any more?"

"Where'd Frank Harris go?"

"The *New York Times*. You still haven't answered my question."

"Humph—it figures. I just got him broken in..."

"Well, you've got me now, and I'm going to keep after you until I get some kind of reasonable answer."

"Wonderful—you're young enough to be my kid Brother."

"We are within months of being the same age. I've read your file. And while you were running around in the Orient, dipping your artistic wick in whichever sloe-eyed female could be persuaded to part her knees, I was busting my ass working for *real* editors to learn my trade. I'm as good at it as you are at writing. Now, are we ready to find out why I ran you down in lower east cow-shit Dakota and had you drag your ass all the way to New York?"

"What 'Real Editors'?"

"Murat Halstead and Whitelaw Reid. Why?"

"'Cause you don't sound like a Na Yawkah. Sounds like you at least know enough to blow your nose once in a while. Sounds like west of Pissburg and east of Chicago. Am I close?"

"Cincinnati—I say you're about dead center. Ten-ring but no 'x'."

Henry nodded after giving Hostetler a long look. "So why am I here in this nest of diseased East-European peasantry? To answer your question—why am I here and not back in, as you so elegantly put it, 'east cow-shit, Dakota,' working with Tod Loring."

"Who?"

"John Alden 'Tod' Loring. He's the man that got Wind Cave elevated from a hole in the ground to a National Park and is now trying to get it more acreage since it's been made into a National Game Preserve. I helped him do a survey a couple of years ago, and I've done a lot of slug work for him—you know, when he tries to squeeze an extra dime or two out of Congress."

"Another local boy that made good?"

"Not really—he was on the Roosevelt safari and he got hold of me after I got back 'cause he remembered I was from 'east cow-shit' and I was interested in conservation, and I had been traveling with the Roosevelts after the safari was over. So he figured I could drop a name or two in the right places."

Karl Hostetler snorted derisively. "Harris said you had a pretty high opinion of yourself. Your name in one or two of the right places fits in nicely."

"Actually, Frank Harris said you were still pissed off about having to do the scut-work on the safari book yourself."

"I was and am. What does that have to do with it?"

"Just thought you might like to know where the idea to have you do it came from—other than my towering ego—and the story behind it."

Hostetler motioned with his fingers—let's have it—for Henry to continue.

"About a year after I got back from the Roosevelt Grand Tour and Safari—or is it the other way around—but in any case, the next year, you people sent me to a writer's conference of some kind, in Chicago. They're all generally bullshit, so you can look it up to see what it was called. Amidst the usual gaggle of hacks and Progressive muckrakers were a couple of people I had actually crossed paths with before, one of whom happened to be Fred Grant, whom I had met in the Philippines and who had done me considerable favors when I was working on the Funston book. So one thing led to another and I offered to buy him a drink. And he, being an old army type of man, accepted most gladly.

"So there we were, half shot in the ass, sitting in the bar of one of Chicago's poshest hotels at some damned writers' conference, and I naturally wondered why General—did I mention Fred Grant was a Major General?—General Grant was present. Found out he was also an author—had written a book or two about his experiences in the army in the Indian campaigns, the Yellowstone and Bannock, as I recall. In any case, he and Adam Badeau were the helpers on Fred's father's *Memoirs*. Badeau had been on Willie T. Sherman's staff when General Grant—Fred's father, the President, not Fred—stole him away, and he was with the General for the rest of the war—wrote the first books about the General's campaigns."

When Henry looked over at Hostetler, he got the distinct impression he was about to be asked where this story was going, so he plunged on before Hostetler could ask. "Fred and Badeau were called in to help on the General's memoirs after he learned he was dying of cancer. That would have been in '84. Century had offered the first contract, and Grant was about ready to sign it when Samuel Clemens dropped by. The story Clemens told was Century's offer was tantamount to highway robbery. Clemens had Fred read the contract to him, since the General's voice was shot. And he immediately doubled Century's offer, with an added promise to sweeten the pie. As it turns out, it was Fred Grant who talked his father into going with Webster, which was Clemens' publishing house. Fred had had far more experience with publishers than his father, and he verified everything Clemens said. And I think you know the rest..."

"As I recall, it was the largest royalty check ever paid to an author," Hostetler said.

"Actually, it was paid to Fred's mother. General Grant, *pere*, died right after he finished writing the second volume. Two hundred and fifty thousand dollars in the first payment, another two hundred thousand later on. Century was going to pay Grant ten percent and deduct publishing expenses to boot. I believe Fred's exact words were 'Don't ever do the shit work for a publisher. All they do is oversee the printing run.'

"I found out Fred Grant died about the week before you wanted me to do my own proof reading. Which removed the possibility of a first-hand account of the subject and thereby the possibility of writing a book about it, which is essentially why I told you and Harris to do certain physiological acts heretofore thought impossible to perform.

"I don't have *that* big an ego, but then again you haven't run all over the world with an ex-President, and the son of another. Nor are you on speaking and drinking terms with most of the kind of people I am. So why am I here in Noo Yawk Shitty?"

"I want to run a book idea past you."

"You could have done that by telegram. Aw, Jesus—don't tell me you're as cheap as goddamned Harris? Don't tell me I'm in goddamned Noo Yawk just because Ryan's is too goddamned cheap to spend the money for a telegram."

"Actually, I was hoping you could leave from here if you say yes."

"Yes to what?"

"Ever hear of Dar-es-Salaam?"

"Yeah, it's the capital of German East Africa, on the coast by Zanzibar, maybe three or four hundred miles south of Mombasa. That's in British East. Why?"

"'Cause that's where I'd like you to go."

"What the hell for? It's a shit-hole from everything I've ever heard…"

"Heard from who?"

"Anyone I've ever talked to about it, or who brought it up." Henry stopped suddenly and added, "with a couple, three exceptions. Come to think of it, they were the only ones who actually lived in German East—farmers. We'd call them ranchers out west. One was even born in England but was brought up by his German mother and went to school in Germany. Formidable son of a bitch, he had been a German officer during the Wahehe Rebellion in the '90s. The natives called him *Bwana sakarani*—the Wild Man—'cause I guess he pretty much goes nuts under fire. I don't think I ever wrote about him in the other book—*The Presidential Safari*—too off the subject. He won a *von*—you know what that is?"

"*Ja. Wie ich es auffasse*—yes, I understand," Karl said.

"Anyway," Henry continued, "it may not be the only time an Englishman was given a hereditary title by the Kaiser, but I'd bet it's one of the damned few times. Still, sounds odd. You just don't expect to find a retired German officer with the name von Prince."

"He's still alive—still in German East?"

"Far as I know. I know Alex and Liesel are—they're the other G.E.A. citizens I met. Alex, and his wife Liesel, Hammerstein. They have a farm just east of Kilimanjaro, around Moshi." Henry raised an eyebrow when he looked at Karl, who was in turn looking at him strangely.

"How the hell do you remember all that shit?" Karl asked. "Christ, it's been—what?—four years since you worked on the book."

Henry shrugged. "No, only two, maybe three. Besides, when you're interested in it, you remember it. They were some of the more interesting people I met over there, a hell of a lot more interesting than most of the British types—bloody bunch of failed Lords, one step removed from pissing out the bottom of the last page of Burke's *Peerage*, and who—by way of getting back to the original idea—were the ones who always told me German East was a shit hole. Except for one, an Englishman named Fred Selous, which makes me wonder whether they were, are, mostly full of shit. Considering most parts of British East we traveled through on the Lunatic Line—that's what they called the Uganda Railroad— were some of the most worthless places I've ever had the misfortune to wander around in. Absolutely horrible scrub bush. I mean, it's probably green for about a week during the year, right after the rains, then it dries out and turns into the most god-awful scrub thorn desert you'd ever hope to see. It would make Arizona in August look like a damned Garden of Eden, not to mention every goddamned living thing there is trying to bite you or skewer you or eat your decomposing remains. So now, you tell me why the hell I would want to go back there…"

"To see if the Limeys were really full of shit? About German East, I mean."

"That's hardly a reason to spend that kind of money, 'cause you know I'm not going to pay my own way on spec."

"And to learn about—that is write about—the Amani Institute, and the seventy schools, and the Central Railroad. Or the odd notion a colonial government is created to *serve* the colonists—all the colonists, including the natives—and not the other way around."

Henry's and Karl's eyes met. Henry remembered what Frank Harris had said in their telephone conversation before Henry had left for New York. *"Hostetler is one of those Midwestern Turner Verein krauts—and don't give me any shit, Henry, I'm from Kansas, remember—who've got the feeling they just have to be more German than the Kaiser. It's the way they prove they can be both German and American. Really took hold after the Civil War when their Union veteran grandaddies could wave the bloody shirt with the best of them to prove they earned their citizenship papers. In any case, it makes some a little zealous—with a capital 'Z.' Now, I don't think Karl would let it get in the way of his good sense, but just be aware of the possibility when you talk to him."*

"Sounds like you've done your homework," Henry said.

"I get tired of reading all the pro-British crap. Comes from knowing too much about the way the business runs…and of having seen how Mother England takes care of *her* little brown Brothers…and of having been on the shitty end of the Limeys' arrogant snobbery in the publishing business for the last couple of decades," Hostetler answered. "How often did you hear the soldiers in the Philippines singing *The Land of Dopey Dreams*? You know, 'Civilize them with a Krag'?"

"Not very often. Mostly they didn't sing at all, and when they did, it was 'Hot Time' or 'Daisey' or somesuch. The idea of soldiers singing as they march along comes from some asshole five thousand miles away, someone behind a desk in a copy room, thinking of 'appropriate' slugs to put with pictures." Henry thought for a second and nodded his chin in agreement with his own words—he had spent months putting "appropriate" words to Jimmy Hare's pictures, pictures in combination with his "appropriate" words had sold nearly three million copies for Ryan's.

"Exactly!" Hostetler exclaimed. "But when you go to the *Journal's* or the *Times'* graveyards and read anything you can find about east Africa, all you get is 'Gee-whiz' stories about the lions attacking the 'natives' building the Uganda Railroad. Every damn thing is about British East Africa—not a goddamned word about German East since about 1906 or 07, about the time of the end of the last native revolt. I think it's about time someone—Ryan's, you, someone—set the record straight. Too much good work has been done in German East to let it go un-noticed." Hostetler's eyes sparkled as he spoke.

"Of course," Henry said off-handedly, "anything praising German East will have a good chance of selling well to what—at least a couple of million German-speaking Americans."

Henry and Karl looked at one another again.

"We aren't in the business to lose money," Karl said.

"Seventy schools?" Henry asked.

"Seventy," Hostetler said. "And the Amani Institute does all kinds of research. Mostly for agriculture and animal husbandry—finds local cures and develops the best methods for planting cash crops."

Hostetler reached across his desk and flipped open the lid of his cigar humidor. He reached in without looking and pulled out two long, thin, almost black cigars, then flipped one to Henry, who looked at it closely and recognized it immediately.

"Where the hell did you get *La Flors?*"

"One of our other novelists. He's a mate for one of the Pacific steamship lines. Brings me a supply back whenever he brings in another manuscript." Hostetler struck a match and carefully lit his cigar, then watched as Henry followed suit. When Henry sat back and blew a cloud of blue smoke into the air, Hostetler asked, "You ever hear of a Doctor Robert Koch? K-O-C-H?"

"Didn't he win the Nobel prize a while back? Ten years maybe, something like that?"

"How about Paul Ehrlich?"

"Same thing?" It was more of a question than an answer.

Hostetler puffed on his cigar. "They both worked at, or visited—whatever you want to call it—Amani."

"And no native troubles since 1907?"

"That was the last of it."

"Interesting." Henry puffed out his cheeks and slowly exhaled. "When does this show supposedly get on the road?"

"Well, they're supposedly having an exposition in Dar es Salaam next year—starts in April or May, thereabouts."

"What—a month to get over there?"

"Give or take."

"Ryan's pays reasonable and usual expenses?"

"Yeah—usual and reasonable."

"You make the bookings?"

"Whichever you prefer."

"You make the booking—Lloyd DOA to get there a couple of weeks or more before the thing starts. That'll give me time to look up some of the people I met before, if they're still there. And anything more comfortable than a cattle boat to make the connections, the more direct the better..."

"All right."

"And *this time*—unlike that asshole Harris—make sure of the name of the damn boat before you send me the telegram."

Hostetler's blank expression told Henry the editor had no idea what he was talking about.

"Last time, good old Frank," Henry continued, "gave me four days to get to the pier from South Dakota. Fortunately, I mentioned where I was supposed to be going to the people at Brooks Brothers and they knew the correct name of the ship and all the rest. If I'd have followed Harris's instructions, I'd have missed the goddamned boat. So don't screw up. Can I go home now?"

"Sure, but *Lucia d'Lammermoor* is playing at the Met. They have a new soprano—really knows how to shred her chemise. I hear she's easy as hell..."

"Stick it in your ass, Karl," Henry grinned. "Someday I'd like to take a look at that file of mine. It must have some really interesting shit in it."

"Oh, it does. I'll be in touch."

"Spend the money—use Western Union—and try to give me more than four goddamned days to get to the dock." Henry put his hat on and took his overcoat from the stand. "Give me five years, and I tell you whether it's been a pleasure."

When he left the office, he did not slam the door.

Karl Hostetler's telegram with the information concerning Henry's booking on the *Lloyd Deutsches Ost Afrika* steamship *Kronprinz* departing Naples on March 17, 1914, and the interconnecting voyage on the SS *Samaritan* leaving New York on February 17, 1914, arrived at the Feller house on December 3, 1913. It was more than the four days Henry had been given for his mad dash to join the Roosevelt party, but strangely, the extended time only made the final going more difficult. This time, however, Henry could reasonably tell his mother as he held her in his arms on the train depot platform something he had not been able to do on most of his other leave takings—he was going back to Africa to work on a book about the many accomplishments of the Colonial government, the schools, the agriculture and the research laboratory. Not about the military. There was no war in German East Africa, and had not been for nearly ten years. And this time he wasn't going to go traipsing through the bush trying to shoot wild carnivores before they could make a meal of him. It was as close a promise of a safe assignment as he had ever been offered. He kissed his mother on the forehead, hugged his father and female siblings, tousled the blond locks of two-year old Katrina, his niece, and shook hands with his brother, Junior, and climbed aboard the Burlington morning Chicago Express. "I'll write," he lied as the train began to roll out of the Mitchell, South-by-God-Dakota depot.

He spent two days in New York being re-measured at Brooks Brothers for suitable clothing, had a nice dinner at Delmonico's with Karl Hostetler and Frank Harris, then ran up to New Haven, Connecticut, and spent the day wandering around the Yale campus while the Winchester Repeating Firearms Factory refurbished his Model '95 to near-new condition. Since it had been on safari with Theodore Roosevelt, several people at the factory made offers to buy it back from him, which he cordially turned down. Thence back to New York for another nice dinner with Hostetler and Harris at a little German place in Greenwich Village, as well as a slightly tipsy arrival at Pier 14 for a meander up the gangplank and a final bottle of bon-voyage Moselle. Henry leaned heavily on the rail of the salon deck and waved a silly wave to his two swaying friends as they negotiated their way to a taxi, blowing him profuse kisses as the ship moved away from the berth into the Hudson River.

Henry spent most of the voyage at the bar or reading the portfolio of articles and pamphlets Karl Hostetler had managed to accumulate— *probably put together by a paid clipping service.* By the time the *SS Samaritan* arrived in Naples, Henry knew far more than he had ever cared to know about the Kaiser's Colonial Empire in general and German East Africa in particular. A couple of things had struck him immediately. First, his hardly-ever-used knowledge of Swahili would have to be dredged out from behind his left frontal lobe and rejuvenated. And second, he was very glad he had had Winchester rebuild the '95 because it looked like the part of German East he was bound for had even better hunting than he had found in British East.

The last time he had seen Napoli, he had not had the time to die, as the old saying went, only enough to hurry from the pier to the train depot. This time he thoroughly enjoyed his layover in Naples. He had a week to eat and drink far too much, especially the outstanding cheeses. A week for also wandering around gawking at the remnants of the European Renaissance perched on every street corner and down every back alley. What the hell—until he got to Dar es Salaam and began earning his keep, he was indeed an awkward, gaping tourist, and he played the role to the best of his ability. The food was splendid, better than any he'd had in the Orient, which was saying a great deal. And other than the fact the place was even more steeped in ancient and gothic Catholicism than the Philippines, the people—the younger ones anyway—were open and friendly, especially the ladies, in a peculiarly chaste and gothicly Catholic sort of way.

At the end of his layover, he climbed the gangplank of the Lloyd DOA liner *SMS Kronprinz* and settled into an opulent stateroom where he slept for the first full day of the voyage to the Suez. Then he began to prepare his notes and questions, based on the information he had read on the way to Naples. That task took up nearly another day, after which he found himself pretty much at leisure.

On the third day out, as he was reading the English version of *La Monde*, the Paris newspaper, in the gentleman's lounge, he was observed observing another of the passengers, obviously a military man, obviously German. When the man noticed Henry watching him, he confronted Henry, who simply told the man the truth. The German twitched his moustache, considered Henry's words, and introduced himself. *Generalmajor* Kurt Wahle, on leave from the Saxon army, was also on his way to Dar es Salaam to take in the exposition, but more to see his youngest, colonist son, who had a farm near Buiko on the Northern Railroad. The two took an immediate liking to each other, and so Henry and the General spent most of the rest of the voyage together, often passing the time on the fantail shooting clay pigeons with one or another of the General's Austrian, frighteningly expensive hand-made shotguns.

Over Mai Wein or a schnapps, Henry talked about his adventures and then listened as *Herr* General talked of his. Where Henry had been a pup in China, *Herr* General had been a sub-altern, a-not-quite-a-lieutenant-yet, in France in 1870. They joked about all of the ensuing times they had been shot at by various and sundry natives, and the list was surprisingly long and disarmingly dangerous—Boxers, Moros, Insurectos, Frogs, Hereros, Wahehe. A generation apart, they were bound together as fellow survivors of some very perilous encounters.

CHAPTER EIGHT

Friday, April 17, 1914
Dar es Salaam
German East Africa

*S*MS Kronprinz *came through the funnel formed by two jutting points of land, and the harbor of Dar es Salaam suddenly opened grandly before them. As the ship drew farther into the harbor and began a turn toward the town to the northwest, the passengers could see a further point of land dividing the harbor into a huge northern pool, nearly round in shape, and the town frontage lined with palm trees. To the south the harbor continued, but lined instead with warehouses and berthing for as far as could be seen on both shores. It looked, in fact, a great deal like the mouth of the Hudson River, or of the Missouri where it flowed into the Mississippi above Saint Louis—on that scale, only African.*

Henry's first impression, as he stood next to *Generalmajor* Wahle at the rail of the promenade deck, was that Dar es Salaam was a much "prettier" town than any of the other African places he had seen. It was much more thought out and orderly, in a Teutonic sort of way. The larger buildings were close to the water, and the water was surprisingly blue, shaded by both the palms and some other larger trees Henry couldn't identify, though he was certain his father would have been able to. There was a skyline, complete with church steeples and buildings of several floors.

The Lloyd DOA pier was apparently directly in front of two of the largest buildings in the bustling town center. Either it had been dredged out or the harbor was surprisingly deep. Henry made a mental note to find out which. In any case, there was little need for a tugboat until the last few feet of the voyage. *Kronprinz* had stopped engines well away from the dock and allowed a little tug to butt its bow against the outboard side and gently nudge the liner against the padded mooring posts, where shouting, laughing Africans tied the ship to the berth. Evidently the Lloyd DOA company had been foresighted enough to build the dock for the use of its ships because when the passengers went to disembark, the level of the pier was nearly level with the passenger hatchway in the ship's side, making it a matter of stepping only two or three steps across a portable iron bridge to be on dry land.

Like every other port Henry had ever been in, but with strongest memories of Manila churned up, the pier was a-throng with white, black, brown, and yellow faces topped with skimmers, huge Gibson-Girl bird-feather head pieces, fezzes, wide-brimmed safari hats, turbans, head scarves—and the occasional gold, or at least brass, ringlet. Rickshaw boys, newspaper peddlers, government officials of several kinds, Native, Arab, and Indian peddlers, and white settlers come to meet someone—all milled about until recognition and pairing with one or another of the passengers brought on a shout and wave and left eddies of movement through the crowd. Near the edge of the pier, Henry and the General stood back from the rushing, coursing crowd and watched in mild amusement as the mob scene played out before their eyes. Henry had reservations at a hotel called the Kaiser Wilhelm—he hadn't really expected any other name—but with the proviso he would surely come up to *Generalmajor* Wahle's son's place when it was convenient.

Henry was watching and musing to himself about the inconsistency of women's styles. With his mother and both sisters as style-conscious as any three females he had ever known, and far more than others, he was more than familiar with present trends—at least those to the west of Chicago. So he was attracted to the fact most of the white women on the dock were still wearing the huge monstrosities on their heads he had seen go out of style three years before, and yet they were otherwise very current, in that he didn't see a mutton-chop sleeve or a pleated bodice anywhere. And the dresses were as short as they now were at home—a little above the ankle—and without mud-bands sewn to the bottom. He speculated to himself the hats, due to their size, even though out of style, were substantial enough to keep the African sun at bay. And come to think of it, bird feathers couldn't be that heavy or birds would all be walking.

Then, from out of the crowd a young man walked up to them, smiling broadly. He was within an inch of Henry's five-foot-eleven. If his hair ever grew out it would probably be blond—his moustache was. He was wearing a safari hat shading his face, a light jacket, complete with cartridges in the cloth chest loops, and very worn boots. General Wahle held out his arms, the young man embraced him, and they patted one another on the back.

"You are looking well, Dicky," *Herr* General said. "Dicky," *Herr* General said, turning to Henry, "this is *Herr* Heinrich Feller, who is an American writer. He speaks excellent Saxon-German so don't say anything in front of him you don't want published. Heinrich, this is my youngest son, Richardt." After Henry and Richard had shaken hands, the General continued. "I have taken the liberty to invite *Herr* Feller up to your farm. I hope that is all right."

"Fine by me, Papa. I'm done with my reserve service for the year, so *Herr* Feller won't be alone—I've invited my new commanding officer to spend some time at the farm after he finishes his inspection tour of the Colony. He's a very good fellow, for an *Oberst-Leutnant*." When *Herr* General's eyebrows rose and his head twisted slightly, Richard Wahle's eyes twinkled, and he went on to explain.

"While I was on call-up for my two weeks annual field duty," he began, "I decided to walk into town for an afternoon schnapps. We were camped right outside of Buiko, maybe a kilometer from the railroad. So, as I was walking along, here comes this fellow striding along, chewing on a stick of sugar cane and whistling. Well, of course I assumed he was a local farmer—he wasn't in uniform—so I walked along with him. We talked for a while, and he told me he was new in the Colony, was taking a little walking tour to see what he could see, and so far was fairly impressed. I explained to him I was on my reserve duty and I was going into town to have a little dram to cut the dust, and when I asked him to join me, he said that would be splendid.

"So, anyway, we get to the *Schutz Polizei* post by the town gates, and I thought it was odd the *Askari* there, a native policeman, came to attention and presented arms as we passed. But you know the native troops, Papa—always trying to look better than the regulars, even for an *Unter-Leutnant*. Anyway, we get to the local *brauhaus*, where most of the *Schutzen Kompagnie* officers have gathered, and when we come into the bar someone yells *"Achtung"* and they all pop up and stand at attention. At first I thought it was a joke on me because they all knew I was supposed to have the duty in camp that afternoon. But then this farmer I had been walking with, and whom I had told about my being absent from camp, says 'As you were, gentlemen.' That's when I realized he was the new *Oberst-Leutnant*.

We take a seat, but I expected him to, at the least, put me under arrest. However, he leans over and says 'What you told me on the road was said between comrades. It goes no further. And I promise I won't tell the new commandant.' So then we had our little schnapps, and he even walked with me back out to the camp, inspected it, and found it adequate. And that, Papa, is how I came to know the new commanding officer of all the Kaiser's Imperial Forces in German East—and how I came to know him as one of the 'good sort,' like you, Papa. And now, Papa, I have a wagon for your luggage. And considering the time of day and the length of the ride, I think we'd best be going if we hope to get to the farm by tomorrow."

They took their leave from one another then, the Wahles shepherding several of Richardt's African workers to handle the General's not inconsiderable luggage. Henry finally located his own smaller pile of trunks and hired his own African crew to cart it to the Kaiser Wilhelm Hof, paying extravagantly for what turned out to be moving the trunks across the dock and adjoining boulevard to the doors of the large building. Here the hotel's Africans took over and moved everything up to his suite. Henry went to the front desk, signed the register, and found everything in proper order—Ryan's was very good at that sort of thing, one of the reasons Henry had never seriously considered any of the attempts by other publishers to entice him away. It was still too early to eat, and he really didn't feel like starting to play the gawking tourist again until tomorrow, so he headed for the barroom.

He had just taken a seat at one of the small tables along the inside wall, away from the very bright rays of the afternoon sun, when he felt someone standing very close behind him. A voice said, "If you come out into the patio garden, Henry, you can sit and talk with both of us. Women are not allowed in here."

Henry turned and looked up into the smiling face of Alex Hammerstein. He rose and clasped Alex's hand warmly. It had been nearly four years since they had seen one another. Henry had spent nearly a month as a guest on the Hammerstein tea plantation just outside Moshi, near the border with British East Africa. Henry considered Alex and his wife Elizabeth, whom everyone called 'Liesel' as foster siblings. They were two of the few people in the world he had continued to write to since the end of the Smithsonian safari. Others in his very select circle of correspondence, were Fred Selous, the African hunter who had introduced them, and Tom von Prince, known throughout German East as *Bwana Sakarani*—the Wild Man.

When a waiter brought Henry's glass, they wandered through the barroom, out of the floor-to-ceiling glass doors, and onto a wide stone-paved veranda covered by a pergola, or *bauer*, draped with vividly red flowers of some kind interlaced with jasmine scenting the air. It was shaded and cool, being on the side away from the sun. Four-place tables were scattered at random. And everywhere, the white female population of German East Africa—or at least a fairly hefty portion of it—sat chatting quietly. The place reminded Henry, not at all surprisingly, of *Unter den Linden* in Berlin, as he was sure it was meant to. A little touch of *gemütliche*, home in deepest, darkest…

Liesel Hammerstein rose as Henry and Alex approached her table, and she simply beamed at them. "Oh Alex—it *was* him. We thought it was you when we were down by the dock, and I sent Alex off to find you." Liesel gave Henry a peck on the cheek.

"He succeeded. So how have my two favorite tea planters in the world been?"

"Very well, thank you very much," Liesel answered. "Everything is going nicely. It actually appears we will make a profit someday before we are both old and gray." She laughed. "You will of course come and stay with us."

"I don't know if that will be possible. For one, I have to cover the Exposition."

"But that doesn't officially begin until July—that's when the railroad should reach Kigoma, over on the shore of Lake Tanganyika."

"I was told it was supposed to begin in May."

"Well *unofficially* it's already open. As you will see. That's why we've come down—to see the Expo' because I'll be busy at the time of the official opening," Alex said.

"Oh?"

"My annual reserve service. July is the month I have to pay my annual dues *fur Kaiser und Vaterland.*"

"Oh, I thought it was already over with. I mean, I met Richard Wahle, and he said he had just finished his. Do you know him, by any chance? His father was on the boat and we got to be friendly. Which is another of my scheduling problems—I've been invited up to his farm as well."

"Of course I know *der Dicke*. And to answer the first of your many questions, he is in a company of the *Schutzen Truppe*—kind of the Colony's answer to your American Militia clubs, or shooting societies, or whatever you call them. I, brave fellow that I am, and educated at the expense of *unser Kaiser* to boot, am in the *real reserves, the Schutztruppen*. *We* assemble on July 1st, the *Schutzen Truppe*, on March 15th. That's why *Der Dicke* is already finished. As to the rest of it, we'll have to sit down and work it out because you know my wife—she will not take no for an answer." Alex winked broadly, bowing his head in the direction of Liesel, who laughed once again.

"Well, there is another thing or two I must do," Henry added, trying to get in a word sideways. "The Amani Institute doesn't happen to be near your place, does it?"

"We go near it on the way back to our farm. Why?"

"It's one of the places I'm supposed to look into."

"Well then, we can all stop in there on the way. I have some things to ask the staff anyway, and it will be easier to talk to them than to write to them," Alex said.

"You did bring your guns with you, didn't you?" Liesel asked.

"Of course. At least the two I always drag around—the one you want to shoot and the shotgun." Henry grinned. Liesel had tried to talk him out of the Winchester on several occasions when he had stayed with them before. "I had Winchester rebuild it, by the way. I think you'll like it."

"You didn't bring your Grandpapa's?"

Henry unbuttoned his jacket and held the left front open so Liesel could see the butt of the Schofield. "Always," he said.

"Then we will have to plan on a little pot meat shooting." She smiled. "Something I can take with your Winchester hopefully."

"How long are you two here for?" Henry asked, realizing the subject of where he was going to rest his head had been taken care of.

"We came down to see the Botanical Gardens. That's what I meant about the Expo's being unofficially open. It's the first showplace to open its doors. And there are some other things we can show you and do. There are some really good restaurants. Liesel particularly likes the Roumanian Café over in the Burger Hotel. And of course there is the Schulz Brauerei—Schulz is from Bavaria, and you know how they are about their beer. And there's the Dar es Salaam Club, which Liesel also likes because they allow women, at least in the club room, which is right next to the bar room."

"How about the Governor's Palace? That's probably the first place I should go. I think Ryan's has arranged an audience or interview or something like that, with the governor for me."

"*Herr Doktor* Schnee?"

"You would know his name better than I would…"

"*Herr Doktor* Heinrich Schnee," Liesel added. "And with any luck, you will avoid meeting *Frau* Ada."

Henry gave her an inquisitorial look, but she demurely took a sip of her wine and said nothing further. *Probably wouldn't be good to be overheard saying unkind things within hearing of what has to be many of Frau Ada's pals*, he thought.

CHAPTER NINE

Monday, April 20, 1914
The Governor's Palace
Dar es Salaam, G.E.A.

T he receiving room of the Governor's Palace, called Government House, was a piece of Teutonic overstatement reminding Henry of both of the other seats of government he had ever seen. He had spent more days of his growing up than he could count kicking dust around the outside of the two-story warehouse in Yankton both of his grandfathers assured him had once been the territorial capitol building. The other had been the somewhat pretentious Provincial government building he had walked past once when he had been taken along to Winnepeg by his grandfather Kevin and his Uncle David on some kind of railroad business. As he judged this place now, he immediately saw the entire Dakota Territorial Capitol building would fit inside this room without hazarding a paint scratch.

He was ushered through the heavy wooden doors by a liveried native who strode before him the full length of the room and then announced in impeccable German *Herr* Feller was present to speak with the Governor. He then bowed Henry into the presence of His *Excelenz Herr Doktor* Albert Heinrich Schnee, and with a sweep of the white-gloved hand, *Frau Ada Schnee. No such luck, Liesel, sorry.*

"Thank you for seeing me, *Excelenz*," Henry said in German.

"You may speak English if you prefer, Mister Feller," *Frau* Ada said, "both I and my dear husband speak it." The accent was very much like the nasal twang of Australia, but not quite. Obviously, *Frau* Ada was not a native German. Just as obviously, she spoke very English English.

Henry's head turned. "May I ask..." he began.

"Oh. New Zealand, actually," *Frau* Ada answered before he could finish his question. "I met my dear husband when he was with the Colonial Office in Samoa. We used to vacation there, my parents and I."

"Ah..." Henry half expected to hear *Frau* Ada use the Imperial Third Person. Instantly, he felt as though she were speaking far down to him from a very great height. He thought of all the stories he had heard of Queen Victoria's supposedly favorite line of disfavor: "*We are not amused*" because it was damned-nigh the same accent.

Governor Schnee was a smallish man, slightly shorter than Henry, with pomaded dark hair and the *de rigueur* Wilhelmine moustache. He was wearing a black cut-away with a starched white wing-collar shirt and cravat. Some kind of Imperial order peeked out from under the lapel, but Henry could not identify it, other than to notice it was *not* the *Eisen Kreuz* – the Iron Cross, which every German soldier he had ever met had sworn to be the only medal worth having.

They exchanged pleasantries of a sort. Governor Schnee asked after his accommodations and was surprised this was not Henry's first time in Africa—and even more surprised when Henry told them he had been with President Roosevelt on the Smithsonian Safari. One or two more polite questions and Henry found himself being escorted back out of the room by the same, very black, African who had led him in. Beyond the great doors, in the reception hall waiting room were three other black men in livery, two of whom were, by the uniform, soldiers or policemen. As Henry was shown to the outer door, he heard the strut-and-announce-guy ask one of the others whether there were any more victims to see *Bibi mkubwa or Daktari theluji*, and Henry had a difficult time suppressing a guffaw. He had decided he would keep his newly reacquired lexicon of Swahili to himself, and was now very glad he had made that decision. It was a priceless little jewel would go immediately into his journal: the servants called *Frau* Ada, something that could be translated from Swahili two or three ways, but essentially meant "Big Mama" and her husband was Doctor Snow, a literal transliteration into English; *Schnee* meaning "snow" in German. Somehow Henry could hear *Frau* Ada's *We Are Not Amused* as he chuckled his way out of the Governor's Palace.

Alex and Liesel were waiting for him in the Schulz Brauerei where they had steins of very good beer and a little braunschweiger and swartzbrot to tide them over until dinner, which they ate at the

Roumanian Café in the Burger Hotel after spending most of the afternoon at the Botanical Gardens. Henry had to admit he was impressed with the place, admitting it was built exactly for that purpose, to impress the tourists in town for the Exposition. *Doktor* Schnee and his colonial officials appeared to know pretty well what they were about. After a pleasant evening in the veranda garden of the Kaiser Wilhelm Hof, they went to their rooms having decided to catch the coastal steamer for Tanga in the morning. Since it would be about a 200-kilometer trip—Henry didn't figure a coastal steamer would be in a great hurry anyway—they figured on an all-day journey, and Liesel said they could buy enough food to take a basket lunch with them and then have a late meal when they got to Tanga, stay over, and take the morning train for Moshi.

Since their farm was not all the way to Moshi, they might make it in one day—if it didn't rain, or if there weren't any problems with large animals on the track, or a grass fire or something like that. In any case, they'd see how far they got and telegraph ahead at one of the watering stops to have someone meet them. It would not be as great an adventure as all that, and nothing at all like a safari. That's when Henry remembered he had to stop at Amani, and so the plans changed once more. *That's what you get when you try to plot an itinerary after a great deal of polite alcohol.*

All in all, the boat trip up the coast to Tanga was pleasant enough. At least they didn't have to sit on hard wooden benches. The little coastal steamer had a first class lounge on the upper deck in deference to the European passengers—Arabs and other Moslems are prohibited the use of alcohol and generally congregated on the promenade deck. The weather was quite nice, though there were several storm fronts in sight on the horizon. And the swell was manageable, a mild three or four feet, amounting to a trifle in the Indian Ocean, which was capable of a great deal more. They steamed around the tip of a peninsula Alex said was called Ras Kasone, then for another two miles or so past rubber and coconut plantations and baobab trees into the main part of the harbor. Like Dar es Salaam, Tanga's harbor front was dotted with palm trees.

To the south of the steamer wharf, the beach was literally smothering in mangroves.

Tanga was laid out in a tidy colonial manner, with streets on a geometric grid, lined with neat white houses uniformly covered with sweet-scented tropical foliage. The place reminded Henry of paintings of tropical paradises in his school books. Even better, the Northern Railway station was on the other side of the wharf, complete with a hissing steam engine and four coach cars idly waiting to depart for points north and west. Alex inquired about the train schedule and was told there was a problem of some kind up the track, so their options appeared to be to wait around for whatever was on the track to get off the track, then travel to the nearest station to Amani and take a chance they could hire some horses. Or to stay in Tanga overnight and then ride up to the nearest station to Amani, hire some horses, and ride over to Amani. Or just go on to Moshi and stop at Amani on the way back, in a month or so.

Henry chose the middle option, knowing Liesel would prefer to stay over and leave fresh in the morning. So they took rooms at the—what else—the Kaiser Wilhelm Hof. They drank a bottle of decent Moselle and went to bed.

After a large breakfast—because they didn't know what they would find on the way and because all they had eaten the day before were the cold dishes from Liesel's travel basket—they boarded the morning train and an hour later stepped off in Muheza. There they hired three mares that looked like they could actually walk twenty-five miles without collapsing and trotted briskly out on the Amani road. It surprised Henry that, unlike most things in east Africa, this was a real road, albeit paved with gravel, but paved nonetheless. The road ran fairly straight until it started up the slope into the foothills of what Alex called the Usambara Range where the road to Korogwe branched off. Near midday, as Henry was looking ahead through the canopy of evergreens lining the road to the green mountains towering in their path and telling Liesel and Alex of the Appalachians and Black Hills, they trotted over a small rise and were confronted by the sight of a line of very white buildings along a ridgeline just across a small dip in the roadway.

"Ah. There it is," Liesel exclaimed. "That is Amani."

As they rode into the compound, Henry was impressed by the size of the place. On the way in they had ridden along several fields of crops, some of them unknown to Alex, and the compound itself was nearly a thousand acres. Alex said it was about 450 and it took Henry a while to realize Alex thought in terms of hectares, so after doing the math in his head, he discovered he was just about spot on. It took him longer to realize that though the compound was filled to overflowing with vegetation, there were hardly two trees or shrubs alike. The profusion was amazing. Three sides of the place were bordered by small rivers, but the name of only one of them, the Sigi, was known to the Hammersteins. In the sun, the stuccoed buildings shone brightly under their tin, thatch, and red tile roofs. Each had a screened porch with overhanging eaves for shade, and these porches uniformly faced east or south-east near the crests of a series of steep-sided ridges.

CHAPTER TEN

Wednesday, April 22, 1914
Amani Institute
German East Africa

Henry and Doctor Philipp Wilhelm Albrecht Zimmermann, who had been Director of the many faces of Amani for over a decade, rode side by side along the crest of one of the higher ridges in the Amani compound. They had spent the better part of the day riding from place to place, and once more Henry was astounded by not only the size of the place—he had grown up in the midst of farms large enough to tax the ability of farmers to work the land, after all—but also the sheer diversity of its studies. Amani was far more than just a place where a few eggheads tried to figure out what kind of leafy plant they were looking at. The place was divided into several plantations, which in turn were divided into fields with different crop types. The soil, crops, fertilizer, irrigation, altitude, rotations, soil recovery, erosion, and propagation were minutely scrutinized, as were animal and insect infestation. There were literally hundreds of variations, originals and hybrids, and that was just for the local flora. Across the Sigi River, and strung out along its banks, was another set of plantations experimenting with imported cash crops from plants brought in from all over the world. Henry was shown coffee imports from Brazil, timber trees from Indo-China, tea from Ceylon and India, camphor from Japan, thousands of Chinchona and Castilloa plants, cotton from India and Texas—Texas of all places, because Amani had found a way to kill off the weevil infestation in Texas seeds, an infestation universal in all other American kinds of cotton seeds.

While *Doktor* Zimmermann could talk endlessly about his charge, his fondest memories were of those other men who had come and used his facilities to help the general population of the world, beginning with the work done by Zimmermann's predecessor, *Doktor* Stuhlman. Stuhlman and two others, the French Algerian Laveran, and the British Indian Medical officer Ronald Ross, had founded the place in the 1880s as the East-African Malaria and Vector-borne Disease Institute. Laveran and Ross had done the first experimentation based on the assumption malarial fevers were transmitted by mosquitoes.

Then Robert Koch had come from his position at the University of Berlin to work on the ongoing intensive research and was the one who had shown malaria was directly connected to the seasonal Great Rains and also the disease had an incubation period of twelve days. Koch had also worked on diseases affecting cattle and made several discoveries ultimately leading to, if not a cure, then at least a course of medication for Babesia, Trypanosoma, and tickborne Spirochaetosis. Those discoveries—and later Paul Ehrlich's development of the .606 treatment—led to their receiving Nobel Prizes in Medicine in 1905.

Zimmermann rambled on for most of the day, with Henry taking notes as the *Doktor* carried on an oral and anecdotal history of the manifold work done at "his" institutes. He always spoke of the place as plural because of all the things going on there at once. The compound was divided into areas for Biological Research, Botanical Husbandry, Tropical Disease Research, a production area to make fertilizers and farm tools, and a school to teach the settlers and the Colony's native farmers the best methods and techniques for planting and cattle care— agronomy Zimmermann called it. One of the things that struck Henry was the way in which the findings of the Institute were shared openly with anyone.

On a daily level, the Institute's work had increased the general welfare of the Colony several times over. Now there were thousands of square-kilometers producing all sorts of cash crops. According to Zimmermann, there were over a hundred thousand acres planted in sisal alone, and then two million coffee trees yielding over a thousand tons of some of the best coffee grown in the world—a fact Henry was more than happy to attest to, having become either spoiled or addicted in a matter of days. Nineteen million rubber trees covered another two hundred thousand acres, thirty-five thousand acres of cotton, sugar cane, tobacco, and cereal grains like Indian corn and millet. And most promising and amazing, only about ten percent of the Colony was presently being scientifically tended. Zimmermann's eyes shown with pride at what "his" place had accomplished. Henry thought he was too damned humble.

They parted with a handshake and a promise by Henry to come back for another visit before he went back to the United States. He would work off the notes he had taken and then flesh out the portions he intended to write into the book. As he rode back through the evergreen woods toward Muheza with the Hammersteins, he talked about how impressed he had been by the place, going on at some length until Alex had finally laughed and said, "Be quiet Henry. If you tell the world about our little secret here, everyone will want one."

They managed to catch the train for Moshi at Muheza—it was only running "a little" behind schedule today. They chatted amiably as the train wound its way through the very scenic uplands of the Usambaras. Zimmermann had been right, of course—they rode through a steady progression of farms stretching away on both sides of the railway. Occasionally, natives along the track waved and called out hello's and sometimes curses as they passed. Henry again had a hard time keeping a straight face when he overheard some of the quite graphic and imaginative shouts. When they stopped to take on water for the engine at Buiko, Alex and Henry jumped off to run to the telegraph office—in the case of Alex, to notify someone at the Hammerstein farm they were on their way and to have a wagon meet them at the Moshi depot, and in Henry's case, to hire a native boy to take a message out to the Wahle's farm to let them know he was going to the Hammersteins' first and would stop by on his way back toward Tanga, time unknown. Then they dashed back to the train and waited while the crew finished a little snack before reboarding and getting under way once more.

As they steamed along, looking out to the north where the first of the Pare mountains rose and ascended in lines of stark rock outcroppings and ridges to what Henry figured had to be at least eight- or nine-thousand feet, Henry asked, "I'm wondering—not that I've grown up around farmers or big farms or anything—but how is it you two can afford to take the time off farming to just walk away for a week or two whenever you want?"

Alex and Liesel looked at each other and then back to Henry before Alex spoke. "Well, we have a very good headman. He knows what there is to do and sees that it's done. You make it sound as though you think we, personally, spend all of our days on our knees in the fields, weeding and planting each seed. Let me assure you that is not the case. Especially since we hired the new headman, who, by the way, said he knew you Mister Two Barrels—*Bwana mbili pipa*. He also said he taught you how to speak Swahili." Alex grinned a Cheshire cat sort of grin, then burst out laughing.

"He wouldn't by any chance be a gray-haired, old, worthless bag of bones named Jayubara, would he?"

"That's highly possible," Liesel said.

"When the...when did he show up?"

"Oh, about three years ago. Said he had finally gotten too old to work for the Aussie outfitter and was walking home, doing odd jobs along the way. Just wandered in and started jabbering about how you had told him about the *wakulima vijani*—children farmers—you had met in German East..." Henry snorted. Then Alex went on, "...he said since he had vast experience as both a headman and as a farmer, and was also a friend of another friend, *Bwana Sakarani*, he thought he would offer to grant us an opportunity to hire him."

Yeah, *that* sounds like Jayubara." Henry and Gemali Jayubara had met on the Smithsonian safari after the African had been demoted from Kermit Roosevelt's gun bearer to a mere porter. Henry had re-elevated him and the two had hunted together for the rest of the safari. Jayubara had also been given the task of teaching Henry Swahili.

"So I did—and damned if he wasn't as good as he claimed to be." Alex continued. "He's been the one mostly running the place since. And we've finally started making money at it."

"How big is Africa?" Henry asked suddenly.

"Oh, I don't know, maybe five thousand miles wide and ten-or-twelve-thousand miles long. Why?"

"What are the chances of this sort of thing happening? How damned unlikely is it to run across such a circle of acquaintances in so vast a space and three years apart?"

"Henry," Liesel said, "this is *Africa*. The strange is the usual here. You're lucky you are in the civilized part. Over on the other side of the lakes, where it's nothing but jungle, it gets really strange, or so I'm told."

"Yes," Alex broke in, "rumor has it over in the Congo, the Catholic Church has relieved their priests from their vows of celibacy—or so we're told."

Liesel nodded in confirmation when she saw Henry's look of skeptical disbelief.

The railway paralleled the ridgeline on an almost flat course. Henry's immediate comparison was to parts of the Rockies, but even more so, because of the very starkness of the ridges, to the *Cordillera Central* on Luzon. They steamed all day, never out of sight of the Pares. At Kisangire a member of the train crew brought Alex a telegram saying they would be met whenever the train managed to arrive at Moshi, no matter how late. And from there it was only a little over an hour by wagon to the farm.

They chuffed into Moshi station early in the evening, having actually made much better time than they thought possible, a mere nine hours to go about a hundred miles so far as Henry could figure—the Northern Railroad didn't put out mile markers with any regularity, or the ones they did put out were considered a meal by some of the local fauna, or considered firewood by the indigenous farmers or herders. Henry kept to himself the same ride would have taken a little more than three hours on one of his grandpa's trains.

They were, indeed, met by two of the Hammerstein's' workers, a man and his wife, who helped unload the baggage and then climbed on top of the trunks in the back of the wagon for the ride back to the farm as Alex drove the mule-team. Just before he slapped the mules into motion with the reins, the male worker said, "There is another guest at the big house, *Bwana*. *Bwana tembo jangili* arrived yesterday and *bosi Jayubara* put him in the back guest room."

I wonder who the hell Mister Elephant Poacher is, Henry thought to himself.

"Not the front?"

"No, *Bwana. Bwana tembo jangili* said it would be easier to leave quickly from the back room."

"Well, Henry," Alex said, "It looks as though you will finally get to meet the Great—just ask him, he'll tell you—The Great Pietr Pretorius."

"Isn't he the one that was supposed to come in to see Fred Selous the last time?"

"Yes. Unfortunately, he was too busy dodging the *Schutz Polizei* to make it. Sent his regrets, though, about two months later, when he dared to show his face again."

"Alex" Liesel said, "that's a very unkind thing to say about Pietr. You know you love him like a Brother."

"You are absolutely right, my dear. Except, of course, it's absolutely true... And, no, I *don't* 'love him like a Brother.' I admire him greatly. I think he is one of the bravest men I have ever met. But if he were my Brother, I'd have my father spank him."

It was nearly noon of the following day before Henry finally met Pietr Pretorious. The first contact took place without the benefit of either Hammerstein when Henry wandered into the veranda of what he called Hacienda Hammerstein, the Texican name fairly well befitting how he thought of the place, even after an absence of nearly five years. He strolled around to the shady side of the veranda, carrying a cup of Alex's excellent coffee. There he found a man sitting, or rather lounging, in one of the rattan chairs, his boots propped up on the top porch rail. He was holding a cup of steaming liquid on his chest with both hands.

"You must be Pietr," Henry said.

The man made no move to rise or to extend his hand. "And you must be their pet American," the man answered, finally moving his boots off the porch railing, leaving a muddy black streak.

Henry suddenly found himself going from cool indifference to slow simmer. The man's voice, demeanor, and attitude all played on Henry's quick-to-toggle "piss-off switch." "I don't know about that," he said evenly, "they fetched me out here as a good old farm-country boy to try and figure out what kind of hog is shitting in their beds and leaving mud on the furniture."

"And have you figured it out yet?" Pietr's voice had a tinge of malevolence.

"Yeah, pretty much. Judging by its tracks, it's what we pet Americans call a 'root-hog.' That's someone brought up so poorly—either in a hog barn or a root cellar—he don't know how, or isn't bright enough to be taught to be anything other than a pig."

"And have you seen this—what did you call him—this 'Root Hog'?"

"Yeah. I'm tracking him."

"And when you find him, what do you think you'll do?" the malevolence was a full step greater.

"I'll tell him to change his ways…or get his ass kicked."

"And you think you're capable of doing any such thing?"

"Yes." Henry's eyes were steady and unmoving. His jacket was unbuttoned. He was leaning casually against one of the porch pillars.

Pretorius's right hand suddenly dropped out of sight, emerging less than a second later holding a large skinning knife. As he began to swing his hand toward Henry, there was an ominous clicking sound. His hand stopped in mid-swing, and his eyes grew large as he found himself staring down the barrel of a revolver of what appeared to be at least 10mm bore or larger. It was pointed dead-center at his chest, and he could see the bullet end of the cartridges in the cylinder. Henry's eyes had not moved or blinked.

"Us pet Americans have an old saying," Henry's voice was quiet and cold. "Never bring a knife to a gunfight."

Behind them, Alex Hammerstein said "I see you two have met. Is there a problem, or are you two just showing off your toys before breakfast?"

Pretorius flipped the knife into the air, deftly grabbing it by the blade and replacing it in his boot sheath. Henry put his thumb over the cocked hammer of the Schofield and allowed it to fall into its un-cocked position before he re-holstered it.

"Just showing off our toys," Pretorious said.

"Good," Alex said, setting his coffee cup on the table and pulling up a chair. "You know how dripping blood on the floor pisses Liesel off." He clapped his hands, and immediately a native servant carried a silver tray loaded with toast, butter, and marmalade out of the house and placing in the center of the table.

Immediately behind the first servant was a tallish African with streaks of gray in the short hairs covering his temples. His weathered face was impassive as he set the silver coffee pot on the table and turned to Henry, extending a hand holding a smaller silver teapot. "Would *Bwana mbili pipa* care for some tea?" he offered. Oddly, he was wearing a European shirt and trousers and oddest of all, shoes.

"Only if the worthless old bag of bones will sit and have some with me so I can watch him to be sure he isn't telling more lies about me behind my back," Henry said in Swahili.

"Oh, *Bwana*, I don't know if it would be proper."

"Sit down, Jayubara," Alex said, motioning for his headman to pull up a chair.

"Yes," said Pretorius, "before you spill hot tea all over your *Bwana*'s American pet."

"Pietr, shut up!" Alex said firmly.

"When have I ever listened to sound advice?" Pretorius answered with a grin. "Besides I'd like to hear how 'Jesse James' here came to be called Mister Two Barrels."

"And while he's at it, maybe he can tell us about Mister Elephant Poacher," Henry quipped, then laughed when Pretorius's eyes turned into cold slits.

Suddenly Pretorius laughed. "*Touché,*" he said.

Considering the near outcome of their first encounter, the following days saw a tense truce of sorts carried on between Henry and Pretorius. To Liesel Hammerstein, who heard all about it from her husband, it seemed as though it was very much like two large male beasts constantly testing the strength and will of the other. If it weren't for the fact both of them were quite capable of inflicting serious damage on the other, it would be almost silly. She could understand it better if it involved something other than what Alex called "bragging rights"—a woman, or a trophy of some kind. But they seemed to be always on the verge of going at one another for no reason at all, other than it would prove one of them was what? Quicker? Bigger? Stronger? Better? None of those things really applied. So, therefore, it was just silly, verging on stupid. And Liesel saw to it she was always close at hand when they were near each other, because her presence seemed to have a restraining influence on them.

Alex Hammerstein, on the other hand, did not consider Henry's reaction to Pietr silly. He did consider it dangerous. They were all of an age, and though Alex wasn't exactly sure who was the oldest, he did know enough about the other two to know they had both experienced something he only thought about on occasion. While Alex had spent over a decade of his life, so far, wearing the uniform of his Kaiser—both during his National Service and his Reserve time, in Germany and the Colony—he had never heard a shot fired in anger. Henry and Pietr had both seen combat, though neither one had worn a uniform. Henry had been in the Philippines, twice, during the Insurrection, and in China against the Boxers, and in Manchuria as an observer. Pietr, even before his constant brushes with the Kaiser's law, had ridden *Kommando* with his father and grandfather against the British—his grandfather, or maybe it was his great-grandfather, even had a town named after him, Pretoria. In addition, they were both experienced hunters. Henry had in fact hunted more places, but for less dangerous kinds of animals; Pietr had hunted fewer places but for mostly very large, very dangerous game. They were two bulls warily circling, looking for any sign of an opening. What Alex feared was Henry seemed to be just a touch more—what... moral? Trusting, perhaps? In any case, qualities lacking to a much greater degree in Pietr, who seemed to revel in living on the edge of the law, with no regard to which side of the line was better. And Alex was truly afraid it would ultimately give Pietr the opening he was looking for, in which case, Alex was in a quandary as to what he would do.

They hunted a great deal, pairing up to be sure Pietr and Henry never hunted together. It was an obvious ploy, and all of them knew it, but Pietr and Henry were both decent enough to acquiesce silently. Because, in the greater part, three of the four of them got along splendidly, absent the fourth. Even when Henry and Pietr traded jibes about the "little American Pop-Gun" and the "Artillery piece without wheels"—Henry's reference to Pietr's double 12.7x70mm Schuler, which the British called the 500 Jeffery—rifle, the only gun Pietr claimed to own. And so the argument would begin.

"I saw Kermit Roosevelt take a 700-pound lion with a 405," Henry stated.

"You *saw* him, or he told you about it later?" Pietr asked unpleasantly.

"Saw, as in, *witnessed*. Ask Jayubara, he was there."

Pietr looked over to Jayubara, who had resumed his original Smithsonian Safari role and was holding Henry's Winchester by the barrel over his shoulder. Jayubara nodded but said nothing.

"Hummph!" Pietr snorted. "I'll concede it's probably enough for a lion. But I wonder if you know what they call the pink stuff between an elephant's toes."

"No idea."

"Slow lions." Pietr said, keeping a straight face.

Henry snorted. "But you still don't need a cannon to kill an elephant when you sneak up on him while he's sleeping," he retorted.

"No. You only need luck and prudence."

Before either of them could say any more, Liesel said, "Stop it! The both of you."

Later in the afternoon, as they were walking back to the plantation house, following a long and unusually unsuccessful stalk, Alex and Henry chatted about other places and times. Suddenly, out of nowhere in particular, Alex asked, "Would you have shot him?"

"Rather than let him carve on me? Yes."

"That's what I thought." They walked on for a few minutes before Alex spoke again. "Pietr is Afrikaans. To someone from Africa, that says quite a lot, but I don't think anyone else would understand. As I recall—and I don't know whether I'm right or not—the only sort you might have seen in America something like the Afrikaans are the Dunkers, though I think somewhere I've read you confuse them or lump them all together and call them Amish. That's not at all the case here. Compared to a strict Dutch Reform Afrikaan, your Dunkers would look like a student of Engels or Marx. Fifty years ago or more, the Afrikaans, rather than submit to English rule, loaded their world into ox-wagons and trekked into the interior. And when English rule caught up with them, they did it again. And finally, when they could go no farther, they went to war with the largest empire in the world and fought them for three years. They revel at flying in the face of change. And Pietr's family was and is right at the heart of it. You will not change him, or the way he thinks, or the way he is because if you try, he simply looks at it as a challenge."

"Does that mean I have to like him?"

"No. It just gives you a point to begin understanding what makes him the way he is."

They walked in silence the rest of the way to the house.

It was near the end of May, early in the evening of the day Liesel had taken what all of them considered to be the biggest Eland buck any of them had ever seen—far larger than any of those Henry had witnessed taken on the Roosevelt Safari, now stuffed and on display in the Smithsonian. Liesel, of course was elated, both because she had tracked and stalked the monster pretty much on her own, having warned off Henry and Jayubara, her other hunting companions; and also because she had managed to take "her" eland with Henry's 405 Winchester. She had followed up the shot with a foolishly high repeat offer to buy the rifle from Henry, who declined just as firmly as he had five years before. Even Pietr's attempt at scoffing at the "little pop-gun" was relatively benign. Since Pretorius carried a double 500 he used for everything—mostly from masochism by Henry's way of thinking— Pietr had refused to even fire the Winchester on the grounds it was a "lady's" gun. Henry figured it was more Pietr didn't want to spoil himself with a rifle that didn't punish him for being an asshole every time he pulled the trigger.

After a huge supper of eland loins, they had lounged around telling hunting stories and other bits of mythology. When Alex brought out a bottle of very old and very good Islay Scotch, they toasted Liesel's success.

"We can expect another guest sometime tomorrow," Alex mentioned. "He's the man I will be working for in a month or so—the new commander of the *Schutztruppe*. Jayubara found out he was in Moshi and is on his way here—on some kind of walking tour of the Colony."

"He's the one *Der Dicke* Wahle was telling about the day we arrived," Henry added. "*Der Dicke* said he seemed like a good enough sort."

When Henry roused himself the following morning, Jayubara was waiting for him on the veranda with his breakfast coffee. Henry was surprised not to find Pretorius already feeding. "Oh, *Bwana Jangili* left last night," Jayubara said, adding a lump of cane sugar to Henry's coffee. "He thought it best not to be near here when the new commander arrives."

"Oh, really?"

"Yes, *Bwana*. He was afraid the new commander might know about his troubles with the governor's tax people and have him arrested."

"Ah. He can do that? That serious, is it?"

"Yes, *Bwana*. As commander of the *Schutztruppe*, he is also commander of the *Schutz Polizei*. And there is a warrant for *Bwana Jangili's* arrest. This I know from my cousin who is with the *Schutz Polizei* in Moshi."

"That's how you knew the new commander was coming here?"

"No, *Bwana*. That was from one of my nephews, who is in the *Schutztruppe* company from Moshi."

"Hmmm. Tell me, Jayubara, do you ever lose track of any of your relatives?"

"No, *Bwana*. Never."

Later, following a light lunch, the Hammersteins and Henry were relaxing on the veranda when a tallish, wiry-thin man, with a pointy nose giving him the appearance of a bird of prey, strode from the gate at the Moshi road up the carriageway to within hailing distance of the house. Receiving a wave from Alex, who was facing the road, he strode to the bottom of the porch steps.

"How have you been, Hammerstein?" he asked.

The voice brought Henry abruptly to his feet. He turned to stand next to Alex and heard Liesel rise and push back her chair. The man, seeing Henry for the first time, grinned. Nearly simultaneously, they both said, "Well, I'll be damned," in English, then met to clasp hands in the middle of the front steps.

"How have *you* been, Heinrich? It's been a very long time," *Oberst Leutnant* Paul Emil Von Lettow-Vorbeck said, smiling.

"Yes it has," Henry said. "Did you ever outline your plans to the *Feldmarshall?*"

"Why, yes I did. And he liked them so much he immediately transferred me to the General Staff school and then had me made commander of the marine detachment on the *Hohenzollern*—that's the Kaiser's yacht you know, Henry."

"Really?"

"No, at least not in that order, but it makes a good story," Paul Von Lettow laughed. He turned to Alex Hammerstein. "You'll have to forgive us for telling in-group jokes at your expense. Henry and I knew one another in China. Peking, actually. We spent several interesting months trying to figure out how to get out of there."

Henry was glad Paul had not expanded on exactly where they had spent so much of such an interesting time. He did not wish Liesel to learn that most of it had been in a brothel, most often in a state of inebriation, and often in a stupor. They had last seen one another at the rail depot as Henry walked to the train for the ride back to Tientsin. Paul had walked with Henry and stood on the depot platform as the train chuffed away. After all those years, Henry remembered the wave and Paul's lips forming *"Auf Wiedersehen."*

CHAPTER ELEVEN

Saturday, June 6, 1914
Dar es Salaam
German East Africa

*B*y the time Liesel was finished with her morning ablutions and they had taken a light breakfast in the dining room of the Kaiser Wilhelm Hof, they discovered there was absolutely no place to stand on the dock, or the promenade, or the boulevard. The entire waterfront was crowded cheek to jowl with natives black, brown, yellow and white. And while the beverage vendors were doing a splendid business keeping the throng cool and reasonably sober, the mass of people was not something any of them cared to rub elbows with when no one knew for certain when the main attraction was to arrive. Paul's latest information was she was coming up from Kilwa and had left there the day before. But no one seemed to know if she was to make any stops along the way, or how fast she was moving.

The "she" in question was the light cruiser *Sieges Majesties Schiff (SMS) Königsberg*, sent out from Germany with a hand-picked crew for the Exposition. Which was all well and good, and exactly as much as anyone seemed to know—Governor Schnee assumed they would find out more when she arrived, supposedly this afternoon. So Henry took Alex, Liesel, and Paul Von Lettow back up to his suite, where they had a small bottle of Moselle. And then they wandered down to the end of the corridor, where they could catch a view of most of the harbor from the window without having to hop up and down Masai style to see anything.

As they watched, the crowd on the waterfront suddenly began to surge toward the end of the pier. The guttural crowd noise could be heard inside through the balcony doors. Henry opened the double windows, and they stepped out onto the small balcony. In the distance, just inside the twin arms of the harbor mouth, was a long, very white, very sleek ship throwing up a bow wave as she steamed majestically into the harbor, plumes of smoke streaming back from her three funnels.

Then there were flashes and clouds of whitish-grey smoke erupting from all parts of her hull and, seconds later, surprisingly loud booms as she fired all ten guns of her main battery in salute. The crowd began to cheer.

It took another hour for the cruiser to stop and be gently nudged into her berth. Once the gangways were lowered to the dock and a guard of sailors positioned to control the throng, the ship was opened to visitation. As the multitude of colonists surged up the after gangway, the majority of the ship's officers walked down the forward ladder to dockside. *Oberst-Leutnant* Von Lettow-Vorbeck was standing at the bottom of the ladder waiting for them.

As the first of the ship's officers stepped onto the dock, Paul dropped most of his pretense of protocol and extended his hand. "Looff, I might have known it would be you in command," he said.

An impeccably groomed and starched officer smiled as he took Paul's hand. "Ah, Von Lettow, how good to see you again. Rumor had it you were in command here, yes?"

"Yes. For once the Kiel rumor-mill was correct. I got here in January."

"Ah."

"I take it you've had a pleasant voyage?"

"Excellent. Took our time. Did a bit of a Mediterranean cruise to Alexandria, then through the Canal to Aden, then down to Kilwa and back up here, with a couple of stops along the way, showing the flag."

Paul turned, "May I present my companions—Alex and Liesel Hammerstein, who are colonists, and Henry Feller, an American writer, who is supposedly here to write about the Exposition but is actually wasting most of his time hunting and drinking beer. Henry, Alex, Liesel, may I present Max Looff, Captain of the *SMS Königsberg*, which was our escort cruiser when I had the marine detachment on the *Hohenzollern*."

There was a nearly strained look on the Naval officer's face while he strove to maintain his martial aloofness in the face of Paul's deliberately loose-jointed introduction. Henry could see the difference pass across Looff's eyes as he struggled to decide how to handle the introduction.

There was the slightest twitch of the ends of his *de-rigeur* Wilhelmine moustache before he turned to introduce the other ship's officers now standing immediately behind him on the dock.

"May I present my First Officer, George Koch, and my Gunnery Officer, Richard Wenig. They are hand picked, which means I have to watch them constantly. George, Richard, this is *Oberst-Leutnant* Paul Von Lettow-Vorbeck, who commands all of the Kaiser's troops—all three of them—in this Colony, and his friend Mister Feller, an American spy, and two fine, upstanding colonists, the Hammersteins."

It was now Paul Von Lettow's turn to be nearly speechless. But then he and Looff laughed aloud. "You haven't changed much," he chuckled.

"Nor have you. Now tell me, where can someone of my outstanding talents get a little schnapps in this town?"

"Follow me," Paul said as he led the way toward the Kaiser Wilhelm Hof.

Over the next hours around a large table on the veranda garden, Henry was soon to discover Max Looff was far less the martinet he first looked on the dock. The Captain had the same sort of sense of humor as Paul, and they both enjoyed planting good-natured barbs. Well into the second, or possibly third round of drinks, they were joined by a young officer—younger even than Wenig, who Henry judged to be about ten years junior to himself—who was introduced as Eberhard Niemeyer, the Wireless Officer. Niemeyer reported the Reserve officers they had been expecting had reported on board and had been assigned as Looff had wished.

Looff nodded approvingly. "Good," he said, "now we can plan our social life for the next few days. I am under instructions from the Kriegsmarine to use the reservists to relieve the regular complement as a training program. We'll break them in the next day or two and then, if everything is going as planned, we can try to get in a little hunting and sight-seeing."

"I would suggest," Paul said quickly, "your first priority should be to pay a semi-official social visit to the Governor."

Looff nodded. "*Doktor* Schnee, isn't it?"

"Yes—*und Frau Ada.*"

"They are a matched set?"

"They are a mismatched set."

"That's not a very nice thing to say, Paul," Liesel said.

Paul shrugged. Max Looff raised an eyebrow.

"I will arrange it tomorrow, then," Looff finishing the topic quickly. He gestured for Niemeyer to pull up a chair and circled his hand over his head to call for another round of drinks. Nothing more of the Governor was mentioned.

"Might I suggest if you want to get in some hunting, Captain," Alex began, "we can go up to my place and hunt from there. The scenery is pleasant, and it doesn't take overly long to get there."

"Really?"

"We can be there in two days. The coastal up to Tanga, then the train to Moshi, and a carriage to the farm."

"Considering everything, like the fact you have to report for your reserve duty by July 1st—why don't we see if we can hunt out of Dickey's place?" Henry suggested. "It's a day closer, give or take, so you can get back quicker. Besides, I think Captain Looff would like to meet General Papa, not to mention I kind of promised to take General Papa bird shooting if he let me use one of his shotguns."

"I take it you hunt as well as spy?" Looff asked.

"I'm an absolutely splendid hunter. But I'm sorry to say I'm only a mediocre spy—Ryan's doesn't pay nearly as well for spying as they do for writing," Henry answered. "You have to be British to be an excellent spy."

"You do?"

"Oh, yes. Just ask them. They'll tell you." Henry managed to keep a straight face.

Paul pretended to cough. "Heinrich was on the Roosevelt Safari. He was born and raised in the Wild West where they have the Red Indians. Not to mention he was in the Philippines during their little carfuffle with the natives. And of course, China, where he was chaperoned by a splendid young *Leutnant* of Artillery."

"China, eh?" Looff said. "That makes us all part of the same, rather small fraternity. I was a guard officer on *SMS Woerth* at Taku and then in the river at Tientsin."

"Well, then," Paul said lifting his glass, "here's to us and those like us."

"Damn few left," Henry and Max intoned.

"Now," Looff continued, "what were you saying, Alex, about taking a coastal?"

"To get to Tanga, Captain, we have to take a coastal steamer to Tanga. Then ride the northern railroad either to near Buiko, where Dickey's place is, or on to Moshi, the nearest town to our place."

"Why would we have to do that?"

"Because it's a couple of hundred kilometers up the coast to Tanga, and there are no roads, at least none decent enough to make any time on."

"No, no, no. I don't mean how far and all that. I mean why do we have to take a little slow steamer?"

Paul, Henry, and Alex all looked at each other. "Because it's there?" Paul ventured, laughingly.

"Ach, you soldiers and spies are such dunderheads. You want to pay to take a slow, smelly boat, one probably run by a bloody Arab or Hindu, when we have a splendid, fast, clean light cruiser waiting our beck and call."

"You can do that?" Henry asked.

"I am the Captain of the Kaiser's Man of War. Even *Herr* Gott has to ask my permission to visit." Looff grinned.

Henry, the ever-unrepentant Congregationalist, mused to himself, *Only a German officer would add "Mister" as part of God's name.*

"Besides which," Looff continued, "One, it will be a training cruise for my reserve officers, and Two, I've got to call on Tanga as part of my itinerary, anyway. I am simply planning to kill two birds—and perhaps a small lion and several antelopes—with one stone, or rather, with one spanking-new Mannlicher-Schonauer 8x56mm rifle I had made for this little trip. I think Wenig and Koch are also suitably armed. Now, *Herr* Feller, who is this 'General Papa' you mentioned?"

"Dickey Wahle's father is here for the Exposition. We came in on the same ship from Naples. He's a retired *Generalmajor* in the Saxon service. Has a couple of really fine, Austrian—Suhl-made—double barrels we were using on the ship. When we came down here from Alex's place, we stopped in at Dickey's for a couple of days and I sort of promised some bird hunting to the General—Dickey always calls him Papa, so naturally I call him General Papa, but not to his face, of course. Anyway, there's a ton of water fowl along the river near Buiko."

"Are there lions and antelopes around Buiko?"

Henry looked at Alex and Liesel. "There are lions everywhere in East Africa, Captain," Alex said. "I'm sure we could scare up a couple for you."

"Ah, good. When do you want to leave for Tanga?"

"After you've made nice to Governor Schnee and *Frau* Ada. And then we can show you the sights for a day or so," Paul said. "And don't look so crest-fallen, Looff—there are some first-class places to eat and drink in Dar that you simply can't miss. Just think of it as being fattened up for the lions." Paul and Max laughed.

Henry looked over at Alex. *Strange,* he thought, *the first thing into my head is something I'd expect to come out of Pretorius's mouth. I really don't think an 8x56mm is enough rifle to handle a lion. And I think Paul knows that, too, otherwise he wouldn't make a joke about it. He has a really refined sense of mortuary humor. Well, shit, here we go again, another job of looking out after a nimrod. Just like Kermit. Only with these three I don't know if any of them have ever fired at anything more dangerous than a nice slow Black Forest stag. Shit.*

CHAPTER TWELVE

Tuesday, June 16, 1914
The Wahle Plantation
Near Buiko, G.E.A.

*T*heir leaving for Tanga was delayed for five days due to the scheduling of the Königsberg's officers' social meeting with the Governor and Frau Ada. That took all of two hours. It was the return conference between the Governor and Captain Looff used up the rest of the time. Henry wondered what could be that important. According to Paul, his meeting with the Governor upon his arrival to take command had lasted, if anything, less time than Henry's preemptive "nice-to-meet-you-now-get-the-hell-out-of-my-office" audience. Henry's descriptive phrase caused Paul to chortle, but he still didn't hazard a guess of what Looff and the Governor were talking about, which caused Henry to immediately suspect Paul knew and was simply not saying.

In any case, the delay in departure gave Liesel Hammerstein the opportunity to throw a welcoming party for the officers and crew of the cruiser. It was another indication of just how little Henry really knew about the inner workings and wherewithal of his colonial friends. Very quickly—in a matter of hours—Liesel had hired a band, rented the ballroom of the Berghoff, hired a caterer, called down some of her servants from the plantation to supervise the hired Africans and Arabs to staff the doings. She also arranged all of the other small bits and pieces necessary to throw a multi-hundred-guest *soirré*, complete to the last bit of red-white-and-black bunting and appropriate naval ensigns to decorate the place. Henry could only guess at the cost of such an affair, but it meant Alex and Liesel were at least as well-heeled as he was—or, they had a typically colonial knack of living ostentatiously beyond their means.

The party was scheduled for the evening before they were all to sail for Tanga. The guests began showing up the day before, and more came during the morning and afternoon of the day. The number and relative importance of the guests was also a surprise to Henry. Especially when two of them walked up to him in the gentlemen's bar of the Kaiser Wilhelm Hof, where he and General Papa were having a small tide-me-over-until-teatime drink, and introduced themselves as Perry Hays and Frank Vining, the American Consul and Vice-Consul in Zanzibar. They were a part of the general diplomatic retinue attending the party. Henry had not been aware his face was known to the American State Department crowd and said as much. Vining, who did most of the talking—and who knew who *Generalmajor* Wahle was—off-handedly said Ryan's had given the Consulate a heads-up and asked them to make certain Henry's stay in German East was "without ripples," whatever the hell that implied.

The evening began to turn a little bleary for Henry after the third or fourth round of well-oiled *gemütlich*. Uncustomarily for him, he decided not to make a drunken ass of himself at Liesel's party, and wandered out onto the Berghoff's wrap-around porch and just sat on the rail. The hired band was doing a surprisingly nice job of playing a variety of popular music interspersed with the usual Strauss and semi-patriotic tunes. The air was cool and after a while his head began to clear enough to allow him to realize he was not alone sitting in the dark. Two others, or more, were leaning on the porch railing, smoking—cigars—and speaking in animated but low voices.

The one farthest from Henry's position was now saying, "…I only have ten companies to guard and patrol the whole Colony, the borders on three sides of which are colonies of probable enemies, though I'm not overly concerned with the military might of either Portugal or Belgium. But the English—ah, the English—and just a little farther south the bloody Frogs, just slavering for a chance at *revenge* for '70. Ten companies for nearly a million square kilometers, and in those ten companies, I have exactly ten machine guns, none of them the latest model. Practically no artillery. You've ten times the artillery power on your one ship, Looff."

Aha! It was Paul's voice, and he is obviously talking to Max Looff.

"Speaking of the '70 war—eight of those ten companies are armed with rifles the Fatherland adopted right after that war, '71 Mausers, in use since we were children. That wouldn't be so bad, but there are two models, the '71 and the '84, and although they are both 11mm, they take different cartridges. Fortunately, the '84s will accept the '71 ammunition, but not the other way around. I have managed to rearm two companies with '98s, but the *Scheissekopfs* in supply sent out more 11mm '84 cartridges instead of 7.92mm, so there is only enough ammunition for a small skirmish with belligerent natives. Fortunately, there are only a very few belligerent natives." Paul laughed derisively.

"I feel for you Von Lettow," Looff comforted. "My lot is considerably easier. I already have my orders. I don't have much to say about it at all. All I have to do is take the envelope out of the safe, pass the codes on to the appropriate people, and let them plot the course."

"Is that what you told the little English twit in there?"

"Can you imagine *that?* The temerity of that little *Anglische scheissekopf* asking what I intended to do with my ship should we—theoretically, of course—go to war with Russia. Hell, why didn't he say Lichtenstein or even San Marino. I think your friend Feller is wrong—the English are not very good spies. I'm going to tell my officers to stay the hell away from Mister King."

"Oh, I wouldn't do that, Max. Norman is so blatantly open about it I've been giving him false information since the second time I met him. He hasn't yet realized we consider *all* diplomats spies, *du jour* if not *de facto*. Besides, he plays a good hand of bridge."

Henry, his head now fairly clear, remembered Looff talking with—actually being talked at by—a man someone had pointed out to him—*It might have been Vining*—as being the British consul in Dar. *Made sense—Looff had looked surprised and hadn't said more than a couple of words before moving away.* This overheard conversation convinced Henry to stay in the shadows as Paul and Max moved back into the ballroom. Then Henry lit a cigar and smoked most of it before he wandered back inside himself.

On a whim, he wandered up to the bandstand and got the attention of the band leader, who bent down to allow Henry to whisper in his ear. Thinking for a moment, the band director nodded affirmatively and whispered something back. Henry took a folded bill out of his pocket and passed it to the director who nodded appreciatively and went back to leading the band through the last repeats of Strauss's *Tales of the Vienna Woods.* Henry set a course through the crowd to where Alex and Liesel were chatting with one of the reserve officers from *Königsberg,* Werner Schönfeld, whose wife was going to go along up to *Der Dicke's* to keep Liesel company. Henry had been introduced to the Schönfelds and had taken an immediate liking to Werner, who reminded Henry of his rancher uncle Fred. As they were chatting, the band began to play a tune very few of the colonials knew. Henry took the opportunity to take Liesel by the hand and began to lead her to the dance floor, telling Alex he was only going to borrow her for as long as the tune lasted.

They began a slow waltz, with Henry holding Liesel close enough for her to hear him. For one of the few times in his life he was glad he had paid attention when his sisters had insisted he learn at least the rudiments of popular dance steps and had dragged him, protesting loudly, around the parlor to the accompaniment of the Victrola. Tizzy had taken all afternoon to teach him to waltz, without the formal sweeps and turns, and Dell had taught him how to two-step and cake walk—though he would never admit it, let alone attempt it. But here he was comfortable enough to go around the floor a couple of times with his surrogate colonial sister, who, as he had planned, asked the name of the tune once they were actually dancing without injuring one another.

"The name, my dear Liesel, is *The Band Played On.* It was popular when I was in the Philippines. And you, my dear somewhat sister, are a strawberry blonde, so I could think of nothing more appropriate on this festive occasion, replete with handsome soldiers and sailors and diplomats—who are nowhere near as handsome—and spies; and, of course the handsomest one of all, the writer." Henry began to sing tipsily with the music:

Casey would waltz with the strawberry blonde and the band played on.
He'd glide 'cross the floor with the girl he'd adore and the band played on.
But his brain was so loaded it nearly exploded
The poor girl would shake with alarm
He'd ne'er leave the girl with the strawberry curl and the band played on.

Liesel laughed delightedly as they waltzed. "I'm not shaking with alarm, Heinrich. I'm shaking with laughter. And I fear you will leave, sooner or later."

"Don't worry. I don't plan for us to explode, either. Besides, my name isn't Casey. Because you know how those Irish are…"

As the tune ended, Liesel leaned to him and kissed him on the cheek. When he looked up, Henry was surprised to see they were the only couple on the dance floor, surrounded by the rest of the guests. Alex applauded loudly and he and Paul shouted, "Bravo. Bravo. Encore." Henry made a exaggerated bow to Liesel and led her from the floor, handing her back to her husband, while the other guests laughed and clapped their hands.

They all boarded *Königsberg* the following morning and were allowed to stay on deck provided they keep out of the way of the crew. The deck plates began to throb as soon as the tug pulled them from their place at the DOA dock cast off its tow lines. The bow began to cut a white curl at its point, and a wake began to stream out to both sides as the cruiser picked up speed heading for the harbor mouth. They slowed as they passed between the points of land, and a small boat came alongside and took off the pilot, who waved a cheery goodbye. Outside the harbor they heeled to the left and began to steam up the coast. All three funnels belched black smoke as they gained headway. Judging by the wind sweeping the length of the ship, Henry figured they were doing 20 knots or a little more.

The ladies took shelter from the sun by ducking into the officer's ward room, while the men stood in the shade of the forward 4.1-inch gun turret just behind the breakwater. All in all it was a pleasant and interesting cruise. Once they were well underway, Max Looff turned the bridge over to George Koch and came down to conduct them on a personalized tour of the ship. They roamed in her bowels literally from stem to stern for the next hours, finally returning to the deck to feel the engines begin to slow. As they swung in toward Ras Kasone point, the Tanga pilot boat came along side and the Arab pilot swiftly climbed the accomodation ladder and gave Looff a wide, toothy grin before climbing up on the bridge. Looff bade them all into the Officers' mess as the claxon sounded the crew to battle stations. In less than two minutes Looff looked out of the hatchway to the bridge, and having received a hand signal from Koch, nodded. Immediately, there were ten terrifically loud crashes moving one after another from bow to stern as the main battery fired its usual salute on entering a friendly harbor.

The salvo coming into Dar had been one of the loudest things Henry had ever heard, far louder than Captain Reilly's field pieces. That had been a mile or so away. Now Henry's ears rang and he felt, but fortunately fought off, an instantaneous desire to empty his bowels at the blast. From the looks on many of the other faces, save Paul Von Lettow-Vorbeck's, most of the others had the same experience.

A little over seven hours after they had cleared the harbor at Dar, they docked at the same berth usually used by the coastal steamer, which they had undoubtedly passed on the way up. Tanga was smaller than Dar, but one wouldn't know it by the throng of upturned heads on the dock. They ran esentially the same drill as they had on arrival at Dar, that is, the aft accomodation ladder was the up stairway and the foreward was the return point to the dock. Once the crew was set, the crowd was allowed to begin climbing aboard, while those officers and men not on duty moved down the foreward ladder and away as quickly as they could.

As Henry stepped down the ladder, following General Papa, the words he heard most often murmuring up from the crowd were "*maniwari na bamba tatu.*" He smiled to himself. He'd have to tell Max Looff the natives considered his funnels the most important part of the ship. It was truly, in the native mind, the "Man of War with Three Chimneys."

The entire party walked across the dock to the depot of the Northern Railroad and checked the schedule. The train was not running late today and was expected in within minutes, according to the ticket clerk. But Alex said the clerk had been trained to give that answer no matter what. They all went to the Kaiser Wilhelm Hof and had a nice luncheon, keeping an ear open for the sound of the engine, which, surprise of surprises, actually arrived within thirty minutes of being on time. By the time the engine was turned around, coaled, watered, and reattached to the cars, they had returned to the depot, had their luggage hefted onto the baggage car, and found seats. And Richard Wahle had wired ahead to have some of his "people" meet them at the depot—the usual arrangement, as Henry was beginning to learn.

Buiko was a little less than halfway to Moshi on the Northern Railway and *Der Dicke's* plantation was only a few miles to the south along the Pangani River where it bent to the east along the base of the foothills at the beginning of the Pare Hills. With the river and the rolling green hills to offer food and shelter, the area was teeming with all manner of game—and, by the way of nature, with all manner of predators to eat the game. The first two days, Henry and General Papa hunted the river bank, bringing in large and varied loads of water fowl each evening.

Finally, on the third day, he could put it off no longer. Henry agreed to take Max Looff out to look for a small lion, and for whatever else happened along. Alex and *Der Dicke* would take Wenig and Koch and try to run down an antelope or two, preferably not too old and tough to eat. Jayubara would go along with Henry, of course, while Liesel and *Frau* Schönfeld would stay at the house with *Frau* Wahle and prepare some of the fowl for a celebratory supper. Henry wasn't sure what they were celebrating, and he was fairly sure being left at the house had not put Liesel in the best of moods. Too bad, that was Alex's worry, not his.

Henry trusted Jayubara to cut some sort of tracks for them, and he was not surprised when Jayubara began tracking lion spoor within an hour of their leaving the last of *Der Dicke's* fields. Henry told Max to load and then made certain his Winchester was loaded and ready. Jayubara was carrying Liesel's 9.3mm, and as soon as he cut track, he had moved it from his shoulder to a position across his chest. If nothing else, the movement told Henry they were fairly close to the cat they were following. That also proved to be true within minutes. As they crossed a small clearing and approached a thicket, they heard a telltale cough, and the hairs on Henry's neck suddenly came to attention as a little tale Jayubara had used at one point in the past flashed through his mind: "*Bwana,*" he had said, "it is said a lion frightens a man three times.

Once when you see its track, once when you hear it, and once when you see it." Henry thought to himself, *now we are two out of three*, about a half second before something very large and yellowish brown came out of the thicket no more than 75 yards away. Henry and Max Looff both instantly brought their rifles to their shoulders. Jayubara, closer to the cat by several yards, leaped sideways to give the men behind him a clear shot, but as he did so, he tripped on a small bush and tumbled into the dust, losing his grip on his rifle. The lion, a large, very pissed-off female, was capable of covering the distance to them in less than three steps, and she had already taken one and a half. Somewhere in that time Henry recalled later he had yelled something on the order of, "Shoot! Jesus Christ, Max, shoot!" As fear clutched at his throat, attempting to squeeze his eyeballs out of his skull, he thought he heard Looff yell something to the effect of, "I can't get the safety off!" This registered just in time for Henry to fire and then empty the remaining rounds in his magazine at the lion, which had begun to leap. The second shot from the Winchester—God only knows where the first one went—evidently passed through the lioness's chest and shattered her spine. She was close enough that the shock of the bullet, and the next one that hit her through the diaphragm nearly stopped her in mid-leap, the fourth and fifth going wherever the first had gone. Nearly stopped her. She had enough momentum to carry her body to within five feet of Henry before she hit the ground.

All Henry could say was "Holy Shit!"

A sensible African hunter would have immediately reloaded his magazine. Henry was not an African hunter. His first concern was Jayubara, who was still face down in the dust with his arms thrown over his head to try to protect what he could from the expected lion attack. When Henry kicked Jayubara's foot, Jayubara only shook his head. Henry kicked his foot harder, finally rasping, "Are you all right?"

At the sound of a human voice instead of a snarl tinged with a blast of hot breath smelling of rotting meat, Zayubara moved his arms off his head and rolled onto his side, looking up at Henry. "*Bwana*," he said, "I think I am getting too old to be doing this sort of thing."

Henry grinned and extended a hand to help Jayubara to his feet. Instead, Jayubara sat looking beyond Henry into the thicket. There was a look of absolute terror on his face while he pointed and said very quietly, like a man staring in the face of death, *"mbogo."* The word turned Henry's blood to frozen mush. He slowly turned—very slowly—to look where Jayubara was pointing. Seventy-five yards away, clearly visible, the *mbogo*—Cape Buffalo—stared out of the thicket at them, its red eyes filled with hate for anything not of its own kind and half of the things that were. From the distance, its horn boss looked to be three feet across. Its black coat was at once shiny and dull with dust. Its potato-sized brain was trying to decide which one of them it was going to kill first.

Max Looff didn't even see the *mbogo*. He was still fiddling with his rifle, still trying to figure out how to get the safety released. Henry's rifle was empty. It would take him longer to reload even a single round than it would take the *mbogo* to reach him. Jayubara's rifle was five yards away in the dirt. By Henry's best guestimation, they were all dead men. It was only a matter of how long the Cape Buff wanted to string out the agony.

Not long. With a snort and a bellow, the Cape Buffalo began its charge. When it was nearly at a run—and only fifty yards from Henry—there were two very loud shots, followed almost instantly by a sound very much like one would expect if he thumped a watermelon with a sledge hammer. The *mbogo* took two more steps, staggered, and stumbled. Blood began to stream from its nostrils as it toppled onto its side. Its legs twitched twice, three times, and it was still.

Pietr Pretorious stepped out of the thicket, snapping the breech of his double rifle shut, indicating he had already reloaded. He looked at Max Looff, who was standing where he had been since the lioness first emerged. Looff's face was pale white, and his hands and knees were trembling.

Pretorius shook his head. "Bloody Nimrod."

He walked over and helped lift Jayubara to his feet. "Just like a bloody *Kaffir*. Fell over your own goddamned feet." He turned to Henry. "Now tell me the 500 Jeffery is an artillery piece without wheels."

"Thank you, Pietr." Henry said.

"I don't want your thanks. It was sheer dumb luck I happened by, that's all." Pretorius stopped suddenly. "There is one thing you can do for me—to repay me for saving your miserable lives…"

"Anything you want."

"Good. Tell the bunch of *Schutz Polizei* that will be here in the next few minutes that you didn't see me."

"Done."

"*Wiedersehen*, Heinrich," Pretorius said as he stepped back toward the thicket, "Try to remember to reload your goddamned pop gun." Pietr disappeared into the brush.

Once Henry was certain Jayubara was uninjured, he sent him back to the house to bring out enough workers to haul the lion and the Cape Buffalo back. Henry sat on the buffalo's carcass as much to keep away the vultures and other predators as to keep his own legs from quaking. He pulled five cartridges out of the loops on his jacket and fed them carefully into the magazine of the Winchester, putting the last one in the chamber by working the lever.

Max Looff came over and sat down next to him. "I made a bloody ass of myself, didn't I?" he said.

"Yes. You did. But so did I. I never asked if you'd ever fired your new rifle. You never have, have you?"

"No."

"So you never learned a Mannlicher safety doesn't work like a Mauser safety, or a Schuler or a Suhl; or for that matter a Winchester, or a Colt, or a Maynard. And no one bothered to tell you, in Africa, once you cut game track, use of a safety can be fatal. This isn't the *Schwarzwald*, or for that matter the South Dakota prairie. And I never bothered to ask you. *My* fault."

"So now what?"

"So now we go find out, in the words of a pretty fair country shot named Selous, whether you've managed to learn anything from the experience."

"What do you propose?"

"I propose we—you—go get us a nice succulent antelope for supper." Henry rose. "Come on, there's bound to be something edible fairly close, otherwise lions wouldn't be around."

Jayubara was not surprised when he arrived back at the buffalo carcass with twenty men and a mule cart to find two young antelope lying beside the lion carcass. *Bwana mbili pipa* and the sailor *Kapitani* were sitting on the buffalo smoking cigars. *Bwana mbili pipa* waved.

Later, after a very nice supper of antelope steak, Henry and Paul sat on the veranda, sipping at glasses of Der Dicke's whiskey.

"That was a very successful hunt, today, wasn't it, Heinrich? Max got to shoot his new rifle and provided us with a splendid meal. You took a very nice lion..." Paul paused. "Who shot the Cape Buffalo? And don't tell me it was you—it was shot with a very big rifle, and you yourself said you had emptied your Winchester into the lion. And Jayubara says he never fired. So? Who, Heinrich?"

Henry put his glass down on the table. He looked at Paul. Finally he answered, "Pietr Pretorius."

"*Ach so*—the one you told the *Feldwebel* of the *Schutz Polizei* you hadn't seen. The one who shot two policemen and is running from the law because of the taxes he refused to pay? That Pietr Pretorius?"

"That's the one."

"You know assisting a criminal is against the law, of course?"

"Yes."

"Even when that criminal saves your life, and that of the commander of the Kaiser's man of war, and an old bag of bones who insists on wearing European clothing?"

"Even then."

"So, what do you think I should do about it? Being as I am commander of *all* of the Kaiser's forces in this Colony, which includes the *Schutz-polizei.*" Paul raised an eyebrow.

"Depends on whether you want to arrest the Commander of the Kaiser's Man of War along with the American writer."

"Looff was there too, eh?"

111

"Standing right next to me when I told the cop we hadn't seen anyone." Henry fell silent.

"Hmmm. Wouldn't do to arrest the Kaiser's officer, would it?"

"No, it wouldn't."

"Well then, I had best simply go to bed." Paul rose, and turned toward the door.

Henry rose saying to Paul's back, "What was just said, was said between comrades. It will go no further."

Henry turned toward the door leading to the back hallway and began walking away. Then suddenly he turned and said "Just a suggestion, Paul, but since the '71 and the '84 are both black powder rifles, there can't be much difference in breech pressure between them, regardless of the cartridge size. Why not have a machine shop make a reamer and ream the short chambers out to the length of the longer cartridge? Try it with one rifle, and if it works, do the rest. That way, at least they could all use the ammunition you have, instead of having to worry about dividing it up."

Henry walked through the doorway before Paul could answer.

CHAPTER THIRTEEN

Tuesday, June 30, 1914
Government House
Dar es Salaam, G.E.A.

Governor Schnee's small office was crowded. It was an anteroom really, off to one side of the great reception hall. Besides the Governor and his staff, there were the officers of SMS Königsberg, both regular and the reservists now serving for the duration of the cruiser's visit; and the Commanding Officer, staff, and many of the company officers, again both regulars and reservists, of the Schutztruppe; and some of the Schutze Kompagnie commanders who lived near at hand to the capital. In all, nearly thirty sailors and nearly twice that number of soldiers jammed the room. They had all been summoned by the Governor, who now pushed his way through the throng and stood behind his desk, sternly looking them into silent anticipation.

"Gentlemen, I have just received a telegram from Kigoma where the radio station has been contacted by the Office of Secretary Solf on orders of Chancellor von Jagow, and the coded message verified by representatives of the *Kriegsmarine* and *Oberost Das Heeres…*" Schnee paused to let the matter of highest verification sink in. "…the message is as follows: 'On 28 June 1914, Archduke Ferdinand of Austria-Hungary and his wife Sofia were assassinated in the city of Sarajevo, Serbia.' For those of you who are unsure of your geography, that is in the Balkans. The message continues, 'The assassin was apprehended immediately. Austria-Hungary has demanded several concessions from the Serbs, but as yet no action of any sort has taken place.' Nor is it expected. This is a rather trifling issue. But the Chancellor feels that, due to the close ties between Austria-Hungary and ourselves, both spiritually and through treaty obligations, any actions against Austria-Hungary taken by anyone will undoubtedly be answered in some form by us. So be alerted. Dismissed."

Schnee turned abruptly and strode out a side door, leaving the officers in stunned silence.

CHAPTER FOURTEEN

Wednesday, July 15, 1914
Governor's Palace
Dar es Salaam, G.E.A.

The three men seated around the governor's desk were the men who would be responsible for carrying out the Kaiser's wishes in the event of war. Only one of them wished, reluctantly, to carry on a war at all, regardless of the Kaiser's wishes. The man who sat across from him thought a war in Europe, or for that matter anywhere else, would be the single very worst thing that could happen to the Colony of German East Africa. Oddly, it was probably the only thing all three of them agreed upon.

The third man sitting at the desk was more of an impartial player in the events that might or might not unfold in the Colony. This man took his orders from a body not in Berlin, but rather in Kiel, and his was the easiest role to describe because there were so few facets to it. In general terms, his role in whatever came had been written into a war plan over a decade before, and it was immutable. This man was present because he represented the most visible symbol of the Kaiser's might in the Colony. He was well aware the other two men did not get along and he had been used as a sounding board by both. Now, as he sat and listened to them exchange frigidly proper dialogue, he was adamant in his determination not to get caught up in any way in their little power struggle. Therefore he was surprised when *Oberst-Leutnant* Lettow-Vorbeck opened the meeting with a question seemingly completely unrelated to the preparations for war.

"So, *Excellenz*, what shall we do about our American journalist?"

"What do you mean, 'what shall we do about him'?" Governor Heinrich Schnee answered in his usual way—answering a question with a question, and then adding his own thoughts onto the end. "I would assume he will leave with the other foreign nationals if war breaks out. There is already a mechanism. Both the American and British Consuls

114

have informed me they have hired Arab dhows to carry the foreign nationals to another port. And the Arabs will fly American flags as neutral hires."

"I know all that, *Excellenz*." Von Lettow answered. "But I think it better suits our interests if Mister Feller were sent where he could take ship for a journey guaranteeing—so much as we can guarantee anything—at least his safe and speedy return to the United States."

"And why would it be in our best interest to do this thing?"

"Because he is a friendly voice, a well-known friendly voice, who was sent here to write a book about the wondrous merits of this place and sent by an editor who is also an 'influential' German-American, one among some millions of German-Americans who I would like to think are allied with us in spirit, regardless of what their sour-pussed President would have you to believe."

"That's all well and good...So?"

"So anything Heinrich Feller writes and publishes will be believed by millions of 'neutral' Americans, and presumably some millions of others, all of whom are being herded and pulled along by their political leaders toward actively supporting our enemies."

"Hmmm. So, what do you propose?"

"That, *Excellenz*, is why I had you ask *Fregattenkapitan* Looff to join us. He knows far more about actually doing something with *Herr* Feller that either you or I."

"For example?"

"The nearest port where he could be put on a ship bound for either the United States or a neutral port in Europe. Definitely not a French or Portuguese ship, and preferably not a British ship, that might be suddenly reassigned to support the Royal Navy."

"What about a German ship?" This was asked by Max Looff, who heretofore had been listening in silence. "Since we are not certain the English will enter the conflict, there is a German ship, the Lloyd DOA liner *Zeiten* that should be able to make it to Naples without difficulty. She is due to arrive in Colombo, Ceylon, in seven or eight days, on her way home from China. She should be able to coal-up in four or five days and is then due to stop in Naples to drop off passengers before heading to Bremen."

"So how would we get *Herr* Feller to Colombo?" Governor Schnee asked.

"We could put him aboard the *Somali*. She has been selected as my tender—though that is not generally known—because she can make 18 knots when necessary and cruises at 15 knots. I intended to send her to Colombo for a load of coal and supplies anyway, so I can just move her schedule up. She should actually be able to leave tomorrow. And to answer your next question, *Oberst*, it's nearly 3,000 miles to Colombo," Looff made a calculation in his head, " a little over eight days, given good weather—on the Indian Ocean, not too likely—so call it a ten or eleven day cruise. *Herr* Feller should be able to reach the *Zeiten* before it's ready to leave."

"We might also wire them there is an important passenger coming to them and to wait a reasonable time for him…"

"Yes," agreed Von Lettow-Vorbeck, "but I would suggest we do it right away, and in an off-handed manner; make it sound as though we didn't care. That way, when the British listen in, it will not sound overly important. And we can accomplish it before—if they come into the war—before they cut the cables and interfere with the radios."

"Agreed," Governor Schnee announced.

Looff rose and saluted. "With your permission, Excelenz, I will be on my way."

"Very well, *Fregattenkapitan*," Schnee said formally, rising to bid the others good day. *Leutenant-Oberst* Von Lettow-Vorbeck, however, remained seated, a fact that brought a small smile to Max Looff's lips as he let himself out of the office. In the background he heard Von Lettow-Vorbeck once more request permission to begin moving the scattered companies of his *Schutztruppen* to the northern border, and Governor Schnee's resounding *Nein… Nein… Nein…* as the argument had been going on for weeks once more reopened.

CHAPTER FIFTEEN

Thursday, July 16, 1914
Room 224
The Kaiser Wilhelm Hof
Dar es Salaam, G.E.A.

*T*he imperious knocking—no, that was too mild—the imperious pounding on his door brought Henry out of his bathroom without the opportunity to put on his tie or jacket. There was no answer to his startled "Who is it?" which he couldn't remember if he had blurted out in German or English. It didn't matter in any case, for when he threw the door open, Paul Von Lettow-Vorbeck immediately walked into the room, followed by a number of uniformed Askaris and trailed by Alex Hammerstein, now in uniform. Without speaking, Paul motioned for the Askaris to gather Henry's luggage.

"What the hell are you doing?" Henry demanded as two large soldiers began to carry one of his trunks out the door.

Paul looked at him, a wry grin on his face, and lifted a finger to his lips. "Sssh. Be quiet and be a good boy, and I will have my Adjutant explain it to you, Heinrich. I believe you already know my Adjutant, *Hauptman* Hammerstein?"

Fifteen minutes later they were parading across the harbor boulevard toward the dark gray bulk of a freighter tied off to the Lloyd DOA dock. Several hundred yards across the harbor, the white hull of the *Königsberg* gleamed in the sun. A thin haze of smoke wafted from her funnels, showing the world she was making only enough steam to operate her internal machinery. The freighter, on the other hand, was spewing a dense black column of smoke. She was obviously simply waiting for the hawsers to be let loose so she could steam out of the harbor. She was also waiting for the last of her very short list of passengers—one—and his luggage to be put on board. Henry, Paul, and Alex followed the line of *Askaris* across the boarding ramp and into the bowels of the ship, thence up a series of ladders until they were directed by one of the ship's officers down a passageway and into a smallish, but comfortable guest stateroom.

As the last of the native soldiers left, Henry put himself in the doorway. "Well," he said, hands on hips, "are you going to tell me what this bullshit is all about?"

Paul Von Lettow walked to one of the cabinets along the bulkhead and began opening doors until he found what he was looking for. He brought out a bottle of schnapps and three glasses and poured a healthy portion into each, handing off one to Henry and Alex. "The powers that be—that is, myself, Governor Schnee, and Captain Looff—have decided to send you out of the Colony..." he began.

"What the hell for?" Henry interrupted.

Paul nodded to Alex, who motioned for Henry to take a seat on the bunk. "You are aware of what's happening in Europe, Heinrich?"

Henry shrugged. "Only what I've read in the papers, which are now several weeks old. But it didn't seem like anything overly untoward."

"Heinrich, the Hapsburgs mean to crush Serbia. They have made demands tantamount to stripping Serbia of its sovereignty. Russia insists, as protector of all things Slavic, she will not allow Vienna to do it. We have a treaty obligation to Austria-Hungary to come to her aid if the Russians come to the aid of the Serbs. Unfortunately, France has treaty obligations to aid Russia. And there are undoubtedly the same sort of obligations to and with the other countries—Romania, Bulgaria, Greece, the Ottomans, probably some others as yet undisclosed. The big question remaining at this moment is whether England will be drawn into a conflict..."

"Alex, what the hell does that have to do with me? I'm a neutral, for Chrissake. If war breaks out, there is already a plan to transport neutrals out of the Colony. I'm sure Schnee knows that. Hell, it came from the American consul in Zanzibar, that fellow Hays. He and the Vice-Consul Vining—he was at Liesel's party, Alex, remember? Vining had it all worked out. They've hired Arab boats and will let them fly the American flag to get neutral and enemy citizens out of the Colony if trouble starts."

"And then what, Heinrich?" Paul asked. "They didn't by any chance mention where all of these Arab boats would go, did they?"

"No, they didn't. But I assume it will be Mombasa, especially if England doesn't leap into a war."

"I repeat...and then what? Will you spend the war in Mombasa? Or will you try to get back home?"

"Home, of course."

"How? You think you will ride an Arab dhow to the United States? Take an English ship? What will you do if England does come into the war? You'll be just as trapped in BEA as you will be in G.E.A.. Unless you seriously think they will allow you to transmit your little messages..." Paul raised an eyebrow and cocked his head, though he didn't really expect Henry to answer.

"Heinrich," Alex said, "what we are offering you is a way out of here. This ship is going to Colombo, Ceylon, for a load of coal and other supplies..."

"For the *Königsberg*..."

"I didn't say that. In Colombo, you should be able to take passage on the *Zeiten*, which is bound for Naples. At the very worst, Italy will probably renege on her treaty obligations with us and stay neutral. So you should be able to find a ship going to the United States much easier there than either here, or Mombasa, or Colombo. And even if England enters the war, which is still fairly doubtful, at the worst, they'll stop the *Zeiten*, but you won't be in Mombasa, and you can undoubtedly find a way to get back to the United States from, say, Alexandria or Malta."

"And why is that so damned important?"

"Because, Heinrich," Paul said, in a tone as though he were talking to a small child, "we need you where you can be heard—even though your voice will be very small, and you will probably be crying out in a very large wilderness in the face of a very noisy gale. In any case, anything you have to say about it is beside the point. Schnee and Looff and I have decided to send you out of German East. Because we are better off—after you get over your piss-off—we are better off with you on the outside than trapped here with us."

Paul finished his schnapps, and he and Alex moved to the cabin door. *"Wiedersehen*, Heinrich. Try to speak well of us." They closed the cabin door behind them.

CHAPTER SIXTEEN

Monday, July 27, 1914
Colombo, Ceylon

Henry Feller jumped quickly from the deck of the lighter onto the cargo deck of the Lloyd DOA liner Zeiten and watched as his luggage was passed, none too carefully, through the portal. He had retained possession of his two most important pieces: his portfolio bag and his gun case. He muttered dire warnings to the native navvies who had attempted to take them from him so that they might abuse them for pay. Over the years he found he was much better off handling the important things himself—which was the same reason he escorted his luggage to his cabin and with no little effort managed to have it stowed without being destroyed by the porters. After locking his guns and portfolios in the cabin safe, Henry gave himself a quick once-over in the mirror and, now certain he was passable, went to make his pleasantries to the ship's bursar and other officers.

He found them in the gentlemen's lounge on the upper deck, a Germanicly ornate place of chestnut and other darker, exotic woods and shining brass—much ornate shining brass. The liner's Captain was sitting at one of the large tables with a group of obviously military men judging by the nearly shaved heads and the skin folds at the back of the neck. It was Henry's way of immediately identifying a military type, though he was too polite to ever tell them how he did it.

"Ah, *Herr* Feller, I see you've made it aboard," the bursar said pleasantly, holding out his hand. "All settled in for the voyage, I hope?"

Henry shook the bursar's extended hand. "Thanks, yes. Everything's been taken care of. Ah, there isn't any new news, is there?"

The bursar shook his head. "Not as yet. The radio is still working and we haven't heard anything. We have the emergency codes, but until we hear differently, it's business as usual. Next stop should be Naples—about twelve days because you can't make any time going through the canal. If anything changes, I'll be sure to let you know."

Henry nodded and moved to the small party formed around the Captain's table. The Captain glanced up at him and motioned for him to be seated. Once he had taken a chair, the Captain made introductions. "*Herr* Feller is an American journalist, gentlemen. *Herr* Feller, this is *Leutnant* Bricker of the 3rd Regiment of Naval Infantry, and the other gentlemen are some of his non-commissioned officers. They are on their way home from China."

Henry leaned across the table and shook hands around. "Out of the frying pan—or should I say wok—and into the fire, *Leutnant* Bricker?" he asked innocently, noting they were getting underway for there was a slight tremor, felt mostly in the soles of the feet, as the *Zeiten's* engines gained revolutions and the ship moved away from the quay.

"You were saying?" Bricker said.

"You picked a hell of a time to go home on leave."

"We didn't *choose* to go on leave—we were sent. Admiral Graf Spee himself made the selections," Bricker said.

"You'll find *Herr* Feller is always asking very direct and embarrassing questions, and then jumping to conclusions, *Mein Leutnant*. It's one of his many endearing bad habits, along with his constant attachment to loose and immoral women…and poor Polish boys far from home—not, however, for the same purpose." The man who had spoken, one of the older men of the group, was looking at Henry with a wolfish grin. What little hair remained on his head was more white than grey, and by the way he carried himself and the confidence with which he spoke, he was obviously a long-term and very senior enlisted man. There was something familiar about him.

"*Herr* Feller and some of us shared the 'facilities' of a certain brothel a few years ago, along with some Americans from their Corps of Marines," he explained to the officer. "Have you ever seen anything of Corporal Daly or Private Plata, *Herr* Feller?" he asked.

Henry shook his head. "No, ships passing in the night. But I have seen—as a matter of fact, I've spent the last few months with—someone else who used to share the 'facilities' of …"*Aha!* "The House of the Morning Dew." *Damn I did remember it.* When he saw the old NCO's look and smile, he went on, "Remember *Leutnant* Lettow?" The NCO nodded. "Well, he's *Leutnant Oberst* Von Lettow-Vorbeck now. He's the commander of all the German forces in German East Africa." The name suddenly also flashed back into Henry's brain, and he grinned broadly as he held out his hand to the old NCO. *Was sagst sie der, Lipz?...Rudolph Lipz...Rudy..."*

"I didn't think it would take you *that* long to recognize me, Heinrich. I don't think I've gotten that old. Hell, it's only been fourteen years." The old NCO turned to *Leutnant* Bricker. "Heinrich and I were both in China in 1900—with Admiral Seymour's column out of Tiensin, then at the Arsenal. That's where Heinrich required lessons in the care and feeding of the *Gewehr* 98," Lipz laughed.

"You were an American Marine?" Bricker asked.

"He was attached to the United States forces and I was on my first hitch with the 3rd, *Mein Leutnant*," Lipz explained. "Though I don't think the Boxers would have bothered to ask about it. It will make for a pleasant—if lie-filled—voyage. We can tell war stories all the way to Naples."

CHAPTER SEVENTEEN

1800 Hours, Friday, July 31, 1914
6.57 S x 39.20 E, the Indian Ocean
SMS Königsberg

F*regattenkapitan Max Looff was looking through his Leitz-Wetzlar 7x50mm naval binoculars at the rapidly receding coast of German East Africa. As he often said, because the Leitz glasses had magnificent optics even in declining light, he could see much farther and with greater clarity than with common naval lenses. His Cruiser and her 322 officers and ratings had steamed out of Dar es Salaam harbor around forty-five minutes ago, and he was now simply enjoying the late afternoon cruise on a placid sea as his vessel cut majestically through the ocean swell on nearly a due easterly course.*

Yesterday, he had not been planning such a hurried departure. There was still much he would have liked to have done in German East. Another hunting expedition with *Leutnant-Oberst* Von Lettow-Vorbeck, perhaps even with his friend Tom Prince and the American writer Feller. He would really like to be the one to take a lion this time.

But the arrival of the *Zabora's* Captain had put an end to those desires. The Captain had come on board immediately after the *Zabora* had been made fast to the dock. A florid, portly little man, he had heaved himself up the companionway and come onto the bridge. His ship had just sailed on the 27th from Madagascar, where he had somehow found out the British South African Squadron of three cruisers had been ordered to Dar es Salaam to blockade the *Königsberg* in harbor—or to sink her in the event of the outbreak of war, which supposedly was only hours away. Surprisingly, the little man's information jibed with the intelligence the *Kriegsmarine* had been passing to Looff. And so it took less than two hours to make their departure, with all hands at battle stations, accompanied by much cheering and waving of hats and flags.

Looff's train of thought was interrupted by the whistle of the voice pipe to the crows nest. The Captain strode quickly to the tube and snapped up the cover of the mouthpiece with his thumb. "Speak," he commanded, putting his mouth close to the bell of the tube.

"Captain," the lookout's voice answered, "I make three ships in formation—dead ahead. Estimated speed 10 knots. They're coming right at us."

"Very well," Looff replied, adding, "good work." He turned to his First Officer, *Korvettankapitan* George Koch, who had the con. "Steady on this course, George. Let's see what we have here, though it shouldn't be too much of a guess."

Looff thumbed open the engine room voice tube and whistled into it. In a few seconds the voice of the chief engineer came through the pipe. "Engine room, aye…"

"This is the Captain. Maintain revolutions for 12 knots."

"Aye-aye, Sir." The tube snapped closed.

Within fifteen minutes the three approaching ships had been identified. In his mind Looff repeated what he had read about them in the intelligence reports: *HMS Hyacinth, 5,700 tons, 11x152mm and 8x76 mm guns, top speed 21 knots, built 1898; HMS Astraea. 4,400 tons, 2x6-inch and 8x4.7-inch guns, top speed 20 knots, built 1893; HMS Pegasus, 2,170 tons, 8x4-inch guns and 2 torpedo tubes, top speed 20 knots, built 1896. All slower than we are, with mostly old guns that cannot penetrate our armor. But in combination, 37 guns and at least two torpedo tubes against our 12 guns and two tubes…*

Looff stood at the portside window of the flying bridge as the British warships passed the *Königsberg* and then turned and took up positions 3,000 yards on each flank and behind, matching the *Königsberg's* speed. They traveled together in this formation, at a stately 12 knots, for nearly an hour, nearly until twilight.

A little after 1900 hours, Looff whistled into the engine room pipe.

This time the voice of *Korvettenkapitan* Paul Koohl answered. "Engine room…"

"Engine room, I want steam for flank speed on my command, but no smoke…*verstehen*—understood?"

"Steam for 24 knots, no smoke. *Jawohl, Herr Kapitan.*"

"Report when you have steam up."

Looff turned to the rear window of the flying bridge. To the southwest the sky was turning black, far darker than mere approaching twilight. Looff watched the squall moving toward them.

"George, when that squall line overtakes us, we will let it shield us from our naval Brothers-in-arms, then, on my command, we will go to flank speed and immediately make a 180-degree turn to starboard, steam for 15 minutes, and then make a 90-degree turn to port. Understood?"

"*Jawohl, Herr Kapitan. 180 for 15, then 90.*"

Looff stepped to the voice pipe and snapped the cover open, then thought twice about it and allowed the cover to snap shut again. He turned to one of the ratings on the bridge and motioned for him to approach.

The seaman popped to attention. "Signalman First Class Ritter, *Herr Kapitan.*"

"Ritter, go find *Leutnant* Niemyer and *Leutnant* Wenig and have them come to the bridge."

Ritter snapped a salute. "Aye aye, Sir."

"And Ritter, stop in the galley and bring some coffee back with you, please."

"Yes, Sir."

It was several minutes before Wenig, the Gunnery Officer, and Niemyer, the Signal Officer, found their way to the bridge. Looff was already sipping coffee when they came through the hatch. He motioned them to the chart table. There, on the chart of the Indian Ocean, their last position and course were penciled.

Looff looked through the aft windows at the rapidly approaching squall. Quickly, he told his officers the plan for evading the British ships. Taking off his steel-rimmed glasses and wiping them with a handkerchief, he added, "This is, of course, in the likelihood we are not yet enemies, NOT an opportunity to open fire. On the other hand, Wenig, I want every possible gun and tube, primary and secondary batteries, brought to bear to target the *Pegasus*. She has the most potential to hurt us. Whatever guns are not dedicated to her should be targeted on the *Astraea*. We'll worry about the *Hyacinth* later—she has bigger guns but they are older models and don't have as much chance of doing us damage."

Wenig popped to attention. *"Jawohl, Herr Kapitan!"*

"Now, Niemyer, I want you to listen for the code sequence E-G-I-M-A. And because it will probably be sent by a flustered *Afrikaner*, it will probably be missent, so be prepared to react to any sequence even close, misspellings, et cetera. It is the code for the start of the war, and I shouldn't have to say if our 'cruising partners' hear it first, they will immediately open fire."

Niemyer also popped his heels and saluted.

Within five minutes after they left the bridge, Wenig reported all stations were manned and the guns inconspicuously brought to bear on their primary targets. Niemyer had taken Signalman 1st Class Ritter with him and announced Ritter was now manning the wireless. A minute after, the engine room called up the pipe all boilers were on line and there was steam available for flank speed on his command. Looff's reaction was as was expected of a German naval officer—he showed no emotion whatever. He had given orders and they had been obeyed, as was expected of a hand-picked crew. Everything was as it should be.

The squall hit as only a tropical storm can. First, a few large drops of rain spattered on the bridge windows. Within seconds, the rain was falling steadily. In a few more seconds, the visibility out of the windows was gone and it was nearly impossible to see the prow of the ship, let alone the escorting British ships 3,000 yards to port and starboard. Looff turned to the engine-room telegraph and swung the handle to the All Ahead Full Speed position. Instantly, the complementary pointer moved to the same position, and the floor of the bridge began to tremble as the 3,400-ton cruiser gained speed and began to slice through the water.

"Mister Koch, turn to starboard 180 degrees."

"Aye, aye, *Kapitan*. Starboard One hundred and eighty degrees. Helmsman, bring us about to 270 degrees."

The cruiser began its turn as soon as the helmsman spun the wheel, leaning heavily as the propellers bit into the waves. As the compass needle approached 270 degrees, the list righted and the bow began to knife through the water. Somewhere nearby in the squall, the *HMS Hyacinth* plodded past on her easterly course, the two cruisers passing one another at a combined speed of nearly 60 miles an hour.

Fifteen minutes later Koch ordered a 90-degree turn to port to a compass heading of due south, 180 degrees. They maintained their heading for an hour, then made another 180-degree turn and slowed the ship back down to twelve knots. In the pre-dawn light of August 1st, they sailed alone on the slightly rolling surface of the vast Indian Ocean, a watery mass approximately twice the size of mainland Asia.

Five days later, they had not sighted another British, or any other nation's, warship. While they were nearing the tip of the Horn of Africa, however, the wireless crackled out E-G-I-M-A, E-G-I-M-A over and over.

They were at war.

Max Looff opened the ship's safe and took out the sealed envelope given to him when he assumed command. In his cabin with his ship's officers, he broke the seal and read aloud the orders from the *Kriegsmarine* detailing his ship's role in the greater scope of the conflict. It was a plan called *Kreuzerkreig*—Cruiser War. Their task was to make war on the commercial and naval forces of the British Empire in the Indian Ocean, as their sister ships *SMS Emden* and *SMS Nurnburg* were to do in the Bay of Bengal and the East Indies, and as Admiral Spee's squadron was to do wherever it might be.

Looff ordered Niemyer to send out, in the clear—unencoded because he wasn't certain if all Germans ships had the war codes—the call for all German ships within hearing of their wireless to head for Dar es Salaam. It was the first time they used their wartime code identifier AKO. Then they set a course for the coast of Arabia and the mouth of the Red Sea.

CHAPTER EIGHTEEN

Thursday, August 6, 1914
The Indian Ocean
Lloyd DOA Liner *Zeiten*
Approx 100 miles SE Cape Gardafiui

The bursar had brought Henry a copy of the radiogram four days ago. Germany had declared war on Russia, which, in a fit of Pan-Slavic pique, had declared war on Austria-Hungary, which had declared war on Serbia, the supposed instigators of the assassination of the Archduke Ferdinand and his wife, Sophia. France had upheld her end of the bargain—like the others, following the dictates of the secret treaties everyone seemed to know about—siding with Russia and declaring war on Germany and Austria-Hungary.*

For the first few days, it didn't seem to make much difference to the crew and passengers of the *Zeiten*, as the nearest French Colony was Madagascar, far to the south and without much of a French naval presence. Italy, their destination, was evidently going to be neutral, reneging on her not-too-secret treaty obligations to join Germany and Austria-Hungary. England was not yet involved. *Zeiten* steamed for the Suez.

Everything changed early on the morning of 6 August. A steward rapped on Henry's cabin door, and when Henry answered, the steward told him the Captain would like to see him and to follow him *bitte*— please. The steward led Henry to the bridge, where the Captain handed Henry a copy of the latest radiograms, two of them. The first stated simply a state of war existed between Germany and England. The second ordered all German flag vessels in the vicinity to steam immediately for Dar es Salaam.

"Shit!" Henry said. It was the only thing he could think of at the moment was appropriate. The Royal Navy had more than enough naval presence in the area to be more than a little worrisome. Henry was not too sure how the Royal Navy might handle neutral passengers aboard a

129

vessel of an enemy belligerent. *Probably worry about it after I survive the sinking—if I survive the sinking. If I don't, then they won't worry about it.*

Henry was still on the bridge—the Captain had not bothered to ask him to leave. So when the lookout hailed down from the top of the radio mast there was a ship on the horizon to the northeast, toward the Aden coast, there followed a flurry of activity. Full Speed Ahead was signaled to the engine room, and the Captain immediately issued directions for a course change, a direct line to the southwest. No pretense, no bullshit. They were going to try to outrun whatever was coming over the horizon and make a dash for the German East coast. If they could. If the other ship was older and slower.

Unfortunately, it didn't appear to be either. It bore down on them rapidly, and its signal light began to flicker. Reading the flashing code, the Captain pulled the handle of the engine room telegraph to All Stop, and the vibrations of the engines died to a murmur. The Captain was smiling when he turned to Henry, whom he noticed on his bridge for the first time in twenty minutes. "It's *Königsberg*," was all he needed to say. But for Henry's benefit he added, "She just signaled AKO. That's her call sign."

The Captain and Henry stood side by side watching as the cruiser steamed toward them, her bow slicing an impressive wave as she parted the swells. When she was nearly close enough to recognize individuals on her bridge, the lookout at the top of the radio mast called down another ship was due north of them. The *Königsberg's* lookouts had evidently also seen the other vessel. A sudden flurry of movement on her bridge and deck and she began to heel over as she turned away to head for the new sighting. Once more her signal light flashed, the Captain translating the code: "God speed, *Zeiten*," he murmured and then ordered, "Send God speed, *Königsberg*." At the same time he pulled the handle of the engine room telegraph around to Full Speed Ahead and the *Zeiten* began, once more, to vibrate, her engines picking up revolutions to continue her course for Dar es Salaam. *Or whatever Royal Navy cruiser happens to be in the way,* thought Henry.

CHAPTER NINETEEN

Wednesday, August 12, 1914
SMS Königsberg
Approx 100 miles off the coast of Aden

*I*n the fast fading light, Lieutenant-Commander George Koch swept the
eastern horizon for any sign of a smoke column or signal flasher, though
*he was certain the Captain of the Somali, their tender—a DOA steamer
converted for the purpose—would not be stupid enough to use a flashing
lamp to signal the world her position. Twenty-five feet above the bridge on
the spotting top of Königsberg's foremast, the seaman on watch with the
Kapitan's binoculars froze in position and pointed toward the darkening
eastern horizon.*

"Smoke… four points off the starboard bow."

Koch had not yet managed to tell the helmsman to steer toward the
sighting when the lookout screamed, *"Alarum! Alarum!* Gun flashes—
It's a British warship!"

The alarm was immediately followed by the rumbling hiss of the
first salvo to arrive, sending geysers of water spouting upwards as tall as
the foremast and rattling shell splinters off the hull and bridge combing.
At the line of the horizon more flashes, and again the hissing shriek of
what Koch estimated as at least 6-inch shells. They were silhouetted
by being west of the enemy ship, and only the miserable visibility of
the half gale blowing out of the west and the usual steep waves of the
Indian Ocean, whose crests were legendary and could easily reach and
run to eighty-foot peaks, kept the British ship, obviously a cruiser, from
scoring hits on them.

Koch could hear boots clumping on the bridge ladder, and
then *Kapitan* Looff strode onto the bridge. *"Kapitan* on deck," the
quartermaster shouted from the wheel.

With a nod Looff immediately took over the conning of the ship
from Koch and slammed the engine room telegraph to All-Ahead Full

Speed. Without waiting for the engine room to acknowledge the order, Looff commanded the helmsman, "180 degrees to port." They would run for the storm.

CHAPTER TWENTY

Wednesday, August 12, 1914
HMS Manchester
Approx 100 miles off the coast of Aden

Commander Adrion Manely, RN, kept his eyes fixed on the lens of the ship's gunlaying binocular, sweeping the horizon one final time on the off-chance his elusive prey might pop out of the nearly opaque rain storm. Finally, he turned to his gunnery officer, Leftenant Lofton Craddick, and shook his head. "Damn," he muttered, "she's gone, Guns." Turning to his quartermaster, Manely ordered Manchester, a six-year-old, 5,500-ton "town" class cruiser on the East India Squadron station, back to 10 knots, and to go to a course of 146 degrees. The change would take them back to the troop convoy they and the other ships of the squadron were escorting from Calcutta to Mombasa, British East Africa. Aboard the transports were 8,000 troops of the Indian and Imperial Services bound for the invasion of German East Africa.

"Sparks," Manely said to his signal officer, using the Royal Navy's familiar term for all such personnel, "message Admiralty. Tell them we sighted and fired on *Königsberg*, time and position, et cetera, et cetera. And tell them we are returning to our place with the convoy, but don't put *that* position in the message—our friend might be listening." He nodded generally toward the point on the horizon where the German ship had disappeared.

Manely turned to his executive officer, whom he always thought of as another hyphenated Smythe, in this case a Dunne-Smythe. "You have the con," he said as he moved toward the bridge door. "If our friend happens to pop up again, I'll be in my cabin composing a report to the squadron commander as to why exactly we were out here chasing after a German cruiser, which wasn't supposed to be here. Almost got her, though, didn't we?"

"Yes, Sir, that we did. Bit of bad luck, that," Dunne-Smythe replied. Then with his usual formality he saluted Manely and said, "I have the con," followed almost instantaneously by "Captain leaving the bridge."

By the time Manely reached the port-side bridge ladder, it was full-dark night and the rain was driving horizontally across the deck of his ship. "Damn and blast," he muttered again, but his muttering was lost in the howl of the wind.

CHAPTER TWENTY-ONE

Saturday, September 19, 1914
The Rufiji River
German East Africa

The crews had replaced nearly all of the coaling slides and gangways locking the Königsberg together with her collier, the Somalia, while the tons of coal bags were shifted from the merchant ship to the cruiser. Now all that was left, was to man the pumps and hoses and wash the accumulated grime and dust of the coaling into the river and scrub down the ship. No work at all compared to the last day's labor of manhandling the bags into the boiler room bunkers.

While the coaling was going on, those crewmen not engaged in carrying coal bags had been put to work transferring canned goods and other supplies to the messes and storage bunkers. The cruiser was nearly ready to put back out to sea and again attempt to comply with its orders: Hunt down and sink whatever allied shipping came to hand. So far, by *Kapitan* Looff's way of thinking, they had barely managed to comply with those orders. Since the beginning of the war they had managed to find and sink only a single British ship—and in so doing had nearly put themselves out of the war. Not through combat at sea, at any case, but by the slow death of engine degeneration, which came as a consequence of burning the absolutely shitty Bombay coal from the freighter's bunkers. Even then, they really had no choice. The German-flagged shipping in the vicinity was neatly blocked up in Dar harbor, locked up when a port official with just a little too much authority and no spine whatsoever had ordered a dredge scuttled in the shipping channel after one of the ancient British cruisers patrolling the coast had sent some shells into town before steaming off.

With the exception of the *Somalia* now alongside and one other liner, hiding out in another channel of the Rufiji—which Looff intended to save as his trump card—his source of coal was limited to what he could carry or hope to capture. And he couldn't carry enough to make it all the way back to Germany, even when steaming at the most efficient speed. It was a puzzle he knew the *Kriegsmarine* expected him to figure out for himself. That was what *Kreuzerkrieg* was all about—provided you could find an English ship...of any kind.

The war had begun badly. After they had heard the radio signal E-G-I-M-A, telling them the war was on, it was two whole days before they saw the trace of another vessel. They had given chase and had found the German liner *Zeiten*, immediately upon which another ship came over the horizon and so they had turned away and given chase again to the German ship *Hansa*. A third ship belched smoke as it made steam for full speed. Looff went to All Ahead Full Speed until they were in range and the other ship hove-to when *Königsberg* put a 4.1 across her bow. It took Looff a long while to control himself when he finally came up to the German ship *Goldenfels*. He had wasted several tons of valuable coal chasing friendly ships whose officers were too nervous or too stupid to listen to their radios. The next ship was a neutral Japanese liner, but at least he didn't have to chase it. Finally, nearly at dusk, he had run down the *City of Winchester*, out of Bombay for Liverpool with a cargo of tea—and several hundred tons of shitty Bombay coal. A radio call brought the *Zeiten* back and the English and Indian crew was transferred, as was the shitty Bombay coal. Then the *City of Winchester* and its cargo of tea was sent to the bottom with two 4.1s below her waterline. *We should have burned the tea and sunk the coal*, Looff thought.

That was the last ship of any sort they saw until they almost ran into that new British 'town' class cruiser while searching for the *Somalia* and had to use up even more coal running into the storm. It was August 19th before they managed a rendezvous with the *Somalia* off Socotra Island, by which time they were nearly out of coal—there was not enough to run the distillation boilers, so there was no drinking water for the days they lay baking in the tropical sun with swollen tongues waiting for the *Somalia* to show up.

The same luck stayed with them until the end of August. They coaled again off Aldabra Island in the Mozambique Channel after searching fruitlessly for a French vessel. By then the shitty Bombay coal had done its work and the engines were crying out for a shipyard. They had radioed *Somalia* for another rendezvous and put into the Rufiji delta to try to figure out what to do and make what repairs they could before the engines went belly-up. They had scraped and reamed the boiler tubes as best they could and taken on nearly a thousand tons of good coal. Now, as soon as the ship was washed down, they could put to sea again.

As though on cue, the radio began to crackle and squawk. A two-funneled British warship had put into Zanzibar Harbor for repair. Schnee or someone else obviously had someone with a radio watching the harbor—probably an Arab who would be just as willing to report the *Königsberg's* location to the British. Looking at his chart, Looff measured the distance—about a hundred and fifty miles. About 10 hours steaming time at a reasonable speed. If they sailed this evening, they could be in Zanzibar Harbor just about at sunrise. Looff gave the order.

CHAPTER TWENTY-TWO

Sunday, September 20, 1914
HMS Helmuth
On patrol outside Zanzibar harbor

S ub-Leftenant Clement Charlewood, RNR, along with a forty-two-year-old quartermaster rating named Brimmely, was manning the bridge of his Royal Navy warship, the former German tugboat Helmuth. Since joining the Royal Navy at Zanzibar the day after the war started, Helmuth was now armed with a decrepit 3-inch cannon of indecipherable lineage and a Vickers .303" machine gun mounted on a swivel on the rear deck of the bridge. As his first order of business after taking command, Charlewood had the engineer weld two pieces of steel upright to the rail on the left and right of the Vickers because he was not particularly anxious to be cut in two by a nervous reservist sailor swinging the gun in a circle as he held down the trigger. With the uprights in place, the Vickers could fire through an arc of only about 120 degrees, which allowed it to cover the stern and points abaft should they ever be snuck up upon. Charlewood hoped—no, he fervently prayed—the bloody cannon would never have to be fired, because if it were, it would undoubtedly pull up all the deck planking and probably recoil over the side.

Up until August 4th, Charlewood had been pleasantly and happily employed by the British-India Steam Navigation Company—BI, for short—and had worked his way up to Second officer on the passenger sloop *Pentakota*, hauling forty or so passengers around to different points in the Orient, India, and East Africa. But when they put in at Kilindi Harbor, the port for Mombasa, British East Africa, Charlewood received two sharp slaps from reality. The first was that Britain—and thus all of the bits and pieces of her commonwealth—was at war with the Central Powers. He couldn't actually remember if that piece of news had come on the heels of or right before learning the German cruiser *Königsberg* was apparently loose somewhere in the vicinity. They had been damn lucky to make it into port in one piece. And, the second:

Oh yes, Charlewood, your reserve commission is activated. Welcome to the Royal Navy, Sub-Leftenant.

He had spent the next six hours rummaging through the Mombasa bazaar looking for some gold lace and an Indian or African tailor to sew a set of shoulder boards for him. That finally done, he was sent down to the harbor and given command of a motor launch manned by mobilized bank clerks. Their task was to patrol the harbor entrance. No further orders. Charlewood was bright enough not to even consider asking what he and his boat were supposed to look for, or assuming they found it, what to do about it.

Several days later he was sent out to Zanzibar, where he was put in command of the ancient, rusted tugboat *Helmuth*, late of the Kaiser's Imperial fleet. Due to the patriotism on the part of her Indian engineer, Kundanlal Raat, who was a British subject—and whose name the new crewmen immediately shortened to "The Rat"—*Helmuth* had been abandoned by her German crew. "The Rat" had claimed the engine had a broken elliptic rod and was therefore unable to comply with the radio message to head for Dar es Salaam when the war broke out. The German crew, less "The Rat" had gone aboard another German craft. The *Helmuth* became His Majesty's Ship and had been fitted out with its present implements of war.

Charlewood and his crew—reservists to a man—spent the next month or so on easy duty, doing what a tug would normally be expected to do. They cleared harbor snags and assisted ships—mostly Arab dhows—off of the sand bars and banks of the narrow Zanzibar channel. They and a coastal vessel, the *Khalifa*—whose crew took great pride in keeping the brass plaque screwed to her bulkhead gleaming and announcing to the world the space was "RESERVED FOR SECOND CLASS PASSENGERS WHEN NOT OCCUPIED BY CATTLE"—shared patrol duties on the harbor mouth and the channels, day on and day off alternately. This morning was their turn to patrol the harbor mouth.

It was a pleasant, nearly serene morning, with just enough haze to give an indication of a hot spring day to come. The sun, now rising over the island, silhouetted the town's minarets and the Sultan's palace. To the west the mist blurred the channel between the coastal islands, shortening visibility to the normal horizon by half. It would do so until the sun was full up and burned off the mist.

Charlewood leaned on the edge of the spray shield and looked toward the small island to the south of them as they steamed at a leisurely 8 knots to arrive at their patrol station before the day's normal rush of shipping began to crowd into the channel. He was about to tell the helmsman to come right a little to keep as near dead-center in the channel as possible when he saw the surprised and frightened look on the man's face. Quickly looking to where the man's eyes were focused, he saw a long, white ship, emerging from the mist.

"Oh, damn and blast," he muttered, mostly to himself, "bloody Union Castle. How the hell many times do I have to tell them this bloody damned channel is closed to them? Signal them to turn around and use the commercial channel, and to slow the hell down," Charlewood called back over his shoulder to a rating standing by the signal light. But even as the light's handle began to flash out the message with its usual irritating squeak caused by years of neglected lubrication and cleaning, as the shutter handle pivoted, the commander of *Helmuth* could see the ship was intent on running all the way into the harbor, channel restrictions or no. Out of the mist now and in plain view, Charlewood looked again and realized his mistake. Three funnels streaming black smoke, her guns swinging toward the little tug, a large red, white and black ensign complete with Imperial eagle and Iron Cross flying, *SMS Königsberg* steamed past, close enough for Charlewood to see the faces of the German sailors manning the guns.

"Oh. My God!" was the only thing he could think to say.

"Should we fire on her, *Mein Kapitan?*" Gunnery Officer Richard Wenig asked.

"No. We have bigger fish to catch." Max Looff took his binoculars from his eyes. "If they fire at us, Richardt, you may use the secondary guns on them." Looff turned his binoculars back toward the harbor and gazed intently. Without removing the glasses from his eyes, he stated, "There she is."

She was their prey, the British Cruiser *H.M.S. Pegasus*, now lying anchored just off shore. Looff recognized her immediately. The last time he had seen her was on the day he had sailed out of Dar. There were several small boats and dhows near her, probably the boats that brought the shipyard crew to her. There was no smoke coming from either of her funnels.

The communications tube from the range finder whistled. Looff opened the cover and said, "Bridge here."

"Bridge…" Wenig heard his senior gunner say, "Range is now twelve thousand yards to the British ship."

"Very well. Report when the range is eleven-thousand." Looff snapped the tube's cover shut and turned to Wenig. "Open fire at eleven thousand yards. Main battery. We'll start with the starboard guns on the first pass."

Wenig relayed the orders to the 4.1 inch gun positions then stood, like his Captain, with his hands folded behind his back, while they waited for the range to run down. It would not be long, for they were moving at nearly 20 knots. The little tugboat with its flashing signal lamp they had passed coming into the harbor was already nearly two miles behind them.

When Max Looff judged they were nearly at their firing range, he ordered the helm brought 90 degrees to port and the engines to go to All Ahead Half Speed. The maneuver brought the starboard side of *Königsberg* parallel to the *Pegasus* and allowed all of the 4.1s on that side to bear on the target. When the range finder tube whistled again, Looff nodded to Wenig, who immediately ordered his guns to commence firing.

The first salvo straddled the *Pegasus*. Wenig was a fine gunnery officer and the crews were all hand-picked men. Two shells from the next salvo hit the *Pegasus*, and three more from the third. The British ship opened fire with her 4-inch main guns. Her salvo was short by at least a mile.

Looff smiled.

CHAPTER TWENTY-THREE

Sunday, September 20, 1914
HMS Pegasus
Zanzibar harbor

Commander J. A. Ingles, RN, sat in his cabin, his feet propped on one of the chairs by his table as he thumbed through one of his favorite books, an anthology of Rudyard Kipling's short stories. He had been rereading The Man Who Would Be King, *more than anything else to look for errors in the Masonic rituals—both by Dravit and Carnahan, and by extension thereby, Kipling—and by the wogs put in charge of Alexander's treasure. So far Ingles, who was 32nd Degree, could find nothing wrong to change his opinion it was a cracking good, true-to-life adventure piece. Too bad Kipling had managed to piss-off her majesty with one of his poems and get himself exiled to the colonies—either Connecticut or Massachusetts. The story had been all over the fleet, with each telling including the queen's imperious "WE ARE NOT AMUSED" third-person royal dictum.*

Where the bloody hell is that bloody wog? Ingles thought as he waited for his Indian steward to bring his breakfast. He was about to go to the cabin door and shout his usual *HINKY BAI*[4] for the boy when he heard the hissing of the shells and felt the deck shake as they detonated. There were, by the sound, at least three. Two seemed to hit on the shoreside and another on the harborside. The explosions were followed almost immediately by the booming of the guns that had fired at them from out in the harbor.

Ingles put his book on the table and immediately left his cabin, heading for the bridge. As he reached for the hand rail at the bottom of the bridge ladder, he heard the shriek of the next broadside approaching. The deck bucked as one of the shells penetrated the stern and detonated in the coal bunker. The second shell hit *Pegasus* just forward of her forward funnel, punching a jagged hole in the deck and detonating in the passageway leading through the officers' cabins. The blast traveled the length of the passageway nearly instantly. Ingles was momentarily

142

aware of a flash of blue-white air as he was lifted off his feet, thrown down the passageway, and bounced off the forward bulkhead. He lost consciousness as he landed on the deck plates.

"Helmsman," Max Looff ordered, "bring us about 180 degrees." Then, into the engine room tube, "Maintain present speed." He turned to Wenig, who was controlling the fire of the main battery from the communications tubes. From the look of things, the *Pegasus* was no longer able to return fire. Her last 4-inch gun had taken a direct hit moments before, and she was burning in several places. There was a great deal of scampering as the shipyard workers escaped by diving overboard into the shallow water.

Wenig carefully scanned the cruiser with his binoculars. "I think she has struck…"

Looff scanned where his gunnery officer indicated. "No, that is just part of her ensign. Continue to fire until she strikes or sinks, whichever, though I doubt an officer of the Royal Navy will strike as long as he has as much as a loaded pistol on board."

Several more broadsides, this time from the port battery crashed out. "Helmsman," Looff ordered, "90 degrees to port. Wenig, have the rangefinder report when we have reached a range of seven thousand yards."

"*Jawohl, mein Kapitan!*" Wenig did not look happy, and when Looff gave him a gesture to speak, he asked simply, "*Warum?*—Why?"

Looff looked over the top of his steel-framed glasses. "Richardt," he said quietly, "their guns are good for six thousand yards, and we don't *know* if they are all knocked out. I'd hate to lose anyone by being wrong. Let us finish her off. They would do the same to us, *ja?*"

"*Ja, mein Kapitan.*"

"*Gut. Sehr gut.*"

The *HMS Helmuth* tried desperately to stay out of harm's way as the crew watched the German cruiser demolish the *Pegasus*. The firing lasted less than an hour, but the British cruiser was reduced to a charred and perforated hulk. All of her guns, both the main battery and the secondaries, were shot to pieces—along with the crews. The bridge was a shambles. Both funnels had been blown from their mountings and were either lying or draped across the equally demolished torpedo tubes. Fires raged from bow to stern, sending clouds of oddly greenish smoke billowing into the air, obscuring the land behind her.

Charlewood knew his duty. As a fleet tug, his obligation was to try to tow the disemboweled ship to an anchorage where she could be salvaged, if possible, but in any case to get her out of the main channel before she sank and blocked all access to the docking facilities. He set a course to bring the *Helmuth* in round-about. With luck they would not be noticed by the German ship now steaming at a leisurely rate for the harbor mouth.

Luck was simply not with them. When they were still several thousand yards from the burning hulk of the *Pegasus*, the first of what Charlewood assumed must be a 47mm shell passed close enough to the bridge of the *Helmuth* to agitate the air. A second soon followed, detonating in the water only a few feet from the stern. Grabbing a cork-filled life jacket, Charlewood yelled for the crew to abandon ship. Continuing to yell the same words over and over, he ran off the bridge to the starboard side railing and flung himself off of his warship and into the water of the harbor.

Most of the crew followed, except for three of the older ratings, who either didn't feel like swimming or, more probably, couldn't swim. These stalwart British sailors leisurely unfastened the lifeboat from its position and, just as they had during lifeboat drill, made a picture-perfect launching, all the while under fire from the German cruiser. Once comfortably launched, they rowed about, picking up the rest of their swimming mates and Captain.

Everyone was accounted for except the intrepid "Rat," who evidently had decided to stay with his engine. Which was too bad for him, because the next set of German shells was dead on target, the shells passing straight through the *Helmuth*'s rust-thinned hull. The first one neatly clipped the Vickers gun from its pivot mount. Another separated the main steam line from the boiler. Unfortunately for "The Rat," he was between the engine and the boiler when the line parted. Charlewood and the rest of the crew in the lifeboat could hear him screaming as he was boiled alive. It took several minutes before the screaming stopped. By that time the German ship was well out into the channel. The Germans had evidently seen the steam cloud and thought it was a fire, for their firing halted immediately.

When he realized the *Helmuth* was not about to sink and the shell fire had in reality done little other than cosmetic damage, Charlewood had his crew row back to the tugboat and re-boarded. It took only fifteen minutes to repair the steam line. Two of the older ratings wrapped "The Rat" in a blanket and carried his body to the fantail where it would be out of the way. After vomiting over the side, they returned to duty.

The *Helmuth* sailed near to the *Pegasus* around noon and waited for nearly two hours for the survivors of the crew to clear away debris and bodies. *Pegasus* had nearly forty dead on board. Then a tow line was passed over and *Helmuth* began to tow the battered ship to deeper water. They never made it. Less than a half hour into the tow, *Pegasus* groaned one final time. There was a rush of air, the cruiser rolled quickly onto her side, and then as quickly slipped beneath the surface.

CHAPTER TWENTY-FOUR

Sunday, September 20, 1914
SMS Königsberg
SSW of Zanzibar harbor

They had left the harbor of Zanzibar far behind and were now steaming to the south-southwest, paralleling the African coast. Max Looff was elated. Without any casualties, without even a close return shot, his cruiser had destroyed a third of the British squadron operating in the area. They were making good time because, after all, he did not know where exactly the other two British cruisers of the South African Squadron were—just as, he was certain, they did not know where he was, though they would surely know by now he had struck and reduced their force by a third.

Quite suddenly the *Königsberg* shuddered and Looff felt her speed drop off. Immediately, the engine room communications tube whistled. Popping the cover open, he had to force his voice to remain calm. "Bridge here."

"*Mein Kapitan*," said the voice of the chief engineer, "the starboard engine has spun a shaft bearing, and at least two boiler tubes have ruptured."

"Shut down the starboard engine and boiler," Looff ordered. "No sense destroying it if it might be repaired." He snapped the communication tube shut and turned to George Koch. "Make for the Rufiji delta at best speed. I'll be in my cabin."

As Looff stepped through the bridge door, the helmsman barked, "Captain leaving the bridge." Looff climbed down the bridge ladder and walked to the outer hatch leading to the cabin passageway. He shut his cabin door behind him, exhaled, and hurled his peaked cap against the far bulkhead as hard as he could, spitting out a loud "*Gottverdammt!*"

CHAPTER TWENTY-FIVE

Thursday, October 1, 1914
Dining Room of the Kaiser Wilhelm Hotel
Dar es Salaam, G.E.A.

It was as though there were no war. On a small stage at one end of the room a small orchestra—twelve African musicians, plus a conductor—were playing Strauss waltzes for the entertainment of the diners, of which there were nearly fifty, mostly couples, mostly married, nearly all colonial government workers or military of some sort. The tables were spread with crisp, clean linen cloths and napkins, and the crystal was, if not the finest in the hotel's inventory, at least better than one would normally find anywhere but at the better European hotels. The Kaiser prided itself in being able to bring a little bit of Germany to this center of the Fatherland's far off Colony, war or no war.

At a small table near the eastern side of the room, Henry Feller and *Leutnant-Oberst* Paul Emil Von Lettow-Vorbeck were finishing their plates of what the hotel was passing off as sauerbraten. It wasn't veal, of course—more likely one of the smaller antelope, springbok perhaps, or even the tenderer parts of a kudu. In any case, it passed nicely as sauerbraten and, considering the circumstances, was a splendid meal, made more so by the fact it was being paid for by the absent Governor of German East, the good *Doktor* Heinrich Schnee. *Doktor* Schnee had sent his apologies for himself and his wife due to pressing government business—meaning the good *Frau* Ada didn't feel like going to dine with some *Amerikaner*. Or she didn't wish to be involved in the passing of any news which might prove unpleasant—such as, in this case, the order to the *Amerikaner* he must take himself forthwith out of danger and go hide in the country. The passing of this bit of information was left to the Commander of German Forces in the Colony, *Leutnant-Oberst* Von Lettow-Vorbeck, which conveniently allowed the wrath of the *Amerikaner* to fall on the *Leutnant-Oberst von*, rather than on the Governor *Doktor* within hearing of his *Frau*.

"Goddamn it, Paul...*Oberst*. That is absolute bullshit. I am a certified neutral correspondent. I should be allowed to go anywhere I wish and report on any goddamned thing I want—subject to your censorship for sensitive information, of course. I should not be sent off like some errant schoolboy, to hide out two miles behind the back of beyond...or wherever." Henry Feller was pissed.

Paul Von Lettow-Vorbeck simply shrugged. "Heinrich, the Governor has spoken. I actually agree with you. I also think it's, how you so amusingly say, bullshit. But I take my orders from the governor. And the governor says you are to go down to *Herr* Cosner's farm and stay there out of harm's way until we know definitely what the British are going to do next. Sorry—it won't do you any good to vent your anger at me—or to argue. I am to see you are sent off to *Herr* Cosner's farm—end of discussion."

"Son of a bitch."

"Referring to me? The Governor? Or someone else in general?" Paul Von Lettow-Vorbeck looked as though he were more amused than insulted. His beaklike nose twitched over his severely trimmed moustache. "Who would you argue your case to? The highest German official in the Colony has told the highest ranking military officer in command in the Colony to tell you to pack your things and get ye hence out of Dar to the south."

"How the hell am I supposed to report about the war if I can't get to where it's being fought?"

"And if you could, then what? How in hell, as you put it, are you going to get whatever you write about it out of German East? Hmmm? Paddle out to one of the Britisher ships patrolling the coast and have them mail it for you? There is no cable, since the British, or the French, or the Portuguese, or the Belgians—or maybe even the Arabs 'cause no one knows whose side they are on—since someone cut it. And the British are blocking all radio traffic, except what might be accidentally picked up by the station out at Kigoma and then sent here by train. You are essentially writing a diary for posterity...after the war...if we survive. That is, essentially, what Schnee said anyway. Your writing will serve as a record, a testament, of what happened here. But you have to live through the experience. And to guarantee that as much as possible, you have to be sent out of the line of fire—that and the fact it wouldn't look good for our Fearless Leader to have our Neutral Journalist accidentally potted by the odd bullet or shell. *Mein Gott, Heinrich,* we tried getting you out of here before the war started and that turned to *Dreck.*"

Paul and Henry had to grin thinking of the ironic turn of events that had sent Henry off to Ceylon to escape the war and then deposited him right back where he started.

"Take my advice, Heinrich," Paul continued, "go down to Cosner's and write up what you have so far. Do a little hunting—there's all manner of game down there. Drink some good home-made beer, eat some *apfel strudel mit slagaubers,* a little *sauerbraten,* some good *Wienerwurst.* Live well. Enjoy life. Make the best of it. In six months, our Fearless Leader will have forgotten why he sent you down there and you can saunter back. And by then we'll probably know with some certainty what the British are going to do." Paul Von Lettow-Vorbeck, commander of the German forces in East Africa, tossed his napkin on the table and rose.

He and Henry Feller walked out of the dining room into the main lobby as the native orchestra softly played the last section of "Artist's Life."

Even wearing his heavy boots, Wilhelm Cosner was no taller than five feet six inches. He was bald except for a fringe of nearly white hair ringing his head like a medieval monk's. To make up for the lack of hair on the top of his head, he sported a luxurious moustache, which he allowed to fall naturally instead of waxing and twisting it into handlebars. Henry remembered the term for such a style as "waterfall," remembering it from his youth when he had seen the same sort of thing worn by the graying men of the GAR. Cosner's shoulders were broad and he was starting to paunch, marks of a man who had put in days of hard labor and had finally begun to realize the good life as a reward for his labors.

He had been in the Colony since late 1907, had, in fact, intended to come sooner, but a relative of some kind—a cousin, uncle, nephew—had written asking him to do something or other for the family in Danzig before leaving, and by the time it was done, the Magic Water Rebellion— the *Maji-Maji* Revolt—had begun and the cousin or uncle or whatever was no longer among the living. As Cosner told the story, Henry silently reflected on how much it sounded like the Ghost Dancing that had gone on when he was just a kid, and how nervous his mother and father had seemed—he had been eight or nine at the time and, as he recalled, it hadn't seemed threatening to him. In any case, Cosner had stayed in Germany until after the army had put an end to the Magic Water affair, and he had then come out to find his land, and his cousin's, or uncle's, or whatever—and most of the rest of the southern part of G.E.A., the Liwale Region—had been turned into a smoldering wasteland by the fighting. Fortunately, Cosner's land was on the northern fringe of the worst of it, south of Kisaki, near the beginnings of the great delta of the Rufiji River. Still, it had taken three years of back-breaking work just to get the land back to the point where it could produce a crop, followed by four years of increasingly good production, thanks mainly to the help of the good people at Amani Institute.

Cosner was an amiable and chatty character. He had learned Swahili and a couple of local tribal dialects, and remembered a cursory amount of English from school in Germany, as well as a bit of Polish and Swedish. He was, like Henry, a language magnet, and also an avid hunter. So they talked of hunting and the situation, and Henry ended up promising to teach *Herr* Cosner American English and maybe a little Texican in trade for a couple of trophy antelope or perhaps even an elephant, and lessons in whatever native dialects came to hand. They had a good deal of time to talk, and to an outsider, their conversations would have borne little resemblance to anything intelligent or intelligible. They got by. Riding first on the Central Railroad to a little nameless station west of Dar, they then piled their luggage onto a springless donkey cart, without padding of any kind, and rode south across a nearly trackless savannah toward Kisaki along the bank of the Mgeta River. On the third day, Cosner turned off of the barely discernable track and told Henry to get their rifles out of the cases. Cape buffalo, rhino, elephant, and the usual big cats all abounded here. The donkey set the pace. Cosner and Henry watched for signs, their rifles carried across their knees, loaded, safeties off.

At night they stayed in native *bomas*, thatched adobe huts with thick perimeter thorn hedges to keep the inhabitants and the indigenous carnivores separated. They usually were offered sleeping mats inside but most often chose to sleep near the outer wall of the hut, close enough to the fire to give them light to shoot by and room to move quickly just in case a wandering jackal, or hyena, or leopard dropped in for a snack.

It was on this part of the trek that Cosner passed along the German East custom of the four beds. When an Askari, a black German soldier, was tired he would send his Askari boy, his *ruga-ruga*, to the *jumbe*, the headman of the village, with a cartridge. This was universally recognized to mean the *jumbe* should make four beds: one for the Askari; one for his rifle; one for his ammunition pouch; one for his uniform. Each bed would also be furnished with a "blanket," meaning a woman. If the *jumbe* didn't immediately comply with the request, the Askari would beat him with a *kiboko*, a hippopotamus-hide strap that could peel a man's hide off his spine with one stroke. The *kiboko* was the punishment of choice in the Colony for offenses not grave enough to warrant hanging or shooting out of hand. Henry wondered if Cosner had ever sent a cartridge ahead of him, but was too polite to ask. And from what he'd seen of most of the native females, he was not at all sure he cared to know, but then again, this was Africa.

A little after the midday meal on the fourth day south of the main track, Cosner pointed south down a long sloping plain to where a thick stand of some sort of trees nearly concealed a substantial building with what appeared to be a red tile roof. It took the donkey nearly an hour to haul them the last kilometers. The nearer they approached the farmstead the more civilized—if that was the word—the land began to look. Cultivated fields spread out in all directions. Henry knew some were tobacco and one looked distinctly like the local tea, rooibos, and another or two of what might have been sisal or hemp. There were others Henry couldn't identify, but that looked like they were doing nicely. Henry had seen enough fields of dying things in his life to know when a crop was doing well and when it was withering.

As they jolted the last kilometer along what looked nearly like a prepared roadway, Henry could see small gatherings of Afrikans and whites standing along the sides of the track. As they passed, the males either held up their hands, murmuring *jambo*, a respectful hello, or doffed their hats in a sign of respect to *Bwana* Cosner, *el Patron*, who in turn nodded a regal nod to acknowledge them. *Herr* Cosner was, after all, if not the local king, then at least the local Margraff. As they neared the house, Henry noted it was a fine, substantial Germanic *schloss*—manor house, its terra-cotta covered adobe now bleached white by the sun. The house was shaded by large local trees of indeterminate *genus*—ebony perhaps or maybe some other species for which Emil Feller, Henry's father, would have paid exorbitant amounts of money to use in his furniture shop.

Sitting on the veranda in a wicker chair behind a green bottle of what appeared to be Mai Wein chilling in a bucket of ice was one of the people Henry Feller least expected ever to see again. As *Herr* Cosner reined the donkey cart to a halt in front of the steps, the man rose, confirming to both Cosner and Henry he was, indeed, wearing the summer white uniform of the Imperial Navy. Even stranger to Henry was the fact Cosner seemed to know the man as well. It was, in fact, Cosner who spoke first.

"Schönfeld, what the hell are you doing here? I thought you had been called up." Cosner turned to Henry to make the introduction. "Henry, this is my neighbor—of sorts—he has the next farm..."

"*Korvettankapitan* Schönfeld and I are acquainted, *Herr* Cosner, but I agree... Werner, what the hell are you doing here? Last I knew, you were on the *Königsberg*."

Schönfeld descended the steps of Cosner's veranda and extended his hand to his neighbor and Henry. "I still am, Heinrich, and the last time I saw you, you were on your way out of German East. And to answer both of your questions at once, I am here recruiting laborers—here and on all the other farms between here and Salale."

"Where the hell is Salale?" Henry asked.

"Down on the Rufiji, near the coast," Cosner answered for Schönfeld.

Henry raised an eyebrow and waited for Werner Schönfeld to explain further. The Naval officer seemed to be considering what Henry Feller might do with whatever information he passed along. Then, realizing there was no means for Henry to pass on anything he might happen to come by to anyone who could do them damage—that and the fact he'd *have to* tell Cosner why he needed laborers—Schönfeld made a conscious decision to tell these two friendly but curious men what he was about.

"I...we...that is, the *Königsberg*...need about a thousand men. We are going to haul the engines to the shipyards at Dar, where they can be refurbished. Then we will haul them back and reinstall them in the *Königsberg*, following which *Kapitan* Looff will wait on the appropriate tides, and make a dash for the sea, and then Germany..."

"You're shitting me..." Henry blurted.

Werner shook his head. "God's truth, Heinrich. *Kapitan* Looff already has the engineers taking the boilers apart, and we are using the davits to hoist the plates onto the deck."

"And what the hell are you going to do if the British decide to shell the shit out of you while you're sitting there with your engines off somewhere else?" Henry asked, only to see Cosner hold up his hand to get his attention.

"It's not that bad an idea, Heinrich," Cosner said. "I don't think the Britishers can get to them. Salale is about seven kilometers—four of your miles—from the nearest mouth of any of six or seven channels, all of which are protected by shoals and reefs. And all the channels are just enough different with shoals and mudflats and sandbars and such to need a pilot. And they are all connected by creeks, so if one were blocked, all you'd have to do is move over into another, and you'd have a clear run to the sea."

"And," Schönfeld added, "we've already taken all of the secondary guns, the 47 millimeters and the machine guns, as well as all the spare Marines—the ones who came in on the *Zeiten*—and sailors and moved them to where they can watch the channels and shoot at anyone who tries to come up. And we've attached fronds and such to the antennas and masts to make them blend in with the rest of the trees along the channels. I don't think the British can see us to know where we are. And they can't shoot at us if they don't know where we are."

"How long do you think it will take you to move the engines to Dar and back?" Henry asked.

"I don't know," Werner admitted. "It's never been done before. It's about a hundred sixty or seventy kilometers from Salale to Dar. There are no roads, so we'll have to build one as we go. I don't know how many streams or rivers… Wilhelm?"

Cosner scratched his pate. "No big ones if you go by the most direct route, maybe a dozen small ones. You could build fords with rocks."

"You both sound like you think it's possible," Henry said.

"We won't know until we try …don't really have a choice. We can't just sit in the Rufiji Delta—we'll rot. We have to try. Our only other alternative is to try to break out of the British blockade with the engines ready to die at any moment. If they do, then we're doomed. The British have three new six-inch cruisers sitting outside the reef. We have 4.1s. They out-range us by nearly two thousand yards. Without rebuilt engines there is no way we can get away. They'll shoot us to pieces." Werner Schönfeld looked to Henry, then to his former neighbor.

"How many men do you need from me?" Cosner asked.

"How many can you spare?" Werner answered.

At the end of a four-day march, the last two and a half days of which were through what seemed like the middle of a pestilential mangrove swamp—though Werner assured him they were only on the fringes of the really miserable portions of the Rufiji Delta—the long column of porters suddenly broke out of the dank thicket into an open space. Less than a hundred yards in front of them was the ghostly white length of *SMS Königsberg* tied off to trees and stakes driven into the murky soil to keep her from being moved by the current of the river. On the shoreline next to her was an odd array of metal plates, some lying flat in the mud, others leaning against tree trunks the suspension lines enabling them to be lifted onto the shore still attached. As the head of the column came to a halt, Henry saw one of the officers waving his hand over his head as the davit operator lowered another plate over the side.

Werner Schönfeld commanded the porters and their overseers to halt and sit. That done, he motioned for Henry to follow him up the makeshift gangplank and onto the main deck. There he sought out *Kapitan* Looff and saluted. He had succeeded in his mission of gathering the necessary manpower for the long cross-country haul. Looff took it all in, grunting occasionally in acknowledgement of some portion of the report, all the while looking over Schönfeld's shoulder at Henry. When Werner had finished his report, Looff asked, "What's *Herr* Feller doing here?"

CHAPTER TWENTY-SIX

Friday, December 25, 1914
Officers mess, *SMS Königsberg*
Near Salale, G.E.A.

Henry didn't have to be reminded Christmas Day just to the south of the equator was the equivalent of the end of June on the 'top' half of the planet. The temperature inside the officers' mess stood at a little over 105 degrees Fahrenheit—close to 40 something Celsius—though the heat made Henry's mental functions too slow to care much about doing precise temperature conversion equations in his head. Most of the officers in the mess were in one stage or another of various tropical diseases. As a consequence there was a great deal of jumping up and rapidly scooting out of the compartment to empty body fluids from whatever orifice happened to be affected at the moment. Since they were all sick at some level, no one seemed to pay much attention. Even Henry, who had managed to stay reasonably healthy, relative to the rest of the men present, was running a fever of something over 101 degrees. In addition, his joints were swollen and painful, making him limp very much like his Grandfather Kevin had. But in comparison to George Koch or Richard Wenig, he remained the picture of health, healthy being defined as someone who could stand up without native assistance and not lapse into occasional unconsciousness.

All this considered, the officers of *SMS Königsberg* nonetheless attempted to put on a festive air for the holiday. Henry had managed to shoot some sort of small deer, or goat, or antelope—it had four legs, small horns, and a hair coat—the species of which he was unfamiliar, and no one bothered to tell him what it was before the *ruga-ruga*—the native laborers—turned it into a fairly flavorful stew. Of course it helped not to think about the cook's hygiene or the methods of preparation.

The Christmas party had two purposes. It was a going away party of sorts for another guest at the officer's mess. And Henry and most of the *Königsberg* officers were going to use it to put the final touches on a little theatrical spoof they had been playing out since the middle of November. At that time they had received reasonably reliable information the British had managed to come up with a seaplane and had also managed to bring it and a maintenance crew and pilot up from South Africa on a requisitioned coastal steamer. Werner had, in fact, been watching through his binoculars for several days as the intrepid flyer attempted time after time to get the beast into the air. Ultimately, the seaplane had managed to clamber aloft, only to splash back down into the channel between the coast and Mafia Island.

Several days later, evidently after the machine had been repaired yet again, it skipped over the waves for nearly a mile before lurching into the air and at an altitude of what Werner estimated to be about a hundred meters, traveling slower than Henry had seen locomotives move across the Great Plains. It flew a stately course up the Rufiji, around the *Königsberg* three times as the pilot aimed what appeared to be a camera over the side. Then it flew back to the coast, where it landed with less than its usual splashing and bouncing, within towing distance of one of the British cruisers. Werner admitted later, it being the first aeroplane any of them had ever seen, his men were too excited to shoot at it, but they did manage a good chuckle or two—that is, until the British ships suddenly let loose a salvo that fell short but was smack on the center line of the path to the *Königsberg*. This meant the hundred or so sick men on board had to go to the bother of getting up steam and moving the damned ship further into the delta, deeper into the primordial slime, until they could anchor in another cross creek.

Several days passed before the seaplane could be coaxed into the air again. This time the Delta Force—the name Looff had given to Werner Schönfeld's troops—was no longer too excited to shoot. It took no time at all to blast the seaplane out of the air. The surprising thing about it was the pilot managed not to die in either the hail of lead, which literally shot the plane apart, or in the ensuing crash into the river, or in the mouth of a hungry crocodile. Flight-Leftenant Cutler had been pulled from the river by some of Werner's troops and bundled off to the confinement of the cruiser, where he had been treated as a not-quite trusted guest of honor ever since. Ultimately, in mid-December, Captain Looff had decided to send him up to the internment camp at

Kilimatinde, via Cosner's farm with Henry, because it was feared if he stayed, he'd probably be taken ill and die. And though it was apparently acceptable for the ship's officers to succumb in that manner, it was not *de rigueur* to let an enemy prisoner of war take the same risk.

As a sub-plot to all of this, Henry had never spoken English around Flight-Leftenant Cutler. In fact, the officers and Henry, with the aid of a couple of the *ruga-ruga* boys, had played an extended and sometimes elaborate game to keep the Brit from knowing Henry was anything but one of the German crew. Now, with Cutler's departure to Cosner's scheduled for the next day, it was time to end the farce.

Cutler had been seated in the position of honor at the opposite end of the table from Looff—it was less of an honor than it appeared because it left room for the others, who might be called on by nature, to scoot away unobstructed. Each officer had contributed something to the dinner. *Kapitan* Looff had ordered out the last of the mess wine to be served, and several of them had exchanged little hand-made gifts. During the meal, the radioman had brought an intercepted signal from the British cruiser *HMS Fox*:

"Kony," we wish you the best of good cheer,

But blame you for stopping our Xmas beer.

Looff passed the message around the table, including Cutler who read it and managed to stammer "I say" before passing it on.

Looff looked around at his officers. "Any suggestions on how to answer?" he asked.

Henry immediately pulled out an only-slightly-mildewed notebook and scribbled a few lines before handing it to Looff. The *Kapitan* read the lines and nodded his head in acceptance, smiling.

"Why don't you read it for us, Feller?" he said.

"*Ja wohl, mein Kapitan,*" Henry answered as he took the notebook back. "Thanks. The same to you. If you want to see us we're always at home. Signed Looff" Henry was looking at Cutler as he read the note in English. Cutler's smile remained frozen as Henry continued. "I'll be your escort tomorrow, Leftenant. You're being sent out of this garden of earthly delights to a farm in the interior, not overly far from here, but but at least it doesn't smell like the bottom of an outhouse pit."

Turning back to the table, Henry hefted his journal bag from where it was hanging from its strap looped on the back corner of a chair and pulled from it a nearly half-full bottle of Kentucky Straight Bourbon. He placed the bottle in the center of the table.

"*Frohe Weihnachten!*—Happy Christmas!" he said.

CHAPTER TWENTY-SEVEN

Monday, March 15, 1915
SMS Königsberg
Near Salale, G.E.A.

Henry leaned on the top of the portside rail just aft of the bridge ladder and tried not to feel the sweat oozing out of every pore of his body. *Nearing his seventh month in durance vile at the bottom of this steaming cesspool, Henry maintained his position in spite of the patch of intense sunlight burning a molten circle through his back and right leg, keeping a nearly mesmerized watch on the Arab fisherman languidly poling his dugout boat across the dank water of the Rufiji. Every now and again, the Arab would slowly draw his pushing pole out of the water and gaze at it for a moment before dipping it back into the river and shoving the boat along for another few feet. Then he'd repeat the process, over and over, slowly working his way downstream toward the point where the vegetation swallowed up the view of the river. He had done the same thing every day for as long as Henry had been watching him. What Henry found most curious, however, was the Arab fisherman never seemed to catch any fish.*

As far as Henry could gather by casually asking non-pointed questions, the Arab had shown up a little after the arrival of the British battleship. Its arrival was announced following the incongruous ringing of a telephone in the middle of an African outdoor toilet. Max Looff, after listening to Schönfeld's report, had taken Henry and acting first officer Wenig and two able seamen to row the launch out to Schönfeld's observation post. The telephone lines ran out to the defense outposts near the mouths of the channels of the Rufiji where Schönfeld had moved most of the ship's 47mm guns—remounted onto improvised field carriages—and machine guns, as well as most of the crew—at least those not sick enough to be immobile.

Henry had never seen a battleship and was not quite sure what to expect. What he saw, looming huge and grey several thousand yards outside the coastal reef, was a very big ship. It had to be at least as big if not bigger than any DOA or White Star liner Henry had ever been on, just to look that large from that distance. With the aid of Schönfeld's binoculars, Henry managed to read the hull number through the dazzle paint streaking the hull, while Schönfeld looked up the ship's particulars in his moldering reference book: *"HMS Goliath, commissioned 1900, four 12-inch, twelve 6-inch guns...scheiss—shit, the gottverdamnt page fell apart. I can't read how many smaller guns or her speed, sorry."* It was obvious, however, *Goliath* was gigantic enough to have a plentitude of heavy guns, enough so she could cover several of the channel mouths of the delta at once. And unfortunately, the channel mouths she was covering were the ones Max Looff hoped to use to slip out of his berth in the pestilential sewer to the open ocean and make a run for it. That was, now, decidedly out of the question. With her engines rebuilt, the *Königsberg* could probably outrun or outshoot any of the British cruisers on station outside the reefs, but she simply could not take on even one of the *Goliath's* turrets on any terms other than mass suicide. They had all been pretty glum as they rowed back into the Rufiji's stinking, slime-covered green dankness.

The Arab was back the next day, and Henry was again leaning on the port rail staring off into the greenness. He watched the man pole the boat for nearly an hour before languidly turning and asking Wenig if he might borrow his binoculars. The request wasn't unusual. Binoculars let the user see things differently from the shimmering green background—even if it were only a different part of the same green background viewed up close. Without looking directly at the fisherman, Henry scanned up into the tree cover, focusing on a bird, or a monkey, or anything else. But he could see the Arab fisherman's face at the edge of the left lens, and though the disguise was very good, Henry recognized the man. *I bet you this is the first time in history a ship has been stalked by a white hunter,* he thought to himself.

Much earlier the next morning, as the Arab fisherman was poling his boat up the channel, a sharp whistle attracted his attention and he looked to the northern bank to where the whistle had come from. There, a white man in khaki-colored linen shirt and trousers and a battered felt hat was sitting on the bank—actually, sitting somewhat back from the bank, out of the way of the odd hungry crocodile—with a rifle across his knees. It was an odd-shaped rifle and there was something familiar about it. The thought crossed his mind he recalled seeing such rifles somewhere else, and then he remembered what and where it was. The white man motioned for him to pole his boat to the bank, and as the prow sucked into the mud, the man rose and climbed down to the edge of the river and held out his hand.

"Hello Pietr," Henry said to Pietr Pretorius, "strange we should meet like this."

Pretorius stepped out of the boat onto the bank and past Henry, climbing to where he could observe anything crawling through the shallows. He was, Henry observed, apparently unarmed, which meant he had a weapon of some sort concealed under his grubby burnoose. His jaw worked reflexively, he looked Henry from head to toe, and then his gaze fell on the Winchester.

"Still carrying your little Ami pop-gun, I see," he said. Henry nodded.

"And how is Ter Roosenveld?" Pietr asked.

"Don't know—haven't seen him since the Safari. I generally don't run around with former Presidents. Besides the last I heard, he was going to drag Kermit off into the Amazon jungle, exploring a river, I think."

"What? Africa is too mild for him?" Pretorious came as close to a laugh as Henry had ever seen.

"Probably—didn't offer a strenuous enough life for his liking," Henry answered.

"You're probably right." Pretorius fell silent for a few moments, then said, "Except for the occasional *chui* or *tembo*—leopard or elephant—a railroad safari isn't all *that* strenuous. Nowhere near as dangerous as being on a German raider within range of many British guns."

"Or as dangerous as marking a channel for the British to use to try to get into range, dressed as a *kaffir*?" Henry answered.

"They were trying to shoot me anyhow. I thought I'd give them a sporting chance."

"I thought it more likely you'd be on their side. As I recall, you weren't overly fond of the British."

"I found it, how shall we say, expedient, to have a change of heart. Besides, the bloody British didn't steal my farm and then chase me all the way across this bloody damned Colony after shooting me full of holes."

"I heard something about that. I recall *Frau* Schnee saying you— what?—declared war on the German Empire and threatened to wipe out all the elephants—after they took your farm for non-payment of taxes or somesuch."

"That was the excuse they used. Actually, they took it after I refused to sell it to one of the little four-eyed bastard's ass-kissing bureaucrats. And I didn't 'threaten' to wipe out the elephants. I did it. I don't make idle threats. That's why they sent the *Kaffir Polizei* to hunt me down. They didn't though. Nearly, but not quite. I stayed ahead of them all the way into South Africa. They had to recruit a good number of new *kaffirs* afterwards too."

Henry just shook his head.

"The British know you're here, you know," Pietr said.

The statement took Henry by surprise. "How?"

"How? Because you're the odd duck out. You're a white man in a black country. And you're not German, like the other white men in this black country. It makes you 'interesting' to anyone in the pay of British Intelligence, which in this case means a man named, oddly enough, Meinhartzhagen—Colonel Richard Meinhartzhagen."

"Never heard of him."

Pretorius snorted. "Why am I not surprised? Oh, don't worry— he's not here. I mean he's not with the good Admiral out on the bloody *Goliath*. He's still up in Nairobi, I think, plotting evil things to do to the Hun. But he knows there is a 'neutral' journalist with the Heinies— though I don't think he has placed you here in this Garden of Eden with the *Kriegsmarine* portion of the German Colonial Forces."

"More like the Garden of Eden's outhouse," Henry mused.

Again Pretorius smiled. "You know" Pietr added parenthetically, knowing full well Henry probably didn't know, "Selous is here, too."

163

"How's that? He must be over sixty. He's too damn old to be in the army. Even the British know that."

"He volunteered. He's an officer, of course—a Captain from what I hear. He's with a battalion just arrived. Call themselves "The Old and Bold," though I think their official name has something to do either with Fusiliers, or Frontiersmen, or something like that. The British are none too orderly when it comes to naming their organizations. In any case, they are supposedly a fine collection of undisciplined but very knowledgable old men who know the bundu, something none of the rest of the British officers I've met can say for themselves. Except Meinhartzhagen of course." Again Pretorious went off on a tangent, "He's an ornithologist, you know."

"Who?"

"Meinhartzhagen. He studies birds. He's written books about them. He's going to make it very unpleasant for *Herr* Schnee and Company."

"Perhaps…"

"You make it sound as though you yourself aren't very fond of the British." Pretorious looked askance at Henry. There was a touch of peril in his look.

"I am an American, Pietr. We haven't liked the British for the last two centuries. I think the only reason we didn't throw them out sooner is we liked the Frogs and Greasers even less."

Pretorious snorted. He was after all, a Boer, and understood such things. "Perhaps you are right. God knows, compared to the Royal Navy, the British army up north is a bloody insane asylum." Pretorious, had evidently decided, regardless of the outcome of this encounter, he was not constrained from passing along the interesting bits he had heard. If Henry proved an enemy, he would deal with it. But he didn't think it would end that way.

"The commanding general, Wapshare, is a red-faced stammerer. He's been in the India army for nearly forty years and hasn't managed to learn any more than a new leftenant would have to know to find a tree to piddle against. There is a story going around he was being pulled around Nairobi by a native who asked him where he was going in Swahili— *wapi ju*—and the old toad thought the bloody *kaffir* was calling him a

Jew so he laid into him with his riding crop and nearly gave himself an apoplectic fit. Another time," Pietr continued, "he was supposedly on an inspection trip, got three sheets to the wind, and instead of inspecting his bloody army, shot a couple of ostriches and spent the entire bloody trip plucking them.

"Then there is a local battalion called the East African Mounted Rifles—EAMR for short. Their drill field is the nearest hotel bar. The first man discharged from them, after two days, was sent off as 'incorrigible.' And the locals bloody-well hate the Indian army people. Every issue there's a new piece of doggerel in the Nairobi and Mombasa papers. I'll see if I can get you a copies—if you're going to let me leave and not turn me over to your friends." Pretorius blinked at Henry. Again the peril in the look.

Henry held up his hands, palms outward. "What we do and say to one another ends here," he said. "I'm officially a neutral."

"Hmm," Pietr grunted. He climbed back down the bank and stepped into his boat. He poled away from the bank and began to move against the current, poling slowly in the direction of the German cruiser anchored around the next bend. He did not look back.

Three days later, a nameless *ruga-ruga* sauntered up to the base of the gangplank and asked one of the German sailors for *Bwana* Feller. When Henry arrived the man handed him a roll of papers wrapped in a grimy piece of muslin. In the roll were three copies of Mombasa and Nairobi newspapers, all months old, but in readable condition.

"And where did you come by those?" *Kapitan* Looff asked, looking over the top of his glasses.

"I traded for them with an Arab fisherman. I figured being an Arab, he talks to the British as much as to us, and I traded a bag of Cosner's tea for them. Well, actually, a part of a bag of tea—the rest went to the *ruga-ruga* that delivered them to take back to him. I thought we could all use a little diversion. I'll be happy to read them for you in the officers' mess whenever you wish. We'll see what the British have to say about us, if anything. And, maybe more important, we'll see what they have to say about themselves."

Looff gathered the ship's officers in the mess. Henry sat at the opposite end of the long mess table from the *Kapitan*. He took the first newspaper from the roll and opened it on the table.

"This one is dated August 15, 1914." *Hmmm, only seven months old.* Henry read of the calls for volunteers, mounted and foot, and an editorial about the Governor General's bloody unpatriotic attitude about the war and supporting the mother country in her time of need. Several columns were filled with reports of alarms. *I wonder if Paul knows—if he had a tenth of the men the British thought he did, he could run them all out of Africa probably.* The last item read from this first paper was a little poem:

> I thought I saw an aeroplane
> Upon the Athi plain.
> I looked again and saw it was
> A Kavirondo crane.

Henry thought immediately of Pietr's tidbit about the British intelligence man being an ornithologist. *I wonder—it would be a way of tweaking those in charge when he couldn't come out and say what he thought. If we all live through this, someday I may get the chance to ask him.*

The last line of the poem brought a few titters of laughter from the officers assembled. There had in fact been an aeroplane sent out from Germany for the Dar Exposition. It had crashed gloriously on its first flight. The nearest German aeroplane at present was in a hanger in, probably, France.

The next paper was dated November 15, 1914. It contained much information of a useless nature about the fighting at Tanga. To believe the India officers who added their commentary on the battle, was to believe the defeat and withdrawal were planned and the whole operation was merely a way to get the other ranks into fit condition following a long sea voyage. Someone, however, hadn't been overly impressed with the operation. Four verses—attributed to someone named Monson who was something or other in the BEA Secretariat—heaped sarcasm on top of debacle:

Steaming down to Tanga
Over the briny main,
See our Major-General
And his brilliant train.
Three Brigade Commanders
Colonels, staff galore;
Majors count for little,
Captains they ignore…

Earnestly they study
Each his little book
Which, compiled in Simla,
Tells him where to look.
Local knowledge needed?
Native scouts of use?
For so quaint a notion
There is small excuse…

Ping, ping, go the bullets
Crash explode the shells,
Major-General's worried
Thinks it just as well
Not to move too rashly
While he's in the dark.
What's the strength opposing?
Orders re-embark.

Back to old Mombasa
Steams "B" Force again.
Are these Generals ruffled?
Not the smallest grain.
Martial regulations
Inform us day by day,
They may have foozled Tanga
But they've taken B. E. A.

The last paper, dated in December, 1914, contained less information than the others except for an interesting letter to the editor. Written by a BEA colonist, the letter complained bitterly about the soldiery and the commanders. The colonists were furious about the imposition of martial law and the "Suffocating Red Tape." The letter went on, "Officers ostentatiously decorated with tabs of various hues and full of their own importance, are pouring into Nairobi. They fill the clubs, where they grouse at the absence of pukka sahibs, pukka golf, pukka polo, pukka bearers, pukka clubs and all the other pukkas they left behind in India."

CHAPTER TWENTY-EIGHT

Friday, April 9, 1915
SMS Königsberg
Near Salale, G.E.A.

Henry Feller *was sitting at the table in the officer's mess, trying desperately not to throw up, when Signalman 1ˢᵗ Class Ritter—he of the yellow skin and sunken eyes—held onto the bulkhead for support as he handed Kapitan Looff a radiogram. Looff took the limp sheet of paper from his signalman and listlessly read it. Instantly, his eyes took new life and color returned to his sunken cheeks.*

"*Mein Gott in Himmel!* It's from *Kronborg*. They are off the coast near Aldabra Island and want to know where to rendezvous with us. The relief ship has finally come!" He jumped up and headed for the radioroom. It was as quick a movement as Henry had ever seen him make.

Within fifteen minutes Looff was back in the mess. "I'm sorry, Heinrich, you'll have to go ashore. We are going to run the blockade, God willing, and meet the *Kronborg* four-hundred miles from here," Looff commanded. Having given Henry his instructions, Looff turned to his officers. "Koch, Wenig—prepare to get up steam. We will pick up Schönfeld and the rest on the way out. We'll go as soon as we have steam enough to move. Dismissed."

Koch and Wenig saluted and left the ward room. Fifteen minutes later, as Henry reached the top of the plank serving as a gangway to the shore, he stopped to shake Koch's hand and wish him good luck, then bounced down the plank and settled onto solid ground. By the time he had found a tent to stow his guncase and journal bag, the air over the cruiser's funnels—the *bomba tatu*—was turning dark gray. Within minutes, Henry heard the anchor chains begin to clatter as the winches pulled the anchors out of the muck of the river bottom and crewmen ran along the deck, casting off the lines held *Königsberg* in place in the channel. The water under the stern of the ship suddenly began to churn and froth as the propellers started to move the tons of steel out into the main channel. Within minutes, she was gone.

"*God speed*, Königsberg," Henry whispered to himself as the stern of the cruiser disappeared behind the green wall of foliage.

Since it was late in the day, Henry went back to the storage tent where he had left his case and bag. There were enough stacks of odd things in the tent to make a fairly comfortable bed, and since he was not really looking forward to the four-day trek to Cosner's farm, he decided to put off starting until the morning. He rearranged some of the mealy bags and lay down, pulling his hat over his face in the false hope it would keep some of the bugs off of him, or at least out of his nose and mouth— he had discovered an insect tasted terrible in direct proportion to the painfulness of its bite.

It was well after sundown when he was awakened by the sound of clanking chains and loud splashes. He started up, waving his hat to part the cloud of bugs swarming around his head, and stuck the top portion of his body out through the tent flaps. The noise was coming from *Königsberg*, now in the final stages of re-anchoring and tying up in nearly the exact spot she had left only a few hours before. Yawning and stretching, Henry sauntered back to the bank and helped two of the *ruga-rugas* put the gangplank back across the gap between the ship and the shore.

When Wenig appeared on the deck, Henry asked for permission to come aboard and bounced up the plank. "What happened?"

"When we got to the mouth of the channel, the *gottverdammt* British were waiting for us. Looked like three cruisers and some other armed vessels. It would have been suicidal to try to get out through them in the condition we're in. So we turned around and came back." Wenig looked dispirited.

"So now what?"

"So now we contact *Kronborg* and tell them where they might land and unload. Knowing full-well our friends," Wenig tossed his chin in the general direction of the British ships, "will then know where she is going and be able to intercept her."

"You think the British have broken your code?"

"No, Heinrich. I *know* the British have broken our code. It's an old code, nearly a year. If we were docked in Bremen or Kiel or Hamburg, we would get new code books every few weeks at the most. But the code we are using is the same one we had last fall when the war started. Of course the British have broken it! That's how they knew we were going to try to come out, and where. If we're smart, when we get on the radio to *Kronborg* now, we will send whatever message in the clear, uncoded, because then they can act on it without having to bother decoding it first, and it might mean they can get a jump on the British pursuit. In any case, that's what the Captain is doing now."

Henry wandered down to the radio room, where Looff was finishing with the message to the supply ship. He was not surprised to see Henry. When Ritter finally said "Done," Looff absently told Henry he had told *Kronborg* to make for Manza Bay, north of Tanga, several hundred miles up the coast, because it was the most protected spot on the coast and it had the advantage of having a ready and waiting manpower pool and defenders, the Tanga Defense Force, part of Paul's troops who defended against a British landing.

"We'll give them a few days, then send a party up there to help unload and carry supplies back here," Looff said.

"Do you care if I go along with them?"

"Heinrich, as you continually tell me, you are a certified *neutral* correspondent. If you want to go, go."

"If someone official shows up from either Paul or Governor Schnee, will you cover for me?"

"No, Heinrich. I won't lie for you."

"Will you just say you don't know where I am at the moment?"

"I'll think about it."

"Thank you, *Mein Kapitan*. That's all I can ask."

"Have a nice walk, Henry."

CHAPTER TWENTY-NINE

Saturday, June 12, 1915
Manza Bay
German East Africa

It had not been a nice walk, nor a short one, even though Henry had left early with two *ruga-rugas and walked back up to Cosner's farm. He laid over there until he figured the rest of the carrying party had started off from the Königsberg. To his pleasant surprise, Herr Cosner insisted on accompanying him, which meant Henry would not have to borrow a mule or horse and he would have someone to talk to on the stretch from the farm to the railroad, while traveling in the relative comfort of Cosner's ox-cart.*

Instead of taking the train into Dar, they continued to follow the Mgeta River all the way to Bagamoyo on the coast. After some asking—and a great deal of head scratching and shoulder shrugging—the natives there decided they, both the Arabs and the locals, had not heard anything about a large carrying party coming from the south, which meant either they were ahead of the *Königsberg* party, or the Arabs were lying, for whatever reason, or the party had not left on time, or the locals just didn't want to tell them. So they kept on to the north, skirting west of Tanga to avoid the possibility Paul might be there, and reached Manza Bay at the beginning of June.

When they crested the last rise before the coast, they could look down over the mangrove swamp separating the beach from the water line. On the beach were several hundred locals, some in uniform, most not, all busily doing things indiscernible from a distance. Out in the water was the fire-blackened hull of a freighter surrounded by some dhows and native boats. Occasionally, they could see crates of things being pulled up from out of the hold and lowered over the side into the smaller boats or simply plopped into the water to be floated ashore.

Another half-hour pull in the ox-cart brought them to the fringes of the working party. The bulk of the party were locals of whatever tribe lived in these parts, supervised by a few white officers and NCOs.

One large section of the work area was dedicated to doing something with cartridges. At one place the boxes were being opened. At another the cartridges were being piled so a group of workers could remove the bullets, then dump the powder onto a large piece of linen. A third group vigorously scrubbed the brass cases clean, and another scrubbed the bullets.

Henry found the whole scene so fascinating he wasn't aware a white officer had walked up to him. Finally, when the man cleared his throat, Henry was reluctantly pulled away from what was apparently a salvage operation.

"*We heist sie?*—who might you be?" asked the officer.

"Excuse me?"

"*Wer bist du?*—Who are you? *Was machst sie hier?*—what are you after?"

Henry stuck out his hand. "I'm Henry Feller, correspondent for *Ryan's Magazine*. And who might you be?"

The officer looked uncomprehendingly at Henry, who suddenly realized he had answered in English. *Nice going, asshole, now he thinks you're a spy.* Henry immediately repeated himself in German. This seemed to placate the officer in some small degree, so Henry added, "We've just arrived from the *Königsberg*."

The officer immediately grasped Henry's outstretched hand. "Aha! From the *Königsberg*." He motioned for Henry to follow and led him to where another pair of white officers were sitting on a mangrove root in the shade of a small palm tree. One of the officers had a bandage wrapped around his leg and had a make-shift crutch now leaning against the mangrove root close at hand. The other was a *Schutztruppe* officer whose campaign hat, with its turned up brim and cockade, hung by its chinstrap on his back.

"*Herr Kapitan, Herr Ober-Leutnant*" Henry's escort said, "allow me to present *Herr* Feller, a correspondent and a member of the advanced party from *Königsberg. Herr* Feller, this is *Kapitan-Leutnant* Carl Christiansen of *Speerbecher A*, and *Leutnant* Kemper. The officer made a slight bow after introducing Christiansen and Kemper, and added

"*Leutnant* Kemper is with *Hauptman* Baumstark's Tanga Defense Force.

"Forgive me for not rising, Feller," Christiansen said, gesturing at his leg, "but this is just about healed and I don't want to start it seeping again. How long before the rest of the *Königsberg* party arrives?"

"Anywhere from immediately to a few days," Henry answered. "We figure we're ahead of them and they have as far to march as we rode."

"Good. Well, as you can see, we almost made it. That bloody British cruiser caught us just as we were coming into the bay to pick up a pilot for the Tanga harbor. Shelled the shit out of us," Christiansen laughed. "But they are typical English. When they saw the ship on fire they assumed it was a total loss, so instead of pressing the attack, they just steamed away."

"What's with the cartridges?"

"Oh, that. We brought several million rounds of rifle ammunition with us, but it got pretty water-logged. So *Oberst* Von Lettow-Vorbeck thought, to be safe, we should take each round apart and dry it out in the sun. Takes the devil's own time, but we've got the manpower to do it, and it will save lives in the long run. The *Oberst* doesn't think the British will try any sort of offensive soon. They're in the tse-tse belt and can't keep their transport moving. Horses and mules die as fast as they can. Supposedly the whole bloody stretch around Moshi smells like a glue factory."

This was the first Henry had heard of the war in the north, and if it didn't sound exactly encouraging, it didn't sound all that bad either. "Anything going on up here since the Brits tried to land at Tanga?" he asked Kemper.

"Not much. Some patrol stuff on the border and into BEA along the railroad. Rotten miserable country that. We've lost men just by running out of water in there. Cut the Lunatic Line in a few places. Took Taveta, but I don't think we're going to try to hold it. That's about it. Been very quiet, really."

Henry was placed in the hands of the first officer he had met, *Leutnant* Nis Kock, who had been Christiansen's second officer. Kock was ordered to make *everything* available to Henry, who Christiansen recognized as an invaluable propaganda tool, both for the furtherance of their careers and as a source to get the story of their adventure out—because an adventure it had indeed been. The first thing Kock had given Henry to read was the logbook of *Speerbrecher A*—Blockade Runner 'A', originally a 3,600-ton British freighter, *SS Rubens*, which had been bottled-up in Hamburg at the beginning of the war and confiscated by the German Navy. The freighter was fitted out as a Danish merchant vessel and re-christened *SS Kronborg*. Her crew was recruited from German sailors born and raised exclusively in the Danish-German speaking provinces of Schleswig and Holstein. They all spoke Danish as a native language, their paperwork was all in Danish, even their pay was in Danish money, and they were paid at the regular scale of Danish merchant seamen. They figured they could fool the Royal Navy possibly for as long as thirty or forty-five seconds.

Henry thumbed through the logbook, reading snatches:

18-2-15: Sailed

19-2-15: Cleared the Skaw (*whatever the hell that is, I'll have to remember to ask*)

South of the Shetlands

Off Cape Verde

Rounded Cape of Good Hope

9-4-15: Anchored Aldabra Island

10-4-15: Message from AKO, rendezvous at Lat 6S Long 45E

13-4-15: Rendezvous pt rescinded. AKO instructs make best steam for Manza Bay.

The last log entry was terse:

18-4-15: Manza Bay, under fire.

In other words, they had made it safely half-way around the world, only to be grounded and set afire within sight of their destination. *I wonder how many of the poor bastards got killed trying this stunt?* It was another of the questions Kock answered. Other than a couple of minor scrapes and burns, and Christiansen's shell splinter in the leg—which occurred on the beach—no one had been lost. Their biggest concern at the moment was whether they were all going to be allowed to try to get back to the *real* war or be put into the *Schutztruppen*. Christiansen and *Oberst* Von Lettow-Vorbeck were arguing about that, and no final decision had been reached, though Henry got the impression Kock was more than willing to try to get back to Germany somehow rather than being stuck in Africa.

CHAPTER THIRTY

Friday, June 25, 1915
Amani Institute
German East Africa

Henry spent three days with the crew of the Kronborg and the Tanga Defense Force. He filled nearly half a journal with notes and copies of messages and, in the case of Nis Kock, an entirely illegal diary. Henry was in fact rereading some of the diary entries when Wilhelm Cosner came into his tent, handed him a cigar already lit, and sat down on the edge of Henry's cot, making it creak in protest.

"Am I to presume the orders you received way back when from the good Governor Schnee are still, by and large, in effect?" he asked.

"I suppose so. I haven't been given any further orders. Why do you ask?"

"Well, judging by the way you've avoided contact with the powers that be—*Unser kleine Schnee*, or the *Obersti*—I take it you are not particularly anxious to meet up with them. Am I right in assuming that?"

"Pretty much."

"Then, were I you, I'd be packing my bags and getting my ass out of here. Because they are *both* due to arrive to look at the loot from the *Kronborg* sometime soon."

"Ah—any suggestions?"

"Amani is only about a two-day ride from here."

"All right."

"I've already borrowed a horse for you. And by the way, don't try to ride it anywhere west of Amani—that's tse-tse fly country and you'll end up walking."

"Sounds like you're not planning on going."

"I'm going to stay here and lie to the Governor and the *Obersti*, at least until they figure it out for themselves. You are good enough to get there by yourself without becoming a meal—uh, that goes for the

177

horse as well, you know. Hide out with Zimmerman for a while and then come back to my place down south. Now, if I were you, I'd get my ass out of here. Take care of yourself, *compadre.*" Cosner shook Henry's hand and walked out of the tent.

Two days later, Henry looped the reins of his rented horse to the hitching post in front of the main building at Amani and went looking for *Doktor* Zimmerman. Compared to his first visit—*God, was it only a little over a year ago?*—the buildings were a-hum with activity. Where there had been only an occasional mule or ox cart, there were now trucks and other motorized vehicles. Henry wasn't sure of the makes, but they were all military, and when one drove by close enough to read the little bits of lettering on it, Henry saw the name Daimler. Each building now had rudimentary loading docks and Afrikans were loading boxes, bales, and odd-shaped bundles onto the trucks.

When Henry finally found *Doktor* Zimmerman, he was dressed in a stained laboratory smock, wearing a battered fedora, also stained, and bossing the loading of truck tires onto the back of an ox cart for a haul to the railroad. Nonetheless, he was delighted to see Henry and they spent the afternoon with the *Doktor* taking Henry from building to building to show him how they had converted the place to a wartime manufactory. In a matter of hours Henry saw the way they were vulcanizing the locally produced raw rubber with locally mined sulfur. They were making a form of quinine from local cinchona bark. They had even begun to make fuel for the motor vehicles from copra—they called it trebol. They could grind lenses for telescopic implements—Henry assumed Zimmerman meant gun sights—and they were beginning to distill alcohol, wine, brandy—and, from the snort offered Henry, a liquid fire product Zimmerman generously labeled as "whiskey." Zimmerman, not being a typical dense egghead, joked the liquor was still a little raw as it had only been made "this morning" and required some aging "until this afternoon."

In one of the buildings Henry watched as African women were taught weaving and knitting. They quickly produced before his eyes nearly a hundred pair of stockings and underpants. Another building held more women preparing cowhide—and undoubtedly other cow-like creature hide—to be bundled and sent off to the *Schutztruppen* where the *Askaris* had already been trained to make or repair their own boots. Yet in another building they were making chocolate bars and cocoa powder; in another, beeswax candles; in another, castor oil and rubber nipples for infant feeding bottles.

Standing inside yet another building, Henry and *Doktor* Zimmerman were watching the production of tooth powder and toothbrushes when a very smartly dressed *Askari* entered, looked around, and marched up to Henry. He stopped, came to attention, and saluted—just who he was saluting was uncertain. "Sir!" he said loudly, "you are *Herr* Heinrich Feller, *ja?*"

Henry nodded.

"Sir!" I am *Ombascha* Jabari Rajabu, *Obersti* Von Lettow-Vorbeck's orderly. I have been ordered to bring you to the *Obersti*. If you do not still have your horse, I have been ordered to secure one for you. If you will, please, Sir, to follow me."

Henry turned to *Doktor* Zimmerman. "Well, *Doktor*, it's been a short but pleasant tour. It looks as though I am about to be cast once more into *durance vile*. But from the looks of this savage warrior here, I don't believe I have a choice." Henry shook *Doktor* Zimmerman's hand and waved for *Ombascha* Rajabu to lead him out of the building.

His horse was waiting for him outside, with two other *Askaris*, larger than Rajabu. Neither said anything as he mounted. Then the three *Askaris* also mounted, leaving a spare horse evidently to replace one they had "secured." Rajabu rode beside Henry, with the other two riding behind. Henry wasn't sure whether it was to make certain he didn't suddenly bolt or as a social sign of respect for rank. *Ombascha* was some sort of rank, after all, and Henry had to admit to himself how damned little he knew about the customs and traditions of the Imperial German forces in this little cess-pit of the world.

They got to the Northern Railroad before nightfall, but they did not stop. They continued to ride south, crossing the Pangani River. At dusk, *Ombascha* Rajabu motioned one of the other *Askaris* forward

and handed the man—as far as Henry could tell in the failing light—
three cartridges. The soldier immediately put his horse to a trot and
disappeared into the gloom.

Within fifteen minutes they rode into a large *boma* where the *jumbe*
bowed and scraped in welcome then showed them to where their meal
had been prepared and the hut where they would sleep. There were four
sleeping mats and a cloth ground cover. As it turned out, the ground
cover was for the *Askaris'* rifles and equipment.

They sat in a circle and ate from a large pot. As far as Henry could
tell, it was some sort of stew. It had meat in it and some crunchy things
he hoped were vegetables, all floating in a thick sauce. Henry pulled his
metal spoon out of his shirt pocket, to the fascinated looks of the *Askaris*.
"If it can't be eaten with a spoon, it can't be eaten," Henry quoted his
grandfathers, who had drilled the habit into him. There wasn't enough
light to give it color, and it didn't taste all that bad. This being Africa
and not Asia, Henry figured it probably wasn't dog—or for that matter
hyena or jackal.

Henry pulled his journal case to him and fished around inside until
he found the bottle of plum brandy *Doktor* Zimmerman had given to
him. "Is the *Ombascha* a Moslem? Or would he like a little taste of
this?" Henry asked.

Rajabu's eyes turned to him, the whites tinged yellow, probably
from the medicines taken in a lifetime of warding off tropical diseases.
Rajabu grinned and said, "The *Ombascha* is Lutheran, *Efendi* and, yes,
he would indeed like a taste."

"Why do you call me *Efendi?*" Henry asked. "Isn't that an Arab
term?"

"It is what we call all white officers. It is Sudanese, I think. When
the *Schutztruppen* was formed many years ago, many of the recruits
were from up north—BEA and the Sudan—and were Moslem and
had used Turkish words, I think, for their army words. They did not
speak the language of the people. To be understood, the *Schutztruppen*
used commands and words familiar to them. *Ombascha*, what we call
a senior private and the German army calls a *Gefreiter*—Corporal—is
one of those, also. As is *Schausch*, which is what we call a sergeant. As

the *Schutztruppen* grew, there were more of the people recruited and the commands were changed to German because the people spoke the Kaiser's language. But we still use some of the old words—like *Efendi* for white officers."

"I am not an officer. Hell, I'm not even a soldier. *Mimi ni mwandishi Mmarekani*—I am an American writer." Henry took a sip of the brandy and suppressed a strong desire to cough. He handed the bottle to Rajabu.

Rajabu looked perplexed. "My Obersti led me to believe you were an officer."

"I was at one time, for a short time, many years ago."

"I do not wish to offend you. You evidently speak some of the language of the people. What should I call you?"

"I am known to some of the people as *Bwana mbili pipa*. You may call me *Bwana*, or Heinrich, or *Bwana* Feller. Any of them will do. I am sure you and the others will come up with something else at least as descriptive as the other."

"If I might be so bold as to ask, *Bwana*," Rajabu said as he passed the bottle back to Henry, "but wherever did you get the name of Mister Two Barrels?"

"It's a long and sad story, *Ombascha* Rajabu—generated by worthless old bag of bones by the name of Gemali Jayubara..."

Rajabu's eyes lit up. "I know this man."

"Oh. You are of the same tribe?"

"No, no—he is M'nuwezi. He is the Senior Schausch of the 17th Company, from around Moshi. I am Wahehe. How do *you* know him, *Bwana*?"

"When I was on a safari in British East some years ago, he was my bearer." Henry took another sip of the brandy. Five minutes of aging had not improved it. He passed the bottle to Rajabu. "So, you are Wahehe. I have heard of them also. From a friend."

Rajabu took another sip and made a face before looking at Henry. "And who knows of us, *Bwana*, well enough to tell tales?"

"The one you call *Bwana* Sakarani. I also met him while I was on the safari."

"Ah. *Hauptman* von Prince. Yes, if anyone knew of us, it would have been *Bwana Sakarani*. He commanded the 17th Company at Tanga." Rajabu nodded in understanding.

"*Ombascha*, you speak in the past, as though *Hauptman* von Prince was no longer with his company," Henry said.

"He fell for the Fatherland at Tanga, *Bwana*," Rajabu said sadly. "He was not alone. Many brave men fell at Tanga. But we drove off the *Anglischers* and their Indian wogs." Rajabu took another sip.

Henry waved away his attempt to pass the bottle back. "Keep it." He didn't feel like drinking any more.

Seeing the other two *Askaris* were already rolled up in their blankets, Henry stretched out on his sleeping mat and pulled his jacket around his shoulders. Evidently, Cosner's story of the four-beds was only partially true.

He awoke near dawn when he heard rustling at the doorway of the hut. The *Askaris* and Rajabu were already awake and seated around another pot of food, still undecipherable. Henry reached into his shirt pocket and produced his metal spoon. This time the *Askaris* paid no attention to it.

Ombascha Rajabu was sitting cross-legged on his sleeping mat. His rifle was lying in pieces before him and he was massaging each piece in turn with a piece of oily rag before reassembling the rifle. He paid no attention at all to the inside of the barrel. Henry asked if he might examine the rifle and Rajabu handed it over warily. Henry had never seen, let alone handled, an 1871 Mauser and found the piece both fascinating and very dated. The bore was huge, larger than his 405 Winchester. The exterior of all of the metal parts was worn bright. There was no rust or pits. The inside of the bore was considerably like the inside of a coal mine.

"Have the *jumbe* bring us a pot of boiling water, please" Henry requested to anyone of the three who might be listening.

Rajabu motioned with his hand and one of the *Askaris* immediately ducked out of the hut, returning in a matter of minutes with a earthen jug of steaming water—or at least steaming liquid of some kind.

Henry pulled his gun case to his side and unbuckled the top. The *Askaris* eyes grew large and very white when they saw the two guns inside. Henry swung a small latch out of the way and flipped an interior partition open exposing the cleaning utensils. He pulled out a rod and a jag shaped like a large needle eye which he screwed onto the end of the rod. Then he took one of the precut patches and threaded it through the eye-slot. After dipping the patch and rod end into the steaming liquid, which might even be water, he grasped Rajabu's rifle by the barrel and inserted the wet patch into the breech using considerable force, and slowly driving the rod and wet patch down the barrel and out the muzzle. Seeing the extent of the crud on the patch, Henry decided to stop wasting time and materials. He unscrewed the patch and jag from the rod, pulled the rod out of the rifle barrel and inserted the patch and jag back into the muzzle. Standing the Mauser on its muzzle, he looked around the hut until he settled on a small gourd. He used it to dip steaming liquid out of the jug, pouring it down the barrel of the upright rifle until hot liquid dribbled out of the chamber. He counted to thirty, slowly, before picking up the rifle and pulling the patch out of the muzzle. A steady stream of black, gritty liquid ran out onto the ground. He then repeated the process until the liquid came out the color of river water. He ran a clean patch through the barrel and then held the rifle up to look through the barrel.

"It isn't good," he said finally, "but at least you can see through it. *Now*, you can oil it." Henry looked at the *Askaris*. "You've seen how I have taught the *Ombascha* the proper way to clean a rifle's insides. Now you do the same for yours. If you are going to lead me into harm's way, I at least want you to be able to shoot your rifles without them blowing up."

It took an additional hour for the *Askaris* to rudimentally clean their Mausers. Henry was not happy with the result, but it was better than nothing. At least they were now reasonably sure the barrels were clear of the largest chunks.

They rode further south for the rest of the day and came to a small town encircled by a large military encampment just as the evening meal was being doled out. There was a Daimler truck unloading crates of some sort outside one of the larger tents, and Henry was fairly certain it was the same truck that had rolled past him at Amani. They turned the horses over to the appropriate officer, and Henry followed Rajabu toward what was certainly the headquarters tent.

CHAPTER THIRTY-ONE

Monday, June 28, 1915
Turiani
German East Africa

Inside the tent illuminated by the flickering light of an oil lantern, Henry found Oberst *Paul Von Lettow-Vorbeck* seated behind a small field desk. His boots and stockings were off, and another white man in uniform, with a scalpel in his hand, bent over Paul's bare feet. Every now and then the man would take the scalpel and make a small cut, bring the blade close to his eye to examine it, grunt with satisfaction, and then go back to his work. Each time he used the scalpel, Paul would set his lips and there would be a sharp little sound as he sucked in a quick breath. Seated on the field cot on the other side of the tent was Generalmajor *Kurt Wahle*, who was in the process of pulling on his boots.

Von Lettow looked up as Henry ducked into the tent behind *Ombascha* Rajabu. The *Ombascha* snapped to attention and gave a crisp salute. "*Mein Obersti*, I have brought the man *Herr* Feller, as you ordered."

"Very good. It only took you twice as long as it should have, but that is to be expected from such a miserable excuse of a soldier as yourself."

"Yes, *Mein Obersti*."

"You may go. Try not to get lost in the camps again."

"Yes, *Mein Obersti*." Rajabu did an about face and left the tent.

The smile on Von Lettow's face disappeared as he turned to look up at Henry. "Heinrich, what am I to do with you?"

"Well, I was heading back to Cosner's when you had your orderly fetch me."

"And how long have you spent at Cosner's since you were sent down there?"

"It's been nearly a year."

"Of which you might have been at Cosner's for what—a week or two, off and on?"

"How do you figure that?"

"I just got done talking to Cosner at Manza Bay, Heinrich. Unlike you, he is a German citizen who can be put in jail—or worse—for lying to me and the Governor. Not that *I* would shoot him, I don't think, but I'll not speak for our Supreme Imperial leader, Schnee. Save yourself the trouble of trying to remember where you've been and what you've been doing for the last year. We already know about your being on and around the *Königsberg* instead of staying *where you were ordered to stay*. So again the question is, what am I to do with you?"

"You could let me do what you and the Governor wanted me to do."

"How is that?"

"You could let me gather the information I need to tell your side of this little campaign in nowhere land."

"And probably get yourself killed in the process."

"I could do that crossing Main Street in Mitchell, South Dakota, U.S. of A."

"How many times do I have to say it, Heinrich? The purpose is to make sure you *don't* get killed in the process—crossing the street or otherwise."

"Which means," Henry said sharply, "at the very best I'll be fed second-hand information about whatever happens."

Paul was silent, conceding the point. He winced as the man working on his feet dug out another small something.

"What the hell is he doing to you?" Henry asked abruptly.

"Removing chiggers. They get under the skin. If they are not removed, they can breed an infection and cripple a man," Paul explained. He motioned to the man with the scalpel. "This is Doctor Taute, Heinrich, the Chief Surgeon for the *Schutztruppe*."

The man looked up and nodded to Henry but said nothing. He continued to work examining Paul Von Lettow-Vorbecks's feet.

"Jesus."

"Oh, it isn't so bad" said *Generalmajor* Wahle. "It's far worse if you let the little buggers stay under your skin. First they itch, and then your feet swell, then they turn black and start to rot. It's better to cut them out right away. You get used to it."

"We still haven't decided what to do with you Heinrich," Paul repeated.

"We?" Henry asked. "It sounds like you have already formed a committee, made up your collective minds and ..."

"We—I and our Supreme Leader, the Governor, and now I think the good *Generalmajor* Wahle, formerly my chief of logistics and now the commander of the Western District of German East."

"What the hell is 'logistics'?"

"Supply, Heinrich. Making sure everyone has bullets and bread and blankets. You know—making it possible to actually fight a war."

"Hmmph," Henry grunted.

"Don't make it sound so simple, Heinrich. When I was at General Staff school, we were taught amateurs study tactics and strategy while professional warriors study logistics—just as Schlieffen, Moltke, Clauswitz, Scharnhorst, and Gneissenau did. And they learned a great deal about it by studying those you may have heard of: Henry Knox, Ulysses Grant, and William Tecumseh Sherman. " There was a tone to Paul Von Lettow-Vorbeck's voice reminding Henry of a teacher talking to a class of First Reader pupils, and, also of how little he knew of German military traditions.

"Heinrich, I remember a quote I was taught: 'It is not I who commands the army but flour and forage are the masters...' Wahle interjected. "Frederick the Great said that, and I was just thinking, it was Moltke used to say the battle of Gravelotte was won at Fort Donelson." Abruptly he came back to the subject at hand. "You could send him with me. We get along, and where I'm going he shouldn't have a problem with wanting to stay close to hand."

"Hmm. That has possibilities," Von Lettow-Vorbeck acknowledged, "but I have another task for him first."

"Goddamn it, Paul," Henry blurted, "don't I have anything to say about it?"

Von Lettow-Vorbeck looked over to Wahle and then to Henry. "No. Actually, you don't. Your other choice is to be taken to Kilimatinde and put in the internment camp. Now shut up and listen. I am going to send you back to Dar, where you will check on the progress of the building of the field carriages for the *Königsberg's* 4.1 inch guns—we usually call them 105mm guns in the *Schutztruppe*. While there, you can visit some of your friends in the Kaiser Wilhelm hospital. Wenig is there, as is Looff, and Koch. You might even meet Schönfeld, though I think the Governor sent him down to Kilwa with the survivor company."

"What the hell happened?"

"Oh, while you were on your little trek up to Manza Bay with Cosner, the British had two monitors and two more aeroplanes arrive. They are shallow-draft monitors, with six-inch guns, and they ran up the channel to within range of the *Königsberg*. Then, using the aeroplanes to spot their shots, they proceeded to blow her into rubble."

"Jesus."

"Consider yourself lucky, *Herr* Feller," *Generalmajor* Wahle said quietly. "If you would have stayed on the Rufiji, you probably would have been killed, along with the others."

"How bad are Looff and Wenig hurt?"

"Looff got peppered pretty badly with splinters when a salvo took out the bridge. As I understand it, his cigarette case and pocket watch saved his life. Otherwise he would have been gutted by a piece of shell. As it is, he should be back to duty in a few weeks. Not Wenig, though—he lost a leg."

"Jesus."

"We've taken the survivors—there were only about seventy unwounded, and maybe that many again who will be able to return to duty—and formed a *Königsberg* Field Company of them and the surviving Marines from the *Zeiten*. As I said, I think they are all down in the Kilwa area, resting and being trained as infantry. I intend to take them into the *Schutztruppe* when they are ready."

Doctor Taute finally rose. "That should hold you for a while. I believe I have gotten all of the little buggers out." The Doctor saluted Wahle and then Von Lettow-Vorbeck before walking out of the tent.

"How the hell did they get the guns off?"

"Your friend Schönfeld. After Koch scuttled the ship on Looff's orders, he had the survivors remove the breechblocks and toss them overboard. When Schönfeld got back to the wreck from down in the channels, he saw the hulk had settled with most of the superstructure out of the water, so he told Looff the guns could be salvaged and sent divers down to find the breechblocks. Then he dismounted the guns and put them on the same sort of sleds they had used for the boilers and had them hauled to Dar—they already had a road, this time. I'm having the ship yard in Dar make field carriages for them. We may not have much compared to the damned British, but we *will* have bigger and better guns—eight of them, I think. A couple others were destroyed in the bombardment."

"I take it, then, you trust me to run loose?"

"No, but I don't have much other choice if I am to get any use out of you at all. And neither do you. Of course you might choose to sit out the rest of the war at Kilimatinde. The choice is yours. I have too many other things to worry about than to try and shepherd you about out of harm's way. I expect you to use a little common sense and just keep your journals up to date. I am going back up north to Moshi to see what I can do to irritate the British. You and the *Generalmajor* will go down to the Central Railroad. There you will go on to Dar, and the General will proceed to his new assignment at Tabora. Once you are done in Dar, you will proceed to Tabora and report to him. What he does with you, I really don't care. As your General Washington once told one of his officers, 'You have been a thorn in my side and a pain in my ass since the day we met'."

"Really?"

"No, but it gets the point across. Don't become either, Heinrich, or I promise you *will* spend the rest of the war at Kilimatinde."

CHAPTER THIRTY-TWO

Wednesday, October 27, 1915
Dar es Salaam
German East Africa

One of the Schwesteren—*nursing sisters*—*transferred the stack of newly laundered linens from one forearm to another, bowed slightly, and pointed into the ward when Henry asked where he might find* Frau Hammerstein. *With the same efficiency of motion, the sister transferred the linens back to her other arm and gave Henry a look of complete disapproval as she passed a glance over his guncase.*

He nodded his head, unseen, as the sister strode away to go about her duties, and leaned the Ruckermann case against the wall outside the ward doorway. He was halfway down the aisle between the rows of beds when Liesel Hammerstein still with her back turned to him, rose from whatever ministrations she had been performing, patted the wounded soldier on the shoulder, and turned to leave the ward. She saw him then, and after an instantaneous pause, she came running to him, throwing her arms around his waist.

"*Mein Gott, Heinrich*, where have you been?"

"Hello, Liesel," he said, wrapping his arms around her and returning her hug. "I've been up at Amani with *Doktor* Zimmermann. This is the first chance I've had to get away."

"We were so worried. Were you near any of the fighting?"

"No," Henry fibbed, "I've had my orders to stay away. The *Obersti* found out I'd been down to the Delta with Werner and read me the riot act. I thought I'd lay low for a while to let him cool off."

"*Ach so.* We thought you might have done something stupid, like go to see the war or something."

"No. Catching hell—excuse me, please—being told my place by Paul was quite enough, thank you just the same. Besides, I'm getting too old for that sort of thing. Warfare is a young man's game. I've seen quite enough of it, world-wide, and don't care if I ever see any more."

Liesel Hammerstein loosened her grip on him but kept one arm wrapped around his back and she led him out of the ward. He reached over and picked up his guncase as they passed through the doorway.

"I'm surprised the *Schwesteren* let you bring that in here" she commented.

"Oh, I got a dirty look or two, but I'm not about to leave it where it can walk off on its own."

They walked arm in arm across the boulevard to the Kaiser Hotel and took a table under the veranda awning. Henry still marveled at how much this spot reminded him of *Unter den Linden* in Berlin.

"Well," Liesel finally asked after they had ordered coffee and a small pastry, "what did you learn with the good *Doktor*."

"Mostly what an amazing fellow he is. It isn't often someone so dedicated to one thing can almost instantaneously refocus onto a whole new set of priorities. When I met him the first time—last spring—he was all soil chemistry and cattle breeding and crop genetics. Now, it's *ersatz* this and *ersatz* that, everything for the war effort. They've found a way to vulcanize rubber—make automobile and truck tires—and they've come up with all sorts of substitutes for medicines and cloth and dyes. And even whiskey, though I'm being generous when I call it that—maybe after it's aged a hundred years or so."

"What did you expect?" Liesel asked. She turned her head slightly. "Heinrich, he's German. I mean *Vaterland* German, not German-East German. Once the call went out from the Kaiser…"

"Liesel, you make it sound almost biblical. And as if the call went out from Kaiser Wilhelm that all the world should be enrolled…"

"You know, Heinrich, my dear, *Kaiser* does mean Ceasar."

"Yes, I know, but you almost make it sound like some sort of crusade."

"It is, Heinrich. It is. Zimmermann is probably the one civilian in the Colony who agrees with Paul one hundred percent on the way the war *must* be fought here, so anything he can do to aid Paul's campaign he will do. Ask him to bring the moon down and roll it over the British, and he will die trying to do it—for Paul, for the Kaiser, for Germany. He knows he probably can't, but he is willing to die trying just the same."

They talked on about the same things over their coffee, and the next and another, until Liesel said she just had to get back to the hospital. They stood and she kissed him on the cheek. "Where will you be? What will you do now, Heinrich?"

"I'll get a room here at the Kaiser again, I suppose. I'll see you and Alex whenever I can."

Liesel stopped. Her face went white and she seemed to stagger for an instant. *"Ach, mein Gott.* You haven't heard, have you?"

"Heard what?"

"Oh, Heinrich, poor Heinrich. I am so sorry. I should have thought. I didn't know."

"Liesel...for pity's sake what?"

"Heinrich, Alex was killed at Jasin...in January. He was wounded during the battle and died a week later. Paul sent a note." She held him again.

"Oh, Liesel, I'm sorry. I'm so goddamned sorry!"

They held one another until she broke away and walked slowly back across the boulevard and through the gate of the hospital.

CHAPTER THIRTY-THREE

Wednesday, March 8, 1916
Tabora
German East Africa

*G*eneralmajor *Kurt Wahle was standing near the railing running between the pillars of the peak of the steeple of the German Lutheran Church. Behind him, less than two meters away, was a similar white painted wooden railing surrounding the church bell. Under the bell was a thirty-foot drop to the foyer of the chapel.* Generalmajor *Wahle was in the tower of the church because it was the highest point in Tabora. Now, if he could just remember not to lean on either railing which may very well have consisted of a couple of coats of paint and little else—this was Africa and the railings were wooden and therefore a tasty tidbit for the vast uncounted numbers of indigenous termites inhabiting this part of German East. It would not do for the exalted commander of the Western District to topple to his death in the face of the enemy, or rather enemies, of the Kaiser, before he could order his beleaguered little army to run like hell to the southeast.*

He put his binoculars back to his eyes and looked west along the line of the Central Railroad. In the middle distance he could see a company of his *Schutztruppe Askaris* ripping up the railway. Scanning farther out to where he expected to see the Belgians materialize over the surrounding hills, some fifteen kilometers away along the mist-shrouded horizon, he saw... Nothing. No dust, no columns, wagons, trucks, artillery, camions. Nothing. Evidently *Herr Oberst* Molitor was taking his morning sip.

The *Generalmajor* scanned to the southwest, even though he did not expect to see anything of the Rhodesians and South Africans. By his last information they were having a terrible time advancing through the trackless, swampy wilderness around the south end of Lake Tanganyika. What did concern him was the possibility of their heading due east, cross-lots, as it were, and cutting off his line of retreat.

Finally, he scanned to the northwest, idly wondering what had become of the British portion of the three-pronged attack on his positions. Again, there was nothing. No sign. *Well*, the *Generalmajor* thought, *that just gives us more time to destroy the railroad.* He took the binoculars from his eyes and put them back into their leather case. Bits of the leather, turned moldy by the constant moisture in the air during the Early Rains, left blackish-green crumbs on his tunic chest. He carefully took hold of the hand rail and descended the steps from the bell tower.

There were two men waiting for him in the foyer of the chapel. One was his son, Richardt—who everyone called *Der Dicke*. Richardt was his aide, made so when the General had been sent west by *Oberst* Von Lettow-Vorbeck. Richardt's *Schutz Kompagnie* had acquitted itself well up on the northern border, but not without loss. When the *Obersti* had rolled the *Schutz Kompainien* into the regular *Schutztruppe* formations to pad out the losses from Tanga and Jasin and Taveta, Richardt had been declared a supernumerary officer, so the *Generalmajor* had taken him on as an aide and no one thought anything of it.

The other man waiting on the General was Henry Feller. He had come back into Tabora the evening before under less than ideal circumstances—though *Generalmajor* Wahle doubted he had been deliberately trying to "stir the soup." He had gone off several days before to visit the outpost line, as he called it, a line holding along the coast of Lake Tanganyika. That was all well and good, and he carried a letter from the *Generalmajor* introducing him and instructing the local commander, *Hauptman* Max Witgen, to offer him all assistance. Feller, being Feller, had interpreted his letter as a *carte blanche* to go and do whatever the hell he pleased, which in this case meant going across the damn lake. He, first, skirted the Belgians, and then infiltrated the Belgian forces from the west, passing himself off as a—of course— neutral correspondent. He even interviewed *Le Colonel* Molitor, the commander, who talked long and openly about his utter disdain for his pig-headed British allies.

Feller then exfiltrated himself back across the lake—without bothering to wake the snoozing sentries on the German side of the line—and took a train to within walking distance of Tabora, infiltrating the sentry line again. The General didn't know whether to have him shot or give him an Iron Cross. The stunt spoke volumes about the skill of Feller's field-craft—and the size of his huge brass balls. Even more about his total lack of brains. *But, the General mused to himself, it was audacious, which is all we have in the face of what we have to face.*

Wahle had called *Hauptman* Witgen back to Tabora, after giving Feller hell for not relaying his gathered intelligence on to the *Hauptman* at first opportunity. Feller, unchastened, gave an incredibly succinct report on the situation across the lake.

Essentially, the Belgians were fighting the war on three fronts. First, within the *Congo Belge*, where the Belgian Congo military, the 10,000-strong *Force Publique* was commanded by Baron Charles Henri Marie Ernest Tombeur, former governor of Kitanga Province—whose name was longer than his military experience. The *Force Publique* was divided into two brigades. One, commanded by *Oberst Leutnant* F.V. Olsen, a Dane, was on the Rusizi River, which connects Lake Kivu to Lake Tanganyika. The second brigade, positioned mostly at the northern end of Lake Kivu in a region known as "The Mountains of the Moon" was commanded by *Le Colonel* Molitor. Between them they had 60 machineguns and 12 field pieces, probably of the French M1897 75mm variety. The Belgian *Askaris* were commanded by European officers, mostly Scandinavians. Pay was low, on the order of less than half paid in the *Schutztruppen*. Discipline was harsh. The *kiboko*—the ubiquitous hippo-hide lash—was the usual implement for the maintenance of discipline. The *Force Publique Askaris* were recruited from the most primitive tribes in the *Congo Belge*, with the generally accepted belief among white and blacks that cannibalism was rampant. There was even a story going around for some time that when rations ran out, the *Force Publique* fed its porters to the soldiers. Needless to say the Belgians were having a hard time recruiting porters.

Then, at least according to *Le Colonel* Molitor, the Belgians were having a hell of a time internally. Kitanga Province had a large foreign population, mostly British and American technicians and professionals who worked for the railroad or *Union Miniére*. The Belgians considered these foreigners to be a rabble of trade unionists, socialists, dissidents, and communists who were corrupting the work ethic of the hard-working Belgians and Africans. The colonial administration was waging a silent war of restrictions and regulations against them in the hope they would simply get tired of being snubbed and taxed and go away.

The other half of the equation was the British—in reality the Commonwealth Forces, mostly South African and Rhodesian—moving in from the northwest and southwest. These forces were commanded by Major General Sir Charles Preston Crewe, a fifty-eight-year-old South African whose military claim to fame was service in the Boer War, and then a term in the cabinet of the Union of South Africa.

Sir Charles commanded from the Colony of Uganda and had sent a small detachment down Lake Victoria to take Mwanza. They had been met by the local *Schutztruppe Kompainie* supported by a couple of hundred locally recruited Africans armed mostly with spears and bows, who had retreated into the bundu pursued by a company or so of the King's African Rifles. Leading the pursuers into some swampy ground and then immediately counter-attacking, the *Schutztruppe Askaris* had stopped the British advance, even though it had cost the loss of the radio masts at Mwanza, thereby cutting half of the contact the Colony had with the outside world. The *Schutztruppe Askaris* had intercepted a message from Captain Carew, the British commander on the scene, who complained bitterly he hadn't the medical means to treat arrow wounds. The British advance had not begun again, nor did it appear likely to resume anytime soon.

The Rhodesians had run into the same sort of trouble. Their advance had bogged down in a morass around Lake Rukwa, and they too had gone doggo. Wahle was hoping they didn't turn and cut cross-lots, due east across his planned line of retreat to a junction with the rest of the *Schutztruppen* somewhere south of Dodoma, or Kilosa or even Morogoro. He had about 5,000 soldiers around Tabora, roughly a third of the German forces in the Colony. He faced close to 20,000 Belgians and Commonwealth troops, who were much better equipped—even though he was expecting at least some of the refitted *Königsberg* guns, and even though the ammunition reclamation from Manza Bay was beginning to trickle into the pipeline.

It was the last part of Feller's report, however, that most likely gave the reason for the lack of Allied offensive movement. Quite simply, General Tombeur and Sir Charles Crewe loathed one another and were not speaking. Nor were they communicating in any other way or planning any sort of combined efforts. Nothing. The British were sitting in the mud southeast of Kigoma, the Belgians were sitting in the mud on the shores of the lakes, and the Rhodesians were sitting in the mud to the southwest. And the Early Rains hadn't even started as yet. Feller was probably right. There wouldn't be any significant Allied movement until after the rains ended—in other words, June or thereabouts. And even then, it was unlikely the Allies would make any sort of coordinated effort. And that meant, at best, the most they might be able to do would be to make three uncoordinated efforts. That raised the interesting possibility to *Generalmajor* Wahle of having local superiority somewhere in his area of operations, possibly more than once. Interesting.

Now, if he could just settle his other problem, which was purely political in that it revolved around politicians—actually, a single politician, the Governor, *Doktor* Heinrich Schnee.

Last December, when it appeared as though the British Navy was about to descend on Dar es Salaam, the good *Doktor* and *Frau* Ada had decided to evacuate the government from the coastal capital to a safer inland location. Tabora was the headquarters of the Western Command, and it was on the railroad, making it easily accessible. *Frau* Ada and the good *Doktor* had up and moved the government to Tabora, taking possession of the largest buildings in the town in the name of the Kaiser—which Wahle had thought a bit much. That displaced the army into much smaller and more scattered offices and quarters, a fact the *Frau* and *Doktor* seemed not to take into account, or for that matter, give so much as a fig about.

Since they had moved in, Wahle had been trying to think of ways to get them to move back to Dar. Now, with Feller's excellent report in his head and hand, Kurt Wahle was fairly certain he had found the means to accomplish his ends. He would send Feller off on a mission to Dar, ostensibly to visit the shipyards, where the *Königsberg* guns were still being refitted, to see how that little project was progressing. If Feller could get into Dar and nose around, he could surely take in whether a British invasion was imminent. If it wasn't, and if Feller could find and talk to the *Obersti*, then he could give the good *Doktor* another of his excellent situation reports when he returned, and hopefully, *Frau* Ada would then wish to dash off to her magnificent Residence, dragging the good *Doktor* with her—out of the hair of and out from under foot of, *Generalmajor* Kurt Wahle. In the worst case, an invasion would be imminent and they would be no worse off in knowing about it. He also wanted Feller to see how much truth there was to the rumor the Allies had a new commander in British East. He had heard it rumored the South African Jan Christian Smuts, quite suddenly for some reason, had been given the command.

Wahle knew of Smuts from his *Gross General Stab* studies of the Boers' warfare against the British, and had contributed some things to the biographic *dossier*. Janni Smuts had never attended a school until he was twelve years old, yet by the time he was seventeen, he had won a degree from Victoria College in Stellenbosch and a scholarship to Cambridge. There he had placed first in both parts of the law tripos, at the same time writing a book about the poet Walt Whitman. Admitted to the Middle Temple, the friendless loner Smuts had returned to South Africa and took up the practice of law when he was twenty-five. Three years later, his friend Paul Kruger, President of the Transvaal, appointed him state's attorney.

When Kruger left Transvaal during the Boer War, Smuts solidified his political position in South Africa by becoming fast friends with Louis Botha and by riding *Kommando*. He took a bunch of less than 400 Transvaal Boers and rode a thousand-mile, ten-month ride through British Cape Colony, cutting up any British army units in his way. The ride won him the nickname "Slim Janie"—Wahle thought very few Englishmen realized '*Slim*' in Afrikaans meant 'sly', not 'skinny'. After the war, both Botha and Smuts experienced epiphanies of sorts and became two of the most vocal pro-British voices in the Afrikaans community. In 1911, when the Union of South Africa was formed from four former colonies, Botha became prime minister, and Smuts served alongside Sir Charles Crewe in the Cabinet. Wahle had concluded his study with an assessment: "Smuts is a physically inexhaustible genius, whose personal courage is legendary. Furthermore, he has the gift of command presence, which, even though he is rude, impatient, and personally cold and distant, galvanizes his troops into acts of uncommon valor and prodigious endurance." Wahle had ended his study with a quotation from the Bishop of Pretoria: "Smuts fears neither God nor man, and particularly the former." If Slim Janie Smuts was indeed in charge, it was Kurt Wahle's estimation the Allies would move sooner rather than later. Slim Janie was not one to brew up tea when there was a fight to be had.

When once he had decided what he was going to do with Feller, the General also decided to shift his other subordinates around. Witgen, who was a good company commander but seemed to have a rather higher self-regard of his own strategic abilities than any of his superiors had of them—especially the *Obersti*—would be sent up to watch over the British south of Mwanza. Major von Langenn would go to Kigoma and do what he could to hold up the inevitable Allied advance on the western end of the railroad. Wahle was very specific about ordering von Langenn to make sure the Central Railroad was destroyed when he retreated back to Tabora, and it was inevitable he would have to do just that. Wahle's main concern was to keep his forces as concentrated as possible. He agreed wholeheartedly with the *Obersti*, so long as the German army remained free to move, the Allies would be forced to devote time, money, and manpower to counter it—in other words divert time, money, and manpower away from the European war to a small and insignificant side-show. It had worked so far. He was facing the equivalent of two European army corps, with not quite one-third of a European-size division. And he had to assume the *Obersti* was doing the same. In any case, Feller would find out.

CHAPTER THIRTY-FOUR

Tuesday, May 16, 1916
Mount Kanga
German East Africa

*I*n the two months that followed, Henry made the rail trip between Dar
and Tabora several times, as well as some side jaunts, on one occasion
to Kondoa Irangi, where Paul had moved his headquarters in order to
watch the British attempting to move through the Early Rains from their
lodgment on Lake Victoria. Henry had convinced Frau Ada when he had
ridden back to Tabora on the same train bringing four of the newly mounted
Königsberg guns to Generalmajor Wahle, the British had no intent of
taking Dar as yet. He and the Generalmajor had waved farewell to the
Kaiser's civil government as it steamed out of the Tabora Station, much to
the Generalmajor's delight.

Another of the side trips was up to the Mombo-Handeni Trolley
Line, a narrow gauge shunt running north from Handeni to Mombo
on the Northern Railroad. *Major* Kraut was the officer in command
there, with about a third of the *Schutztruppen* holding the British
eastern advance—that portion of the British offensive taking place east
of Mount Kilimanjaro and down the line of the Northern Railroad
with Tanga as an objective. Eventually, of course, Slim Janie Smuts
would succeed. There was simply no way *Major* Kraut and his five-
thousand *Askaris* and farmers-in-uniform could hope to stop the British,
Nigerians, South Africans, and Indians coming against them. But they
could bleed them—unless, of course, the rains killed them all off first.

While Henry was running back and forth across the Colony, Kraut
managed to fight a splendid little rear guard action along the Northern
Railroad. Kraut had learned from somewhere the British had formed
a mounted force—not surprising considering Slim Janie's experiences
riding *Kommando* a decade or so before—to outflank or cut off Kraut's
defenders. *Major* Kraut fought small-unit actions every five kilometers
or wherever the ground afforded him concealment and advantage. He

forced the British to deploy their infantry and send their mounted troopers off on wide sweeping marches. The result was the dismounting of the British mounted forces and the animal-borne supply train by the tse-tse flies. In a matter of days, the British troops were reduced to less than half rations, and the line of advance was literally blocked by piles of dead and dying oxen, horses, and mules. Kraut received a report from one of his ubiquitous sources one of the British Doctors attached to the advance was supposed to have said the only veterinary supplies needed by the army was a resupply of pistol ammunition for putting the stricken beasts out of their misery. Kraut mused that the good Doctor did not define who or what he meant when he referred to the stricken beasts.

The occurrence of the mass of freshly dead animals had the unforeseen effect of bringing out every kind of scavenger and predator that made little distinction between two- and four-legged meals. For days on end the Commonwealth Forces lost more men to disease and animal attack than it did to German fire.

Eventually, after one of the larger scale actions across Richardt Wahle's farm outside Buiko, which left the place in ruins, Kraut had turned and started his retreat down the Trolley line, leaving Tanga to the British. It had taken them only twenty-three months to capture the first sizable town in German East—on the second attempt.

Henry caught up with Kraut again after the end of the Early Rains. The *Schutztruppen* were dug in along the Lukigura River at a little cluster of thatched huts called Ruhungu, in the shade of Mount Kanga, where they had been pushed by the British after leaving Handeni. Kraut and his troops were in good spirits despite having lost a number of men during the retreat. They had tested the fighting abilities of the Indian soldiers at several brush piles and had found all but the Gurkas lacking in skill. Now they had been supplemented with two of the *Königsberg* guns, which had been dug in nearly at the summit of Mount Kanga, about 6,000 feet above the plain. The mountain was high enough to afford a splendid field of fire. Ammunition was relatively plentiful. And the mountain was covered by lush vegetation—compared to the plains surrounding it. All told, it was a pleasant little field exercise for the gun crews.

Henry and Major Kraut sat at the door of Kraut's tent, and from a distance of a half-mile or so watched the guns spit shells onto the British positions below. They were sharing a bottle of Amani's finest *ersatz* liquor—neither of them could bring themselves to calling it whiskey, though it was very much indeed alcohol. Kraut was telling how they had left a little present for the British in Handeni when they retreated—over a hundred porters all in various stages of typhoid fever. The story reminded Henry of some of the tales from his youth about the handing out of infested and infected blankets to the reservation Indians. Nasty similarities.

"But, my good Major," Henry said, trying to sound far more jovial than he felt, "that story is not why you dragged me up the side of this mountain to watch artillery practice."

"Oh no, *Herr* Feller," Kraut chuckled, "the real interesting show is about to start now the heat of the day has abated and the main players can function."

Henry gave Kraut a quizzical look. The officer rolled his eyes and after turning his head as if listening to something in the distance, simply said, "Ah, here they come."

Off in the distance, and well below them, Henry could hear the stuttering, buzzing sound of an overworked motor of some sort. He was wondering how large a truck it would have to be to have a motor large enough to be heard at the apparent distance Kraut was pointing to. But Kraut didn't seem to be pointing *at* anything except a sound. Finally, in frustration, Henry shrugged and said, "What?" Kraut pointed down slope and told Henry to look for movement against the darker spots of the background. Finally, with the motor sounds growing louder all the while, Henry saw a grayish-light blue oblong, perhaps still a mile or two away and moving far slower than Henry had expected. Two aeroplanes flying close together were coming nearly straight toward them—or at least straight toward a point a couple of thousand feet below them.

Henry's total experience with aeroplanes of any sort had been his seeing a picture of President Roosevelt taking a ride, or returning from taking a ride, or something like that, with one of the Wright Brothers or a newly minted Army Aviator just before they had all gone off on the Smithsonian Safari. And then there had been the dauntless Leftenant Cutler's aeroplane blown out of the air by Schönfeld's Delta Force guns. That pretty much summed up his aeroplane knowledge.

"They can't get off the ground during the heat of the day," Kraut said, "so they wait until it cools a little, and then, with any luck, they can get into the air. Their landing field is on the other side of Handeni so it takes them a while to use up enough petrol to get light enough to climb so they can drop their bombs."

Kraut seemed to be enjoying the show. He sat back in his field chair and put his heels up on the edge of his field table, balancing the glass of Amani's finest on his tunic chest. "My intelligence sources—Arabs mostly—tell me the British have an entire Squadron, Number 26, here. And the aeroplanes are BE2s—whatever that means. In any case, they are not the best the Royal Flying Service has to offer. On a good day, down slope and with a strong tailwind, they might be able to do 80 or 90 kilometers an hour. We could probably shoot them down with rifle fire—they're only made of wood and cloth and piano wire, of course. I've been told the flyers call them 'pigeon traps' because of all the piano wire. Supposedly, if you turn a pigeon loose between the wings and it can find its way out, you are missing some wires." Kraut laughed.

The aircraft circled around for a long time, burning off weight. Finally, one began to climb leisurely, staying five or six hundred feet above the treetops on the mountainside. Twice during the climb its motor coughed and died, and the pilot was forced to turn around and gain speed going downhill until he could restart the motor, which coughed and protested and belched so much blue-black smoke out of its exhaust pipes Henry thought for a moment it was on fire. Finally, the aeroplane managed to work its way to the top of the mountain, where, after circling for a while as the pilot tried to see the *Königsberg* guns, two small objects fell from the side of the aeroplane. These landed in a dense thicket about a half kilometer from the nearest gun, detonating with the sound of wet firecrackers. The bomb noises were met by the cheering of several thousand of Kraut's *Askaris* and the answering, deafening crack of one of the *Königsberg* guns as it sent another unmolested shell into the British positions below.

"That must have been Bell," Kraut commented. "There was only the pilot in that one, and Bell refuses to fly with anyone in the observer seat."

"Who's Bell?" Henry asked, thinking to himself Kraut's intelligence service must be pretty good at its job to be able to furnish the German commander the names of the individual British pilots.

"Oh, like your Selous and Pretorius, another of Mother England's innumerable white hunters. The natives call him *Karamoja*. His particular claim to fame is he hunts *tembo*—elephants—with rifles most sane humans consider stark madness to use. The story goes, and I have no reason to doubt it, he actually took *tembo* with a 6 millimeter of some sort. He claims it isn't all that difficult if you know where to aim. Personally, having taken several *tembo* myself, I think he's a raving lunatic. But he appears to be far more dangerous with a rifle than he is with an aeroplane."

Kraut looked down slope where the other aeroplane was turning to rejoin the first. "That appears to be it for the afternoon's entertainment. I don't think the one with two men in it can get enough altitude to attempt to do anything—they haven't hit anything yet and they've been trying every day for the last week. Look's as though they are going home and saving Mother England the cost of the hardware." Kraut waved his hand after the departing aeroplanes. "Until tomorrow, then. *Schlaf wohl*,—sleep well."

Notwithstanding the afternoon's entertainment on Kanga Mountain, the German East Colony to the northeast was in the process of losing one of its greatest assets through another stroke of audacity—on both sides—that Henry came to realize was the earmark this campaign in nowhereland.

Near the end of the third week of June, as *Doktor* Albrecht Zimmerman was taking a breath of fresh air on the veranda of the main building-turned-factory, he leaned on his veranda railing and watched a familiar figure walking into the Amani facility. The *Doktor* had not seen the white man leading a squad of soldiers since the beginning of the war. But considering the *Doktor* saw few white men at all, the sudden appearance of the man he knew as the local parish priest was a happy occurrence. Father Pearce had been at Amani hundreds of times before the war and had spent innumerable pleasant evenings over a meal, a little wine, and much enlightened conversation.

Zimmerman strode down the steps of his veranda and greeted the Father, who jokingly but warmly said "Professor Zimmerman, I presume."

"However did you get here?" Zimmerman asked.

"Oh, I walked from Monga."

"Monga! But, that's in British hands."

"Why, yes, it is," the priest admitted, quietly adding, "And now I think I'll take possession of this facility in the name of his Britannic Majesty."

Zimmerman suddenly looked at the *Askaris* who had walked in with Pearce. They were dark, but they were not African. Zimmerman realized this too late. They were Sepoys—British Indian soldiers. And because the former Father, now KAR—King's African Rifles—Major Pearce was so well known by everyone in the area, none of the natives had thought it necessary to give warning. Amani and its facilities were now in British hands.

When the word of Amani's fall reached Kraut, Henry decided on his own hook he should take the word to Paul himself, but before he could leave, he was once more intercepted by a courier from the *Obersti* and sent back to Dar-es-Salaam to give an assessment of the situation to Governor Schnee—and parenthetically, though he was certain Paul had to think long and hard about it, to prepare the Governor to once more evacuate the town and rejoin Paul at Morogoro.

That the passing of all this information and the gathering of intelligence went far beyond the pale of "neutrality" didn't cause Henry any particular qualms. There had been, after all, several times during the last months and years when he could have simply made it convenient to be transferred into Allied hands. For instance, he had no particular reason to come back from his little scouting foray into the Congo Belge.

Yet he had. And he had brought considerable information of military importance with him and had freely given it to his friends, who just happened to be opponents of the Allies. Wahle and Paul discussed this between themselves and neither could think of a way to change what was Henry's apparent choosing of sides. By Henry's own admission, the British—at least—knew he was in the Colony. Realistically, what would happen would happen. When the end came, if they survived, perhaps they could do something to help, thereby guaranteeing Henry, who was supposedly their voice, would live long enough to actually tell the story. But until that time came, and if their luck held, they had other, far more pressing things to concern themselves with.

CHAPTER THIRTY-FIVE

Thursday, July 20, 1916
Morogoro
German East Africa

Henry Feller was sitting on a packing crate on the platform of the Central Railroad Depot at Morogoro, slowly munching on the remnants of a piece of ersatz rye bread and some farmers cheese. He was wishing for one of Liesel Hammerstein's famous sausages, but that was not going to happen, so all he could do was bask in the memories of the delicate flavors of Liesel's famous wienerwurst and pretend. He was intently watching the main road and the growing cloud of dust telling him there was a large number of moving things—men, perhaps, for he didn't think it was a driven cattle herd, though it might be. The dust cloud was rising, which meant whatever was creating it was heading his way.

There had been rumors for the last two days the *Obersti* was bringing all of the *Schutztruppen* he could gather to Morogoro ahead of the British—technically the South Africans, if the intelligence he had heard could be believed, for there were damned few "British" troops involved in this small corner of the war. Rumor also had it Paul had decided to fall back to the Central Railway and put up a defense along its length. Knowing how many troops Paul had available, Henry thought that happenstance highly unlikely, on the order of one-in-no-chance-at-all. Also, somewhere off to the west, or maybe the southwest, *Generalmajor* Wahle was operating with his own column and the odd *Askaris* and colonial rifle companies he had managed to get out of Tabora before it fell to the Belgians, as they raced the British western division to the prize by a few hours. To the north, *Major* Kraut was still causing the British Eastern division all the trouble it could care to muster.

And during the rains in late March, another relief ship, the *Maria von Stettin*, had slipped through the Royal Navy blockade and dropped anchor in Sudi Bay on the southern coast. There, several thousand porters managed to unload the 4,000 tons of war material—a bloody-great windfall, according to Paul: five million rounds of rifle and machinegun ammunition, over a thousand shells for the *Königsberg* guns, as well as a battery of 77mm field guns *and* a battery of mountain howitzers with ammunition for them, medical supplies, and even a crate of *Eisen Kreuzen*. Two of which were meant for Paul, who passed them out to others instead. The Royal Navy finally showed up and belatedly shelled the *Maria* until she appeared to be consumed with flames. Then, as they had done with the *Kronborg*, the British sailed away up the coast to shell towns willy-nilly as they passed. The *Maria's* crew promptly re-boarded, put out the fires, and sailed for parts unknown.[5]

Henry chewed on the bread and cheese as long as he could. Making it last was a good exercise in passing the time, and when the last of it was washed down with the last dregs of a bottle of what was generously called *Mai Wein* he could see the head of the marching column with its leader slowly peddling along on a bicycle. A further ten minutes put Paul Von Lettow-Vorbeck peddling along within hailing distance of Henry. *"Vie gehts, Heinrich!"* he called out, raising his hand from the handlebar in greeting.

Henry raised his right hand palm out and called back *"Hu jambo, Bwana Obersti"*—Hello, Mister Colonel. Paul laughed. Their conversations were becoming a pastiche of mixed phrases in three or four languages that would try the soul of most academics.

"What brings you here?" Paul asked in English.

"Here?" Henry continued, "as in Morogoro? Or figuratively as in 'how came I'?"

Paul laughed again. "For a writer, my friend, you are a linguistic nit-pick."

"As a writer, my friend, I took the last train 'here' to try and find a decent meal—which didn't happen, I'll have you know—and to see if the latest rumors washing through the former capital of this fair Colony have any truth to them."

"Und...what rumors are those?"

"That you are falling back to the railroad to defend it to the last man."

"You've been talking to *unser* Fearless Leader Schnee again, yes?"

"Actually, to Missus Fearless Leader, *Frau* Ada. She is quite miffed, by the way. The Royal Navy shelled her palace and broke some of her dishes and crystal."

"She is safe?"

"She is safe, but highly pissed off—her words. She swears she will never again speak to any Englishman."

"And *Unser* Supreme Fearless Leader?"

"The Governor is also alive and well."

"Damn. Oh well, better luck next time."

"He also sends his best regards and asked me to tell you to be sure to let him know where you are marching to so he can join you—sounds like he thinks you need his sage military advice, in addition to sounding like he plans to abandon Dar... again."

Oberst Von Lettow-Vorbeck shook his head, but said nothing. He was well aware Henry knew of the bad blood between them. Still, it was one of the things Paul had never bothered to try to pry out of Henry—just how Henry felt about, or more properly, what Henry thought about the situation. Henry was a past master at playing the neutrality game. Paul was certain Henry had strong opinions, and just as sure he would never divulge them unless he felt like it, regardless of the fact it did not seem to bother him to pass military information, and he had in fact apparently managed to somehow compartmentalize that sort of thing in his rationale of neutral conduct. However, the *Obersti* did *not* know if Henry had learned of the real reason for the taut feelings between the commander of the Kaiser's troops and the appointed leader of the Kaiser's Imperial colonial government.

The ill feelings had started in the usual game of power-power-who's-got-the-power arising in every Colony of every empire since the dawn of time. They had played out their roles supremely well before August of '14, and even understood each other's positions with respect to the welfare of the Colony—at least in an abstract, debating society sort of way. Paul had wished to prepare its defense; Schnee had wished to keep it at peace. The positions were not mutually exclusive, provided there was no war with other imperial powers.

But that had ended in August of '14, and by Paul's way of thinking, the military defense of the Colony immediately took precedence over everything else. Thus he and Schnee were immediately at loggerheads because that little *Wiesel* Schnee could not see the declaration of war changed everything. Schnee was determined to keep the Colony on a peacetime footing and even went so far as to attempt to open talks with the governors of Uganda, BEA, and the Congo Belge seeking to form a coalition of neutral colonies based on the now dated Berlin Treaty of 1885. Schnee, the simpering dunderhead, adamantly refused to listen to any interpretation of the treaty conflicting with his own, such as the not so incidental fact *any* action for neutrality had to be agreed upon by *all* the signatory parties, and there had been fourteen or fifteen of them. Knowing the territory-greedy Belgians and the Portuguese made neutrality as likely as finding a baboon who could sing Wagnerian opera, and that was without mentioning the French, British and Italians.

Still, the little *Wiesel* Schnee kept attempting to negotiate in private with the other colonial governments, going so far as to make private arrangements with the Royal Navy to have Tanga and Dar spared bombardment. But from the sound of Henry's information, that part of the Greater Schnee Scheme had fallen apart. Perhaps with *Frau* Ada now officially "pissed-off" at the English, the Supreme *Wiesel* would be forced to realize he would have no power at all if his Colony were occupied by the Allies and he would be sitting in an internment camp somewhere.

As they chatted, the head of the *Schutztruppen* column swung into town and turned west along the railroad tracks. There was but a single field company, about two hundred *Askaris* and their German officers, followed by one of the *Schutztruppe's* precious field guns with its ammunition wagon. Henry didn't recognize any of the officers, so which field company would remain a secret until he asked. Or so he thought.

As the head of the column strode past, marching at an easy route step, Henry could hear the German officers and NCOs singing loudly:

Der Schwur erschallt, die Woge rinnt,
Die Fahnen flattern hoch im Wind:
Zum Rhein, zum Rhein, zum deutschen Rhein,
Wir alle wollen Hüter sein

It was one of the later verses of *Die Wacht am Rhein*, the marching song of all marching songs of the German army for nearly half a century. Now, as the German officers finished their singing, the *Askaris* took up another. Henry recognized the tune—it was the *Schutzetruppen Marsch*, but instead of singing it in German, the *Askaris* were belting out the words in Swahili:

Tunakwenda, tunashinda
Tunafuata Bwana Obersti
Askari wanaendesha, Askari wanaendesha
Tunakwenda, tunashinda.

Roughly translated, it meant: "We're on the way. We're winning. We're following our Colonel. The troops are marching. The troops are marching. We're on the way, we're winning." Whenever the end of a verse was reached, the company drummers would swing wildly into a purely African beating. Then everyone, officers, NCOs and *Askaris* would blast out the final line:

Haya. Haya Safari.

That it was the 9th Company suddenly was made apparent when an *Ombascha* marched up to the *Obersti*, came to attention and saluted. "*Mein Oberst, Hauptman* Heidenberg wishes to know whether the company can make camp."

Von Lettow-Vorbeck returned the salute. "Tell *Hauptman* Heidenberg the company may camp. You may also tell him to make certain every man has water and to check everyone's feet."

"Thank you, *Obersti*, I will tell him."

"And *Ombascha*..."

Another salute. "Yes, *Mein Oberst*. Thank you, *Mein Obersti*."

"Don't fawn—it is unbecoming of a Wahehe. Off with you."

"I see you and *Ombascha* Rajabu are still at it," Henry said.

Paul smiled. "It passes time, my friend—it passes time."

If their relationship could have been anything other than commander and subordinate, they could have cut the pretensions and acted like the close friends they had become, just as Henry and Jabari were becoming. But Paul had already seen one Rajabu die following his orders and he had no illusions about Jabari's expectations for surviving this war. Hell, he had no illusions about *any* of them surviving, except possibly someone like Wenig and others who were out of it due to a lack of limbs or other necessary body parts. *Ombascha* Omsha Rajabu had been chopped into crocodile food by multiple British machineguns as he tried to swim a stream in order to scout out the British positions at Jasin. He had gone into the water on Paul's orders, knowing he would probably be killed. And he had been. Now his Brother, Jabari, was in the same position. They were Wahehe. Warriors. It simply was not in them to *not* attempt such actions or follow such orders. Paul and Jabari kept a correct and proper distance between them, but they toyed with each other. It was their way of asserting their closeness, without being overt about it. Paul was not surprised Henry had immediately seen through their little gambit.

Jabari—the name can mean The Bravest One, or, None Braver, in Swahili—Rajabu was the third child and second son of his father's favorite wife. His father's *tembe*—farm—was up in the hills northeast of the Wahehe's main town of Iringa. Counting cattle, his father was neither poor nor wealthy. The *tembe* was far enough removed from the main traveled route to Iringa to have put it out of harm's way when the Wahehe revolted against the Kaiser in the tenth or eleventh summer of Jabari's life. When the Wahehe swore faithful allegiance to the Kaiser after the warrior *Bwana Sakarani*—the Wild One—*Hauptman* von Prince swore a blood oath against Mkwana, the Wahehe leader, and after Mkwana had blown his own brains out rather than be captured, Jabari's older Brother, Omsha, had gone into the *Schutztruppe* to represent the family as a token of faithfulness and had served the Kaiser for all of his years, rising to the rank of *Ombascha* and serving as the *Oberst's* orderly, a place held by only the best and bravest. Omsha had fallen at Jasin, cut nearly in two by a burst of machine gun fire as he tried to cross the Sigi River on a scouting mission for the *Obersti*.

When word of Omsha's falling had reached Jabari's father's *tembe*, it had been left to Jabari to leave the mission school to go and replace his fallen brother in the *Schutztruppe*. As a sign of his earnestness, his father had given him a pair of *ruga-ruga*, younger lads from the nearby village, to carry his equipment, and had also sent his younger sister by his father's third wife, the half-Arab one, to go with him to cook and mend his uniform and make him as comfortable as she might.

Jabari had joined the 9th Company in the hills outside of Taveta, proud to stand watch over the only piece of English territory captured and held by the Kaiser's army. Here he had shown his bravery when the *Anglischers* and their *ruga-rugas*, the South Africans, had attacked, crashing through the bush like a herd of stampeding cattle. They were so easy to kill. And they ran away so well Jabari and his comrades chased them through the worst of the thorn scrub just to hear them shriek as they were torn at by the long, pointy barbs. It was funny—even more so than the angry bees at Tanga that had nearly driven the Indians into the ocean. They had all laughed for many hours. *Hauptman* Heidenberg was elated. He raised Jabari to Omsha's rank of *Ombascha* on the spot and recommended him to the *Obersti* for an Iron Cross.

The *Obersti* had no Iron Crosses to give, but he said he would find some sort of reward for Jabari nonetheless, for he could see he was very much like his Brother Omsha, who had been very brave indeed. And he would replace Omsha as the *Obersti's* Orderly—a great honor. His sister was very happy and very proud when he told her what the *Obersti* had said.

In the weeks following he served the *Obersti* as well as he could, and they grew to know each other very well. Jabari often talked to his sister about the *Obersti* and how he kept so well from showing the heavy, heavy weight of his responsibilities, a weight bearing down on him like a great invisible *tembo* only he could see. The *Obersti* showed many signs of understanding, and Jabari silently thought to himself the *Obersti* would have made an excellent Wahehe. Often, at the end of day's march, he would come into the *Obersti's* tent to find his commander seated on his field cot and cutting chiggers out of his feet. And after the ship had brought ammunition and supplies, the *Obersti* had given Jabari an *Eisen Kreuz*, a Second Class, and also a First Class for their father in memory of Omsha.

"Why don't you go with *Ombascha* Rajabu, Heinrich? You can settle in with him and that way you can stay ahead of *Frau* Ada," Paul suggested. It was one of the nicer orders Henry had ever been given. He followed Jabari to his area near the 9th Company's camp. They chatted as they walked, as they had many times off and on since their first meeting at Amani.

"The British *ruga-ruga* Crewe came down from the north, *Bwana* Henry, and we had many good battles along the way. All the way to Kondoa-Irangi. And then we led him into the Nguru Mountains where the valleys are narrow and the ridges very high. And we fought him every day. It was great fun."

"Why do you call them *ruga-ruga?*"

"*Ruga-ruga* do their master's bidding. That is what they are for. To do your bidding so you may be a warrior all of the time and not be a porter some of the time and a warrior only the rest. They are South Africans. They do the British bidding. So they are *ruga-ruga*. And because they call us *kaffirs*. We are not *kaffirs* nor are we *ruga-ruga*. We are *Askaris*, Wahehe *Askaris*. Soldiers. Better soldiers than the British *ruga-ruga* will ever be." Jabari bobbed his chin with certainty, before continuing.

"We lost some warriors, but they lost many, many more. And we left them all of our sick to tend to. But one of their *daktaris* came into our lines and spoke with the *Obersti*. I was there when they talked of it. He was a very brave man, the *daktari*. He asked me if I used tobacco and he gave me some of his to chew. I will never forget. He said it was Turkish. He called it Latakia. It smelled very fine when he was smoking his pipe. He told the *Obersti* if the *Obersti* didn't want to take the sick along, the *Obersti* should just give them to the *daktari* and be done with it because if we waited, he could not save some of them. So the *daktari* took all of the rest of the sick back with him. He was a very good and brave man. If he was not a *daktari*, he would be a very great warrior." Again the head-bob of certitude.

The *Ombascha's* tent had already been set up and a cook fire was starting to set its sticks to coals. Jabari ushered Henry into the tent and bade him sit on the animal skins spread on the dirt floor. He was offered a sweet—a fig dipped in honey—and a small glass of a clear liquid Henry assumed was some of the potent distilled liquor provided by the Amani Institute. Jabari left him there to go about his duties. He did not return for the better part of an hour, and Henry had nearly fallen asleep when Jabari came back into the tent leading a female.

She was tall, only an inch or two shorter than Jabari's five-feet ten, and a well set up young woman of perhaps twenty years. Her nose was straight, set between piercing black eyes. Her thin lips were turned up at the corners in a slight grin, even as she averted her gaze, as though intently watching some small crawling thing on the dusty ground between them. Her skin was a deep rich brown, shaded on the darker side of baking chocolate, with tinges that might be called ebony. Her teeth, what could be seen of them in her slight grin, were white, straight, and even. Her Swahili bore the traces of a German accent learned in the Colonial schools under the rigid discipline of the *Schwesteren*.

"This is my sister," Jabari said.

"Does the sister of *Ombascha* Jabari Rajabu have a name?" Henry asked in Swahili.

"I am called Zanta." Her voice was contralto and clear.

"Ah…'Beautiful Girl'…very appropriate."

"I take that as a compliment, *Bwana*."

"Please do, Zanta. And you needn't call me *Bwana*—I've been through all this with your Brother. My Christian name is Henry— Heinrich in German. My family name is Feller. I am *Mmerikani*. I am a *mwandishi*, a writer."

Henry motioned for her to sit beside him, and she looked to her Brother for guidance. Jabari nodded and took his own place on the opposite side of Henry. "*Herr* Heinrich is a writer of books and a correspondent to newspapers and magazines. You would do well to treat him with respect."

Zanta nodded to her Brother and bowed her head to Henry. "How can you be a writer and correspondent if there is no cable or radio because of the war?" she asked.

Henry pulled his journal bag toward him and unfastened the straps, careful not to expose the Schofield. "Do you speak or read English?" he asked.

Zanta shook her head. "No. I speak German and Wahehe."

"Not Swahili?"

"Yes, Wahehe, the language of the people."

"Oh, is Wahehe a dialect of Swahili?"

"No. Swahili is a dialect of Wahehe" she said firmly with a head bob of certitude.

CHAPTER THIRTY-SIX

Wednesday, September 20, 1916
Dar es Salaam
German East Africa

T he first person Henry saw as he entered the hospital ward was Richard Wenig, who was sitting up in his bed reading a small leather-bound book. His crutches were leaning against the wall next to the head of the bed where he could get to them should he feel the need to use the toilet at the other end of the ward, or to roam to some other part of the hospital. He didn't notice anyone standing at the foot of his bed until Henry said, "Vie gehts, Richardt?"

"Heinrich, you old sod. Still alive and kicking?"

"Mostly. You look a hell of a lot better than you did the last time I was through here."

"Well, Heinrich, they have assured me if I can be a little patient—like until the end of the war—it shouldn't be too difficult to outfit me with a new leg."

"Ah, I'd hold out for one made of whale-bone."

"Oh really?"

"Oh yeah. I think you'd probably make a fortune on the stage playing Captain Ahab. You know—'Damn Thee, Whale! With my last breath I curse thee!' You know—Moby Dick...The White Whale...Captain Ahab..."

Wenig looked on, unknowing, trying to decide whether Henry was drunk or only crazed.

"Never mind, Richardt. You had to be there."

Wenig shrugged.

Changing the subject quickly, Henry asked, "Where is *Frau* Hammerstein?"

"She's not here today."

"You mean she actually took a day off?"

"Er, yes." Wenig looked disconcerted, adding quickly, "She went to a wedding."

"Oh, anyone I know?"

"Er… Major Buller—British fellow. He was captured and they brought him in here from up north. I think he was wounded around Handeni…" Wenig's voice trailed off.

"Well, how does Liesel know him?"

"Oh, she was his Nurse."

"Ah. Who's he marrying? Anyone I know?"

"One of the Nurses."

It was Henry's turn to look confused. "I thought all of the Nurses—other than Liesel, I mean—were *Schwesteren*—sisters.

"They are."

"Richard, you're attempting to be evasive as hell."

Wenig swallowed hard. "I don't know how you'll take it, Heinrich."

"Take what, fer Chrissake?"

"That Liesel's marrying a British officer."

"What?"

"That Liesel Hammerstein is marrying a British officer, Major Redmont Buller, whom she nursed back from nearly being dead. The wedding is today. I believe it's in the ballroom of the Berger Hoff Haus—is that right?"

"The Berghoff."

"Whatever."

"Why aren't you there?"

"Because we heard you were coming in, and I said I'd stay here to talk to you. We weren't sure how you'd react."

"Because of Alex?"

"Because of Alex."

The Ballroom of the Berghoff was undecorated. An altar of sorts—a table with a white cloth cover—was set up at one end of the room. The presiding official was the German colonial equivalent of a justice of the peace. The groom, dressed in a clean but patched khaki field uniform was standing before the official. His right arm was in a white sling. The best man, also wearing a patched but clean khaki field uniform was leaning on a crutch, standing to the groom's left.

The bride, her strawberry blond hair held in place with a net, was wearing a white blouse and a dark gray skirt. The maid of honor looked vaguely familiar...*Ah, Richardt Wahle's wife.* No one in the wedding party noticed when *Leutnant* Richardt Wenig was pushed into the ballroom in a wheelchair. The tallish man who was pushing the chair parked his passenger along the aisle and carried a large oblong package, wrapped none too carefully in white paper, to a sideboard. Leaving the package, he returned and took a seat beside *Leutnant* Wenig.

The ceremony was abbreviated, the civil service cutting right to the cusp of the matter without any religious folderol: "Do you, Redmont? Do you, Elizabeth? Pay the clerk. Kiss the bride. Next!"

When the happy couple turned to leave, they discovered there were perhaps ten people attending their nuptials. None, of course, of the *Schwesteren*—because Catholic nuns do not attend ceremonies not of the Church, especially a civil ceremony smacking of *Evangelische*, such as it was—and only a few of the ambulatory patients, mostly British or Commonwealth. The surprise was the man seated next to Richardt Wenig's wheelchair. As the happy couple left the altar, he rose and stepped into the aisle in front of them. The bride's eyes grew large when she saw him.

"Heinrich!"

Henry stepped behind Wenig, his hands on the handles of the wheelchair. He looked a long look at Liesel, then a brief glance at her new husband. "Congratulations," he said, flatly.

After what seemed to be an endless awkward silence, Henry asked, "Well, aren't you going to introduce us?"

Liesel looked flustered, quite uncharacteristic for her. Her right hand was resting on her new husband's left arm—his right being suspended in the linen sling. Henry tried not to stare, but still looked automatically to the wounded limb. Evidently the tunic and shirtsleeve had been cut off at some point hidden by the sling. The right wrist was bare, and showed the edge of bandaging, but the portion of the upper arm exiting the other end of the sling was covered by the tunic sleeve. There were also traces of bandage just above the top of the tunic collar, and an angry red pucker line ran up the side of Liesel's new husband's neck to disappear in a tuft of grayish hair considerably shorter than the rest of his brown mop, which was parted high up on one side and combed carefully. He was ruddy and wore a full 'Sir Garnet' moustache also sporting a considerable amount of gray. All in all, he looked to be at least as old as, if not some years older than Henry, and thereby considerably older than Liesel, who now blushed and stammered her way through a formal sort of introduction.

His name was Redmont Wentworth Townsend Buller. He had been in the army (this time) since 1915 and in Africa since his eighteenth year, when he came out to serve on his father's staff in South Africa and stayed on after the close of the second war against the Boers, ultimately ending up with a farm near Taveta in BEA. As it turned out, he was actually a year younger than Henry, thirty-three. Rather than leaping into the war in 1914, he had waited until the arrival—well after Tanga, in the spring of '15,—of a unit that struck his fancy, spurring him to join along with several of his friends and neighbors—the 25th Battalion of Royal Fusiliers, known officially as the "Frontiersmen." He was quite surprised to hear Henry had heard of it and referred to it by its unofficial title, "The Old and Bold." Henry, in his turn, also noticed Major Buller was *not* surprised to find an American writer in German East.

They sauntered onto the Berghoff veranda where Henry managed to produce a bottle of passable *ersatz* champagne. As Major Buller prattled on about his battalion, Henry would occasionally, though sometimes only momentarily, bring him up short by dropping a tidbit of information seemingly impossible for him to know. Buller would stagger in his narrative and then manfully barge on while eyeing Henry oddly.

Finally, Buller could stand it no longer. "Old sod," he asked, "just how did you come by what it is you know? That one wouldn't think you'd know?"

"Well," Henry said slowly, thinking carefully through his words, "I'm not a spy, if that's what you mean. I'm a writer, and a neutral to boot. It means I hear things and I also know any number of interesting people. For example, I know Paul Von Lettow-Vorbeck and Max Looff, as well as Fred Selous and Pietr Pretorius. And I've seen your white hunter-aviator, *Karamoja* Bell, at work. And I know that your Colonel *Mein*hartzhagen knows I'm here and what I'm doing."

"And how do you know that?" Buller asked skeptically. "I don't think more than a dozen people know what Meinhartzhagen does."

"Because Pretorius told me when I met him in the Rufiji delta when he was marking the channel for the Royal Navy and I was on the *Königsberg*. I've talked to any number of assorted Allied and German types, including your not-so-friendly ally *Le Colonel* Molitor. Because it is what Paul Von Lettow and Governor Schnee want me to do…that is, report objectively. They are at odds, by the way. And the strangest part of it is I agree with them both, just as I have been led to believe your Governor in BEA also does—this war is a colossal waste of life and will be the ruination of two good colonies, and in the end, regardless of how gloriously or cravenly it is fought and decided, it will, in the greater picture of the war, not amount to a hill of dung—or as one of my favorite generals, Fred Grant, once called it, 'a pinch of owl shit'." Henry lifted his glass. "So here's to the survivors. May they be plentiful, but I don't hold much hope for it."

Major Buller clinked his glass against Henry's but said only "Here, here."

Henry looked to Liesel. "Let's go get your wedding present before someone steals it." He took Liesel's arm and, pushing Wenig's chair at the same time, led them back to the sidebar of the ballroom and the oblong package none too carefully wrapped in white paper.

Using her finger to tear the paper wrapping loose, Liesel was surprised to find Henry's Ruckerman gun case, replete with its multitude of scars and bruises and moldering leather straps. She unfastened the straps and then worked the little knob latch. When she lifted the top she found a clean, well-oiled, but often used Winchester Model 1895 rifle in 405 caliber. Nestled in the plush-lined compartments of the case were the cleaning materials—rod, worm, brushes and jag with several properly sized cleaning patches and a small bottle of oil. Held securely by elastic straps in the lid were one full and another partial box of Winchester cartridges. There was a small calling card stuck in place under the buttstock. Hand lettered, it said simply, "Have a good life. Happy hunting. Henry."

Liesel's eyes immediately filled with tears. She choked, finally managing to whisper, "Thank you." She put her arms around Henry and kissed him on the cheek, then lay her head on his shoulder. Henry held her gently and said offhandedly to her new husband, "I'll let her explain it to you. She's wanted that damned old gun for years."

What Henry had not told was the rest of his adventure in arms. At this point in the war, money had very little use in German East. Barter, however, and a thriving black-market trade in the Arab quarter could secure most anything anyone might want or need, provided the price was right. Essentially, the price of what Henry wanted, or needed, ended up costing two for one, because he also needed the services of someone with enough skill to do a bit of machining, or a bit of thieving. In the end, it really didn't make much difference.

Originally, his plan had been to trade his double twelve bore for the machine work needed to change Max Looff's Mannlicher rifle, which Looff had left with him when the war intervened following the cape buffalo fiasco. However, when Henry finally talked to one of the machinists at the Dar shipyard who was knowledgeable about guns, he discovered a simple reaming of the 8x56mm Mannlicher chamber to 7.92x57mm Mauser simply would not work. There were too many differences in the various dimensions and angles to do the job. It would require a complete rebarrelling, and there just were no barrel blanks available.

So that left Henry with the choice of carrying around yet another rifle with no ammunition supply available—or seeing if he could work a deal. A few shadowy phrases in a few shadowy alleys with faceless men in burnooses ultimately netted Henry a well used and often abused, Mauser *Gewehr* 98, with a stock repaired with wire-wrapping around the wrist and a barrel probably never cleaned. But it was chambered in 7.92x57mm, and it cost him only his double twelve and the Mannlicher.

He, of course, told no one of the 45 Schofield in his belt. No one. He considered it his insurance policy, just as his grandfather had.

When he got back to Morogoro, the rifle drew an odd look from Paul, who said nothing. Jabari took the rifle and returned with it cleaned and sporting a repaired stock of some local wood, dense as hell but serviceable, and a bandoleer of cartridges put up in 5-round brass charger clips. Henry carried the rifle, and Jabari pretended he had a *Bwana* gunbearer. It was all good fun. Henry guessed Paul considered if Henry got himself killed, the *Schutztruppe* would have gained one more modern rifle to use.

It was during one of the many fireside discussions with Paul after his return from Dar, that Henry learned more about Liesel's new husband. He had been found after one of the multitude of attacks made upon the *Schitztruppen* on the way to Handeni. He had been shot through the throat and arm by an Askari's 11mm 1871. Abandoned by his compatriots when they scampered off into the thorn scrub, he had nearly bled out when Doctor Taute found him and had him carried back into the German lines. Two other captive officers—as Paul recalled, one from the Indian Army and the other from the KAR—identified him, and it became immediately apparent he was what Paul called a VIP prisoner. In other words, someone worth trying to save because he was one of the sons of General Sir Redvers Henry Buller, VC, GCB, GCMG[6], the one-time General Commanding of the British Army and commander of the British Forces in South Africa during the first part of the Second Boer War.

Sir Henry had not been a lucky general. He had won the Victoria Cross while a Leftenant Colonel of the 60th Rifles, the King's Royal Rifle Corps, during the Anglo-Zulu War in 1879. He had fought in China, South Africa, the Sudan, and Egypt. He had married well, taking as his wife Aubrey, the daughter of the 4th Marquess of Townshend. He had been on the Gordon Relief Expedition and on an investigating commission in Ireland before being named the Quartermaster General of the Army and then to Adjutant General of the Army in 1891 as a Lieutenant General.

He and his son were sent to take over the Natal Forces in 1899, and he was defeated by the Boers almost immediately at Colenso, where he earned the nickname "Reverse Buller" and was replaced by Lord Roberts, though he remained as second in command long enough to be defeated again at Ladysmith and Spion Kop. He returned to England to take command at Aldershot—without his son, who stayed in Africa. There, he ran afoul of the Broderick government and was summarily dismissed on half-pay in 1901. His request for a court martial was refused, as was his request to appeal to the King. He refused a seat in Parliament under the Balfour government in 1905 and died in retirement in 1908.

Wahle had known him, and Paul had met him on one of the jaunts to England with the Kaiser. And because Sir Henry Buller always remained a popular figure in England, mostly because of his shabby handling by the likes of PM Broderick and the unpopular Roberts, it was only common-sensical to give his son the best treatment possible for whatever might be made of it down the road. So his marriage to the widow of a brave German officer, the Adjutant to the German officer commanding, was not considered as anything other than a boon to the Kaiser's war effort, such as it could be under the circumstances. Henry got somewhat drunk after the discussion.

CHAPTER THIRTY-SEVEN

Friday, October 6, 1916
Near the Rovuma River
German East Africa

*S*lim Janie's offensive began in earnest after the end of the Early Rains. Though it was never as coordinated as it might appear to later students of the campaign, it was finally enough to force the disparate portions of the Schutztruppen *back upon, first, the line of the Central Railroad, and then more slowly to the southeast in the general direction of Lindi and Kilwa. This part of the campaign traversed the region already wasted from the Maji-Maji troubles ten years before. But Paul had to accept it because there was nowhere else to go.*

The roughly one-third of the German forces that had been annoying the Allies in the northeastern portion of the Colony under Major Kraut fell back and joined Paul's main body at Morogoro. A massive section of the Central Railroad was then destroyed.

Meanwhile General Wahle's one-third retreated slowly from the Tabora region south of the railroad. Somewhere to the southeast of Morogoro, *Herr Gott* willing, Paul and Wahle would meet and combine forces and the *Schutztruppen* would be, mostly, together for the first time since Tanga.

They—meaning the *Schutztruppen* with Henry tagging along—had marched south for the better part of a month. They had almost reached Lindi when they found out the British had already landed there, and so the march was diverted to the west toward the Rovumu River and Portuguese East Africa border. If it disheartened Paul, he tried mightily not to show it. It was, after all, part of the game-plan he had talked about to anyone he felt had the need to know, repeatedly: to make the British expend far more of their forces than they could afford, and in a theater not worth the effort, thereby perhaps making a difference on the Western Front in France.

They were nearly to Nangomba where they thought they might be able to resupply. The column, as was usual, marched at a route step, singing their marching songs. The officers rendering the German army classics like *Annemarie*, **Mein Kamerad, schlaf wohl im kühlen Grab!**, *Rote Husaren, Erika, Die Soldat*—one of Henry's favorites—*Der Trommelbube, Es Leiben die soldaten*, and *Ich hatt' einen Kameraden*. More often than not, the colonists that had come from the *Schutze Kompainien* would sing the *Kaiserjägerlied* and always, of course, there was *Die Wacht am Rhein*. The more miles they marched, the more of these songs Henry recognized, but always in the back of his head was the one he heard most often, the marching song adopted by the *Askaris* and the only one he knew in both German and Swahili: *Haya Safari*.

Paul had an explanation, of course. Regardless of how seemingly silly it was to sing while marching through what was essentially an arid, parched landscape, with clouds of dust rising from the boots of the soldiers and the bare feet of the *ruga-ruga* as they slogged along across the bundu, Paul explained it was all part of a very old but very rich tradition. Singing was considered calisthenics for the lungs. The singing of marching songs as a training method had been employed in the German army since at least the time of Frederick the Great—who, according to Paul, had written some of the army's favorite tunes like *Die Alte Desauer* and *Ansbach Dragoner*. Every lad who had come through a *kaserne*—a local training barracks—knew the cadences and words of the great German songs, most of them military songs, but some—like the hunting songs and the drinking songs—were just simply good tunes to march to. As well as drink to.

Besides, it passed the time. And it gave the soldiers something to do rather than think about what a miserable position they were in. Or how far they had to go.

Henry knew their world was contracting around them, square miles at a time, as they abandoned vast tracts to the Allies. What he lacked was a mental map of just how much they were giving up. He simply had not seen enough of German East to have an overall idea. And as they retreated to the south and east, he was still vaguely aware that off to the west *Generalmajor* Wahle was fighting what amounted to a splendid rear-guard campaign to hold the Rhodesians and Belgians off their flank, so there was still a large part of the Colony in dispute off to the west.

The spirits of the *Askaris* remained amazingly high. Paul did everything he could to keep them healthy and as well-fed as possible. Their high spirits often came from the fact their counterparts in the Allied army were in such low spirits as to be easily dealt with. With the exception of the KAR and the Gurkas, the Allied soldiery was held in scorn by even the *ruga-rugas* and the family members who marched with the column.

As they marched toward the Rovuma River, Henry marched along beside *Obersti* Paul. The longer he marched, the weaker he felt. Cold sweat began beading on his forehead. At one point Paul looked over at him and said, "Heinrich, you look like shit." That was just before Henry's eyes rolled back in their sockets and he did a very good imitation of a potato sack as he collapsed to the ground.

In the seventeen days that followed, Henry was conscious on only a few occasions. During those times, he vaguely remembered snatches of conversations going on about him but he was too weak to participate in: Zanta and Jabari discussing his chances of survival… Zanta covering him with blankets as he shuddered with chills… Zanta holding his head up as she forced him to drink some sort of evil-tasting potion… Zanta under the blankets with him on one side and Jabari on the other to drive the chills from him… Zanta. Always Zanta.

They told him later he awoke on the eighteenth day. His first desire was to eat.

Zanta was there, sitting by his pallet and watching him.

CHAPTER THIRTY-EIGHT

Wednesday, November 1, 1916
North of the Rovuma River
German East Africa

Though Henry had come back to consciousness, he was still far too weak to move about on his own, and the fact of the matter was, he was unsure whether Zanta and Jabari could manage to keep up with the column with him as a burden. Not to mention that Jabari was, first, a soldier and if his duties called, he would be forced to abandon Henry, leaving Zanta to carry on as best she could—which would be impossible, even if she had the help of the ruga-rugas. As Henry lay on his pallet waiting to hear what his fate would be, he said to himself, *If these were Sioux or Arikara or Crow, any of the Plains Indian tribes, they'd build a damn travois and move the whole shootin'-match. This thought was followed immediately by a desire to kick himself right squarely in the ass, as he yelled for Jabari to come to him.*

"Go cut two poles about five meters long," he told the *Ombascha*. When Jabari began to question, Henry told him to just go and do it, he would explain as Jabari, Zanta, and the two *ruga-rugas* worked. It took longer to find and chop suitable wood than Henry thought possible. Then again, they were in an area of the bundu, where tall, straight trees simply didn't grow plentifully. But once wood was found and cut, and once the multitude of thorns were whacked off with a bayonet, Henry had the poles lashed loosely together and then a blanket folded over them forming a sort of hospital stretcher at one end. He then ordered them to tear one blanket in two and padded the long ends of the poles by wrapping them with the cloth. That done, Henry lay down on the blanket and told the *ruga-rugas* to place their usual loads on the blanket at his feet and to lift the padded ends of the poles onto their shoulders. They looked at him strangely but obeyed. When they had Henry and the rest of the load hefted into place, Henry called out *"Vorwärts Marsch."* Immediately, the *ruga-rugas* began to move forward at their usual marching pace, dragging Henry and their usual loads along behind them, with Zanta walking alongside and carrying her usual bundle of domestic goods all stuffed into her cooking pot, all perched on a cloth pad on her head.

Henry looked up at her, striding along next to him. "Why don't you put that bundle on here with the rest?" he said.

"It would be too heavy for the men to pull."

"Bullshit. Their loads are about thirty kilos each, plus me—that's probably about another seventy. That's a hundred and thirty kilos they're sharing, but old Mother Earth is helping carry half of it. I've seen Indian women move a whole damn village like this all by themselves."

"Indian women do not do that here."

"Red Indian, American Indian, not brown Indian, Indian Indian. And not here—back home. They used to move the villages from one end of the reservations to the other for hunting, least ways if the government agents would let them—and sometimes even if they wouldn't."

"Why would they have to ask the government for permission? Were they not warriors?" Zanta asked as she strode along. When she received no answer, she looked down to find Henry asleep. *He is still very weak*, she thought.

When *Obersti* Paul first saw the travois with Henry aboard, he didn't know what to think. He had never seen anything like it. Still, it allowed the *ruga-rugas* to haul far more than by packing boxes on their heads. Within days, nearly half of the *ruga-rugas* were using the strange American Indian device. Even better, the travois left tracks that might confuse the enemy following the column into thinking they had carts. In any case, it was worth the effort because it allowed the column to carry along all of its ammunition, both for the small arms and the artillery, and all of the medical supplies, and a goodly portion of the niceties, the luxuries he allowed on the march—coffee, soap, alcohol, cooking spices, and condiments—all those little things made the march more than a simple flight of escape.

Still, even with the improved logistic capacity made possible courtesy of the Dakota Sioux, Paul found he had to order strict adherence to a few rules of engagement. Machinegunners were held to bursts of no more than three rounds—no hauling back on the trigger and firing an entire belt of cartridges. *Doktor* Taute was forced to issue strict orders all bandaging was to be retrieved, washed, and disinfected. Every day each company conducted an ammunition count, and woe be to the Askari who could not produce the exact number of cartridges he had been issued.

On the positive side, more of the sick and wounded could be moved with the column instead of being abandoned to fare for themselves in the bundu. The vast majority of these returned to duty, so the effective strength of the column remained reasonably constant. And essentially, the long march into the southern end of the Colony served as a period of intensive training in independence for *Schutztruppen*. By the time they reached the line of the river just south of Mahiwa—Henry never did catch the name—and climbed to a relatively secure position atop the northern edge of the Makonde Plateau, a table land running south nearly to the Rovuma River on the border with Portuguese East, the *Schutztruppe* was a well-organized smooth-operating force in being. They were cautious of the Allied forces behind them, mostly British Commonwealth, but they were downright disdaining of the Portuguese rabble in their front. They came to a halt on the plateau and camped, waiting for the western column to be heard from. The last they heard, *Generalmajor* Wahle was bringing his troops to join them, coming across the mountains somewhere between Lupembe and Mahenge, provided they could reach the Kilombero River and then get across. If not, they would either be surrounded and trapped, or wiped out. In any case, they had done a masterful job of occupying the attention of Slim Janie for several months across several hundred kilometers of bundu. Paul would give *Generalmajor* Wahle until the middle part of December to bring his column in. If they hadn't arrived by then, the *Obersti* would have to go on without them.

CHAPTER THIRTY-NINE

Saturday, December 9, 1916
On the Makonde Plateau
German East Africa

*A*fter three more weeks being hauled around on the bed of the travois, *Henry was finally able to stay conscious for most of the daylight hours. In other words, he no longer nodded off between syllables. His temperature was still running slightly above normal but not as elevated as it had been at its worst during his time on the Königsberg. Zanta roamed about the camp looking for specific trees and bushes. She stripped the bark and roots from these and boiled the gathering into a vile-tasting concoction she forced Henry to drink twice, sometimes three times a day. Surprisingly, he recovered. By the middle of December he was able to walk around the camp without assistance, provided he rested often, usually in Paul's headquarters tent. What he found the most irritating about being sick was his loss of desire for tobacco, in any form, and a very diminished desire for alcohol.*

He was sitting at the door flap of Jabari's tent on the afternoon of the fourth day of what he had begun to call his "ambulatory period," as opposed to his earlier "comatose period," when Zanta walked up to him and tossed him a bar of the yellowish soup used by the *Schutztruppe*.

"You are going to take a bath. You smell very bad. You have not bathed since you have been sick. Come with me."

She led him to the edge of a small stream that furnished water to the camp. Doctor Taute had marked off sections of the stream for laundry, bathing, watering of the few animals still alive with the column, and drinking water. All of the sections ran downhill with the natural flow of the stream, drinking water being the highest and nearest the camp, laundry and bathing the lowest and farthest from the camp.

When Zanta and Henry arrived at the edge of the stream, Jabari was already seated on a rock and holding his M71 Mauser rifle on his lap. He waved to them and shouted, "No crocodiles!"

Zanta waded into the stream carrying her universal utensil-water jug-cooking pot. She turned slowly in the current. "Take off your clothes and get into the water," she commanded.

"What?"

"Take off your clothing and get into the water," she repeated. "You smell very, very bad and I am going to scrub you down."

"It's not proper."

"What is not 'proper' about it?"

"My being naked in front of you."

"That is ridiculous. Who do you think wiped the shit off of you when you were sick? Who do you think held the gourd for you—and held your organ, too—so you could urinate? Who do you think wiped off the vomit? Who do you think put your pistol in your kit bag so it would not be found? Take off your clothes and get in the water. Now!"

Henry dropped his pants, pulled his shirt over his head, and got into the water. He had given up wearing underwear a long time before on the pungent advice of *Herr* Cosner, who had warned him wearing a clothing layer under his outer garments was a fine way to trap moisture against his skin—though Cosner had put it rather more inelegantly: "You'll rot your balls off." Now he kept his back toward Zanta. He felt her hands on his back, slippery with the strong-smelling soap she used to scrub him. She had no cloth or sponge, only her hands, but she was very thorough. There was nowhere on his hide she did not scrub. When he would not turn for her, she simply reached around and began to lather his front. He tried to move away into the deeper part of the stream to hide himself under the water, but at its deepest the water came only to his hips.

"Turn around," Zanta commanded again.

"I think we would both be embarrassed if I did..."

"Turn around—now!"

Henry turned slowly, keeping his eyes lowered. He was blushing, his face hot and red in embarrassment. Just above the surface of the water, his manhood stood at rigid attention, made worse by the realization Zanta had shed her clothing while his back was turned. She stood in the stream with the water coming just to the level of her pubic "y." Her skin was shiny wet. Her breasts were round and firm and larger than he had thought they would be. The cool water and light breeze had caused her nipples to stand as erect as his John Thomas—*where the hell did that come from... ah...Emma Fontaine...that's what Emma had called it damn near twenty years ago.* If Zanta was embarrassed, she didn't show it. Nor did she acknowledge his condition. She simply scrubbed the soap between her hands and continued to lather his front. He prayed she would stop before reaching his middle, but she didn't. When she touched him, soaping his crotch, he just couldn't contain himself and with a deep throated groan, he released years of pent-up pressure, his organ twitching and spasming over and over into the stream. He thought he was about to die of embarrassment, but when he finally forced himself to look at her, she was standing with the soap in her outstretched hand.

"Now you lather me," she said as she handed the bar to him, adding quietly, "*Zawadi ni zawadi*—a gift is a gift."

Bathing Zanta went considerably better than he thought it might until it came to soaping her front. At the first touch of his hand to her breast his erection returned full force, and he once again blushed deep crimson. Again she seemed not to notice. She took the soap from him and ordered him to douse his head into the water, then she lathered his wet hair with the soap. The result was a small island of grayish-brown scum floating down the surface of the stream. She repeated the process until his hair was clean. Then he did the same for her, nearly losing control again when her midsection rubbed against him as she bent over and soaked her own hair. The touch of her skin caused him to give off a little yelp, almost as though he had been burned.

He was still sporting an erection as they climbed onto the bank and began to dress. Zanta gathered up her kanga, a piece of vivid blue-green cotton, and quickly wrapped it around herself, pulling it taut and then tucking the top loose corner over the opposite end, just above her right breast. She picked up another piece of the same size and, folding it deftly, wrapped it around her still wet hair to form a cross between a turban and a head scarf. Henry, meanwhile, had pulled his shirt back over his head and had fastened one of the buttons before grabbing his trousers and hopping into the legs. His erection made it difficult to button the fly, and when he finally managed to tuck himself in and complete his dressing, he found Zanta looking at him.

"If that is going to happen every time we bathe," she said, "we will have to do something about it."

By the time Henry had pulled on his stockings and boots, she was gone. Jabari, who had been sitting on his rock all the while, said nothing at all.

"Let's go see the *Obersti*" Henry said to him. "I have an idea I want to run by him."

CHAPTER FORTY

Tuesday, December 12, 1916
On the Makonde Plateau
German East Africa

Ombascha *Rajabu and Henry waited until Paul had finished his daily foot treatment and heard the reports of his quartermaster and commissary officers before entering the headquarters tent.*

"*Mein Obersti,*" Jabari said, saluting, "*Herr* Feller has an idea he would like you to hear."

Paul pulled on his stockings and rolled the tops of them down his skinny shins before looking up to Henry. "Well?" He pulled on his ankle-high shoes—he was the only German officer Henry had ever met who did not wear the usual high-top German army boots—and pulled the laces tight before tying them. "Let me hear this idea of yours. And by the way, you look and smell much better."

"I've been wondering if they taught you much of American history as it related to Germany in your *Kadettschul* or your War College or whatever?" Henry began.

"Other than things like Moltke's little line that the Battle of Gravelot was won at Fort Donelson—wherever the hell that is—I can't say it was the most emphasized subject, no. What does this have to do with anything?"

"Bear with me," Henry said, raising a finger to beg for indulgence. "Have you ever heard of Baron Von Steuben?"

"Something to do with your Revolutionary War, I believe?"

"Yes. Actually, the Baron was a *Ombascha* in *Gross Fritz's* army and was given a title and a promotion by Ben Franklin in Paris before he was shipped to America to General Washington as a 'Baron' and a 'General' to boot. He became Washington's training officer.

"Heinrich, I reiterate, what the hell does this have to do with anything?"

235

"Paul... *Obersti*... what is the biggest problem you have at the moment, logistically speaking?"

Von Lettow-Vorbeck thought for only a moment before saying, "Ammunition. We can get *ersatz* for damn near everything else, but once we are out of cartridges, it will be over... unless we can capture enough arms and ammunition to re-equip. That should be pretty obvious."

"So anything you could do to cut down on the superfluous use of ammunition would be a help, right?"

"What are you going to do, Heinrich? Show me how to make cartridges from buffalo dung and tree bark?"

"No, I would like to show you how to apply all of those interesting little facts I learned in Common school. America only has a little over a hundred years of history to study, so it can get to be pretty detailed, almost mythological when it comes to the more important figures—like the good Baron, the drill-master of Washington's army. And to show all the rest how to *not* use so damn much ammunition every time you see a bloody enemy sneaking through the bundu. In other words, I'm offering to become the *Schutztruppen's* Baron Von Steuben. I have this screwy notion I owe it to you. And I won't even mention the bigger, philosophical stuff. Call it a debt of honor, if you've got to put a reason on it."

"Other than the obvious fact you are a 'neutral,' just how are you going to be the Von Steuben of the *Schutztruppen?*" Paul asked, though without rejecting the notion out of hand.

Again Henry held up a finger. "How many companies have you got here?"

"Ten."

"In that case I would need to borrow fifty men—the best shots—five from each of the companies, preferably NCOs. Plus one senior NCO, who could be given credit for the whole thing if it works."

"To what end?"

"Marksmanship training, a la Baron Von Steuben's methods. And to divert Colonel Meinhartzhagen's attention away from me."

Paul's head whipped around to give Henry a withering look. No comment, just a look.

"Christ, Paul, I've known about Meinhartzhagen for more than a year—since I was down on the Rufiji."

"The men have already received marksmanship training."

"No, the men have been handed five cartridges and shown how to load their rifles and to get them to go off. *That* is not marksmanship training. It is a way to make noise and smoke and entertain them for a little while. When they finally get into a fight, they blast away at the enemy and occasionally hit one who accidentally gets close enough, or is unlucky enough to get in the way, using up hundreds of cartridges to do it."

Henry continued immediately without giving Paul time to interrupt. "Now, imagine if they could be shown how to use their rifles and the sights on them to actually hit an enemy at ten times the distance, and with only one or two shots. It wouldn't cure your ammunition problem, but it sure would put off the inevitable, which, I was under the impression, was the strategic purpose of this campaign—to make the enemy pay a far greater price than the prize was worth and to use up far greater resources than he thought were necessary."

"So how would you do this thing?"

"I wouldn't. I am not allowed to take sides. I am a 'neutral,' remember. I could merely observe and criticize while a Senior NCO trained other NCOs in Von Steuben's system."

Paul motioned with his hand. "What pray tell *is* this Von Steuben system you are so enthralled with?"

"Simple. Five men from each company, fifty men organized into a training group or platoon, or whatever you want to call it. Show them how to use their rifles. How to use and adjust the sights. How to estimate range. How to control their breathing. How to hit a damned target. And then how to clean their rifles—not just the outside of it for inspection, but the working parts and the bore. Did I mention it would cost fifty cartridges per man?"

"No, you did not."

"Well, it would. Then once the fifty were trained, they would go back to their companies and show the rest. But in the mean time, you'd have to issue orders to their officers they were to do most of the initial shooting—until the rest of the men were shown what was expected of them."

Paul snorted. "And how long will this training—and the expenditure of 2,500 cartridges—take?"

"How long do we have?"

Paul scowled at Henry. "I have sent word to *Generalmajor* Wahle if he isn't here by the end of the month, we will have to move without him. In other words, roughly three to four weeks."

Henry looked at Paul. "Once it's organized, I can do it in two weeks. That will give the trained men the other two weeks to show the rest what has to be done."

"I think you are crazed."

"Hey, I'm an American. We can do anything. Besides, if I fail, what have you lost?"

"Two thousand, five hundred rounds of ammunition."

"Granted. But you'll use that much up in the next skirmish anyway."

"All right. Two weeks. No more." Paul turned to Jabari. "*Ombascha* Rajabu, see the men are gathered by tomorrow morning. I will send a senior NCO to make sure everything stays under control."

Jabari saluted. "*Jawohl, Mein Obersti.*"

Paul pointed to the tent flap. "Out. I have work to do."

Henry walked slowly back to *Ombascha* Rajabu's tent. He had already formulated in his mind how he would begin the instruction without seeming to be the instructor. Mostly it would depend on the Senior NCO Paul sent. Jabari was going to be busy for the next few hours, so Henry sat down on a packing crate outside the tent flap and began organizing the next two weeks into a practical schedule. He pondered, remembering how he had taken the ten farm boys on his team and started them from scratch, realizing this would probably be more difficult because the *Askaris* all in all knew less about shooting than his prairie hunters. So which would come first? He thought of the shooter's litany—sight picture, trigger control, breath control. Sounded good to him. As he sat and pondered, he felt more than heard another presence join him.

Zanta's voice said, "Would you like something to eat? I have a stew made."

"I thought we might wait for Jabari. The *Obersti* sent him off to make the rounds of the companies, so he'll be gone for a while."

"If you insist." Zanta moved around him and took a seat on the ground cloth she always had in front of the tent opening. "Would you like me to help you learn to speak the language of the people properly?" she asked.

"I thought I already had a fair grounding in it."

"You know many of the words, but you have not been taught the soul of the language, why the words are used as they are in different ways."

"Interesting—is that because of the dialects?"

"Somewhat. But also because it is a very old language. It was being used on all the shores of the Indian Ocean for more than a thousand years. According to the *Schwesteren* at the school, the first mention of it as a language is in what they called 'the Greek Source,' a surviving manuscript in the Alexandria library, written in the second century of Our Lord. Even then it was a commercial language, for trade here is equally old. From the east there came the Wahindi—the Indians—Maparisi—the Parsee—Magoa—Goans—Mabaharani—Iranians—and even Wachina--Chinese. These were joined in trade to the Wangazija—Comorians—Waarabu—Arabs—and Washihiri—Yemeni—and from the south the Watumbatu—Bantus. And it is alive in all of these places, because trade is alive still. And all of these groups have sub-dialects—Kiamu, Kimvita, Kiunguja and Unguja, Kitumbatu, Kibarawa, Kisetla... "

"How do you know all this and keep it straight in your head?"

"How do you know the difference between English-English and American English and Australian English?"

"I was raised using it. And I use the language to make a living. And I have met enough different people from those places I recognize the differences."

"And you do not think I can answer the same way? Because, according to at least some white Europeans and all the Arabs, I am an African and a woman to boot? And so I am incapable of knowing the subtleties of my native language? But that is why there is a Kisetla dialect, you know. It is the language as spoken by the white settlers. We laugh at it a great deal."

"What were you studying in the school?"

"I was studying to be a teacher of children."

"I think you will be a very good teacher... of anyone."

Henry popped awake, suddenly aware something had moved under the blanket covering him. His heart raced suddenly, and he tried to remember where he had left the Schofield. The inside of the tent was pitch black, meaning all of the fires had died down, meaning it was the middle of the night. Without moving, without changing the pattern of his breathing, he tried to hear a sound that shouldn't be there. Terrified he was sharing his sleeping mat with a snake or a rodent of some kind— in particular, a rat—Henry ever so slowly moved his hand under the blanket. What he touched was very warm and very smooth. But before he could shout, Zanta's hand pressed over his mouth as she whispered a shush in his ear.

"Jesus H. Christ, you scared the shit out of me," he whispered when she removed her hand.

"Oh, I am sorry. I thought you looked tired and should get some sleep before we started to take care of your problem."

"Jesus, I thought it was a snake or something," he whispered, still muzzy from sleep.

"No, it is not a snake. I do not know what you call it in your country, but it is definitely not a snake."

Henry turned on his side, facing her voice. He could feel the heat of her under the blanket. When he moved to pull the blanket over his shoulder, his hand found her side. She was apparently wearing nothing but her skin, which was very warm and very smooth to his touch. He began a cautious exploration, moving his hand slowly down her side to her hip and then down her thigh as far as he could reach. Then he began to move his hand in the opposite direction, back up over her hip to her waist and higher. She was equally smooth and equally warm there as well. Quite tentatively, he moved the tips of two fingers across the outside of her breast, hearing her take in a little gasp of air as his fingertips passed across the nipple, which grew firm under his touch.

Then he felt her fingers working at his waist and realized she was trying to unbutton his trousers. He spent the next seconds deciding whether to let her continue or to just get up and shuck his clothing before crawling back under the blanket. *But what if I wake Jabari?* he thought, and whispered as much to her ear in the dark.

"Do not worry," she said, "Jabari is not here. He is with his woman over in the 17th Company camp."

"I didn't even know he had a woman."

"Oh yes, of course he has a woman. Jabari s a warrior, a Wahehe, after all. It is his obligation to care for his Brother's woman and her children."

"Does that include climbing into bed with her?"

"I do not know what you mean. It is what a man and woman do. If he did not like her, he would not bed her, but it has little to do with the way a warrior lives or dies, other than it is the way he passes his seed to the next generation. They have been together since the beginning of the war. She was Omsha's woman before he was killed and Jabari took her as his own when he came to the *Schutztruppe*. She has one of Omsha's sons with her and a daughter by Jabari."

"And if Jabari dies? Like Omsha? What then becomes of his seed?"

"His children are raised by those who will best teach them their father was a warrior."

"And who would that be?"

"Why, the women and the surviving warriors, of course." Zanta had finally managed to unbutton his trousers and began to tug at the tails of his shirt, moving it up across his body to be pulled over his head. He sat up to oblige her, and she flipped the shirt toward the edge of the tent. Henry flopped over onto his back so she could maneuver his trousers down his hips and legs. Finally, she tugged off his socks.

"Wheww… How long has it been since you've washed these?"

He lay back down on the sleeping mat and pulled the blanket over them, shoulder high—it was after all December, mid-summer in these parts. She began to manipulate him and he ran his hands up and down her back from neck to buttocks, stopping only long enough between passes to knead her silky flesh.

She buried her head in the nape of his neck. "Have you ever killed another man?" She asked.

The question took him completely by surprise. "What? Are you trying to see if I am 'warrior' enough for you?"

"Jabari has said you have been in many wars and battles. But, I think it is possible to be in many battles and never come face to face with an enemy. Have you?"

"Yes, but I take no pride in any of them… except maybe one… "

"How many?"

"I've never put a count to it. Let's see…at least three Moros—those're Philippine Muslims—and unnumbered Chinamen, so I guess it's a number somewhere between four and fifty."

"And Simbas?"

"Yes. At least one, which is quite enough, thank you."

"And much other game?"

"Yeah. Deer. Antelope. Buffalo—American, not African. Too hard to count the rest, but probably 'several thousand' over a lifetime. Why is this so important?"

"Because you are truly a great hunter and a great warrior; your seed will live long with the people."

Before Henry could even think of an appropriate answer, Zanta had thrown her leg over him and, holding his manhood firmly, mounted him and pushed him into her in one deft motion. It was so smooth and so silken it took only the slightest movement of her hips and he began his orgasm that seemed to go on for an eternity, while she ground her pelvis against his. Finally, when she felt he was spent and gasping for breath, she rolled off without ejecting his organ and lay next to him, stroking his shoulders and back. He finally dozed off, still half erect inside her. Twice during the darkness before dawn he came awake still wrapped in Zanta and felt himself stir. Their second and third couplings were not as feverish or as quickly finished. He thought Wu Hu, his once upon a time sixteen-year-old, Chinese, sexuality instructor-cum-pillow dictionary, would approve. Zanta certainly did.

CHAPTER FORTY-ONE

Wednesday, December 13, 1916
On the Makonde Plateau
German East Africa

When the sun cracked gold, tinged with orange, above the eastern edge of the Makonde Plateau, Henry emerged from the tent feeling as fit and relaxed as he had in the last ten years. It was, in fact one of the first mornings he did not long for a drink or a chew. He buckled his borrowed belt with its attached bandoleers around his waist and slung his Gewehr 98 on his shoulder. After taking a last sip of his coffee, he left the tin cup sitting on the packing crate serving as a seat and table in front of Ombascha Rajabu's tent door, and looked up to see a cluster of fifty black faces staring at him in wonder. At roughly the center of the gaggle was an old Feldwebel, black leathery skin and bone, white fringing his ears where the hair had been allowed to grow out, a fringe that would probably be cut back to nothing before they marched again. Jayubara.

"Good morning, Feldwebel." Henry said. "Are these the picked men?"

"Yes, Bwana."

"Do you know of any place near the camp where we might fire without endangering the camp?"

"Yes, Bwana."

"Lead on."

Jayubara led the group out of the western end of the campsite and into the head of a slightly sloping, dead-end wadi—a shallow gulley or water course—ending in a sheer wall nearly sixty or seventy yards wide. Two men were sent to scrounge wooden poles, and two others to draw three hundred meters of rope—they were told to tell *Hauptman* Benedek, the quartermaster, the rope would be returned when they were finished. Then Henry pulled a pair of shorts and a shirt out of his kit bag and had the men gather tufts of the dry, brittle foliage passing itself off as grass. He stuffed the shirt full of the grass and fastened it to the top of the shorts with thorns. The affair made a passable man-sized dummy. By the time he was finished, the two details had returned with the poles and the rope.

Paul Von Lettow-Vorbeck finished writing his report of activities for Governor (the little *Wiesel*) Schnee. He wondered again just why he had to write such a piece of garbage every day when the *Gottverdammt Wiesel* was living in a tent—actually three tents—less than a half kilometer away, other than the *Wiesel* commanded it to prove on a daily basis Paul was subordinate to him. So every day Paul wrote a one-page synopsis of all of the things that had not happened in camp the last twenty-four hours and sent one of the *Askaris* to deliver it. This last was a special detail concocted by *Feldwebel* Jayubara and several of the other senior NCOs. Each day the most slovenly Askari found at inspection was packed off to the *Obersti's* tent to be his runner *du jour*. Because it was considered a left-handed honor, the men, and later whole companies, actually vied with one another to see who could have their chosen slovenly soldier selected for the duty. Jayubara said off-handedly the men enjoyed the joke because they didn't particularly like the Governor. Paul refused to ask any further questions about what all went in to "selecting" a candidate. Some things were better off not being known.

In the back of his mind, Paul had been wondering why there was a lack of gunfire coming from any part of the camp—though there were the very faint sounds of shots from well away across the plateau as the daily hunting parties gathered meat. If Heinrich was training the men to shoot, why was there no shooting? Paul knew Heinrich was at work because he had already fielded complaints from *Hauptman* Benedek and a couple of others before noon. It seems Heinrich had been issued a very good portion of the available rope, and apparently his men had requisitioned two tent poles and a load of laundry—khaki shirts, mostly—all of which had brought howls of protest to the *Obersti's* ear.

Paul pulled his field hat down on his forehead to shade his eyes from the midday sun. Unlike some of his officers, he always kept the side brim turned up and secured with a cockade. He refused to allow the brim to flop down—the favorite style for the *Askaris*—or turned sideways, and always gave those he caught doing so a pungent and short piece of his mind. He wandered out the western end of the camp until he saw activity down in a wadi, where a large number of men were gathered in no apparent order, standing around in a circle and watching something on the ground he could not see. He moved along one side of the wadi as it steepened, and when he was well above the group but still out of hearing, he sat in the partial shade of a large thorn bush and observed. Heinrich was seated on a bread box facing the same way as Paul, so could not see the *Obersti* above and behind him.

Feldwebel Jayubara had ten of the men lying on the ground in a row. The other forty stood behind them in a loose gaggle. Jayubara squatted beside the man at the end of the line and said something to him. The man brought his rifle, a *Gewehr* 98, to his shoulder in a classic prone position and lowered his cheek to the stock. Jayubara said something more to him, and he slowly squeezed the trigger. When the rifle made a metallic snap, the man cycled the bolt as though loading another cartridge and repeated the motions. He continued to repeat his actions at least ten more times before Jayubara moved to the next man, and then that *Askari* began as the first one had.

By the time Jayubara had reached the last man in the line and began to give him instructions, the first, who had continued to aim and snap his rifle throughout the exercise, had snapped off fifty aimed "shots" at what appeared to be a man-sized target Paul estimated to be over two hundred meters down range against the dead-end of the wadi. As the last man in the line began the snapping of his rifle, the first rose from his position and yielded his place to one of the waiting men standing around behind the line. When his fifty snaps were completed, each prone man did the same, while Jayubara endlessly moved from man to man and from one end of the line to the other until all had snapped their rifles fifty times. While waiting for the last man of the fifty to finish, Jayubara stepped to Heinrich's side, and they talked until the last man rose. Then everyone stood about, expectantly waiting to see what would happen next.

Jayubara pointed to one of the men who snapped to attention. The man was given a melon, the size of a man's head and, following some instructions, jogged down range to the man-sized target and secured the melon where the target's head would be if it were, in fact, a man. After the Askari had returned to the group, Jayubara beckoned to Heinrich, who unslung his rifle and dropped to the ground. Taking his own classic prone position, he loaded a stripper-clip of five cartridges into the magazine and closed the bolt. Looking at his sights to make certain they were set to the desired range, Heinrich went into slow motion, breaking the act of shooting into distinct steps while Jayubara lectured on what he was about. Finally, Henry dropped his cheek to the stock, and the rifle froze into position. Quite suddenly, the rifle barked, and the melon exploded. The fifty *Askaris* jabbered. They were impressed by the skill of the American, who wasn't about to tell them he had paced off two hundred paces to the dummy, a reasonably short range shot, and had decided to demonstrate by using the melon for its visual effect—and because he wasn't sure he'd dare ask Zanta to patch his shirt should he perforate the target.

Whatever Heinrich was attempting to demonstrate had apparently been satisfied with his single melon shot, for he unloaded the four remaining rounds out of the magazine by unhinging the floorplate. Then the entire procedure began again. By the time Paul rose and quietly left the edge of the wadi, the fifty *Askaris* were working through their two-hundredth snapping of their rifles.

As he moved to leave, the *Obersti* was seen by Jayubara, who walked up the side of the wadi and saluted. "They have done well on their first day, *Mein Obersti*. They did not think it possible to hit a man's head at two hundred meters, but *Bwana mbili pipa* showed them it could be done, and did it by doing just as he had had them do. They all now know about sight picture and how to set their sights for range. They will next learn how to clean the rifle so it will always shoot straight. This we will do every day, whether they fire or not. *Bwana mbili pipa* says after seven days it will be a custom, and after fourteen, a habit. Tomorrow we learn about the squeezing of a trigger like the squeezing of a soft woman's breast. *Bwana mbili pipa* has a very good way of teaching, I think."

On the eleventh day of the training, according to Baron von Steuben, *Obersti* Paul Von Lettow-Vorbeck was interrupted in the writing of his morning report by his orderly, who told him *Bwana* Feller wished to give him a demonstration of what had been accomplished so far. Paul followed *Ombascha* Rajabu toward the wadi to find the firing line now moved nearly another two hundred meters closer to the camp. He could just barely see the five man-sized dummy targets staked out at the other end of the wadi. Here at the open end of the wadi there was enough room for half of the students to fire at one time, and, indeed, *Feldwebel* Jayubara had divided them up into two relays, the first of whom were lying in prone positions along the firing line.

Heinrich sauntered over and asked Paul if he had remembered to bring a pair of binoculars along. When Paul admitted he hadn't, Jayubara handed him a pair of Leitz 7 power field glasses, much to Heinrich's apparent amusement. Without further discussion, Heinrich turned to Jayubara and instructed the *Feldwebel* to have the first relay load five cartridges.

"You will note, *Mein Obersti*," he said to Paul, "the men are all using their own rifles now. Not like on the first day, when they were all shown the principles using a '98. We are not going to fire for record here because there are not enough targets—and because I don't have anymore spare shirts." *And Zanta told me she would patch only two of these five.* "The range is four hundred paces. *Feldwebel*, please have the first relay stand."

Under Jayubara's orders, the men lying on the ground rose. "Five men to a target, beginning on the left... One round... Standing. You may commence firing whenever you are ready." Jayubara gave the order and within seconds five rifles fired, two sharp cracks from the *Gewehr* 98s and throatier booms accompanied by thick clouds of black-powder smoke from the 71s and 84s. Paul, watching through the binoculars, saw the center of the target dummy dance with the impact of five bullets. When he looked back at the line of shooters, they were all still in position. They had not begun to dance around in delight at having survived shooting their weapons. Each five-man group repeated the exercise. In the first relay of twenty-five shots, there were only three misses.

Then the line of shooters was told to kneel and the shooting began again. Kneeling, the shooters had only two misses. The same for sitting position. Then five men were sent down range to fix melons to the tops of the target dummies. Instead of returning to the firing line, they moved off to the side of the target line. Now each man in the relay had two chances to hit the melon from the prone position. Each time a shot exploded a melon, the men already down range would replace it. None of the first twenty-five shooters failed to hit the melon, fourteen of them hit it on the first shot.

The second relay fared slightly worse than the first. Paul wondered if that was because Jayubara had put the best shooters in the first relay to impress him. Yet the shooting was still outstanding: nine misses in the first three positions, and twelve first-shot hits from prone, with total destruction of the enemy melons accomplished. In other words, not one of the fifty students failed to hit every target most of the time. Compared to the way most of these men fired less than two weeks before, it was a remarkable achievement. It was made even more so when Heinrich explained they had only used twenty of their allotted fifty cartridges. Each man still had thirty rounds left. So Paul was taken off guard when Henry asked if they might finish the training with a field exercise—it was, after all, still three days until the end of the two weeks they were allowed.

"And what sort of field exercise might that be, Heinrich?" Paul asked, amused.

"A bull hunting trip—break them into ten five-man squads and let them go out and see if they can hunt up some bulls."

"What the hell kind of bulls?"

"Why *John Bulls*, to be sure." Henry chuckled at his reference to the favored American term for things British.

Jayubara and Henry stood before *Obersti* Paul Von Lettow-Vorbeck early in the afternoon of the fourteenth day of the training.

"Now, *Mein Obersti*," Henry began, "you will have to issue firm orders the graduates of Baron von Steuben's Marksmanship class are to be allowed to train the other men of their companies. And it will cost some ammunition and a few shirts and melons."

"I assume I will be happy to do so after hearing the *Feldwebel*'s report on the results of your little 'bull' hunt?"

"Yes, I think I can safely assume that." Henry said with a straight face.

"*Mein Obersti*," Jayubara began, "the fifty men were divided into five squads of ten, rather than the ten squads of five. This was done after we received reports of a large British probing force moving against our positions on the Plateau, evidently in an attempt to cut off the head of *Generalmajor* Wahle's column from rejoining us. We felt the larger squads would be more efficient and less likely to be ambushed, especially as they were to operate within supporting distance of each other."

Hearing no objections or comments, Jayubara continued. "The first day, we moved to positions overlooking the probable British line of march. The second day was spent engaging what appeared to be perhaps two battalions of the enemy. We know one was a South African battalion, and we think the other may have been Nigerians. In any case, they maintained enough cohesion to remove all of their dead and wounded from their positions so we could not gather insignia or papers to be more specific. We began engaging them at the extreme edge of visibility, which in most places in the scrub thorn, was between one and two hundred meters. The primary firing members of the squads were those men armed with *Gewehr* 98 rifles, with the men equipped with 71s and 84s acting as perimeter guards and fire support. In all each man expended between twenty and twenty-five rounds of 7.92 x 57mm cartridges, for a total of 350 rounds fired. In addition, once the British were retreating, we expended another 200 rounds of 11mm cartridges. That gives a total expenditure of 550 rounds of ammunition of all types. By the blood trails and confirmation of at least two observers for each shot, we estimate we inflicted between 250 and 350 casualties on the enemy. It may have been more, but I don't think so. The brush was too thick to get in good shooting. We had one man cut a finger on a ruptured cartridge case. We also met the head of *Generalmajor* Wahle's column and escorted them back here. The *Generalmajor* should be seeing you shortly. So far as we could tell, he has about four thousand men remaining."

Jayubara smiled broadly. "… and most of his machineguns and artillery, plus many captured pieces and ammunition."

CHAPTER FORTY-TWO

Sunday, December 24, 1916
Near the Makonde Plateau
German East Africa

*C*orporal Aaron-Nicholas Van Doorn lay panting under the rear tyre
of the Bulldog lorry and listened to the bullets smacking against the
metal side above his head. He was dripping a cold sweat from the end of his
nose, which he tried to press as far into the dust of the track as he could. He
had been running through the thorn scrub for a couple of hundred meters
twitching instinctively as the enemy bullets snapped viciously past his head,
expecting all the while to feel the impact of a round hitting him in the back.

After several minutes of heavy breathing, he rolled onto his back
behind the tyre and looked right and left to see how many men he had
remaining with him. There had been nearly a hundred in his company
when they had clamored down from the lorries less than an hour before.
Now he could recognize fewer than a dozen faces and forms. All the
rest were from the other companies of the 3d Pretoria Pals Mounted
Infantry Battalion, plus a few black faces of the *kaffirs* from whatever the
hell Nigerians had been on the other flank of the movement. He scoffed
to himself at the incongruity of the names. The 3d Pals, eight hundred
and sixteen of them, had been recruited in 1915 in the Pretoria area
and had lasted as mounted infantry until shortly after their arrival in
the East African theater. As they marched around the flank of Mount
Kilimanjaro, they passed through a tse-tse fly belt, and that ended the
"Mounted" part of the title. As far as Van Doorn knew, there were
two horses that survived in the battalion's kraal, and by his way of
thinking they should both be shipped back to Transvaal and put to stud
in repayment for valiant service. It was the least that could be done
for them, as it had been done for over three hundred of the original
human members of the battalion, who had discovered the wide variety
of diseases contractible by man in East Africa.

Corporal Van Doorn shouted to the men close enough to hear, asking if they knew what had become of the other officers. No bloody sense asking about Captain du Toit. The Captain had been standing behind Van Doorn when his head had exploded. Van Doorn still had a good-sized chunk of the Captain's brains clotting on the brim of his field hat.

Slowly the volume of fire coming from the enemy lessened and then, after a few sputtering shots, ceased. That meant the bloody Heinie *kaffirs* had either run out of targets or were bloody fooking gone again, just as they had for the last nine hundred fooking kilometers.

It had been another absolute cock up, right from the start. They had been sent out to ambush the head of a Heinie column coming in from the West. Simple job, the fooking Brigadier had said, just ride out, set up an ambush, and shoot the shit out of them. Either kill them all or force them to surrender. But in any case, keep them from joining old Von Lettow. Fookin' simple—except their ambush had been fookin' ambushed before they could set up.

They had deployed. Standard deployment procedure, two companies abreast in the front line and one back as a reserve, with the Niger wogs over on the right in the same formation. Then they headed into the velt—slow going because the thorn shit was so bloody thick. Half a kilometer or so into the bush, the first bullets found them. The Heinies had to have been using 98s 'cause you couldn't fooking see their smoke, like you could've if it was their *kaffirs* shooting the old 11mm's. It had to have been just the NCOs, or maybe they had one of their *Jäger* Companies in there. In any case, the shooting was terrifyingly accurate, and from farther away than Van Doorn and his pals could see. Within seconds the Captain, and the First Sergeant, and probably at least one of the Leftenants, were dead and gone. They had advanced maybe fifty more meters when the men on the flank realized they were taking deadly aimed fire from the left, and they broke, going to ground, or trying to. The bullets sought them out standing or lying down, so it didn't really matter much. So everybody got up and ran the hell away, all the way back to where the lorries had dumped them. There they found the lorries under fire, with most of the drivers hit, and three or four of the

Bulldogs with all the tyres shot out and radiators holed. But at least the big metal bastards offered protection from the bullets—until they began to take fire from the other side. That's when the Niger wogs broke and streamed back down the track. A whole battalion running all fooking clustered together, presented too good a target for the Heinies and the rifle fire lifted from the survivors under the lorries to the fleeing *kaffirs*. Now Van Doorn could see the puffs of powder smoke as the rest of the Heinies shot into the fleeing mass. But as soon as he took his SMLE III and fired at the smoke from behind the tyre, two Mauser rounds answered. One kicked dirt into his eyes from right fooking under his forend, and the other smacked into the metal wheel on the other side from his head. So he gave up on the idea of trying to return fire and watched as the track behind the line of lorries was rapidly covered with bloody bundles.

The survivors lay in the track for nearly two hours, until someone—possibly one of the surviving officers—thought to send out a patrol to see if the Heinies were still out there. It took the six-man detail nearly an hour to cautiously crawl to their forward positions, and another half hour to even more cautiously creep to where they thought most of the enemy fire had originated. There they found many firing positions, well concealed behind or beneath patches of scrub and small trees. All of them were scraped out of the hard soil, with the dirt mounded toward the direction of the track. The positions were meters apart but extended in a loose semi-circle large enough to contain four companies in line. In other words, it had been a pre-set ambush. No one thought to actually count the firing positions, because the volume of fire and the number of casualties indicated a body of Germans at least the same size as their force—two battalions—not the fifty positions nobody bothered to count. When the patrol returned to the track, the lorries capable of being moved had already been turned around, and everyone loaded aboard. The recovered bodies of the 3d Battalion rode in stacks in the last two lorries, which were among those being towed back to the Commonwealth lines. The Nigerian dead were left where they fell, to satisfy the jackals.

Two days later, Corporal Aaron-Nicholas Van Doorn was made First Sergeant—he being the senior surviving NCO of his company. He would be effectively in charge until an officer could be assigned to the command.

CHAPTER FORTY-THREE

Friday, March 2, 1917
Near the Rovuma River
German East Africa

Obersti *Paul Von Lettow-Vorbeck led his army off the Makonde Plateau shortly after the turn of the year. The delay allowed the tired troops marching in under* Generalmajor *Wahle some days rest to repair their boots and replenish their ammunition. Wahle's arrival had been a good-news/bad-news event on a couple of levels. It meant most of the North and West of the Colony were gone. But it also meant for the first time since the very beginning of the war Paul had the whole of what remained of the* Schutztruppen und Schutzen Truppen *all together and under his direct command, including those portions containing the* Königsberg Kompainie *and the remnants of Schönfeld's Delta Force, which had heretofore been farmed out to Max Looff for coastal defense.*

The British had landed at Lindi, which was really no surprise, but they were doing their usual plodding approach, and it would be no problem to stay ahead of them. If they had mounted elements on their side, Paul had another of the ubiquitous tse-tse fly belts between them, and the Brits would be reduced to walking in short order. No, they'd go west and south, in easy stages staying ahead of the Commonwealth forces until they reached the Portuguese East border. Then they would have to see what came next.

Generalmajor Wahle also brought in some other odd news. *Hauptman* Max Witgen, of Tabora fame the year before, had finally decided he could have more effect on the war by taking a force of two companies off on its own and raising hell behind British and Belgian lines. To give him credit, at least from everything filtering in about it, he was being true to his purpose. He was now several hundred miles away, operating well north of the former central railroad, bypassing main Commonwealth bases and, indeed, raising hell in the rear areas. There was even a rumor—unsubstantiated—he had reached Lake Victoria.

Paul quietly admitted to Henry even though he didn't like Witgen, he did wish him a long and fruitful march. Witgen was, after all, willfully or unwittingly, carrying out the spirit of Paul's campaign. He was forcing the Brits and Belgians to commit far more troops than they wished in a campaign that, in the end, was meaningless, and might thereby have an effect on the broader outcome of the war. Not much of a chance, but you had to play the hand you were dealt. Simple surrender would amount to allowing the enemy to send upwards of twenty thousand troops where they were needed more desperately than here.

So they marched every day just far enough to stay ahead of their pursuers—except for the occasional artillery shell fired after them in a fit of Allied pique. Jabari had pretty much taken to living with his steady lady, though, as Zanta explained, it was a custom for Brothers and sisters to remain close and to visit each other far more often than other members of the same family or clan. The Wahehe were a patriarchal people. Even though divorce was made easy, when a man and woman divorced, the children went with the father. And when a man married, he symbolically married all of his wife's relatives. When he married a woman who already had children, the children became his responsibility, and he inherited their relatives as well. That is why the clan structure, though loose and shifting, was very important.

Henry and Zanta took up housekeeping. Though he was at liberty to roam anywhere in the column, he never strayed too far from home. The truth was he had no need; his world had shrunk to a moving piece of territory the length and width of the column. Anywhere much beyond was *terra incognita*. He would roam out on the flanks and take enough game to keep his "family" fed, but in turn he would provide barterable services in trade for replacement cartridges. He was glad to see the sun begin to set for it meant he could go home to Zanta. He had never felt this way about a woman. She was at once a companion, a teacher, a guide, and a lover. His biggest worry was the war would end before he could make a decision about what the hell he was going to do when it did. It would be the biggest decision of his life and would determine what he did beyond the war.

She was Wahehe. This was her world. So would he try to persuade her to leave it? Or would he renounce his world to stay with her? If he persuaded her to leave, what would he take her into? How would anyone in Mitchell, South Dakota, react to an African woman, a black African woman married to a white man? Hell, who was he trying to kid? How would anyone in New York react? How could he or how would he tell her about Harlem? Jim Crow? Poll Taxes? Let alone lynchings. Yet could he leave her? Could he just walk away? Nice to have known you, good bye? He thought not.

After the daily meal and after all the chores of living in the column had been completed, they would snuggle on the sleeping mat and tell one another of things they found interesting, but most often they answered each other's questions about themselves—where they had come from and how they came to be who they were.

"My Uncle Fred has a ranch up in North Dakota right near an area called the Badlands, over on the border of Montana. The Lazy S Ranch—he called it that because his last name is Schilling and his wife, my Aunt Dorcas, always joked about him being such a lazy ass.

"Anyway, the state is divvied up into River West and River East. It's mostly grasslands, called prairie—pretty good, actually real good, farming country. They grow a lot of wheat there—miles and miles of wheat fields. It's something, watching the wind blow across the wheat, all green in early summer, then all golden yellow before harvest. It's like watching the wind blow over water, sort of eddies and ripples and waves.

"We lived well away from Iringa, which is the tribal home of the Wahehe, in a region often called the Mpwapwa after the main market town," Zanta said on another night. "But it is not a Wahehe town. It is very nice—many beautiful mountains and wide lush valleys. We lived high in the mountains, twice as high up as the other tribes. It is pleasant, with not so much rain, but enough. I once heard my father say there were one hundred and twenty clans of Wahehe living in the highlands.

Unfortunately, we were bordered on the north by the Ugogo, the region of the hongo squeezing Wagogo."

"What's a hongo?"

"It is a tax the Wagogo *mfalme* levied on food and water."

"How the hell could they tax food and water?"

"By having the *mfalme* claim to use magic to control fertility and rainmaking, and by dispensing 'medicine' to the ignorant and telling them it will protect them against natural disasters. These were the same ones who were given the power to decide on circumcision and circucision—female circumcision—and what all had to be included in initiation ceremonies. They also offered protection against supernatural undertakings and witchcraft accusations, and they were arbitrators in homicides and serious assaults. They had much power over the ignorant."

Another night—Henry's turn: "My Grandmother's house—my Mother's mother—was a big old place in a town called Yankton. It was about..." Henry stopped, thinking of how to translate distances... "a kilometer from the railroad depot where my Grandfather's office was. The house was big enough so each of the children had their own room, plus Grandpa and Grandma's room—on the second floor until after all the children were grown up and moved away, then they moved into one of the back rooms on the first—ground—floor. The place was always painted light yellow for as long as I can remember, but the trim color was changed whenever Grandma felt like it. The thing I remember most about it was this big old linden tree right by the steps of the front porch. It was damned near the biggest tree in Yankton. When I was a tadpole, we used to drag some of the porch furniture down onto the lawn in the summertime and sit out in the shade under that linden. Me and my cousins and some of the Welsh kids—my Dutch Uncle's kids. We'd play out there, and Grandma would always have cold lemonade for us. Sometimes she even had sodapop—sassparilla or cherry fizz. And there'd always be fried chicken and fixin's on Sundays."

Henry fell silent remembering.

And there was always the teaching of the language of the people for some part of the night. "In the language of the people you have fewer distinctions than in German or English. You must remember, Swahili developed over centuries to help primarily in trade, not in communication. It was to make trade easier.

"There are root words with prefixes telling the extent of the meaning you are trying to convey. 'Hehe' is a root. Add the prefix 'wa' and you have wahehe, the ethnic hehe people. Add the prefix 'ki' and you have kihehe, the language of the wahehe. Add the prefix 'u' and you have uhehe, the region or the land of the wahehe. And add the prefix 'm' and you have an individual hehe, a mhehe. As the *Schwesteren* taught us in the mission school, *Hehe ist der Wortstamm des Namens und kann durch die morphologischen Präfixe Wa (Ethnie), Ki (Sprache), U (Land) und M (der einzelne Angehörige) erweitert werden.*" Zanta chanted this by rote.

"I think I like your explanation better," Henry said as he rolled close to Zanta in the dark.

"And why is that? The *Schwesteren* were very good teachers."

"Yes, but it is easier to get into *your* habit than theirs."

Zanta thought a moment before she exhaled sharply and smacked him on the buttock. Then she kissed him. Then he returned her kiss, and then she felt his hand creeping up the inside of her thigh.

The Swahili lesson would have to wait.

"I think I am with child," Zanta said as she filled Henry's plate with a serving of antelope stew. In an instant Henry knew circumstances and situation had determined his decision. He nodded but said nothing. "I will know certainly in another month, I think," Zanta continued. "I have not had the bleeding for two months now, and if it does not come again, then I think it is certain. Anyway that is what *Daktari* Taute told me." Zanta stopped speaking and looked at Henry who was looking at her. "You are not pleased?"

"No, I'm very pleased. Just speechless," Henry finally managed to say.

"Oh. I thought you might be angry."

"Why would I be angry?"

"Well, because this is not a very good time or place to have a child."

"Tell that to the child. I don't recall giving it a choice."

"No we didn't, did we?"

Zanta remained quiet until the meal was finished. As she gathered up their few eating things and began to carry them from the tent— the washing was done communally by the women who gathered each evening around the large water boiler supervised by the medical staff— over her shoulder she said quietly, "I will not make you stay if you wish to leave."

When she returned from the evening washing she found Jabari and his woman and another Wahehe soldier—the one named Makenda— and his woman waiting in the now crowded tent. Zanta put the basket with the clean utensils on a ground cloth and stood looking at all of the rest of them.

Henry walked to her and took her hands in his. "Tell your Brother what you told me," he said.

"I told Heinrich I think I am with child," she said, barely audible, then blurted "I also told him he could leave if he wanted." She averted her eyes.

Henry did not let go of her hands. "You all will have to help me with this," Henry began. "Zanta has been trying to teach me some of the ways of Wahehe, and I think I understand about a tenth of it. Somewhere along the line though, I have heard it is the husband's responsibility or obligation or whatever to acknowledge he is the father of a woman's child. Am I right?"

"If you are married to the woman, it is not necessary unless there is a divorce," Makenda's woman said. "If the woman has been married before and has had children by another, then the new husband must recognize the children as his own or they will be sent to their mother's family."

"So marriage is the main difference?" Henry asked.

"In most cases."

"What's it take to get married in these parts, then?"

"Well, first there is the bridewealth."

"How much is that usually?"

"In our clan, speaking for myself, it depended on the age and the desirability of the woman—that is to say, how many warriors were interested in her as a bride. It could be as little as five and as many as twenty-five cows."

"How much is that in hard money? Reichsmarks, talers, whatever?"

Henry was answered with a stupefied look.

"The bridewealth is always paid in cows, Henry," Jabari said. "It has never been paid in any other way."

"Well, that's a problem, then. I have plenty of money—when I can get to it. But I'm kind of short on cows at the moment. In fact, I think even the *Obersti* is pretty short in the cow department at the moment. The question remains: what does it take to get married in these parts, when you're short on cows?"

"You could contact the family and take an oath to pay the bridewealth in the future," Jabari's woman spoke up.

"But your village is—what—five hundred miles to the north up in the mountains? So how do I give an oath to the family?"

Jabari looked at Henry oddly. "I am Zanta's Brother. I speak for the family. What is your oath?"

Henry exhaled deeply. He drew Zanta to his side and together they faced Jabari. "I acknowledge this child as mine for all to know. And further I swear when the war is over I will provide a home for Zanta, my wife, and our children. And further, I will build a *tembe* and on it have cows enough to give the family however many cows they determine at that time to be a worthy bridewealth." Henry looked directly into Jabari's eyes. "Is that sufficient?"

Jabari smiled. "It is acceptable. From this time, I accept you as Zanta's husband, and speak for all the family. This I have said before witnesses, as have you. I believe that is how it is done in these parts."

"That's it? We're married? That's all there is to it?"

"Not quite," Jabari said, smiling, "But it will have to do. I don't think you are going to talk the *Obersti*'s chaplain into marrying an African woman to a *Mmerikani* man. But other than that, as far as the people are concerned, yes, you are married. Oh yes, and you may kiss the bride. Then we can all have a sip of this." Jabari pulled a bottle of *ersatz schnapps* from his breadbag while Henry and Zanta did as they were told.

CHAPTER FORTY-FOUR

Wednesday, May 16, 1917
Headquarters, 3rd Pretoria Pals Battalion
German East Africa

*F*irst Sergeant Aaron-Nicholas Van Doorn got the word officially from *Major Van Deventer at noon on the same date the 3rd "Pretoria Pals" Battalion of Mounted Infantry was to be disbanded, and he, as a consequence, had all of the survivors' paperwork to complete so it could follow them—all one hundred and twelve of them—to whichever new commands they were sent.*

Thanks ever so much you bloody fooking arsehole, thought Van Doorn. *Well, at least the fooking moron won't be my fooking CO any more. And it could be worse—it could be the paper for everyone that started out.*

By three in the afternoon, he had them all lined up in front of his tent, and so he began to call out their names from the roster. As he called them forward, they signed the forms requiring their signatures, and then he handed them the rest of their records, shook their hands, and said goodbye. There were damned few he did not know, and a great many who would never answer a roll-call again, unless it was commanded by Saint Peter. Ultimately, he signed his own forms, stuffed them into his record folder, and without looking back, walked off toward brigade headquarters.

Of course the fooking Brigadier is nowhere to be found, but the Brigade Adjutant is sitting behind his field desk with another officer. "I suppose I'm to report to you, Sir," he said, handing the adjutant his folder.

The adjutant tossed Van Doorn's military history casually onto the top of a pile of other folders. "Righto," he said, allowing Van Doorn to stand at a semblance of attention. *Because I didn't bloody fooking 'pop-to and stomp' like I'm supposed to when reporting to a fooking officer.* Then, finally, the adjutant very casually motioned for Van Doorn to stand at ease. "You were in college when the 3rd was recruited, weren't you, First Sergeant?" he finally began.

"No, Sir. Trade school, Sir."

"Ah. Electrical whatever?"

"Actually, wireless and telephony, Sir."

"Ah. Well, that will work out nicely then…"

"Sir?"

"Your next assignment, First Sergeant," the adjutant said, gesturing to the other seated officer. "This is Leftenant Lambert, Royal Engineer Signal Service. He's to be your new commanding officer, if everything works out well."

The other officer, Leftenant Lambert, looked First Sergeant Van Doorn up, down, and sideways. He was older than the adjutant, his hair was thinning on the top, and he wore wire-bound spectacles. His uniform, what there was of it, was far less than perfect, far less perfect in fact than the much-patched shirt and shorts so casually worn by First Sergeant Van Doorn. He looked as though he was uncomfortable as an officer and would rather have been teaching somewhere musty and out of harm's way. Van Doorn knew the type; he had studied under many of them.

"First Sergeant, you say you were studying electricity, wireless, and telephony?"

"No, Sir. The adjutant said I was, Sir."

"Well, were you?"

"Yes, Sir."

"So I take it you know the difference between American Morse and Continental Morse?"

"Vaguely—I know they're different in aspects, as is American Naval Code, but I've never seriously studied the differences."

"But you know Continental Morse?"

"Yes, Sir."

"Can you tell me what you might have learned of the Fullerphone?"

"Sir?"

"The Fullerphone, First Sergeant. Have you ever heard of it?"

"Only theoretically, Sir. That is to say, I've never handled one. As I understand it, it's supposed to be a portable, battery-powered device, which can be operated at rather low amperage over quite a distance—

I've heard fifteen to twenty miles—and it can use the same wires as a regular, that is, a Bell patent telephone without interfering with the signal already on the wire, and vice-versa…Sir."

From that point, the adjutant lost interest because Leftenant Lambert and First Sergeant Van Doorn began to speak in tongues. In the end, Van Doorn was transferred to the RE Signal Detachment of the 6th South African Division and left with Leftenant Lambert to go have a look at a Fullerphone, whatever the bloody hell that might be. The adjutant gave very little thought to either of them beyond that point.

As they walked toward Leftenant Lambert's automobile—which appeared to be very nearly like the American Ford Model T, though it was covered with enough dirt identification was at best uncertain—they talked through the project Van Doorn quickly realized was to be his new point of interest. Leftenant Lambert explained Captain Fuller's telephone had been developed the year before for use on the Western Front. It had worked splendidly in the environment of the rat-warren of entrenchments, with one large drawback. The Germans had developed a system, or a machine of some sort, which could listen in on the electromagnetic signals given off by the Fullerphone, evidently without actually tapping into the wire. Unfortunately, they had never been able to capture one of the German devices, so just how the bloody Hun was doing it remained a mystery. Lambert thought it might have been more on the order of listening for the signal activating the buzzer—the Fullerphone used a buzzer to send Morse code when the distance or interference was too great for the Fullerphone to be voice activated, its usual method. Anyway, the buzzer had been added in the later Marks of the device and it was after they started going into use the Hun began to overhear them. That was Lambert's theory anyway.

"Well, Leftenant, I don't think that will present too great a problem here," Van Doorn answered. "I've never known the bastards to use a radio or even an electrical signaling device of any kind. They use mostly runners and couriers… from what I've seen."

"Right-o. That's why I was sent here from France. General Smuts thinks we might be able to come up with a way to use the Fullerphone here in much the same way it was originally intended to be used in France—that is, to spot artillery."

"Sir?" Van Doorn was vaguely aware every now and again there were supposed to be people out there communicating with the gunners, but he had practically no idea how they went about what it was they were supposed to do. He said as much.

"Well, we'll have to take care of that lack of knowledge then, won't we, First Sergeant?"

"Yes, Sir. I suppose, Sir." It didn't sound all that appealing to Van Doorn, who made a mental note to see about getting out of the bloody RESS just as quickly as he could. But he began to immediately change his mind when Leftenant Lambert began rambling on about one of the subjects Van Doorn considered his pet interest. The Leftenant's ramblings also confirmed Van Doorn's first impression the Leftenant was a bit of an effete egghead, but was, therefore, probably malleable. *Not like fooking Major Van Deventer.*

In any case, they could at least talk to one another knowing the other was well grounded in a subject of mutual affinity. It was while the Leftenant was explaining the problems he was having trying to set up some sort of a communication system for the artillery Van Doorn was suddenly aware of a solution the academic Leftenant had overlooked.

"Why don't you just earth the antenna?" he asked.

"Never thought of it."

"Well, it worked for Marconi," Van Doorn added somewhat caustically. He remembered it as one of two interesting points in an otherwise forgettable lecture. The other thing he remembered was the lecture contained a bit of information on his hero, Lee Deforest.

Right after he entered trade school at age eighteen in 1912, he had been browsing through the library and had come across some oldish copies of American journals. One was *The Western Electrician* and then an even older issue of *Electrical World and Engineer.* It was in these magazines Van Doorn first read about Lee DeForest and conceived himself to be a kindred spirit and not merely because they were both ladies' men. DeForest was working on his third marriage, while Van Doorn was yet to find his first, but no matter. He followed DeForest's life and career avidly, and was not at all surprised when DeForest had moved his operations to Hollywood, California, where he was beginning to work on adding sound to motion pictures for the burgeoning movie industry. Then the war had come along and Aaron-NicholasVan Doorn's dream of going to Hollywood to work with De Forest was sidetracked into the 3rd Pretoria Pals in a fit of beer-inspired patriotism.

The artillery pieces looked peculiar. Van Doorn couldn't quite put his finger on it, but they were obviously not regular field guns. When he asked one of the gunners about it, the man was quick to point out the fact they were naval guns slapped onto makeshift field carriages by the shipfitters in Zanzibar. *Why Zanzibar you ask, chum, because they were salvaged from the bleeding HMS Pegasus, the bleeding cruiser that had been caught in the harbor in '14 when her bleeding commander disobeyed his bleeding orders and shut down her bleeding boilers so that when the bleeding* Königsberg *arrived she got her bleeding ass shot to pieces and sunk. But they had salvaged her guns, 4-inchers, and here they were, complete with crews of bleeding survivors, in the middle of bleeding Africa, instead of in the real war with the Home Fleet."*

It was rather more than Van Doorn cared to know. His concern was more on the order of accuracy and distance. He had faced some of the *Königsberg* guns and knew from residual fear the 105s could outrange these 4-inchers by a considerable distance. It seemed to him his best ally in this little problem was going to be his skill in fieldcraft, all of the velt antelope hunting he had done in his often misspent youth. He let the officers try to figure out what they were going to do, while he took the gunners back to the R.E. lorry and cracked out several bottles of his private stache of Durban brew. The sailors were appreciative, and Van Doorn came away from the initial meeting with the feeling if it came to them listening to the officers or to him, he would be calling the shots, because he and the sailors shared the bond of having been shot at, and the officers had not.

First Sergeant Van Doorn lay at the base of some odd sort of tree shaped not unlike a candelabra. Leftenant Lambert lay to his right, directly behind the tree, *putting the fooking tree between him and the fooking Hun positions.* Van Doorn succeeded in keeping himself from scoffing derisively at the thought. Between them was the Fullerphone, a Mark III, in its wooden case. Van Doorn looked through his binoculars. He could make out movement a mile beyond them and at the base of the slope. He fiddled with the focus and then could see khaki and what appeared to be light-colored, fez-type headgear. From the amount of dust rising around them, the *kaffirs* were digging some sort of position, or a shit hole, not that it really mattered.

Van Doorn opened the cover of the Mark III and pulled out the hand set. He then seated one end of his jerry-rigged antenna wire into one of the sockets drilled into the side of the case and drove the other end into the ground. Pressing the hand set to his ear, he squeezed the toggle switch with his thumb.

"Can you hear me?"

Feldwebel Jayubara sat atop a large rock and casually watched the detail from the 12th *Kompainie* finish digging two mutually supporting machinegun positions. His rock was fifty or seventy-five meters in front of the positions so he could see them—or not—as an enemy soldier would. When they were satisfactorily difficult to see against the background, he called for the guns to be brought up from the carts and emplaced. The 12th *Kompainie* was manning this position as an outpost—it being almost ten kilometers from the main line—and as a reward for capturing the guns from the enemy in one of the innumerable nameless clashes punctuating the last weeks since they had moved south and west from the Plateau camps toward the Portuguese border. Jayubara had thought it odd the captured British Vickers guns were so like their own Spandaus, until *Bwana mbili pipa* had explained to him they were both invented by the same man, a Mmerikani named Hiram Maxim. Jayubara thought that odd as well but said nothing. The only real difference was the ammunition—the British bullets were slightly smaller than the Spandaus'.

The guns were nearly in place when Jayubara heard the artillery shell whistling toward them. He yelled for the *Askaris* to take cover—which meant lying on the ground or in the gun pits—as he threw himself close to the side of the rock and covered his head with his arms. The shell was large and very loud and it struck very close to the positions, raining down dust and chunks of things, and sending pieces of hot, sharp, metal singing through the air around them.

When the dust settled, Jayubara rose to see if anything was left. Both of the gun pits were still there, the guns and Askari occupants unscathed. Twenty meters behind the pits, however, two of the carrying party had not been so fortunate. One had been turned into a red smear on part of the crater wall where the shell had exploded. His companion was mostly still intact, except for the large channel gouged through him by a piece of the shell. He also was quite dead. Jayubara ordered the body carried back to the cart to be hauled back to camp. The *Obersti* would not be pleased, but he would understand. War was mostly a matter of good or bad luck.

"Lucky shot," Van Doorn muttered. He spoke into the handset again, giving new directions to the gunners five kilometers north of them. By the time the guns had been re-set and the adjustments made, many of the *Kaffirs* had moved away from the target area to their cart and moved off to the southwest. Van Doorn had been right about the luck. It took him the rest of the afternoon to correct the gunners back to where the first shot had landed. The whole process was going to need further study. He crawled back down his side of the ridge after pulling the antenna out of the dirt and replaced the handset. He slung his SMLE Mark III and allowed the Leftenant to carry the Fullerphone as they trudged back to the South African lines and the attached battery of the *Pegasus* guns that had become their new home.

They crawled to the base of a large termite mound, not the largest, but one of many dotting the top of a low sand ridge. The crawl took them nearly an hour, and Van Doorn had to shush the fooking Leftenant several times so his whining wouldn't give them away to anyone or anything within hearing. Van Doorn had his rifle, of course, but just like a fooking officer, the fooking Leftenant only had his Webley 'n'

Scott 455 revolver. He wouldn't be worth a fook if they spooked a lion or a rhino.

Once they were in position, it took another hour before they saw any sign of movement to their front. *At least this time the fooking Leftenant remembered to bring along his own fooking binoculars.* Van Doorn wiped a drop of salty sweat from his right eyebrow with his right forefinger and flicked it into the dirt, keeping his hand behind the mound while he did it.

"That's not a legitimate target," Leftenant Lambert said as he took the binoculars from his eyes.

"The fook it's not," Van Doorn said flatly, "it's a pack of Hun *Kaffirs* gathered around the well."

"We don't make war on women and children. Remember, we are the civilized ones, not the bloody Huns."

"The fook you say—they're fooking *Kaffirs*, for Chrissake."

Leftenant Lambert, belatedly recalling his original conversation with the Brigade Adjutant on the day of his first meeting with First Sergeant Van Doorn, remembered the adjutant saying: "Oh he's a good enough man"—*Damn, that should have been a warning*—"but he's a bit of a loose cannon, doesn't take discipline at all well—doesn't take any criticism well. Argumentative, tends to be dour, has a temper. Typical goddamned Afrikaner. Once he takes a notion, any attempt to get him to see reason, he takes as a personal challenge. But, as I said, other than that, he's a survivor, and he apparently knows a bit about wireless."

"Van Doorn, I don't think you heard me. I said those appear to be camp women, and I order you not to use them as targets. That's a direct order. You are not to fire on those people."

First Sergeant Van Doorn frowned. He put the Mark III handset down on top of the carrying box. *It'll do me no good to argue with a fooking officer.* Having made up his mind on the matter, he rolled over and unslung his SMLE Mark III. The safety was already off, so it was just a matter of swinging the muzzle around. First Sergeant Van Doorn shot Leftenant Lambert in the face. He'd have to think of some sort of story when he got back—an animal attack or some such, but he'd worry about that later. He leaned his rifle against the termite mound and retrieved the hand set.

"Can you hear me?" he said as he keyed the toggle-switch.

Zanta awoke earlier than Henry, her usual practice because she had more things to do in the morning than her man. She wrapped her kanga about her and tucked one corner to hold it in place, then hefting the earthenware water vessel onto her head-pad, she walked out of the tent where her Brother's woman, Kamaria—Like the Moon—was waiting with her own water vessel and the shoulder-pole so they could carry both comfortably and talk together. The column had passed a small *boma*—a farm protected by a surrounding thorn hedge—the evening before, which was only about a kilometer away, and one of the women had noticed the well-head. They headed there now, chatting of their latest adventures and about their men, and Zanta finally admitted to the rest of the 9th *Kompainie* women she was indeed pregnant, and yes, her man the Mmerikani had said he would acknowledge the child, which made them both very happy. When they got to the well-head with its single-handled pump, they had to wait in line to draw water. They were fourth and fifth in line when they heard a strange whistling sound coming toward them.

Henry awoke suddenly when he felt someone shaking his shoulder, and when he opened his eyes, he found Jabari leaning over him on the sleeping mat. "My Brother," Jabari said, "You had better come with me."

That's all. So few words to do so much to change the direction of a man's life.

He followed Jabari to a *boma* where a crowd of women were wailing. There were seven bundles of kangas strewn at random on the ground. One was wearing a kanga just like Zanta's. Jabari's woman was kneeling beside it, keening.

Even in death she was beautiful. Henry found himself rejoicing that the very small piece of shell that had killed her had not disfigured her. It had been quick, like the sudden snapping off of an electric switch. Her face bore no sign of pain or even of surprise.

Henry knelt down next to her and touched her face. Then knelt beside her and kissed her lips for the last time.

A little less than an hour later, as he approached the outpost line, he saw *Oberst* Lettow-Vorbeck sitting on a large rock. Paul motioned him over, Henry leaned against the boulder, and Paul slid down to stand next to him. He noticed Paul held his pistol in his hand.

"I can not let you do what you are planning to do, Heinrich," he said quietly but firmly.

"What are going to do, Paul? Shoot me to keep me safe?" Henry said.

"If I allow you to go stalking out there," Paul tossed his head in the direction of the bundu toward the British lines, "it would be a crime. It would mean I was sanctioning your act of vengeance. I don't and I can't."

"What if I go unarmed? What if you give me two men and I lead them to whoever is doing this. Would you 'sanction' that?" Henry gave Paul a hard look.

When Paul Von Lettow-Vorbeck stared back, he found himself looking over the edge of the abyss to discover there were demons down there, and it honestly terrified him. He had known Henry Feller, on and off—mostly off, he had to admit—for nearly twenty years, but the eyes he looked into now were like nothing he had ever experienced. This was an eyeball-to-eyeball look into the face of death. No pity, no compromise, no compassion. Whatever Heinrich wanted to stalk was dead, but just didn't know it yet.

"What do you mean by 'whoever is doing this'?"

"I think it should be pretty goddamn obvious. The Limeys have someone spotting for their artillery, calling in the shots. It started when they shelled the 12th *Kompainie* a couple of weeks ago, and then when they got in that barrage at the *tembe*, and now this one on the women at the well. It doesn't appear it makes a helluva lot of difference to them what the target is so long as it belongs to us. They're dogging us with those goddamned guns, and the only way they could be doing it is if they have an observer spotting targets for them. Because they know we can't answer. We have no means to make 'indirect fire' I believe it's called. So our only option is to get whoever's observing and calling in the shots. That means stalking the bastard."

Henry never raised his voice. He was cold reason and logic personified. "And don't give the 'I'm a neutral, you're a belligerent line' of bullshit. It got real personal for me a little while ago. The son of a bitch killed my family, God Damn him. And I *will* have his scalp on my lodgepole before I'm done. No matter what you think you can do about it. Now, you tell me—what can you reasonably do for me?"

Paul thought for a moment before speaking. It made sense, even if Heinrich was looking for some sort of excuse to play out his reasons for personal revenge. "Heinrich, before I give you an answer, any answer, I want you to go back to your tent and get roaring drunk. Then I want you to stay that way for at least three days. Then, after you have done this thing for me, we will talk again, and I will decide. Paul handed Henry a liter bottle of *ersatz schnapps.*

For the next three days Paul continued to receive reports from *Ombascha* Rajabu on Henry's state of inebriation. Heinrich had indeed followed his advice and had literally destroyed his tent before becoming gut-wrenchingly sick. And that had been on the first day, followed by two more of the same. On the next day he had simply stopped drinking and had spent most of the morning thoroughly cleaning his Mauser. He and Jabari appeared before the *Obersti* a little after noon.

CHAPTER FORTY-FIVE

Friday, April 6, 1917
Near the Rovuma River
German East Africa

"How do you plan to do this thing?" *Paul asked.*

Henry sat opposite Paul. "First, I'll need a good map, if you have one... or someone who knows the territory. Then I'd like to 'borrow' Jayubara and Makenda—he's an NCO from the 23ʳᵈ *Kompainie.*"

Paul had a slight grin. "It sounds like old home week—your former bearer on a couple of hunts and one of the witnesses at your wedding. I'm surprised you didn't ask for Jabari as well, since he has as much to avenge as you do."

Henry looked nonplussed.

"There is very little that goes on in this army that I do not know about '*Bwana mbili pipa,*' Paul said.

"I asked for them because they both have safari experience, which is stalking experience. Besides, if I took Jabari along, you'd have no one to act as your foil. You need him more than I do. To let you know that I'm being straight about it, I'll take only 5 rounds for my Mauser and I'll use them only if we wander into dangerous game of the four-legged variety, and I'll let you count the rounds before and after.

"When the column moves,' Henry went on, "we'll hang behind and try to intercept whoever is spotting for the artillery. We know roughly where he has to be, and we'll try to put ourselves in position to get a shot at him, or them. No promises on how long it will take because that depends on the situation and the terrain. Fair enough?"

Paul thought for a moment before nodding. "Fair enough."

Makenda, a short, stocky NCO, was not at all pleased when he was told not to wear his field fez with its shiny Imperial Eagle badge. But he seemed mollified when

Jayubara assured him that he had been chosen because the *Obersti* and *Bwana mbili pipa* knew him to be a very good shot and a worthy stalker.

Henry, Jayubara, and Makenda squatted around a large map. It was far less of a map than Henry had hoped for, but at least it showed the main roads, tracks, and water courses, even if it had only rudimentary references to elevations or vegetation. In addition, the *Obersti* had shown Henry the day's route of march. Using his fingers as a ruler, Henry traced an imaginary line along the route of march and about two kilometers on both sides. He expected that somewhere along the imaginary line the observer would find a position. In all there seemed to be six or seven possibilities, which meant they would have to move at least three times. Movement, by Henry's thinking, was inherently dangerous because if they were seen, the spotter could easily call the artillery in on them and the hunter would immediately become the hunted. So he chose one of the last sites an observer might set up for their initial position. If they heard artillery, it meant the spotter had set up earlier in the line of march, and they could then backtrack to an interception point—if they were lucky, and hurried—and catch the spotter as he moved to maintain observation on the column.

They left camp before dawn and walked until they had covered seven or eight kilometers before veering off the track to a point just below the place they thought a spotter would be. Then they waited, one man staying awake while one or both of the others dozed. The only frightening time was when a lioness took an antelope eighty yards away and began to drag it directly toward them. But she finally stopped and grunted for her cubs. They watched the young lions demolish the carcass without their being seen themselves. Perhaps the lions could not smell fear—or were just too well-fed to care.

Near noon, they heard artillery fire—four shells—muffled by the distance. Then nothing for nearly an hour. When the artillery fired again, the sound was still distant, but the detonations of the shells was much closer and the head of the marching column was in sight on the road two or three kilometers away. The shells were coming down beyond their range of vision, toward the back of the column, so the spotter had to be still back that way, but it was time to get ready. Even if they were successful, it would still be a ten-kilometer walk to camp and a meal. Henry sent Makenda over the little hump of ground and told him to find a position a hundred or so meters behind where they expected the spotter to come to. He left Jayubara in place, and crawled to the crest of the ridge to see if he could overlook the same place. They all thought the observer would use the ridge as cover for movement, so one of them should be in a position to get a shot. If he came. If he did what they thought he would do.

They lay in the dust the rest of the day, until long after the tail of the column had passed them on the road. There was no more artillery fire. The only activity in the hours before sunset was the meandering of a troop of baboons. Just before sunset, Henry realized the error in their planning. They had figured out only one-half of the variables of the equation and had forgotten the most important part: the artillery guns could fire only so far and then had to be moved and readjusted. If the column marched out of range of the guns, they couldn't shoot, no matter where the observer was. Henry would not make that mistake again.

The next dawn found them already in position. The terrain closed in on both sides of the road, the high ground to the south being well within shooting distance of the high ground to the north. The defile thus formed would be a logical place for artillery to catch the column with nowhere to take cover. They stayed just behind the crest of the southern ridge, using Henry's field glasses to scan the crest of the northern ridge three hundred and fifty meters away. With the glasses they could see nearly three miles of the road on both sides of the defile. A little after dawn the head of the column approached the defile and passed through. Henry had just about given up hope when he heard the first shells whistling in and watched the explosions bracket the road a kilometer east of their position. He moved the field glasses slowly, looking at the base of every bush and rock and termite mound along the northern crest, but could see nothing.

Van Doorn watched the first shells bracket the road and waited. He was going to allow the Hun *kaffirs* to think they were safe and get back into the road and nearer the narrows before he called in the next set of shells. That didn't take overly long since the Hun officers were reasonably quick getting their *kaffirs* up and moving. He brought up his glasses—the Late Leftenant Lambert's glasses—to see how far they had to go to the narrows where the road ran between two parallel ridges, the feature that had brought him here in the first place, when a glint of sunlight off something shiny caught his eye. The glint was perhaps a hundred and fifty meters off the road to the south and just at the crest of the southern parallel ridge. Van Doorn smiled to himself because he knew it had to be some Hun trying to spot him. He toggled the handset. "Can you hear me?"

Henry slipped back off the crest and shrugged. *The sonofabitch had to be out there. The salvo had bracketed the road. No amount of lucky shooting on God's green earth* … Then he heard the shells whistling in. But they sounded different, and instantly he realized why. He was up and moving even as he yelled RUN! leaping down the back side of the ridge in long, fear-driven, strides. On the fourth stride Makenda passed him, his eyes wide, white, and wild. The salvo straddled their position on the ridge with ear-splitting explosions. As Henry ran, he could hear fragments singing past and saw small branches clipped loose from the thorn bushes dotting his path. As the sound of the fourth explosion died away, he stopped running to hear if any more shells were coming. He stood, bent at the waist, his hands on his knees, as he gasped for air. Makenda stopped fifty meters beyond him and was walking back toward him when he pointed back up the ridge. Henry eyes followed Makenda's finger.

Jayubara was walking slowly down the ridge. His knees were wobbling and his right hand held tightly to the front of his uniform jacket, which was wet and red. As he came closer Henry could see he was holding the torn edges of the jacket front together. It was a moment before Henry realized that Jayubara was also holding himself together. A razor-sharp fragment of one of the shells had cut neatly across his abdomen. On both sides of his clenched fist portions of his intestines were trying to protrude along the slice.

"I think I am getting too old for this sort of thing, *Bwana*," he said between clenched teeth.

They had no choice. If Jayubara lay down, he would probably die. If he even stopped moving, he would probably die. If they left him to get help, hoping to catch the tail of the column, the hyenas and jackals would be on him instantly. No, the only choice was to walk to the column's night camp. Not counting the distance to the road, it meant a walk of ten, perhaps fifteen kilometers. Henry figured they had a one-in-five chance of getting Jayubara back alive. And if they could do that, then he had a further one-in-three chance of living.

As they reached the road with Makenda and Henry supporting Jayubara between them, Jayubara began to chant as he slowly hobbled along. At first Henry thought he was praying to whatever God or gods were in his particular pantheon, but the words stealing out from between his clenched teeth, slowly took a familiar form. Each step punctuated by a word:

Left, *tunakwenda*;
Right, *tunashinda*;
Left, *tunafuata*;
Right, *Bwana*;
Left, *Obersti*;
Right, *Askari*;
Left, *wanaendesha*;
Right, *Askari*;
Left, *wanaendesha*;
Right, *tunakwenda*;
Left, *tunashinda*;
Right, *heiya*;
Left, *heiya*;
Right, *safari*.

Endlessly, one foot before the other. Endlessly, holding in his guts. The song, always the song. Sometimes in German, but mostly in

Swahili, until the campfires came into view and Henry sent Makenda running ahead to get help.

"How did it happen?" Paul asked.

"The sonofabitch spotted us. I think he saw my field glasses," Henry said after he had taken a long pull from a bottle of *ersatz* schnapps. "It won't happen again."

"No, it won't. I'm not going to let you go out and get yourself killed to no purpose. At least on the march, we can accept the casualties, then. When and if we go into camp again, then I promise I'll think it over, but until then, you are not to go stalking. Is that clear?" Paul raised his eyebrows and waited until Henry answered.

"*Jawohl, Mein Oberst.*"

CHAPTER FORTY-SIX

Sunday, July 29, 1917
On the Rovuma River
German East Africa

Henry had begun regular attendance at the usual open-air Sunday services conducted by Reverend Hoernbacher, the Obersti's head Chaplain, or one of what Henry thought of as the "Acolytes" which sometimes included Werner Schönfeld. Mostly it was to kill time and try to make some sort of connection with something larger than the column of Askaris marching and singing its way across the nearly featureless bundu of the last few miles of German East Africa.

The head of the column had already come to and crossed the Rovuma River just west of its junction with the Lugenda, and it had scattered the Portuguese garrison stationed there to defend the border. The haul had been impressive—artillery, machineguns, rifles, explosives, and ammunition for all. In fact, they had stopped the march long enough to celebrate for a day after the rear guard *Kompainie* had sent in a runner saying the British pursuers were not moving.

So when Henry was called to Paul's tent after divine services, he figured it was to have a tot of *ersatz schnapps* or possibly some of the captured Portuguese port. He found *Generalmajor* Wahle and *Ombascha* Rajabu waiting, along with the *Obersti*. None of them looked particularly happy.

"Heinrich," *Generalmajor* Wahle started without preliminary greetings, "these were part of the load captured by the 14th *Kompainie* on the other side of the river the other day."

Wahle handed Henry a stack of newpapers. The papers were not in the best condition, given they had been captured in equatorial Africa. And most of them were printed in Portuguese. Other than for a few isolated words that seemed to cross-reference to his seldom-used store of Texican, Henry shrugged—indecipherable. But about half-way down in the stack were some papers that looked more promising, one in French, the Paris *Le Monde*, and two in English, one the *Times of London*. And EUREKA! The *New York Times*, a Sunday edition no less—well, at least part of it.

Henry avidly opened the *Times* to the editorial page and scanned for Frank Harris' byline. What he found instead made his hands shake and a feeling of nausea begin to rise in his throat. He wanted to scream No, no, no and hurl the paper away from him. Instead, all he could manage was "Oh those stupid bastards. That's what they get for voting for a goddamned Democrat." Then he let the paper fall out of his hands. He felt almost overwhelmed by the feeling that he should cry. His country had come into the war on the side of the goddamned Allies, the bastards who had murdered his wife and child.

Generalmajor Wahle put his hand on Henry's shoulder and patted him, very much like a father would do for a hurt child.

"Now what?" Henry asked.

"Well," Paul began, "since you are no longer a neutral journalist traveling with this army, but an alien belligerent, I don't see how we can keep you with us. It would put you much further in jeopardy than you are now, because the war will eventually be over and someone would, then, undoubtedly ask what you had been doing here with us. I think it's safe to say a great many of your people—judging by the tone of those newspapers—would call you a traitor. This whole conversation is made academic, however, by the fact that the internment camp at Kilimatinde has been overrun for nearly a year, so there is nowhere to send you in any case. What is left, I'm sorry to say, amounts to two choices for me. I can have you shot as an enemy spy. Or I can allow you to try to get to the British lines. I would send you to the Portuguese, but your chances of survival there would be about the same as if I sent you to the Belgians. In other words, you'd probably be eaten. Since I will not do the first, and I might add the easier solution, I am left with no choice at all. I will allow you to take your journal bag, since it is still the one best hope we here have of ever being remembered. And I will give you one Askari to try to protect you from harm by the indigenous flora and fauna. Besides, he is a worthless soldier, who never follows orders. *Ombascha* Rajabu will go with you—he's your Brother-in-law anyway. But I'd like him back, eventually. Go get your things. You are leaving while there is still enough light so you can get well away from here before dark."

Fifteen minutes later, Henry slung his journal bag over his shoulder, allowing it to ride at hand level on his right hip. If Paul knew the Schofield was in the bag—which he probably did—he said nothing. Jabari carried Henry's 98 Mauser and wore a set of carrying equipment that obviously held a full load of ammunition. He also carried two breadbags stuffed with rations, such as they were.

Paul came out of his tent and shook Henry's hand. "It has been most interesting, Heinrich. You have done well by us, in your way. *Auf Wiedersehen.*"

Generalmajor Wahle also shook his hand. "You take care, Heinrich. Live to write about what you have seen here. That's an order."

Jabari and Henry strode out of the camp.

After they had walked for nearly an hour, Jabari finally spoke. "The *Obersti* says the British lines should be twenty or twenty-five kilometers to the northeast, but it is very open and bad country, and so he told me to take a far longer route to avoid being seen. There is a rearguard outpost, I think the 4th *Kompainie*, watching the British lines, and he says we should be able to reach them in four or five days if we circle around to come in from the northwest where there is higher ground. We will be able to see how things stand better from there I think."

It was the longest speech Henry had heard from Jabari since Zanta had been killed. Henry nodded, and they veered to the northwest toward a line of low grass-covered hills, perhaps ten kilometers away. As they crossed a dry stream bed in the second hour of their march, Jabari suddenly handed Henry his 98 Mauser and walked quickly to a tree root, which in wetter season would have been under water in the stream. He pulled a M71 Mauser out from its hiding place, did a quick check to make sure everything was where it was supposed to be, and then pulled a cartridge pouch out of the same spot. He slung the rifle and hefted the cartridge pouch onto his shoulder. When he rejoined Henry, he unbuckled the belt of cartridge pouches from his waist and handed them over to Henry as well.

"There are many dangerous animals between here and there," he said.

"And you just happened to know you would be passing this way when you hid the Model '71, right?"

"Something like that."

"What would you have done if I had not chosen to take the long way around?"

"I would have had to tell the *Obersti* I had lost one of his precious rifles and a pouch of cartridges as well. I don't think he would have been happy."

Thursday, August 2, 1917
The Bundu
German East Africa

At mid-morning of the fourth day of their walk, Henry and Jabari lay on a sand ridge covered with dry, yellowish grass, and watched the 4th *Feld Kompainie* cook their morning meal. They were both perturbed because of the nearly complete lack of security on the part of what they assumed was a first-rate *Kompainie* of *Askaris*. Jabari was muttering dire threats under his breath about how he was going to have a strip of flesh torn off the ass of the *Schausch* in charge for being so careless. They watched for a while before deciding to move along the ridge until they could find a spot where they might see the British outpost line. Not wanting to draw fire from either side, they moved very cautiously, and Henry had Jabari stash the black-powder firing 71 Mauser and carry the 98. They were out to avoid trouble, not look for it.

They had crawled nearly a half mile—Henry was beginning to rethink his life in non-metric terms—and were moving silently through thorn scrub when Henry heard a strange and very foreign sound coming from perhaps a dozen yards in front of them on the ridge. Henry immediately held up his hand to stop Jabari and placed a finger on his lips for absolute silence.

Ahead of them, out of sight in the thornbush, they again heard a strange click-click sound that reminded Henry of someone throwing an electric light switch. Almost immediately they heard a voice—an English voice—say, "Can you hear me?"

Van Doorn watched in amazement as the Hun *kaffirs* boiled their coffee. *I had had far less trouble creeping into this position than I thought I would, especially while dragging along a fooking kaffir porter to carry my tucker. The fooking wog thought we were on a fooking picnic in Hyde Park, evidently, until I pushed the muzzle of my SMLE against the fooker's gut and told him to shut the fook up. Fooker had almost given away our hide. The Hun* kaffirs *were usually very good troops, but this bunch was showing a total cock up. Well, I'm here to make these Hun bastards pay for it.*

He toggled the handset switch. "Can you hear me?"

Henry gave Jabari hand signals to show he couldn't see anything through the thornbushes. Then four artillery shells passed overhead to land in the 4th *Feld Kompainie* camp. After an interval of silence, they heard the sound and voice again. This time it said "Down five." Very soon, four more shells passed overhead, and there were four more detonations in the 4th *Feld Kompainie* camp, if anything was left of it.

As the shells whistled over, Jabari suddenly knew what he must do. He rose and moved to his right. As he did he screamed a Wahehe obscenity concerning Wagogo women and goats in Swahili, and then he threw himself sideways, firing his Mauser from the hip toward where he thought their target might be. He was off by several yards, and as his eyes passed behind the trunk of a large thorn tree, he caught, for just an instant, a flicker of motion, followed as quickly by a blue-white flash. The bullet passed less than an inch in front of his eyes and low enough on the bridge of his nose to gouge a channel through the bone, spraying blood and bone onto Henry, who was just rising in an attempt to stop him from moving. Jabari fell heavily backward and lost consciousness after hearing Henry shout, "Don't Shoot! I'm an American!"

Van Doorn watched impassively as the shells fell among the Hun coffee boilers. *Right on the fooking money.* He toggled his handset, but before he could say "Fire for effect" his fooking wog porter shouted something and pointed to their right. He squinted, trying to see through the scrub. Finally he barely made out what might have been some Hun *kaffir's* head peering over the ridge—*God the fooker was close*—not ten yards away. Van Doorn brought his SMLE up and snapped off a shoot, grinning when he saw red mist fly.

"Got you, you fooking *kaffir*." He said just before another man, a white man, stepped out of the scrub.

"Don't Shoot! I'm an American!"

The incongruity of hearing the man yell in English caused Van Doorn to bring his SMLE back down to his waist. "Step over this way, unarmed, with your hands away from your sides," he commanded.

When the man appeared, he was doing as Van Doorn had said. He had some sort of bag slung over his shoulder, but no visible weapon, not even a military belt. He was wearing the sort of clothing a hunter might wear on safari. Nearly six feet tall, he had a disreputable looking hat—in the American movies, like *The Great Train Robbery*, Van Doorn knew were called Westerns, it would be called a cowboy hat. The hat was pulled low on his forehead, though it allowed some brown hair to show on the sides—not a military hair cut. His boots were of the hunting type too. Very well used but quality.

But what the fook was a goddamned American doing here? And why should I care."

He signaled the man to halt when he was still ten yards away or so. They stood there, eying each other. *I really didn't feel like fooking around with this. It would mean an extra trip back to the lines, probably hours answering questions, then another long stalk to find some more Hun* kaffirs *to bring down hell upon. It just wasn't worth the effort.* He looked down and realized he had not worked the bolt on his SMLE. He did so now as he said to the man, "Sorry, chum, but I don't feel like taking prisoners today."

When he looked up and started to raise his rifle, the man's hand was down in the bag hanging by his side.

Strange memories were running through Henry's head. He was twelve years old again and his Grandfather Gus was standing behind him, saying, "This isn't Creedmoor. Pick your target. Use two hands. Rest the trigger guard on the forefinger of your left hand." The Schofield came out of his kit bag in his right hand. In one fluid motion, practiced thousands of times over decades, his right thumb locked onto the serrated top of the hammer, pulling it back until it locked in the full-cock position, and his left hand moved to meet the trigger guard as his body crouched to align itself with the center of the man's body. It was over twenty years since Henry had first been big enough to handle the Schofield's heavy trigger pull, and now as the sights came up to the level of his eyeball, his elbows locked against the side of his ribs, the Schofield roared. The 250 grain, 45 caliber, soft lead bullet, traveling at a sedate 800 feet-per-second caught the South African dead center in the sternum, shattering the bone into small, lethal fragments. The bullet, now flattened to nearly three-quarters of an inch, followed through the chest cavity, blowing out the right atrium and a portion of the aorta before sieving a large chunk of the left lung. Van Doorn had a stupefied expression on his dead face before his body appeared to deflate and topple over backward.

In a less heated moment, Henry would have grudgingly admitted he had managed to make a pretty good shot. Now he walked over and prodded the body with the toe of his boot. He could again hear his Grandfather. "Good shooting."

"There, you bastard," Henry said to the dead South African. "I don't take prisoners either." He reached behind him and seated the Schofield under his belt in the small of his back.

He walked quickly to where a *ruga-ruga* was kneeling beside Jabari and pressing a dirty sock over the bloody bridge of Jabari's nose. The sock was already soaked, and blood was running down Jabari's face and into his ear. The *ruga-ruga* looked up at Henry. "He still lives."

The *ruga-ruga* was looking on, his eyes wild and frightened, as Henry walked back to the South African's corpse, bent down and, taking his hunting knife out of its sheath in his boot, grabbed a handful of Van Doorn's hair, and sliced neatly around the scalp until he could rip the hair and skin free. He wasn't certain it was the way the Indians actually took a scalp, but it was satisfying nonetheless.

Henry walked back to where Jabari Rajabu lay. "You are safe," Henry said to the terrified *ruga-ruga* as he tossed the scalp casually onto his lap, "provided you do exactly as I tell you. If you do not, my spirit will send a *chui*—leopard—for you, and you will be eaten slowly and painfully."

Henry wasn't sure how much the *ruga-ruga* would believe, if any, but what the hell, it was the best he could muster on a moment's notice to keep the frightened man from simply bolting into the bundu. That fear departed when the *ruga-ruga* said, "He is also Wahehe. I knew when he called out a clan curse." Then picking up Jabari's Mauser he checked to see if it held cartridges and asked, "What must I do, *Bwana*? If I do not wish to find out if you are enough of a *mfalme*—tribal medicineman—to bring on a *chui*." The *ruga-ruga* grinned, proud of his little joke.

Henry unslung his journal sack and laid it on the ground beside Jabari. "You will take this with you and keep it safe," he told the *ruga-ruga*. "Then you must help this man get back to his village—without being seen by the British or the Germans. And then you must stay with him until his wounds are healed and he no longer needs your help. This you will now do. When you have reached his village, which is east and north of Iringa, you will take that," Henry motioned to Van Doorn's scalp on the *ruga-ruga's* lap, "and you will tie it to the end of a high pole and raise the pole in front of his hut. If you do not, all of the spirits of a nation of great warriors called the Sioux will descend on you and kill you so slowly you will beg a thousand times for them to put an end to you quickly. And you can ask him," Henry nodded toward Jabari, "if I am enough Wahehe to make it happen. Do you understand?" It was a curse Henry remembered from China, but it still sounded pretty good. The *ruga-ruga* bobbed his head repeatedly.

Jabari opened his bloodshot eyes. He looked at Henry who told him what the *ruga-ruga* was to do.

"When you are healed, my Brother, I would have you live a good, long life. Find yourself many willing maidens. Make many, many *kitoto*—babies. And always remember your sister and me." Henry squeezed Jabari's shoulder before rising.

"And you, *Bwana?*" the *ruga-ruga* asked.

"I will go to the British and tell them I escaped from the Germans and if they manage to find his body before the jackals and hyenas do, the Germans killed the white man and took you away, and when I saw my chance I ran away." *And maybe they will believe me.*"

"Yes, *Bwana...*"

"Go, now."

CHAPTER FORTY-SEVEN

Tuesday, November 20, 1917
St Albert's Hotel
London, England

*I*t had been so remarkably easy, far easier than Henry ever thought it
would be. He had stumbled into the British lines less than a mile from
where he had left Jabari and the ruga-ruga, *and he had undergone a cursory*
inspection by the two soldiers at the King's African Rifles outpost. Escorted
by a corporal, he had been passed back to the reserve line, where he was asked
two or three simple questions by a British Leftenant, who then sent him back
to battalion headquarters in a motor truck—an American Mack, which the
Tommy driver called a Bulldog.

In less than two days he was back in Lindi, and from there he was
hustled onto a British destroyer and taken up the coast to Mombasa,
where he was transferred to a British-India steamer bound for Naples.
Naples was reached without incident in eight days, in time for another
transfer to another British ship, a former Cunard packet, which six days
later docked at Southampton. An afternoon's train ride had brought
him to London, where, he seemed to be expected. Then he checked into
the St. Albert and was handed the key to his rooms by a very polite and
proper concierge. The concierge made no mention whatsoever Henry's
entire baggage train consisted of a German Army bread bag, a very worn
khaki jacket and shirt and equally abused khaki trousers tucked into a
pair of battered boots. After all, there was a war on. In all of that time,
never once was Henry searched or asked any questions at all about what
he had been doing for the last three years. It was very much as though
at least the British didn't particularly care. He had stashed his Schofield
in the bread bag, and so far as he knew, he was the last person to look
into it.

On the way to his rooms he stopped in the hotel bar, coming away
with a bottle of Laphroaig. In his room, he had just taken the first
healthy swallow when there was an imperious pounding on his door.

Probably the maitre-de telling me it's against the rules to walk out of the bar with a whole bottle while there's a war on…

Two men—in uniforms looking strangely familiar to Henry, until he realized they were very much like the one he used to wear back in his National Guard days—were standing in the hallway. "Are you Lieutenant Feller, Henry A.?" said the larger one, wearing the three stripes of a Sergeant on his sleeve.

It took Henry a moment to realize these were, indeed, Americans. *The chevron point is at the top, not the bottom like the British, or the Germans.* "I'm Henry Feller. But you're mistaken about the rest—I haven't been a Lieutenant for about ten years."

"If you're Feller, Henry A., Sir, I'm to place you under arrest. You are to come with me."

"What?"

"You are under arrest, Sir. The charges are failure to report for federal induction, two counts, failure to muster as ordered, and failure to make or to avoid making an overseas movement. The Judge Advocate of the American Expeditionary Forces has issued an order for your arrest, dated 1 May 1917, and amended, and he has further ordered you be brought before a hearing, preliminary to a court martial, at the headquarters of the American Expeditionary Forces. Do you understand what I have just told you, Sir?"

"Very little of it, Sergeant. I don't suppose my saying there has been some kind of horrible mistake made would influence you at all, would it?"

"No, Sir, it would not."

"Where, Sergeant, are the headquarters of the—what did you call it?"

"The American Expeditionary Forces, Sir. The AEF for short."

"The headquarters of the AEF, then?"

"Chaumont, Sir."

"And where exactly is that, Sergeant?"

"About fifty miles from Paris, France, Sir. Southeast, Sir."

"Well, then, Sergeant, may I bring my bottle and my bread bag?"

"You may bring your bread bag, Sir. I'm not sure whether the bottle is allowed."

The equally large private who had said nothing at all up to this point, cleared his throat and nudged the Sergeant in the ribs with his elbow. The Sergeant pretended as though he had not been nudged.

"I think with the two of you guarding me," Henry said, "we can make sure the bottle doesn't arrive at the headquarters of the American Expeditionary Forces at Chaumont, France, to embarrass any of us."

"Yes, Sir , I think we can guarantee that."

"Well then, Sergeant," Henry said, picking up his bread bag and putting the bottle inside, "lead on."

CHAPTER FORTY-EIGHT

Wednesday, December 5, 1917
Headquarters, American Expeditionary Forces
Building A, Chaumont, France

Colonel (Temporary) J. Brandon Edgely, Assistant Judge Advocate, Judge Advocate General's Corps, United States Military Academy, 1908, and Harvard Law, 1913, was busily scanning through a pile of courts-martial requests and transcripts. Most were tales of the rather tawdry things one would expect of enlisted men—robbery, rape, the occasional murder, black market sales, that sort of thing. Colonel Edgely was almost happy to see the great bulk of the charges were against National Army and National Guard personnel. Apparently the higher standards of the Regular Army of the United States were reflected in the sort of things one might expect from the untrained and untried. Colonel Edgely would never have allowed himself to fall into the unconscionable practice of referring to them as 'temporary' soldiers or as 'enlisted swine' which he had so often heard them call themselves.

But it did seem to reinforce his beliefs the Army would have been much better off if it had not had to accept the "non-regulars" into its fold. Statistics seemed to indicate regulars were far less likely to find themselves at odds with the Articles of War than the often free-thinking elements of the "temporary ranks." And, by his way of thinking, the National Guard types were far worse in a number of those faults than the National Army inductees—draftees.

Take for example this "officer and gentleman by designation of the governor." A Lieutenant who had failed to report for duty, not once, but twice, when his state National Guard regiment was called into Federal Service. First, he had not appeared for duty on the Mexican Border in 1916 and then had further failed to report when his regiment had been federalized in April 1917. In other words, he had deliberately absented himself from duty against his country's enemies and had further failed to present himself by the time his regiment was sent overseas. Colonel Edgely was righteously pissed off by such actions and was determined he was going to hold this flagrant dereliction of duty to the highest standards and penalties prescribed by the Articles of War. The best part of it was this particular officer was now sitting in his outer office, apparently blithely unaware his life was well and truly on the line.

Colonel Edgely had never conducted a capital case before. His career would definitely be enhanced, possibly even earning him a permanent change of grade within the JAG Corps, which would put him ahead of dozens of his fellows after the end of the war. Colonel Edgely smiled.

Lieutenant Colonel Edgely's clerk rapped on his office door two days after his interview with Feller, Henry A., and a day after the confirmatory order had come from Paris. General Pershing himself had an interest in the matter because he, General Pershing, remembered Feller, Henry A., as a troublemaker from the Philippines, and had in fact thrown the sumbitch off of Mindanao at one point. Edgely was given *carte blanche* to proceed with whatever action he deemed appropriate, including summary charges. In other words, the General Commanding had said to go ahead and shoot the sumbitch if he wanted to—after a courts martial, of course—so Lieutenant Colonel Edgely was in a particularly fine mood.

Edgely was about to ask what his clerk wanted when his office door opened and the commander of the 84th Infantry Brigade strode into the office. Edgely and the 84th commander did not get along well. Some would say they disliked one another intensely, but they were both officers of the Regular Army establishment and therefore kept their personal feelings in check. Edgely was thankful the Army had at least been wise enough to appoint regular officers to most of the important slots in the command structures of the National Guard divisions, though the 42nd Rainbow Division was an orphan of sorts.

The summer before, it had been decided to send two divisions to France as quickly as possible. For reasons more political than military, one of the divisions would be from the Regular Army, the other from the National Guard. The First Division was pulled together from existing regiments, most of which had served on the Mexican border the year before, and it was quickly brought up to wartime strength by transferring men from other units. It was ready in a very short time and shipped out for France in June, only two months after the United States entered the war.

On the other hand, none of the nearly twenty National Guard divisions could be made ready in anything like that amount of time. Once the army realized that sad fact, it was decided to put together a single National Guard division containing elements from as many of the state organizations as possible. When all was said and done, the 42nd Division was organized on the regular army structure of two infantry brigades of two regiments and a machinegun battalion each; an artillery brigade of three field artillery regiments (two light 75mm and one heavy 155mm) and a trench mortar battalion; an engineer regiment; a signal battalion; a medical regiment with attached hospital trains; and assorted other trains. In all, twenty-six states sent elements to the division at Camp Mills, New York, but it took them more than a month to get organized and another month to stop fighting with one another. The New Yorkers and Alabamans had gotten into a colossal brawl over some half-remembered battle fought by their grandfathers—during the Civil War for Chrisake—that took an entire company of MPs to break up. Finally, they shipped out beginning in October, arriving in France in November, after a less than pleasant time of it on the high seas. And since arrival they had been stuck in a variety of cantonments all over France for further training under the watchful eye of French officers. At least the last months had served to winnow out some of the worst of the National Guard types who were replaced by Regulars.

The Commander of the 84th Brigade was a case in point. Old Army to the eyebrows, a West Pointer whose father had been a senior general officer, he had come in as the Division Chief of Staff and had wangled his way into a combat command. In Edgely's mind, it was probably more by way of his family associations than from his skill, because he had acted mostly like an over-eager puppy yapping after promotion during his time in Mexico, and there was no other real experience in his file. So far as Edgely knew, the commander of the 84th had not heard a shot fired in anger in his short time in the Philippines or since. Still, he had been more than adequate as the Division Chief of Staff—for instance, he had supposedly come up with the nickname for the division, but one knew how those stories started after all.

"I hear you are holding an officer by the name of Feller, Henry A., who claims not to be an officer. Is that correct?"

"Why yes, Colonel, it is. In fact he 'claims' many other things. For instance, he claims to have been trapped in Africa by the Germans since the very beginning of the war. And he also claims to have resigned his commission in the National Guard in 1909 or 10, sometime in there, to go on a safari with President Roosevelt, of all things. The man has an astonishing capacity for lying."

"Is that so?"

Oh, yes. I've never heard such a line of bullshit in my life."

"And you've investigated his claims and found them to be false?"

"Oh, we'll get to that at the time of the courts martial."

"And you don't expect any complications?"

"Heavens no. It's an open and shut case. The man refused two separate call ups, one for the Mexican Border and one after the Declaration of War—tantamount to an unauthorized absence to avoid overseas movement. He'll be lucky if he's not shot for cowardice."

"Where was he arrested?"

"London, England."

"And you've held him for how long?"

"A week, ten days—something like that."

"And he was originally in the…?" The Colonel commanding the 84th Infantry Brigade made a rolling gesture with his hand.

"Er, South Dakota National Guard, I believe, Colonel."

"The element presently in the Rainbow Division?"

"I believe. Probably…"

"But you didn't bother to inform anyone at division you had him in custody? Someone who might possibly know him from past service?"

"I didn't think it would be necessary until we actually started courts-martial proceedings."

"Ah, well I think you'd better have him brought here."

"Colonel?"

"I said, have him brought here. Now. That's an order, Lieutenant Colonel. I'll wait."

Lieutenant Colonel Edgely told his clerk to have the duty MPs bring Lieutenant Feller to the office.

Henry was brought from his cell—the Army called it arrest to quarters. If he had been one of the enlisted swine he would have been in the stockade or guard house or whatever the hell they called it now. Henry's cell had actually been a small single room, furnished *a la* the Spartan Hoplites—foot soldiers—but somewhat better than sleeping in the open under a blanket of stinging, biting, sucking insects. When he and his MP escorts arrived at the Assistant Judge Advocate General's office, the little Light Colonel who had kept him standing at attention for the better part of an hour the other day and had not allowed him to take a leak when he had to, looked unhappier than he had on that occasion. *Come to think of it, he hadn't been as much unhappy, as just plain pissed off, with me as the target of choice. Now he looks like his pet dog just died. Maybe that means he isn't going to get to have me shot today and has to wait for dawn tomorrow...*

There was another vaguely familiar officer form standing by the window with his back to the door, who neither turned around nor uttered any sort of comment when Henry was announced by the MP Sergeant. Henry moved to the front of the little Light Colonel's desk and stood essentially at ease. *What's he going to do, have me shot for not acting like a soldier? Well, I'm not a soldier and I haven't been one since 1909. So piss on him.*

The little Light Colonel waited for several long moments, until he finally realized Henry was not going to stand at attention or salute. "Lieutenant Feller," he finally said, "there seems to have been a bit of new information concerning your case."

"It's Mister Feller, not Lieutenant Feller," Henry answered.

"Goddamn it, Feller," Edgely blurted. He was about to spend the next seconds berating Henry, again, when the other officer, without turning from the window, interrupted.

"I have a letter—*that voice, I'd know that voice anywhere*—which was sent to me by the rather strange and convoluted route of the British Colonial Office diplomatic pouch, to the British Liaison Officer with the Rainbow Division, to General Menoher, the Division Commander, to me. It's dated several weeks ago, and it took this long to arrive because of the distance it had to travel. It's signed by a Colonel Richard Meinhartzhagen DSO MM and some other letters. And I have been reliably informed by our staunch allies at the War Office, he is presently serving as General Allenby's Chief of Intelligence in Palestine, though before that he held the same job under General Smuts in East Africa. It's a very interesting letter, going into great detail about certain operations in the East African Theater of War, especially in the time before the United States became involved. Begins right at the beginning, so to speak, and pretty well covers it right up to the time he was transferred to Palestine—sometime last autumn. If you don't mind, I'll read the first few lines:

> We became aware of the presence of an American writer, Mister Henry A. Feller, in German East Africa, about the time of the opening of the Dar es Salaam Exposition. We were advised of his presence by Messrs Perry Hays and Frank Vining the American Consul and Vice-Consul at Zanzibar. Further, Norman King, the British Consul in Dar es Salaam informed the Foreign office Feller had been sent out of German East by Governor Doctor Heinrich Schnee and Colonel Paul Von Lettow-Vorbeck before the outbreak of war, but had the misfortune to have his vessel rerouted back into Dar es Salaam by the German Navy. Thereafter we found it impossible to make contact with Feller as the German administration was doing an excellent job of keeping him under wraps and any contact would have jeopardized both him and our agents. Nor was a later contact possible when Feller was allowed to attend the wedding of Major Redmont Buller, the son of former General Commanding, Redvers Buller, when he married the widow of a German officer in Dar es Salaam.
>
> During this period, however, Feller was instrumental in the success of the activities of one of my agents, Pietr Pretorius, in charting the channels of the Rufiji Delta in our successful action

against the German cruiser SMS Königsberg. Feller had ample opportunity to expose Mister Pretorius and did not…"

"Need I go on?" Colonel Douglas MacArthur tossed the letter onto Lieutenant Colonel Edgely's desk and walked to the office door. "Major, could you come in here, please?" he asked politely.

When another officer entered, Henry gasped and gaped, but managed to say nothing, realizing he was being given the benefit of a first class show of some sort in the theater of MacArthur. The officer who entered the small office was six-feet-four and weighed nearly two hundred and twenty pounds. His uniform was impeccably tailored. His leather Sam Browne belt and boots were highly polished. He was in all respects what the Well-Dressed-National-Guard-Field-Grade-Officer should look like. He came to attention and snapped a perfect salute.

"Major Anderson, tell Lieutenant Colonel Edgely what took place in your presence in Mitchell, South Dakota, in the spring of 1909," Colonel MacArthur instructed, turning to Lieutenant Colonel Edgely and throwing in an aside, "Major Anderson is the Executive officer of the 117th Ammunition Train—that used to be the 1st South Dakota National Guard Infantry."

"Sir!" Major Dodger Anderson said. "At the time, I was the First Lieutenant of Company F of the 1st Regiment, Infantry, South Dakota National Guard. Henry Feller was the Second Lieutenant of the same company. The Company Commander was Captain Otis Jividen, since deceased. At that time Lieutenant Feller was notified he had been chosen by his publisher—he's written several books, as you might know—to go on the Smithsonian Safari with former President Roosevelt. He wrote out his resignation immediately upon receipt of the telegram. I hand-delivered the resignation to Captain Jividen the same day. That was in March of 1909. As I recall. Sir!"

Both Major Anderson, known to all as 'Dodger'—a name given to him a quarter of a century before by Henry Feller on the playground of the Mitchell Common School—and Colonel Douglas MacArthur, both made a valiant effort to not return the unbelieving stares greeting them from Henry Feller. Henry had last seen Dodger on a daily basis in 1912, when they had, as they had done for nearly twenty years before, hunted deer in the creek beds northwest of Mitchell. And early in the spring of 1913, they had shared a pail of beer the night before Henry caught the train taking him on his return journey to Africa.

Henry had last spoken to Douglas MacArthur shortly after Lieutenant-General Arthur MacArthur's funeral services in Milwaukee, Wisconsin, also in 1912, while Henry had been on his way to Minneapolis to visit his Uncle David Welsh's grave. It had been the latest, and saddest, crossing of their paths since they had first met and grown to like one another in Manila. They had even shared—not at the same time, of course—the attentions of a young and passionate Filipino opera singer called Tamanti.

Seeing them both at the same time, now, for the first time in years, Henry was torn between the urge to either cheer or cry. And his face told them he was having a hard time deciding which to do. Dodger tried mightily to keep from grinning, and failed. Douglas remained the soul of composure.

"It seems," Colonel MacArthur said, "*Mister* Feller has apparently been telling the truth. Just to confirm some of the other parts of his story—or as you say his remarkable capacity for lying—I have taken the liberty to send a telegram to Colonel Roosevelt to see whether Mister Feller ever actually went on that safari. Now, unfortunately, there is no way to confirm—other than by way of British Intelligence and the Foreign Office and, of course, the State Department—as yet, his presence with the German forces in East Africa, because it seems our British and Belgian allies can't seem to find them—and our Portuguese allies *wish* they could not. When last seen, they were somewhere in Portuguese East Africa heading for parts unknown. But, given all of this material, Lieutenant Colonel, I would say it boils down to what you are going to do to remedy the—as our English allies are so fond of saying—the 'compleat cock-up' you've made of this matter. I shouldn't have to tell you you have detained an eminent civilian journalist, without charges being filed, without adequate investigation into the facts of the case, without due process even under the Code of Military Justice and the Articles of War. In fact, if I were Mister Feller, Lieutenant Colonel,

I'd wait for the end of the war and then I'd sue your ass off in a Federal Court. Fortunately for you, I believe Mister Feller remembers the basic elements of his oath as an officer and will be satisfied to simply be reinstated and have these foolish, foolish charges dropped and expunged from his records." MacArthur turned to Henry and raised an eyebrow. "Am I right?"

"Do I have a choice?" Henry asked, drawing a surprised scowl from MacArthur and Dodger Anderson, which immediately turned into grin on Dodger's part.

"No, not really," Douglas MacArthur said. "You're back in the Army, Henry. We can sort the rest out later."

Before Lieutenant Colonel Edgely could protest, MacArthur said, "While you're about doing the paper work to reinstate First Lieutenant Feller into the Army of the United States, post-dated to whenever, you might as well cut the paperwork transferring him to the 84th Infantry Brigade, 42nd Division. I think I can put him to use somehow, even if he is a little long in the tooth for a First Lieutenant."

CHAPTER FORTY-NINE

Monday, July 22, 1918
Near the Marne River
France

To say the mental displacement Henry underwent had not been oppressive would be considered the understatement of the century. He likened it to breaking a new horse while riding a roller coaster on a lifeboat—ups and downs and reverses in all directions all of the time.

Douglas had appointed him to command the brigade headquarters platoon, about fifty men from at least as many places. And some of them were so new to the United States, let alone her military establishment, his occasional reversion to giving commands in German or Swahili—well at least the German ones—were understood and followed with no more than the occasional chuckle as he mumbled, "Sorry."

One way in which he was damned lucky was his platoon First Sergeant, Luther James, had been on the 1ˢᵗ South Dakota, A Company's shooting team and had been the newly minted corporal who had come in two places behind Henry when he had been beaten out in the individual rifle match the year Company F had taken the state championship. Quite often Luther James and Henry would share a bottle of Van Rooj—the AEF pronunciation for the common red wine of France—and tell war stories. A couple of times Dodger would even join them. James was one of the few who realized just how bent and out of focus Henry's life had become, and he was—along with, strange as it may seem, Douglas MacArthur—someone who went out of his way to try to straighten Henry out before the occasional miscues caused him troubles far out of proportion to his crimes.

Dodger, of course, was another of the select few because he was directly responsible for the first of Henry's brushes with authority. In this particular case, they had both run over to the 83ʳᵈ Brigade to coordinate some training item or other before they moved into the Luneville sector of the line to replace—the army called it "augment"—

some French troops who had been in the line for several months. They had been joking with one another at the 83rd Brigade billets, joking around as they had since they were ten years old. Only, this time, when they noticed him, there was a bespectacled Colonel standing there with his hands on his hips, looking exceedingly pissed off—and apoplectic red to boot. It didn't help that Dodger saw him first, and instead of saluting said, "Uh oh, I think that Colonel looks pissed," to Henry, who replied, "Yeah, no shit, Dodge."

A little over fifteen minutes later, Colonel MacArthur had finally arrived to end Colonel William Donovan's infamously New York-Irish harangue. The two recalcitrant perps had been left to mop the remnants of their hides from the floor and timidly slink off into the night. At least that was the impression they hoped they had left with Colonel Donovan, because they might, by some wild stretch of the imagination, meet him again in this lifetime. The real result was they practiced a semi-serious ritual of proper rank address from that point forward. Following the basic outlines as set down by Colonel Donovan, one became "Major Dodger, Sir" and the other became "Lieutenant Henry Old Buddy." If Colonel MacArthur disapproved, he didn't say, provided both of the idiots played the army game when there were other witnesses around who could cause trouble.

Following their trench training around Luneville, they moved to the Baccarat sector where the Rainbow took over a sixteen-kilometer section of the front line and its support positions. Henry's platoon took its first casualties there, four dead and seven wounded, during an artillery barrage. Then they moved to the Esperance-Souaine sector, then over into Champagne. They knew the Germans were on the offensive, but most of the action was taking place up north.

That all changed in the middle of July. The second part of the German offensive broke through the French lines and began to gain ground. Reluctantly, General Pershing agreed to feed American divisions into the line to bolster the flagging Allies. They moved up to the River Marne, and for the first time in a year or more, Henry heard the sound of Spandaus firing—this time, at him. And artillery going in both directions over his head. For three days, they, along with other

American divisions—the 1ˢᵗ, 2ⁿᵈ, 3ʳᵈ, and 26ᵗʰ —made a stand along a stretch of the river and stopped the German drive on Paris. Then they hunkered down as shells rained down on them.

After those three days they attacked, pushing toward the Argonne and Meuse Rivers, and that was even worse. Henry rapidly became sick to death of seeing the ambulances and piles of coffins and fresh graves. They were finally pulled out of the line and turned their sector over to new American troops anxious to pull the Kaiser's moustache. *Let 'em. I just want six hours of uninterrupted sleep.*

Henry and Dodger managed to find billets in the same French hotel in a nameless pile of rubble on what had once been a poplar-lined road. They pitched a piece of canvas they stole off a French Renault camion to keep off the rain that began to fall at about the time the first American set foot in the billet. Dodger found a wreck of a dining room chair buried under some debris to give them enough firewood to boil their coffee and warm the space under the tarp by a few degrees. The rumor was field showers might be set up along with a delousing station, but they both decided warmth and the chance to sleep took priority over cleanliness and cooties. The trouble was, even as exhausted as they were, they simply had too much adrenaline flowing to sleep. Instead they sat under their tarp and talked, sharing a can of 'gold-fish,' the doughboy's favored name for the tinned salmon ration.

Henry couldn't for the life of him remember at a later date what had brought their conversation around to politics and the war, because they had never, ever, discussed politics back home. But now Henry ranted on, roundly blaming the Progressives and their present-day demons, the Democrats, in particular the head Democrat, President Woodrow Wilson for all the ills of the war and society. And suddenly, Henry found himself lying there, with Dodger's hand clapped over his mouth and Dodger whispering in his ear, "Damn it, Henry, shut the hell up."

When Dodger took his hand away, all Henry could think to say was, "Jeez, Dodge, I didn't know you were a Democrat."

"Goddamn it, Henry, I'm not. You should know that. But you don't have a blessed idea of what's been going on since the war started."

"So tell me."

"You ever hear of George Creel?"

"Who?"

"Wilson's information guy—he's got some kind of government title, but what it really means is he's in charge of propaganda."

"No shit?"

"Look, Henry—Jesus, I hope there's no one listening to us." Dodger looked around and then snuck a peek under the edge of the tarp to see if anyone else was in the billet. Satisfied they were alone, he went on. "When Wilson found his excuse to get us into the war, anyone who was in the military, Regulars or National Guard, could have told you we were completely unready to fight a war, and had been for years. Hell, the government didn't do a damn thing to get us ready, in spite of everything Generals Funston and Wood said or could do…"

"Fred Funston?"

"Yeah, General Frederick Funston—he was commanding the Southern Department of the Army when that old greaser Pancho Villa attacked Columbus, New Mexico, and Wilson called up 15,000 National Guard. Funston was supposed to command the AEF. Unfortunately, he did a face-first into his soup at dinner one day—heart attack. That left old Black Jack, who had chased Villa all over north Mexico, with yours truly sweating in a rear-echelon billet in El Paso, Texas, by the way. We were called up for a year in '16, then discharged in April '17, and recalled damned near the next day when we declared war on Germany-and-friends.

"Anyway, as soon as it was official, Wilson names this George Creel guy to be his information czar, what amounted to mind-control and head-hunting. Creel had good training as a muckraker—you remember them, don't you?" Dodger didn't bother to wait for Henry's nod before going on. "Ah, I remember what they call it—the Committee on Public Information. That's the name of the bunch he's in charge of. Henry, my lad, he's a goddamned zealot with a capital Z. He can literally tell artists what to paint, what kind of music Tin-Pan-Alley can write, what movies the studios can make. He has a campaign going to de-Germanize the country. There ain't any more Schmidts, just Smiths.

There ain't any more sauerkraut, it's Liberty Cabbage. There're Creel's Four-Minute Men talking all over the damned place. They shut down all of the radio stations, and all of the amateur radio people had to turn in their stuff—get it back after the war, of course—maybe.

"And then they passed the Sedition Act and under it, Henry old bud, you could have been arrested and either fined or put on trial for what you were just saying before. In fact, you could have been put on trial for your goddamned *life*, 'cause that's one of the penalties the," Dodger looked out from under the tarp again to make certain they were alone, "Democrats consider part of the law for speaking your mind. Henry, it ain't the same country you left. This goddamned war has changed it in more ways than I've got time or energy to name. Anyone opposed to the bastards has been put on the hotseat. Eugene Debbs, the guy that ran for President, is in jail. The Wobblies are in jail. Anyone who opens his or her mouth is looking for jail time. Your best bet, my friend, is to keep your thoughts to yourself and soldier on. Maybe we can fix things after the war. But we got to win the son of a bitch first, and of course we have to live through it, too. Let's get some sleep."

CHAPTER FIFTY

Thursday, September 12, 1918
167th Infantry Forward Trench
The St. Miheil Salient, France

There were many times in his life when Henry Feller had been frightened. He had been caught in a cattle stampede while working on his uncle's ranch in his fourteenth summer. That had been frightening. He had been shot at by numerous Filipino insurgents on Luzon. He had been trapped with Admiral Seymour's bunch in the Hzingtsu Arsenal, with several thousand murderous Chinese adherents of the Harmonious Fist—Boxers—waiting just outside, ready to cut up everyone inside into so much dog food. That had been frightening. He had been in his first big gun fight with Moro ladrones on the Island of Mindanao. That had been frightening. He had been shot at on four continents while plying his trade as a military journalist and correspondent. Each individual case had been frightening in its own fashion.

But now, in the pre-dawn dark of this goddamned filthy, stinking, oozing trench, watching the doughs—only the newpapers called them "doughboys"—getting ready to go over the top into no-man's-land, knowing he was going to go with them, he was beyond being *only* frightened. He was scared shitless. Fifteen seconds before, for the eighth time in less than two minutes, he had checked his Colt 1911 pistol and his 1917 Eddystone rifle, to make sure they were loaded and locked. He looked around him to see his men, thirty some surviving members of the 84th Brigade Headquarters Detachment, also wondered as to their future and would have been comforted to know they had one.

It wasn't their first time over the top. They had done it in the Meuse-Argonne offensive, when the Rainbow had been seconded to the little one-armed French general at a shitty little hovel they called Red Cross Farm. The Frog had sent them and his other American 'augmentation' in without artillery preparation and they had walked into a hornets' nest, while his *poilus* sat in the support trenches and drank Van Rooj.

307

Henry simply did not know how he had managed to survive. But he had. And now he was going to attempt fate to do it again.

Henry counted himself to be among the already dead. To his mind there was absolutely no way in hell he could come out of this one alive. He was resigned to the inevitable, but even that didn't make him any less scared. The only thing giving him any pause at all was watching his immediate commander, Brigadier General—the promotion had finally come through—Douglas MacArthur.

The night before—*was it only six or seven hours ago?*—he had been summoned into the General's dugout. Actually, the phrase Douglas had used and passed on by way of a runner was "the Lieutenant may attend me in my dugout in fifteen minutes." It was as though Henry was some sort of medieval page waiting on his knight errant. *And*, Henry smiled to himself, *that is, more than likely, exactly how Douglas thought of it.*

He had *attended* his General and had found Colonel Flagler, commander of the 167th Infantry, the Colonel of the 168th –but for the life of him Henry could *not* remember the man's name—along with Colonel Charlie Rhodes, the Brigade Artillery commander, already present. When he came into the dugout, MacArthur had looked up and introduced him saying, "Lieutenant Feller will command the runners I am going to take along with the first wave. I don't believe the telephone lines will be any more useful this time than they were the last, and probably less so, because in spite of First Army's continued insistence we go in without artillery preparation, I intend to see the orders from Chaumont[7] so stating are lost.

"Colonel Donovan's regiment will lead the 83rd Brigade's attack with the 166th in the second wave. I—we—will go in with the 167th—if I didn't put your Rebels in the first wave, Flagler, I'm sure I'd never hear the end of it.[8] The 168th will be my second wave. They served my Father well in the Philippines and I'm certain they'll do well now.

"Colonel Patton's tanks will support the advance. Be aware they will be operating mostly to our left flank, as the mud there should be shallower. We—Colonel Patton and I—both intend to accompany the first wave on foot. Lieutenant Feller will be near at hand to me to employ his runners as communicators. We will jump off at 0500 hours. The artillery preparation will commence at 0100 hours. Colonel Rhodes and I have worked out a plan of fire which I pray will give our advance ample support."

MacArthur did not entertain questions. He then told Henry to wait on him and ducked into the rearmost cubicle of the dugout. Five minutes later, he re-emerged—wearing a private's uniform under his trench coat, no helmet, and carrying a riding crop as his only defense.

CHAPTER FIFTY-ONE

Thursday, September 12, 1918
800 yards from the village of Essey
The St. Miheil Salient, France

*H*enry was lying on his stomach, trying to be as inconspicuous as possible as he watched General Macarthur standing on a small piece of high ground forty or so yards from the shell crater, where the survivors of the Brigade Headquarters Platoon had taken shelter. He isn't even wearing a helmet...just his piss-cutter[9] and that damned silly-ass purple muffler his mother knitted for him.

Henry looked around and took a rapid nose count. In the two hours of the attack so far, they had come about 800 yards, as far as he could figure, and were still about 800 yards short of their objective, the remnants of the village of Essey. Such as it was. Compared to some of the villages he had seen on his way to the new American sector, Essey was still in pretty fair condition for there were still portions of buildings—mostly walls—left standing. He had seen places called villages that were only recognizable because the rubble was a little more orderly and a little deeper amidst the universal moonscape of shell craters. Eight hundred yards in two hours was a veritable foot race by Western Front standards. Henry had seventeen men of his original thirty-four remaining with him. Of those original thirty-four, two were wounded slightly, and he knew three were definitely dead—he had their ID tags in his tunic pocket.

MacArthur was looking intently off to his left at something or someone out of Henry's field of view. He beat his riding crop against the side of his boot as he watched. Hearing something behind Henry, he turned and waved, giving the "come-to-me" hand signal to whoever was there. Henry slid back down from the rim of the crater when his ears heard the familiar and unmistakable "ticka-ticka-ticka" of a Spandau machinegun firing. He had heard them too often in Africa to be interested in trying to locate this particular one, or to expose his Mark

One Eyeball Locator to its fire. He was, therefore, startled unpleasantly when the six-four, two-hundred-twenty-pound frame of Major Dodger Anderson jumped over the edge of the crater and almost landed on him.

"What the hell are you doing here, Dodger? Major, Sir?"

"Lieutenant, Henry, old buddy," Dodger answered after catching his breath, "what the hell would the Ammunition Train be doing following the first wave of an attack, do you suppose?"

"Ah, let's see—could it be you were bringing up, let me guess, ammunition?"

"By God, you're right. You bettcha. You're a pretty fart smeller."

"Dodger, Major, Sir—has it ever been pointed out to you that's why God invented Sergeants and privates?"

"Henry, Lieutenant, old buddy, you are truly one ignorant shit. I, in the splendor of my exalted field grade rank, am the Executive Officer of the 117th Ammunition Train. It is, therefore, my job to tell all of those Sergeants and privates, most of who are bright enough to not walk into enemy fire if they can avoid it, to 'grab those ammunition boxes and follow me.' So, lo and behold, here I am. Which brings me to the question of where is the General, whom I suppose it would behoove me to report to, so I can get the hell out of here back to my safe dugout?"

"Anyone ever tell you that you are 'prolix'—that's a word that means you talk too much."

"Only when I'm scared shitless. Some Heinie sumbitch with a machine gun tried to shoot me just now."

"I heard. For your general store of information, Dodger, Major, Sir—machine guns are bad for your health."

"No shit?"

"I never lie." Henry snuck a quick peek over the crater rim and ducked back down. "General's over that way about forty yards. You can't miss him—he's standing out in the open talking to another equally crazy officer. You'll be able to tell right off he's our General—he's the only one wearing a purple muffler."

Dodger gave Henry a strange look, uncertain whether his leg was being pulled. Henry said nothing but made the sign of crossing his heart with his right forefinger and grinned.

Dodger slithered over the rim of the crater, listened intently for the sound of the Spandau, and not hearing it, rose to his feet, and sprinted to where MacArthur and the other officer were still standing in the open. The General gestured to where he wanted Dodger's carrying party to take their loads of ammunition, shook Dodger's hand—the Douglas shake—with his left hand patting Dodger's shoulder the while.

The German counter-barrage began just as Dodger started to sprint back to Henry's crater. The nearest German guns, those with the shortest range, were the 77mm light field guns. They fired a reasonably high velocity shell. Because of the short range and the velocity, they didn't give a great deal of time—if any—for the target to take cover. They were known as "Whiz-bangs" for that reason, a term contributed to the language by the British Tommies, who universally hated them.

Henry heard the first Whiz-bang hit and felt the ground shake. When he looked over the rim of his crater he saw Dodger on the ground trying to crawl toward him. Dodger was missing most of his right leg below the knee, and his right arm and side were bloody. He left a trail of bloody mud in his wake as he inched his way toward Henry's crater.

Without thinking, Henry dropped his Eddystone, stood and leaped over the crater's edge. He ran full speed to Dodger and without stopping reached down and grabbed him by the back of his tunic collar and the straps of his musette bag and gasmask. Then he continued on in a straight line toward the next shell crater. As he moved, dragging Dodger, he heard the sound of the next German shell coming toward them, a much bigger shell, probably a 150mm. At the same instant he heard the Spandau open fire, and there was no mistaking it—he was the target. The 150mm landed with a strangely dull, muffled explosion as he heaved Dodger over the edge of the crater.

The Spandau continued to fire, long bursts of ten or fifteen rounds. *Must be nice to have that much ammunition*, he thought, remembering Paul Von Lettow-Vorbeck's stringent "No More Than Three Shots" rule. A line of machine gun slugs stitched along the ground, coming directly at him just as he hurled himself sideways at the crater.

He almost made it. Nine of the ten bullets in the burst missed him, kicking up mud and clods of other things. But the tenth 7.92 x 57mm bullet went through his body on the right side, fortuitously just under his lung and just over his liver. It broke the last rib and followed it around to exit three inches above his belt and six from his spine. All of this in less than half a second. Henry sat down heavily upon impact and toppled sideways into the crater, hoping the German gunner would be satisfied and go search out more lucrative targets than two wounded doughs. The 150mm shell, on the other hand, had contained gas, now seeping over the edge of the crater. It smelled musty, like old damp straw—phosgene. Dodger was still conscious.

Trying hard not to panic every time he looked at Dodger's wounds—the leg was gone, so the Whiz-bang must have clipped it off as it hit, and the arm was mangled at the elbow. *He'll be damned lucky if he doesn't lose it.* But the splinter wounds in the side looked to be superficial—there was no frothy blood or the sound of air escaping the lungs. Henry reached under his tunic and pulled his web belt out of his trousers. He looped the belt around Dodger's leg where it ended just below the knee and drew the belt up tight enough to make Dodger groan through clenched teeth. Henry looked around the crater for anything to make a handle to complete the tourniquet. Finding nothing useful in the crater, Henry finally pulled his Colt Automatic out of its holster and began to disassemble it. When he had extracted the barrel, he checked it for length against the width of the web belt and discarded it, using the slide instead. This he looped as a handle in the belt and twisted it until the bleeding from Dodger's stump slowed, then stopped.

He propped Dodger into a more comfortable position, then reached into his First Aid pouch and pulled out his sealed-in-tin Carlisle dressing. He unsealed the container and put the dressing in Dodger's good hand. Turning his back, he told Dodger to "cover the exit wound so I can lie down without getting it full of all this stinking, filthy French shit." That done, Henry flopped onto his back, just in time to see whispers of greenish white stuff slowly waft over the edge of their crater. At the edge of his aural sensibility, Henry again smelled the odor of damp straw—phosgene gas, known as 'white-cross' from the markings on the artillery shells.

"Dodger, Major, Sir," he said, "we'd best be putting on our gasmasks." Not waiting for an answer, he began yelling, "GAS...GAS...GAS" as loud as he could between stabs of pain, just in case anyone near at hand had not noticed the greenish white clouds descending on them. The bullet may have missed his lung, but it still had bored a hole through his body, and it was beginning to throb unmercifully.

Henry popped the star-snap fasteners on his mask bag and pulled the mask free. He tossed his helmet to one side, pulled the mask over his face, fit the nose clip and pulled the straps tight while testing the fit by pressing a hand over the air outlet. The mask expanded and contracted as he breathed in and out through the mouth piece. He put his helmet back on.

When he looked at Dodger, he froze. Dodger was attempting to put his mask on with one hand. That was bad enough, but what Dodger either couldn't see or didn't want to admit was his mask was riddled with holes.

Shit...shit...shit...shit...shit.

Henry pulled his helmet back off and pulled his mask over his head. Kneeling beside Dodger, he unfastened his gas mask bag, pulled the strap over his head, and set the mask and bag on the ground. He gently removed Dodger's helmet and pulled the mask over Dodger's head. Dodger tried to stop him. "Give it up Henry—I'm a goner."

"You ain't a goner until I goddamn-well say you are, you ignorant shit. I've seen men hurt ten times worse than we are. Seen 'em do incredible stuff. Hell, I seen an *Askari*—big, black sumbitch—with his belly split open like a melon by a piece of shell and he walked ten frigging miles holding his guts in, and all the way singing, fer Chrissake—singing that damned silly marching song, *Der Trägen und Askari: Haya, haya, Safari.*

"Besides, I'm not giving it to you, I'm just letting you borrow it. When I pull it on, you count to thirty, slowly, and then I'll take it back. I figure I can hold my breath for thirty seconds."

"And then what?"

"And then we wait here until somebody comes and gets us. Unless you think you can outrun that Spandau with one leg."

"Jesus, Henry, it sure hurts, you betcha it does."

"Yeah, it does that."

Lying side by side, they shared Henry's gas mask for the next five interminable hours. Most of the time was spent with Henry telling war stories from his adventures in German East. Dodger, sliding in and out of consciousness, had a hard time believing his friend, and said so. So Henry kept asking him, "Dodge, have you ever known me to lie?"

Around noon, long after the combat had moved hundreds of yards away from where they lay, a stretcher party from the 117th Ambulance Train found them and carried them back over the 800 yards of their advance to the trench they had climbed out of at 5 AM. From there they were carried along a communication trench to the forward 84th Brigade Field Hospital where their wounds were dressed. They were tagged, and they were put aboard an ambulance for transport to the 42nd Division Field Hospital.

Dodger would find out two years later his best friend had lied. Try as he might, Henry could not hold his breath for thirty seconds. At least not toward the end of their five-hour wait in the shell hole.

Having been a hunter and the number of animals of all sizes he had taken, and field dressed, Henry had known from the first his bullet wound was not fatal. The circumstances, however, might very well be. In addition to the through-and-through gunshot wound to his right central torso, Henry had ingested several nanoliters of phosgene gas. It was less than a lethal dose, but more than enough to cause him great discomfort until some months later the scar tissue created in his lungs had sloughed off and was discarded in his sputum. And he and Dodger had lain in a veritable sea of necrophilic matter churned into a gluey soup by nearly four years of artillery fire, a soup seeping into every open pore and orifice of Henry's body looking for a place to begin generating gas gangrene.

It meant he stayed in the American First Army Hospital at Chaumont for an extra two months, breathing camphorated steam and spitting up green pus. It was, perhaps, the least favorite of his memories of his service on either side in the Great War, which was over by the time he was released back to duty on 9 December 1918.

It was while in the Chaumont Hospital Henry once again slammed head-on into the military establishment and the Articles of War. One afternoon as he lay in his bed, weakened from a particularly violent bout of "phlegm expectoration"—the polite way of saying coughing-his-lungs-out-and spitting-up-green-shit-into a bucket—he was approached by an officious little Captain of the Quartermaster Corps armed with a sheaf of forms and a list of all the equipments Lieutenant Feller, Henry A., 0-197843, had been issued. Particularly of note was one pistol, Colt, M1911, caliber .45, serial number such and such. The Captain wanted to know where it was and /or what had happened to it. When Henry explained what had become of the pistol, he was told by the five-foot four-inch Captain of the Quartermaster Corps his improper use of the weapon meant it would be charged against his pay and allowances. At which point Henry told the Captain if he wanted the pistol back, Henry knew exactly which crater it was in and would be more than happy to draw him a detailed map of how to find it. The QMC Captain was not amused.

From that point tempers degenerated nearly to the flash point where Henry was about to throw caution to the winds. *What's the worst thing they can do to me—courtmartial me?* But from Henry's blind side came, once again, a familiar stentorian voice.

"What seems to be the problem here, Captain...?" General MacArthur asked.

After the QMC Captain had explained the problem in minute detail, General MacArthur held out his hand for the disposition form and endorsed across it "Lost or destroyed in combat—BG Douglas MacArthur, Commanding 84th Brigade."

"Sir...?" the QMC Captain started to protest.

"Good day, Captain," the General said. "Please continue about your duties. You are dismissed." Without further regard for the little man, General MacArthur stepped over to Henry's bed and took a seat on the edge of the mattress. "How are you feeling?" he asked, real concern in his voice.

"Well, Sir, the bullet wound is healing nicely. The gas is… unpleasant… but they say it will heal after a while."

"Excellent prognosis." MacArthur paused. "I put you in for a DSC—a Distinguished Service Cross—for what you did for Major Anderson. Unfortunately, it was turned down—not enough witnesses. Sorry."

"Not a problem, Sir. I wasn't trying to be a hero anyhow—just trying to stay alive."

MacArthur held up his hand. "But you were a hero, Lieutenant. What you did for Major Anderson was a heroic act. And you should be rewarded for it."

"I was, Sir. I'm alive and so is Dodger—I mean Major Anderson, Sir. That's reward enough. Mission accomplished."

MacArthur stood and placed his hand on Henry's shoulder. "Well, nevertheless, I'll see what I can do about it at a later date." He strode out of the ward.

CHAPTER FIFTY-TWO

Sunday, April 20, 1919
Building B, GHQAEF
Chaumont, France

The Model R Hupmobile four-cylinder staff car bounced along the cobblestones of the highway, slowing to turn into the grand gateway shielding the higher beings of the General Headquarters, American Expeditionary Forces, from the outside world and the enlisted riff-raff. The weather had been wet and muddy, a typical Rhineland late spring, but it cleared and warmed the afternoon they had received the call to proceed forthwith to Chaumont. At least it wasn't bitterly cold as it had been the last time the Lieutenant who was sitting in the front seat had taken this highway. That time the trip had turned into an extended and frustrating trek to rejoin his command after his discharge from the First Army Field Hospital in December.

At the time it should have been a simple matter to catch a ride on one of the hundreds of GMC or Mack trucks heading up the highway toward the German border, that is, the River Rhine, and the Army of Occupation with its headquarters in Coblenz, Germany. Four days later, Henry had finally stumbled across the officer he was looking for, now sitting serenely in the back seat of the Hup, watching as the car moved past huge, empty fields of freshly mown grass, fields large enough for thousands of men to stand in ranks therein—which is essentially what they had done—and have some dozens of prominent dignitaries look at them while their commander handed out the victors' laurels—the few scraps of cloth, as Napoleon had called them. The Lieutenant, whose hospital ward had been only a half a mile or so from this very spot, had been able to hear the cheering when he wasn't coughing up green slime into a bucket.

The officer in the back seat leaned forward. "You may pull across the courtyard and stop in front of the main doorway, Private."

"Yes, Sir," the diminutive driver said, grinning when the Lieutenant murmured, softly enough for only him to hear, "Don't tip the damn car over, Cohen. The Army will make you pay for it now the war's over."

Private Aaron Cohen, late and hopefully soon again, of Brooklyn, Noo Yawk, was one of the survivors of the Headquarters Platoon of the 84th Brigade. Like all the other survivors—there were seven of the original fifty-six, though not all of them had been killed, only wounded badly enough to be sent home and discharged—was happier than hell when Lieutenant Feller had returned to Headquarters, and when they got out from under the thumb of that dipshit second looey, Tibbets, the Adjutant had stuck them with. Even when the Lieutenant had been grafted into being the CO's junior aide, he still remained in charge of the HQ Platoon, and that made life a helluva lot easier on all concerned.

Cohen had joined the army in July of 1917, straight out of his job as a meat grinder for Nathan's Kosher Meats. Now he wasn't so sure he wanted to go back to it, not after everything he had seen in France. Though he was the first to admit, after three or four glasses of Van Rooj, that having been a meat cutter had pretty much kept him from hurling his cookies on several occasions. Maybe in a few years he'd be able to philosophize about his experiences with his brother, Isaac, the rabbinical scholar, but for now he mostly wanted to forget what he had seen, and just go home, thanking God he was alive. He had been in the shell crater when the Lieutenant was hit and had dragged his buddy from the Ammo Train into cover, and he had ended up in charge of the rest when Corporal Mienkiewicz had tried to get over to the CO and had been cut in half by the same machine gun that got the Lieutenant. Cohen didn't remember much of anything after that. But General MacArthur had gotten him a citation for his records and he could wear a little silver star on his rainbow ribbon—or whatever the hell they called it. His being a Private though, meant an Officer would have to run the platoon. And Tibbets had been a real asshole. So they were all really happy to see their bedraggled, muddy, wet Lieutenant when he pushed the billet door open in Adhenau. That asshole Tibbets would have had them all pop to attention and salute and whatever other chickenshit stuff he could think of.

Lieutenant Feller had stuck his head in the door and grinned when he saw Cohen. "No offense, Cohen, but Jesus Christ, I'm glad to *finally* see someone I recognize." And then they had all swarmed around him, slapping him on the back and saying as how glad they was he was alive and come back. And he had fished a bottle of *real* booze out of his bag and gave them all a snort.

Cohen now drove the Hupmobile carefully around the driveway forming the perimeter of the courtyard of the four-story building that, he figured, housed the part of GHQ AEF the General wanted to go to. Fastened to the wall at the top of the steps leading to the entrance was a square sign painted white, with a big black letter "B" painted on it. Cohen mused, it was there so non-chauffeured field-grade officers could find Building B without getting lost. When the car came to a stop, Cohen set the hand brake, jumped out, and ran around to open the door for the officer in the back seat. Cohen played the army game for officers loitering around the entrance to the building. He held the door with his left hand, offered a perfect salute with his right as General MacArthur alighted from the runningboard. Lieutenant Feller stepped out of the front seat without Cohen's assistance and awaited his General's wishes.

MacArthur smoothed his uniform and, with a wave of his swagger stick, led Feller up the steps of the Headquarters building. Feller called back over his shoulder, "Park it, Cohen, and don't let anyone steal it."

The statement drew a few odd looks from the "stoop sitters". "Yes, Sir," Cohen called back, saluting.

Feller returned the salute and followed his General into the building.

Inside, beyond a reception area with its requisite directory, was a wide corridor leading toward the rear of the building. Marble staircases flanked both sides, and intersecting corridors led to both wings. Before Feller could move ahead and look up the office number on the directory, however, a hatless, grey-haired, slim officer wearing the four stars of a full General on his epaulets rose from one of the couches in the reception area and walked quickly toward MacArthur, his hand extended in greeting.

MacArthur's face lit up in delight. "Peyton, Old Man, it is so good to see you," he said warmly. "Whatever, are you doing here? I thought you'd be stuck in Sodom-on-the-Potomac."

"I'm just passing through here. I'm on my way to see General Liggett in Coblenz and General Bliss in Paris, then I'm heading right back to the States. Perhaps we'll be on the same ship?"

"Do you know something I don't, Peyton?"

"As a matter of fact I do, Douglas."

Henry Feller was standing two paces behind and to the right of his general when MacArthur suddenly realized he had forgotten his manners. Before pressing the other general officer for more information, he turned and motioned toward Henry. "May I present my junior aide, Lieutenant Henry Feller."

Henry snapped a salute, which the other officer returned before extending his hand. Once they were close enough to shake hands, the other general suddenly grew a look of recognition as Douglas MacArthur continued the introduction.

"Lieutenant Feller, this is General Peyton March, Chief of Staff of the United States Army." MacArthur then noticed the look of recognition on March's face, and his own took on a look of bewilderment.

"I believe Lieutenant Feller and I are already acquainted," March said.

"Yes, Sir," Henry said, nodding agreement. "We met the first time, I believe, near the Chinese Cemetery, just north of Manila. Must have been in...what? January? No, February, of '99. The General was, at the time, also an aide to a general."

Peyton March shook Henry's hand nearly as warmly as he had shaken Douglas MacArthur's.

"And was still, even when *that* general's son, a freshly frocked Second Lieutenant just out of West Point, arrived in the Philippines," MacArthur went on. "It seems as though we have *all* known each other for almost a fifth of a century."

"If I might be so bold, Feller," March said, "aren't you a little long-in-the-tooth to still be a Lieutenant?"

"No offense, Sir, but I'm strictly a 'part-time' officer. I will cease being a Lieutenant just as soon as I can shed the uniform and go back to being a writer. In fact, I hadn't intended to even be a Lieutenant, again, until *this* General MacArthur rescued me from the clutches of the Judge Advocate who intended to see I was stood before a firing squad."

Douglas MacArthur laughed. "True. True. It's truly an amazing story, General. Lieutenant Feller here deserves several citations for his accomplishments, but I don't think my boss would go along with at least one of them."

"Which one is that?" General March asked.

Henry was fairly certain March had heard of Pershing's withholding of the Medal of Honor from MacArthur while awarding one to Colonel Donovan, a regimental commander in the 83rd Brigade, for far less heroic action, at least by Henry's way of thinking. So March couldn't be certain whatever MacArthur said didn't come from some bitterness, albeit Douglas's esteem for John Pershing.

MacArthur grinned slyly. "Why, the Iron Cross First Class, of course," he said, laughing, but at March's perplexed look. "It seems General Pershing also remembers Lieutenant Feller from the Philippines. If I hadn't stepped in, I think he would have gone along with the desires of the Judge Advocate, that little lawyer fellow."

The conversation lasted a few more minutes, dominated by MacArthur and March. Lieutenants do not interrupt Generals. But Henry left the encounter with an invitation, by way of accompanying his General, to dinner with the Chief of Staff and a promise that, there, he could tell his entire story in detail.

From there they had found the third floor office and were met by an extremely judicious Colonel who handed MacArthur a sheaf of orders informing him he had been relieved of command of the 42nd Division. He should proceed as soon as possible via government transportation to Brest, France, from there to embark for the United States of America, where he would assume command of the United States Military Academy at West Point, New York. General MacArthur thanked the Colonel and led Henry out of the office.

As they walked down the marble stairs to the first floor, MacArthur quietly said "I don't know whether I should cheer or cry. Leading the Rainbow in combat has been the best experience of my life, and now it's over. I think General March had something to do with it, with choosing me for the command. I think it is meant to salve not getting the Medal of Honor."

"Possibly," Henry agreed, not sure whether MacArthur was either interested in, or even wanted, his opinion. *Well, in for a penny,* he thought and plunged on. "You're still the most decorated soldier in the AEF, Sir, and I don't recall seeing anywhere in those orders you've been reduced to your permanent grade in the Regular Army. You are going as a Brigadier General, with a good chance of getting your second star in the Regulars if you do your usual outstanding job." Henry tried very hard not to sound like a sycophant, but that *was* his assessment of the orders, regardless of being a lowly Lieutenant.

"You don't think Pershing withheld the Medal out of spite, then?" MacArthur asked offhanded.

"I think General Pershing is fully capable of both holding a personal grudge and setting impossible standards for his subordinates, since you put it that way, Sir. But, no, in this case I think he simply felt you had enough *other* decorations and by his standards you didn't do anything all exceptional 'above and beyond' what he expected from you in your position."

"Did I ever tell you what he said to me when he gave us the order to attack at St Miheil?"

"No, Sir, you didn't."

"Oh, of course not. You were already in the hospital by then. He said, 'Give me Chatillon, MacArthur, or a list of 5,000 casualties.' And I replied, "All right, General, we'll take it, or my name will head the list." MacArthur paused having trouble finding his voice.

"The challenge was daunting, my friend," MacArthur finally managed. "Embedded in the Cote de Chatillon were 230 machine gun nests. Protected from artillery by pillboxes. Protected from advancing troops by coils of barbed wire often 25 feet deep. The night before the attack, I organized a small patrol to probe for weak spots. We had not gone far in the darkness when the enemy opened up with everything he had available. I discovered a thin spot in the wire where we could hope to cut through. Then I whispered 'Get up when I give the signal—I will lead you back to our lines.' But when I gave the command, no one stirred. I crawled along from shell hole to shell hole. I took hold of each man and shook him. They were all stone dead, my friend. I made my way back alone, with God's help. The next day we took our objective." MacArthur fell silent here and made no further comment on the subject.

Coming from anyone but Douglas MacArthur, Henry realized, the statement would have sounded like pure puffery, but Henry also had no doubt at all it was a verbatim restatement of the original conversation.

Since it was now only a little past three in the afternoon, and their dinner engagement with General March wasn't until seven thirty, it meant they would have to find something to do other than sit in a *bistro* and slug down cheap wine or expensive cognac. As they approached their Hupmobile, Cohen, who had been leaning on a fender smoking a cigarette, saw them coming and flipped the butt away before bracing to attention and saluting. *There must still be other officers watching*, Henry thought. Henry and MacArthur returned Cohen's salute, and Douglas climbed into the back seat through the opened rear door.

Before Cohen could run around the car to the driver's seat, however, Henry stopped him. "Sit on the right, Cohen," Henry ordered. "I'll drive."

"Gee, Sir, I don't know if I'm allowed to do that," Cohen protested. "I think it's against regulations."

"Cohen," Henry asked, "who are 'they' going to turn you in to? Your Division CO? Why don't you ask him? He's sitting in the back seat, waiting for us to get this show on the road."

"I don't know, Sir…"

"Of course you don't know, Cohen—you're only a private. You're not supposed to know anything. Just get in and shut up."

Reluctantly, Cohen climbed into the front seat, shaking his head and watching as Henry stepped on the Bendix starter button and adjusted the spark until the engine fired. Henry quickly pulled away from the other staff cars clustered around one side of the courtyard and drove swiftly down the cobble driveway and out the gate, turning right onto the main highway heading into the center of Chaumont.

"Ever been into Chaumont, Cohen?"

"No, Sir."

"Well, I was here from September until December. The last month they even let me out of the hospital so I could walk around and either get my strength back or die of pneumonia, they never explained which." Henry heard General MacArthur's snort from the back seat. "The enlisted billets are in the center of town in one wing of the Hotel Carcassonne. But even better might be getting a room at the Transient NCO quarters at the Hotel Reine."

Cohen turned on the seat so he could be heard over the sound of the Hup on the gravel road. "That'd be nice, Lieutenant, but I ain't no NCO." Cohen's voice was trying not to sound too bitter. He had been up for Corporal, but that asshole Tibbets, who was from someplace down south—Louisiana or Alabama or someplace like that—had taken an instant dislike to him. According to Tibbets, Cohen was just a little New York Yankee Jewboy. So, no Corporal.

Lieutenant Feller feigned stupidity as he said, "Oh, yeah—I forgot."

Cohen shook his head and suddenly felt someone tap him on the shoulder. That someone could only be his division commander, General MacArthur, so when Cohen turned on the seat to look at what the General wanted, MacArthur was found to be passing him a fairly hefty envelope. As Cohen took the envelope from General MacArthur's hand, the General asked Lieutenant Feller if he knew where there was a tailor in Chaumont, and when the Lieutenant said sure he knew right off where one was, the General said to take them there. Then the General said that way Sergeant Cohen could get his uniform properly prepared, because it was lacking a lot of the things that it was supposed to have on it—like the wound chevron and the Sergeant stripes and the overseas stripes and the Rainbow patch.

When Cohen looked in the envelope, all that shit was in there, including an extract from the orders promoting him to Sergeant. And the General said he could use those to get a room at the NCO billet so it wouldn't cost him hardly anything.

"I think you'll be interested to know, Sergeant," said the General, "that Lieutenant Tibbets, who is a fine young officer, has been reassigned to the duties he was trained to perform—as a platoon officer in a negro company in the Service of Supply. Furthermore, Lieutenant Feller here is leaving with me—I've been reassigned. Therefore, you'll be in charge of the Headquarters Platoon until the Division re-embarks for the States. You're a credit to the Rainbow, Sergeant, and I'm proud to have commanded men such as you."

And then the General shook his hand and patted him on the back, and the Lieutenant, grinning like a damned idiot, even though this was the first he had heard he was going back to the States, shook his hand and said congratulations. It was a story Aaron Cohen loved to tell at VFW Post 107 and to his kids and grandkids and great grandkids until the day he died in 1975.

They dropped newly minted Sergeant Cohen off at the NCO billet, and then Henry drove out of Chaumont to a site he had found on one of his walks from the hospital. Chaumont—actually the town's full name was Chaumont-en-Bassigny, but no member of the AEF was ever known to call it that—sits on a ridge running between the rivers Marne and Suiz. In places the ridge drops away precipitously, and Henry chose to pull the Hup off the road at one of the steeper spots. The view was stupendous. In one direction they were looking down into the valley of the Marne, in the other, literally separated by only the few yards of the road's width, was an equally impressive view of the valley of the Suiz. To the west, toward the next major town, Troyes, the railroad crossed the river valley on a spectacular masonry viaduct whose arches appeared to be several hundred feet above the river. Behind them rose the huge grey stone Gothic *Basilique St-Jean-Baptiste,* eight or nine hundred years old, Henry couldn't remember which. After admiring the view, Henry drove them back into Chaumont by side streets, barely wide enough to allow the automobile to pass. Henry pointed out the same architectural feature the Medical Corps Doctor who had been his escort the first few times he was allowed out of the hospital had pointed out to him: the bulging towers of the houses that showed the shapes of the large spiral interior staircases on the outside of the buildings.

They arrived early at *Hotel Le Terminus Reine* with its adjoining restaurant *La Chaufferie*. They were bowed and scraped to. Actually, Douglas was bowed and scraped to Henry just followed along, making sure he wasn't suddenly inundated by his General's glory. One of the bower and scrapers was the head waiter who had been around the AEF long enough to recognize American insignia and rank. They were shown to a smallish table and there sampled a bottle of some of the local Van Rooj—the dough's fractured French for red wine—chatting until MacArthur saw General March enter the place escorting a lady, and waved to them.

CHAPTER FIFTY-THREE

Sunday, April 20, 1919
La Chaufferie, Hotel Le Terminus Reine
Chaumont, France

*A*s March and his companion moved toward the table, Henry first
noticed the obvious differences in their ages. The female was thirty-ish,
with dark bobbed hair of the newest style fad, covered by a small hat. She
had vivid dark eyes and a moon-shaped face. The collar of her coat was mink
and silver fox laid on in two rows to form a stripe effect. The coat cuffs were
mink. The lady was, by her outer garments in any case, well heeled. Henry
vaguely remembered his mother's silver fox coat had made his father blanch
when he received the bill.

When he appeared to attend them, the lady shrugged out of her coat
and casually handed it to the waiter for him to store until it was called
for. From the look on the waiter's face, Henry could see the man did not
like to be treated as a coat-rack, but the waiter held his tongue. With
her coat removed, Henry could see her other garments also reflected
money—and plenty of it. Her silk dress was obviously Parisian in cut
and style, and the setting in the multi-strand pearl choker held a center
gem Henry guesstimated to be worth about five years' pay for a First
Lieutenant. The dress and pearls adorned a female who was neither
slim nor plump, but who seemed to exude her femininity much like the
Parisian *parfum* that scented the air around her as she moved to take
the seat.

"General Douglas MacArthur and Lieutenant Feller, his aide," he
said as he held the chair for her. "This, gentlemen, is Missus Louise
Brooks. We happened to run into one another after I left you, and
I thought it might make for more civilized dinner conversation if she
joined us."

Missus Brooks nodded graciously to MacArthur, who, Henry
noticed when he glanced his General's way, suddenly had that old
familiar look in his eyes—the look of a stag in rut.

General March seated himself next to Henry, explaining he wanted to hear all of the strange details of Henry's hinted-at story. "I'm an old red-legged cannon-cocker. My ears went bad on me years ago, so I think I'll sit here to better hear what you have to say," he said as he slid into the seat next to Henry. "Now tell me, Lieutenant—what was so strange about your service Douglas there could make a joke about your not being able to receive…what was it? The Iron Cross First Class?"

Through the soup, a bit of *fromage,* and two more bottles of Van Rooj—which General March relayed to Missus Brooks as being the Doughboy pronunciation for *Vin Rouge*—a small offering of fish, a very nice serving of veal, a little more *fromage,* a small serving of *paté,* coffee throughout, and a most excellent cognac. Henry regaled General March with stories about his service in the South Dakota National Guard, his being trapped in German East Africa, his time with the *Schutztruppen,* his release by Paul Von Lettow-Vorbeck, and his subsequent arrest and rescue, reinstatement, and wounding. As he was telling his story, two things struck Henry about General March. One was the General's real interest in his problem, and the other was the fact General March's eyes reflected a very quiet but nearly overwhelming sadness.

In the background, Henry heard the constant chatter between Missus Brooks and MacArthur. From what he overheard, Missus Brooks was, or had been, married to a banker and was now in the process of waiting out some legalities having to do with her children's—there were two, a boy and a girl—trust funds. She had moved out of his house and come to Paris, where they had a suite in one of the hotels. She had lived in Paris for most of the last two years and knew *everybody*— Pershing, March, Tasker Bliss, Hugh Scott, Marshall Foch, General Haig, General Allenby—all of a class. She loved to entertain, maybe even *lived* to entertain, and there was considerable mention of "Daddy," her step-father, providing the wherewithal to keep her in a style to which she was obviously accustomed. Missus Brooks didn't strike Henry as being either overly bright or a particularly good conversationalist. Henry wondered what had toggled Douglas's horny switch. He was pretty sure they weren't playing footsy under the table. She was no raving beauty—she wasn't ugly, by any means, but she was no Lilian

Gish either. She was louder than necessary in a condescending down-her-nose, I'm-rich-therefore-important sort of way so it was impossible to not overhear her.

Once Henry had managed to tell General March everything he could about his service—March had pulled a small notebook from his tunic pocket and jotted notes from time to time, repeating the names and dates and other facts back to Henry to make certain he had heard them correctly. Then they joined the other conversation in progress. In fact, just in time to hear Douglas MacArthur order a magnum of *Champagne Pommery Cuvée Louise* 1907. Henry was happy he did not have to drive them anywhere after drinking most of it. About midnight they staggered back to their adjoining rooms. The hotel did not offer suites—Douglas MacArthur had been a snorer of the first stripe in the Philippines and probably hadn't improved with age.

The walls between the rooms were about the same thickness as a piece of writing paper. Henry was nearly asleep when the music of human conjugal pleasures began to filter through the wall. Toward the end of the gasping and groaning and squealing, Henry was tempted to applaud the performance, but managed to control his champagne-induced urge and simply pulled the pillow over his head so he didn't have to hear the encore.

It took them another day for Sergeant Cohen to drive them back to the Rainbow Division Headquarters and get their travel papers and get their kits prepared for packing and loading. On the way, Henry asked his General about Peyton March's sad eyes.

"Oh heavens, my friend, you have no idea—Peyton had only one son, his wife died right after his return from the Philippines, he never remarried, raising the lad all by himself. A splendid young man—joined up at the outset of the War and volunteered for the aviation section of the signal corps. He was killed in a flying accident last spring, just before Peyton was made Chief of Staff. "

Henry was sorry he had asked.

The Chevrolet six-cylinder truck with their trunks—most belonging to General MacArthur—was sent on ahead, since it would take the truck at least an additional day to cross France to Brest. Henry,

MacArthur, and the other members of the staff were a day in making their farewells. This included MacArthur's official printed farewell address to the assembled Division, distributed to all of its various and widely spread-out posts by his junior aide. Thereby Henry missed the teary-eyed farewell given to whatever troops could be assembled to hear it.

CHAPTER FIFTY-FOUR

Monday, April 28, 1919
Aboard the *USS Pueblo* (CA-7)
Atlantic Ocean

T he trip to Brest was unhurried and meandering. They were driven to
Troyes, where they boarded one of the French National Railway trains,
changing in Paris to the Brest Boat-Train, running again for the first time since
1914. After many stops, many whistle shrieks, and much violent swaying
of the carriages—not much larger than the quarante et huit [10] boxcars
transporting the enlisted swine and draft animals. They arrived in Brest
then taxied to the pier where, surprise of surprises, they were united with
their luggage and assigned to their cabins aboard the USS Pueblo. Henry
wasn't certain, but he was nearly convinced the Pueblo was a renaming of
one of the ships that had hauled troops to the Philippines in '98. She was
about as small, and even with only a battalion of the 117th Engineers sharing
the berthing deck, as crowded. During the night, Henry felt the engines begin
to make power, and by morning they were well out in the Atlantic, with the
Ile de Seine just peeking over the horizon on the port side.

By the fourth day out, the *Pueblo* had admitted her age, but she had
fairly new engines for they were making fifteen knots or more. She
had begun service as the Armored Cruiser *Colorado* in 1903, and had
been overhauled and renamed in 1916. She was now "CA-7" and they
could put on full cruising power when they got out into the Atlantic
proper. They were essentially crossing the lower end of the English
Channel, and there was just too much shipping crossing their path to
make decent speed. When they cleared the traffic, they were planning
on a steady pace of 20 knots because the sailors were just as anxious to
get back to the States as the soldiers. By the afternoon of the next day
out, the ship's speed made standing at any part of the rail facing the
bow a bracing experience. Her four funnels belched a steady stream
of black smoke trailing above their wake. Scuttlebutt, the shipboard
rumor system, had them making the crossing in less than ten days.

On the morning of the eighth day out, Henry woke up with a slight fever and a scratchy throat. By the noonday meal, his nasal cavity was producing mucous faster than he could blow it into a handkerchief, a tissue paper, or over the rail. When he looked at himself in a mirror, his eyes were puffy and watering. His forehead felt hot to the touch. *Goddamned cold*, he muttered to himself before dosing himself with a copious pour from the illegal bottle of Calvados he was smuggling into the United States, contrary to the Volstead Act. Other than making him nauseous, the liquor didn't do him a helluva lot of good.

By early evening, his knees and ankles were swelling, and his elbows and wrists ached almost unbearably. During the night he kicked off his covers but was immediately chilled when his sweat soaked pajamas were exposed to the air. He stumbled out of bed to close the portholes, only to find they were already dogged shut. He did not make it back to the bed.

The colored mess steward making his morning rounds, found him on the deck. Henry had lost control of his bowels and had emptied the contents of his stomach onto the deck. The stench was what had attracted the steward, and he immediately sent up a yell for help. It took three other sailors and the steward to roll the dead weight onto a stretcher and negotiate their way to the infirmary through the labyrinth of passageways. There the ship's Doctor had him cleaned up and then performed a hasty examination.

When Henry awoke, or came to—he was never certain which—the ship's Doctor told him he was running a fever of a little over 102 degrees. By then, all movement was painful. Henry's first question to the Doctor was whether or not it was polio. The Doctor was certain it wasn't. If it was polio, Henry would have lost use of whatever limb, or limbs, were affected, and be numb, not in continuous pain in all his joints. The Doctor didn't know exactly what the hell it was, but no, it was not polio. At first, he thought was Spanish Influenza, but the one part of Henry that did *not* seem to be affected was his lungs. There was no sign of pneumonia, even considering the gas scarring. They would keep him in sick bay until they docked in New York, and then they would transfer him to the Hospital at the Brooklyn Navy Yard. And no, he wouldn't get his discharge until *after* his release from the hospital. Henry, in his present condition, was simply too weak to protest.

The *Pueblo* steamed through the Narrows on the morning of the ninth day—scuttlebutt for once being dead nuts on. Henry, even with a fever of 103+, saw the Statue of Liberty out of sickbay's portside porthole and guessed they were heading for the Brooklyn Navy Yard. He was lifted onto another stretcher and carried to the deck by four sailors. At the bottom of the gangplank, waiting for a Cadillac ambulance to back up to them, Henry caught the eye of a Chief Petty Officer. The Chief moseyed over to the stretcher. Henry asked the Chief to please hand him his musette bag lying on the stretcher beyond his reach. The Chief found it for him and Henry pulled out a paper-wrapped package about the size of a bottle of Calvados. The Chief leaned down close to hear over the background noise of the dock.

"Chief, I have a confession to make. I was going to try to smuggle this into the country. It contains an illegal substance, but I don't see how that will be possible now. So I'm turning it in to you for disposal." Henry surreptitiously passed the Chief the package.

The Chief quickly tucked it into his medical aid bag. "Yes, Sir. You've done the right thing. I'll see it gets disposed of, Sir."

Henry and the Chief nodded to one another as Henry's stretcher was loaded into the waiting ambulance.

CHAPTER FIFTY-FIVE

Monday, May 12, 1919
Brooklyn Naval Hospital
Brooklyn, New York

Commander (Medical Service) USN Floyd D. Carter, head of the Epidemiology Department, leaned against the marble windowsill in the Doctors' annex, wondering why the Navy had decided he should be concerned with the Army officer presently abed in his ward. The Lieutenant was an anomaly. He had been brought in on the order of the Navy Department two week before. The memo from the ship's Doctor on the—Carter looked at the note—the USS Pueblo, old CA-7—stated the ship's Doctor did not think the officer was suffering from Spanish Influenza. But rather than take a chance...

So now this Army Lieutenant was taking up a bed that could be used to save someone who *was* afflicted by the Spanish Influenza, like the *other* 187 patients presently in the ward, many of them in far more serious condition. Since the beginning of the epidemic, in August of 1918, Commander Carter had watched several thousand sailors suddenly sicken, develop pneumonia, and in all too many cases, die. In a matter of hours. The disease, oddly enough, targetted the young and healthy. Carter couldn't recall having treated anyone over the age of forty here or at Brooklyn General, where he was a visiting Doctor. But he was certain there had been deaths in that age group as well, only fewer of them. He put the total number of deaths to the back of his mind, not wanting to think of just how really bad the Flu epidemic was. Yet there was the nagging notion if he had had hundreds die in one Navy hospital, in one city, in one country, there was probably no way to know the exact total of deaths worldwide, but undoubtedly in the millions. Such thoughts, however, didn't help him treat the sick men in his ward here and now.

Lieutenant (Medical Service) USNR, Michael Trautman, one of the many Naval Reserve officers assigned to duty in Commander

Carter's ward, was also leaning against a handy flat surface, in this case a table. He was perusing the thin manila folder containing the records of the Army officer someone in the Army had seen fit to finally deliver. He tossed the folder onto the table and looked over to his commanding officer.

"Shit," he said, "that doesn't tell me any more than I already know— less in fact. There's nothing in there about his being in Africa."

"I noticed that, too," Carter said. "That, and the fact it's a great military void for most of the time covered by his records. Nothing at all from 1909 until 1917, late in 1917, when he was assigned to a command in the 42nd Division."

"Maybe some of his records were lost?" Trautman wondered.

"It's a possibility."

"Now, if this were a Navy or Marine Corps record jacket," Trautman went on, "there would be another explanation."

"And that would be?" Commander Carter asked.

"According to Rocks and Shoals[11]," Trautman began, "if he had been acquitted by a court-martial, he would have had his record jacket expunged and a new one made up. I really don't know if the army does the same thing or not. But it might explain the new record jacket and the absence of so much stuff." Trautman shrugged.

"So where did Africa come into this enlightening conversation?" Carter asked.

Trautman's face took on a blank expression. He was trying hard to remember having mentioned something that odd, but he, as well as Commander Carter, were on the verge of exhaustion. The ward was meant to handle a maximum of forty patients, not nearly two hundred, less the few who had died during the night—more paperwork to do before they could catch a catnap…

"Oh, yeah—he told me." Trautman finally remembered where he had picked up that bit of information. "He said he had been in East Africa until '17. I never got around to asking what he had been doing there. Why?"

"Because after forty-six years of eventful life, I have suddenly, within a month, run into the first two people I've ever met who have actually been in Africa." Carter pushed off from the window sill and walked to the large coffee urn setting on a soapstone sideboard. He took two cups from a tray and poured them both full of Navy coffee. He handed one of the steaming mugs to Trautman. "I went up to Hartford about a month ago, to the Veteran's Hospital up there, to hear a lecture by one of their visiting Doctors. He's been doing a lot of work on the epidemic and has a hell of a background in epidemic diseases, most of which he studied in East Africa, where he was with the British Army from 1915 until sometime in 1918. The gist of the lecture was, if you study some of the more virulent African diseases, you should be able to spot Spanish Influenza right off, because they're not similar in most cases."

Trautman took a sip of his coffee and made a face. The black fluid was strong enough to float a battleship. "So you think our special case is more in the purview of Doctor...? He gestured.

"Oh—sorry. His name...I have it somewhere. I'll have to look in my notes."

"And then?"

"And then, I think we will give the good Doctor something to work with, as well as free up a bed at the same time..."

CHAPTER FIFTY-SIX

Wednesday, May 14, 1919
Hartford Veterans Hospital
Hartford, Connecticut

D octor Robert Valentine Dolbey, until recently Major R.V. Dolbey, *Royal Medical Corps, finished reading the transfer report come into the hospital with the patient.*

Stapled to the official transfer were letters, notes and a treatment record from the Director of the Epidemic Medicine Department at the Brooklyn Naval Hosital, the patient's first stop. He had been admitted after taking sick aboard the ship bringing him back to the United States—bit of bad luck, that. There was also a note from another of the Naval Doctors with additional information not found in the man's records. Essentially, the Doctor had said the officer had been in East Africa for three years—odd, Dolbey couldn't recall ever having met any Americans while he had been with Slim Jani's column—and the Naval Doctor, a Jewish fellow by his name, had thought whatever was wrong with this patient might have been caused by exposure to or something picked up there and dormant. In other words, the naval Doctors didn't have the time or knowledge to fool with unknown diseases and had passed the case on to Hartford and its eminent tropical disease specialist. How very wonderful, indeed.

The patient had come in by ambulance that morning—meaning they had hustled him out of the Brooklyn Naval Hospital in the middle of the night. So he had bounced along in the ambulance all night to arrive here when he had. Bloody nice of the Navy to do that for him. Still, better than riding in a springless two-wheeled cart pulled by a pair of oxen across a mud track for some hundreds of miles. That had been the *mode du jour* for moving wounded and sick across the bundu. It was a bloody miracle any of them had survived. Of course, many had not. Dolbey had often thought it would have been far more merciful to let them die quickly and in peace where they fell, like his friend Fred Selous and so many others had, when they chased old Von Lettow all the way across German East, from Kilimanjaro to the Rufiji and beyond, all the way to the border of Portugese East.

It had been a beastly place to fight a war. They had taken ten times the losses from disease than they had from the Hun. And then the very flora and fauna had been against them—well, no less against them than against the Hun in any case. The lions were particularly bad, as were the cape buffalo and rhinos—and along the coast the elephants. Dolbey shuddered, remembering the screams and shrieks of the outposts that were suddenly set upon by a lion pride. In the mornings they would find nothing but blood trails and scrapes where the beasts had dragged away their victims.

Dolbey's shoes squeaked on the highly polished floor of the hallway leading through the ward. He had ordered the patient prepped when he came in, and was glad to see two of the competent Nurses were on duty in the ward. They had reported to work at Hartford fresh out of their nursing schools, the younger one from the University of Connecticut and the older—a widow who had gone back to school to receive her certificate when her husband had been killed in France—from Massachusetts General. Dolbey wondered how the younger Nurse had managed to have herself assigned so close to home, and when he had asked, he found out she had graduated fron Connecticut but was actually from a small town in Kentucky, whereever that might be, somewhere to the west among the red Indians, he supposed. In any case, compared to some of the other Nurses on this ward, these two were competent and seemed to actually care about the patients.

The patient, an army lieutenant according to his records, was lying in his bed apparently dozing when Doctor Dolbey entered the room and picked up the record package from a wire hanger wrapped around the metal bed frame. He glanced at the particulars—temperature 102.5, pulse 98. Starting with the top of the officer's head, Dolbey began a very careful and thorough examination. Chest: lungs sounded as one would expect from someone who had, according to his records, been treated for inhalation of phosgene gas, but not the usual sounds of pneumonia. Abdomen: no swelling. No liver sensitivity. Oho! Entrance wound scar above the liver on the right side. No obvious exit scar. Probably around back. Genitalia: no lesions or superation—the officer may not be pure, but he is at least careful. Hips: sensitivity to lateral and direct pressure. Knees: swelling. Obvious sensitivity—quite apparent by the swift inhalation of breath and stifled groan. Ankles: swelling. Only slightly less sensitivity to pressure. Feet: Ah! Interesting. Small scars. Many small scars. A quick re-check of the ankles and knees. More small scars, so small they were missed on the first look.

Doctor Dolbey quickly jotted some notes on the record sheet and hung it back on the bed. He dug his pipe and tobacco pouch out of his jacket pocket and carefully filled his pipe with his favorite Latakia. Using an old issue trench lighter he puffed his pipe to life and sat down in the chair next to the bed to wait until the patient regained a semblance of consciousness.

As the pain from his hips and knees slowly subsided, Henry Feller opened his eyes to find himself in a strange hospital room and enveloped in a cloud of aromatic smoke that smelled very much unlike the camphor the Navy people had spread all over hell and gone in the Flu ward. He had his last completely conscious thought, just before two very large white hats had grabbed him and began to move him off of his bed. That was the last thing he remembered completely, other than the endless bouncing and the noise of a motor. He had gone back under when they had begun to move him again, and he vaguely remembered a female voice trying to cut through the fog of his private hell. Christ, this damned disease was worse than being shot.

Henry eyes began to focus on shapes farther away than the end of his own nose. Slowly, he realized someone was in the room with him, and so he carefully moved his head to bring the side of the bed into focus. Sitting in the chair was a slim man in a white hospital smock, unbuttoned to reveal the tweed jacket underneath. His legs were crossed, and he was writing on a tablet held on his knees while puffing on a large pipe, the source of the aromatic smoke. His hair was combed straight back, thinning at the top and greying at the sides. Henry quessed he was in his late forties or early fifties. And something about him told Henry he was not an American.

Dolbey looked up and noticed Henry was back in the real world. "Ah," he said, "back amongst us I see." *British.*

"I'm not sure," Henry answered, "I suppose that depends on where *us* is."

"Right-o." the man chuckled. *"Kwa muda gani una matatizo haya—* how long have you been sick?" he asked suddenly.

*"Leo tarehe gani—*what day is it?" Henry answered without thinking. Then he looked at the man with questioning eyes.

"Just checking. Your records didn't mention BEA, and so I thought it would be easiest to see if you understood Swahili, which you obviously do. When were you in BEA? And, oh yes, it's Wednesday, the fourteenth of May."

Henry looked at the Doctor. "First things first. They hauled me off the ship on April 28th. So I guess that means I've been sick for a little over two weeks, sixteen days, something like that. As for the other, we may have a problem. Up until the summer of 1917, I considered you my enemy."

"Oh, really? And could you explain to me how I managed to offend you so badly when I believe this is the first time we've ever met?"

"I wasn't in BEA, at least not this time."

"Well, it's plain to me that you were somewhere in Africa, somewhere along the Swahili Coast, to be more specific."

"German East."

"Oh?"

"The first time, BEA—that was in 1909 and 1910—I was with President Roosevelt's safari. This time I was trapped in German East when the war broke out. I tried to leave but the war breaking out caused our ship to head back back into Dar. I was, am, a correspondent, a writer by trade, and I was kept out of harm's way by Governor Schnee and *Oberst* Von Lettow-Vorbeck—until you people moved in and we had to beat tracks down south." Henry stopped. *"Ninaona kinzunguzungu—*I feel dizzy."

"Nauseous?" the Doctor asked.

Henry nodded.

"Had the runs?"

Again Henry nodded.

The Doctor so noted on the tablet. Then he reached into the pocket of his smock and pulled out a bottle. From it he poured several pills into his hand. "Open your mouth," he commanded, popping two into Henry's waiting maw.

Henry made a face, tried to grab for the water glass on the bedside table, and nearly fainted. Dolbey took the glass for him, and holding his head, allowed him to drink enough water to swallow the pills and get the taste out of his mouth.

"Nasty little blighters, but they should ease the spasms and allow you to sleep for a while. I'll have the Nurses put you on regular dosings for a couple of days, and then we can tell one another war stories." Dolbey stuffed his pipe and tobacco pouch into his jacket pocket and started toward the door, stopping when Henry called after him.

"I don't have influenza, do I?"

Dolbey turned. "No. You have a couple of very nasty things wrong with you, but *not* the flu. Get some rest. You're not the first one I've treated for this, but it has been a while—going on three years. If it makes you feel any better, you're still alive. That's a good sign. Rest."

The Doctor left the room. Henry could hear his shoes squeaking as he walked away down the corridor.

Sometime during the following day, or possibly even longer—there was no clock in the room and Henry's watch was whereever the hospital people had put it, or stole it, but in any case not near at hand—he woke suddenly when he felt a cool hand touch his forehead. He started, instantly awake. There was a slender female, of medium height dressed in a grey uniform, with a crisply starched white cap pinned to her strawberry blond hair. *Nurses cap, ergo, a Nurse.* Even when his body twitched, startled, she continued to keep her hand on his forehead until she was satisfied whatever she was trying to find out had been found out. At that point she stuck a thermometer in his mouth and put her finger to her lips to keep him from talking until she removed the glass tube after what seemed like an eternity. Henry had no choice but to remain silent and watch her. *A "strawberry blonde," as in "Casey would waltz with…"* And she was fair looking—no raging beauty, but fair to look at. After she had pulled the thermometer out of Henry's mouth and written something on the tablet, she took the water tumbler from the table, handed it and two more of the Doctor's little pills to him, and ordered him to take them. They went down much better this time.

Henry smiled at her and asked, "Do you have a name, Nurse?"

Without much reaction of any kind she simply said, "Missus Feeny."

Henry looked at her and said, "Must have been easy on your mother, then. You know, when you were growing up—'O, Missus Feeny, dear, get up. It's time to go to school. Oh Missus Feeny, dinner's ready.'" He grinned.

The Nurse still did not react. She busied herself folding linens. But as she went to leave the room, she stopped and smiled at him, "It's Mary Evelyn Feeny, if you must know." Then she left.

Mary Evelyn Feeny had been born Mary Evelyn Doyle in a house two long blocks up from the Charles River in Boston. Her father was a policeman. She was the youngest of six girls in the Doyle family of eleven children. Two of her older Brothers had also gone to the cops, and another worked for the New Haven Railroad. Mary Evelyn had grown up a strict Saint Ann's Parish Catholic and had attended the parish school. When she was sixteen she met Walter Edward Feeny— Wally—one of Saint Ann's former altar boys and the outstanding scholar of the school. Wally and Mary Evelyn knew from the second or third time they had spoken to one another they had both found the other person to share the rest of their lives with, and they planned accordingly. Wally was nearly two years older than Mary Evelyn, and his brains won him a scholarship to Norwich University up in Vermont, which, though it wasn't a Catholic school, was grudgingly admitted to being a pretty good engineering school. While waiting for Wally to finish his degree, Mary Evelyn took classes at Boston University whenever she could squirrel away the cost of tuition from her pay as an operator at Bell Telephone.

Wally graduated in 1913. They were married a month later. They rented a house in Roxbury, just a block off Columbus Avenue, and settled into marriage and Wally's career as a construction engineer. There hadn't been any children—not because they hadn't tried—but they were still young, and they had their whole life to raise a family. Then the War came, and Wally couldn't resist the Siren call of the drums. He was commissioned in the Corps of Engineers, and when the 26th Yankee Division sailed for France, the 101st Engineer Regiment and First Lieutenant Wally Feeny went with it.

On May 11, 1918, at 10:22 AM, Mary Evelyn Doyle Feeny had answered the front door to find an army chaplain and another officer and his wife standing on the porch. The chaplain handed her a telegram from the War Department—she found out later if Wally had been only an enlisted man, she would not have had to meet the chaplain, for the telegram would have been simply delivered by a boy from Western Union. From that point, her memory of events remained fuzzy. About a month later she had received a letter from the Colonel of the 101st Engineers, as well as one from First Sergeant Sidney Rosen. The Colonel's letter had confirmed Wally was dead and he had died bravely doing his duty, etc., etc. Sid Rosen's letter was a bit different. Sid was a construction foreman and he and Wally had worked together on a couple of Wally's projects for the city of Roxbury. His letter told her how Wally had simply been in the wrong place at the wrong time: He had been there, supervising a detail, and the German shell had come down, and then he hadn't been there. They had tried real hard to find everything they could, Sid had said, and they had made sure his grave was marked and all his information had gone to the graves registration people…Oh yes, and all the boys was real damn sorry he had got killed.

By the end of summer, Mary Evelyn had decided no amount of crying and wailing was going to bring Wally back. She would have to get on with her life and try to do something that actually meant something. So she went back to school. Wally had taken out the government insurance when he went "Over There," and there was enough to find a smaller place to live while she finished her nursing degree at Mass General. She had the advantage of being older than the average wide-eyed student, and she knew far more about life and its rough spots than she cared to, so the school work was no real challenge. She spent most of her spare time socializing with the instructors rather than the other students, who never seemed to figure out how she managed to get such good grades and yet never seemed to be in a tizzy over exams and papers and the other usual impedimenta of studenthood. Not that she really cared what the other student Nurses thought. She graduated at the top of her class in April, 1919.

It was policy at Mass General's school not to place new graduates near to home because they usually ended up quitting as soon as they discovered what a wretchedly difficult job nursing really was. Mary Evelyn was placed with the Veterans Administration Hospital in Hartford, Connecticut. She was a diligent young woman, who really cared about her patients, most of whom bore the physical and mental scars of having recently served in the World War and most of whom had barely survived the experience. One of her favorites was the one in 4-D with the crippled arm and one leg. She would look in on him often, and since he was still undergoing therapy, which was both protracted and painful, she always managed to be near at hand while the therapist was working on him. But lately she found herself more often than not being too late to be first at assisting the Major.

Another Nurse, Ruthie Hannaford, some years younger than Mary Evelyn, insinuated herself into the unspoken assignment of being the Major's personal angel of mercy. *Fine*, thought Mary Evelyn, *that will give me more time with the other patients in the ward, including the new one, in 2-A, who made a rather spectacular entrance.* He had been carted into the ward after a long and arduous trip via ambulance from the Brooklyn Naval Hospital. *Why in heavens name hadn't they just put him on a train? It wouldn't have taken any longer, and it would have been considerably easier on him.* And then their visiting specialist, the British Doctor who was here working on the flu epidemic, read the new patient's file and made him his own special project, contrary to what the hospital administrator would have liked him to do. That part of it included having Mary Evelyn and Ruthie attend him every four hours or so and keep dosing him with some non-standard—that is, unauthorized—medication Doctor Dolbey had apparently brought with him from God-knows-where.

What really made Mary Evelyn Feeny's job difficult was she had the responsibility of reporting the general condition of the patients in the ward to Missus Dora Thatcher-Dunne, the administrator. Missus Thatcher-Dunne was a career bureaucrat, at best. Her main concern was every "t" was crossed and every "i" dotted precisely as prescribed in the operations bulletins, and there was an adequate paper trail generated by her office to prove beyond the slightest shadow of a doubt that if anything at all went wrong, Dora Thatcher-Dunne would emerge with a spotless record. Mary Evelyn Feeny, needless to say, detested the administrator, but could see no way around her duties and responsibilities except to report everything going on. To do anything less would place her in the administrator's line of fire, and she needed the job.

Now when Mary Evelyn stopped at the Nurses' station at the beginning of her shift, she found the usual stack of memos posted for the edification of the nursing staff. These usually amounted to lists of petty complaints Missus Thatcher-Dunne made about the way the ward was being served. On the top of today's stack was a memo about the administrator's discovery the bed linens in the storage area had been improperly folded and stacked. Before she could get to the portion of the memo detailing the "proper" method of folding and stacking, she felt a hand touch her shoulder and a British-accented baritone voice quietly say, "Nurse, put those stupid memos down and bring Nurse Hannaford to 2-A—that's a good lass."

If anyone else had used that tone or manner, Mary Evelyn would have turned him to ice with one of her frigid glares. But Doctor Dolbey was neither offensive or condescending. It was just the way he was.

"Right away, Doctor," Mary Evelyn said, hurrying off to find Ruthie.

They caught up with Dolbey as he worked his way down the corridor, looking in on the patients in the ward, and then they followed in his train as he opened the door to 2-A. The patient was sitting up in bed, playing solitaire on an upturned tray. He looked up when the Doctor entered and then did a very odd thing. He raised his right hand, palm out, and said what sounded like, "*Jambo Daktari.*"—Hello, Doctor. Then Doctor Dobley did the same thing and said, "*Jambo Leftenenti. Uhali gain?*"—Hello Lieutenant, how do you feel? To which the patient replied, "*Naona afadhali kidogo*"—I feel much better than yesterday.

Doctor Dolbey saw the patient nod imperceptibly toward the pair of Nurses standing behind him and turned to find them with looks of absolute bewilderment on their faces.

"Ah," he said, "terribly sorry—forgot you were there...and you don't speak Swahili, of course." He paused. "You don't, do you? Speak Swahili, that is." Both Nurses shook their heads. "I didn't think so. I don't think the Leftenant will mind if we speak English." Dolbey looked back to Henry, who was smiling. With his face hidden from the Nurses, Dolbey winked.

He walked to the foot of Henry's bed and jotted a quick note on the tablet. Then he pulled the blanket up to reveal Henry's bare feet and legs. He gently lifted the left foot by the heel and had the Nurses look at it closely. Henry noticed Ruthie Hannaford's eyes grow large and Mary Evelyn Feeny blanch when she saw what the Doctor was pointing out to them.

"Unless I miss my guess," Dolbey stated, "those are the scars from when you or someone removed a family or two of those beastly chiggers, right?"

Henry nodded. "We averaged about a dozen a day."

"Right-o. If you hadn't cut them out—well, you had to—or they'd have gotten under the toe-nails and feasted. Nasty little buggers. We had men end up losing their toes and feet from clawing at them and having it go septic."

The Doctor gently put Henry's foot back on the bed, casually mentioning the other looked just like it. He put his hand under Henry's left knee, and in spite of the obvious pain it caused, flexed the joint so he could look at Henry's leg. Again he told the Nurses to take a close look. This time Ruthie nearly screamed and stepped quickly back, and Mary Evelyn looked very much as though she were going to be ill.

"Don't shrink away," Doctor Dolbey ordered. "It's going to be your job to administer the treatment."

Swallowing rapidly, Mary Evelyn Feeny, whose face was now white, grimly set her lips and again looked closely at Henry's left leg. "My God, Doctor, what are those?"

"Those, my good girl, are what is known in East Africa as 'guinea worms,' the female *dracunculiasis*. They are carried into the host body by drinking water containing *cyclopes*, that is, water fleas, which are themselves infected with the *dracunculus medinensis* larvae. Once inside, they penetrate the walls of the intestinal tract and take up housekeeping. In about six weeks, they migrate, boring into various areas just under the skin, usually the extremities, sometimes the scrotum, and then they turn into the little whitish worms we have here. There the males fertilize the females and then die. Eight months or so after that, the pregnant females, which these are, break through the skin and begin to lay their eggs, preferably somewhere wet. The larvae are then ingested by the water fleas, and the cycle begins all over. Another of East Africa's delightful oddities explained to absolute perfection. You needn't applaud. Simple prostration before me will be adequate."

Doctor Dolbey dug his pipe and tobacco out of his jacket and went through his usual packing and lighting ritual. He seated himself in the chair next to Henry's bed and puffed contentedly for a while. "You've been out of Africa how long, old boy?" he finally asked.

"Late summer—actually late winter, we were well south of Lindi by then—of '17."

The Doctor mentally computed the time. "Actually, you're quite lucky then. It might have taken much longer for the symptoms to appear—up to fifteen years actually. I don't suppose by then you'd have been lucky enough to stumble across someone who actually knew what was happening. That would have been fatal, as you bloody-well know." Henry nodded. There was no denying the truth of the statement.

"What it amounts to, old sod, is when whoever was extracting the little ladies for you the last time, they either burst one or missed one. I think the likelihood of it being a burst one is right. The larvae sprouted and took to migrating randomly before they died. The pain and swelling, as well as the fever, are caused by that. You've bloody-well got guinea worms in your knees and hip joints. We'll see if we can medicate them out. If not, we'll have to go in and do some worm hunting. I'll show the lasses here what to do to get rid of the new crop. Any questions?"

Henry began to shake his head, then stopped. "Not a question so much as a request…"

The Doctor made a gesture with his hand.

"Can you move me into a room with other people? I'm going a little stir-crazy talking to myself all day."

"Not yet, considering what has to be done in the way of treatment. I wouldn't want to scare my flu patients. For that matter, I wouldn't want to make them sick by having them watch. After we've culled the new crop—there aren't many, only six or seven on one leg and three on the other—then we'll see. I'll see if I can find someone in the ward to match you up with, but no promises. Fair enough?"

"Fair enough. *Asante, Dakatari*."—Thank you, Doctor.

The procedure for removal of guinea worms was simple enough. It was just a question of whether Mary Evelyn or Ruthie had the stomach to do it. Three times a day Henry's legs were washed with tepid water and mild soap. The moisture drew the worms out until they bit into and could be attached to a small stick of wood. Then every day the worms were wound onto the stick a few centimeters at a time. The first few days were nightmarish for the Nurses, but after that they adapted, and the last worm was finally removed on the sixteenth day of treatment. By then, most of Henry's joint pain and the last vestiges of fever had also disappeared. Considering the medication and the bed-rest, Henry felt better than he had at anytime in France, let alone German East. During the last days of his treatment, Doctor Dolbey had dropped by and asked if his records had the correct home address, which Henry took as an indicator that the Doctor was going to move him into either a ward or a room with another patient.

Then, on the morning of the day after the last guinea worm had departed, Henry's game of never-ending solitaire was interrupted when Ruthie Hannaford's pert little rear-end backed into the room. Ruthie was tugging on the headboard of a bed. As she pulled it through the door, Henry caught a glimpse of Mary Evelyn Feeny pushing on the foot rail. The bed obviously held a patient, but because it was cranked flat, Henry could see only the mound of a torso covered by the blanket. Even when Ruthie and Mary Evelyn were turning the bed to move it into the room on the other side of the table and chair, their bodies blocked Henry's view. Finally, Ruthie went to the foot of the bed and turned the crank to raise the head. The motion reminded Henry of how he used to crank his Grandfather's Oldsmobile, back before electric starters. He was jerked suddenly out of this reverie when Major Anderson said from his bed, "You son of a bitch—you *were* lying to me."

"I take it you two know one another," Mary Evelyn Feeny said.

When Henry looked at her, she noticed his eyes were glistening, as though he were about to cry. He saw that she was smiling. It was the second time he had ever really noticed her smile. It was a very nice smile.

CHAPTER FIFTY-SEVEN

Wednesday, August 6, 1919
Mitchell, South Dakota

Henry Feller, former First Lieutenant in the Army of the United States, carried his suitcase, a medium sized leather affair bound by two straps and buckles. It contained all the worldly goods he cared about. That is to say his other new suit of civilian clothes and the remnants of his uniform—the rest of his kit had been donated to an Army-Navy store in Hartford right after his discharge physical. The suitcase also carried his Schofield revolver, which, considering all things, had been packed with his clothing rather than taking the risk of having it stolen at this late date, after all of the effort he had put into keeping it out of sight for the better part of two years. He had been pleasantly surprised to find it under his socks, exactly where he had stashed it in his newly issued duffle bag, along with his German bread bag, when he had been divested of his worldly goods by the Military Policemen on the way to Chaumont, France, in 1917. Now, when he left the Hartford Hospital, he had kept only enough of a uniform to make the short trip to Camp Edwards, Massachusetts, for out-processing. And during the process he was careful not to eat or drink or generally slop anything onto himself that would necessitate the purchase of something else from the Officer's Sales Store.

He had been traveling off and on for over a week, ever since he had caught the train at Camp Edwards in Bourne, Massachusetts. It was probably the last train out of the camp judging by the rumors floating around about the place closing its gates.

He had stopped off in Pennsylvania to see if he could look up some of his kinfolk in a little town called Elgin and its neighbor, New Breslau, but was disappointed in all but one instance. He had managed to sit and talk for a while with his grandfather Kevin's sister, his Great-Aunt, Margaret Agatha, known as Sister Agatha at the Carmelite Convent in Harrisburg. She was a pleasant woman, in her mid sixties, who remembered her older Brother lovingly. She told him of the day Kevin had come home from the war the first time and had given her two china-head dolls bought somewhere. She had sent the dolls to Henry's grandmother Ellen when her mother had passed away and after she had decided to dedicate her life to God, Holy Mother Mary, and the Church. Henry told her he would look for the dolls when he got back home. As he recalled, his Grandmother Ellen had given them to his Mother, who had passed them along to his sister, Theresa, who everyone called "Tizzy." Sister Agatha had chuckled at that nickname.

In Chicago, he had tried to find Jimmy Hare, his first boss and mentor, but his name wasn't in the book, nor was he listed in the city directory. The old studio was a tenement, but Henry's memory of Polish wasn't good enough to find out if anyone knew where Jimmy had gone. In Milwaukee he stopped at the cemetery and left a small bouquet on General Arthur MacArthur's grave. And in Minneapolis, he'd done the same at the Colonel's, Uncle David and Aunt Theresa Welsh's grave, not surprised to see how meticulously the grave and its large carved marble stone were cared for. In Yankton, he was caught between great sadness and the consoling idea Grandpa Kevin and Grandma Ellen were once more together. By the newly-chiseled date on their headstone, Grandma Ellen had gone less than a year before. He arranged with the Pastor at Saint Aloysius to have their graves tended. Then he walked past his Grandparent's house, but did not stop when he saw the old Linden tree had been removed.

Henry had been talking himself through this homecoming for days. He had deliberately saved it for a surprise, wondering if his family would even recognize him after nearly eight years. He mulled over what his first words would be after all the years of silence, and of course how he would explain to them why it had been impossible for him to correspond with them from all the isolated places he had been. It was, after all, not like he'd been at home much since he left school. Excepting for the time he was finishing the books, he had not been home at all. And he knew, and had explained to his Mother often enough, that he was notoriously bad when it came to writing personal stuff.

Instead of going to the front door, he walked around to the kitchen Dutch door and pounded on the upper frame until he heard someone inside hurrying to see what the banging was all about. He heard the latch click, and the top of the door swung open suddenly. A balding man, just starting to jowl, dressed in an old shirt, baggy trousers, and an unbuttoned vest stared out the kitchen at him. The man reached up, pulled a pair of glasses down off his pate, and nestled them on the bridge of his nose. He looked curiously at Henry for several moments before asking, "Who the hell are you?"

It was not the first question Henry had expected upon his joyous homecoming. Well, in spite of the ravages of age, his Brother was still as surly as he'd ever been. "Hello, Junior," Henry answered. "Where're the folks?"

Junior's face went white. For a moment Henry thought he might be having a heart attack, but finally he stammered, "Jesus Christ—you're supposed to be dead."

"I'm not. I came pretty close to it on several occasions, but I managed to keep most of a whole hide. You can pinch me if you don't believe it." Henry held out his hand to his Brother and chuckled. "So, where're Mom and Pop?"

Junior unlatched the bottom of the kitchen door and motioned for Henry to follow him into the house. Not much had changed in the kitchen. There was new linoleum on the floor, or it might be a painted floor cloth. Anyway, it was glossy enough to be new, and Henry couldn't be certain what it was made of. The old table and chairs were the same as he remembered them, and he idly wondered if his old typewriter was still stored away in the attic.

Junior pulled out a chair and took a seat, motioning for Henry to do the same across the table from him. "You'd better sit down," he said.

"Everyone gone shopping or something?" Henry asked.

"No, I'm the only one here, now."

"Yeah, I can see that, but where's Mom and Pop? How're Tizzy and Del doing?"

Junior shook his head. "They're all gone. I said I was the only one..."

"Yeah, that's what you said, but when will they be back? I'd like to see them, to say hello, to tell them what's happened since..."

Henry's voice trailed off as Junior continued to shake his head from side to side. There was a stricken look on his face.

"Goddammit Henry, they aren't coming back—*they're all dead!* Junior's voice thickened. "They all died while you were off wherever the hell it was you went. Tizzy had an appendix burst. Del died having a kid. Dad's heart give out, and Mom died last year, mostly from the Spanish flu—but a lot from pining after the way you just disappeared— and after she died Grandma El just gave it up and went, too."

Junior scowled at Henry. He had spent most of the last years shedding tears over graves, and he simply didn't want to have to do it any more. The memories were too painful and too plentiful—memories of the family he had grown up in while his prodigal big Brother was off getting famous.

CHAPTER FIFTY-EIGHT

Thursday, September 9, 1919
Hartford Veterans Hospital
Hartford, Connecticut

Former Major Dodger Anderson was sitting up in bed reading a magazine when former First Lieutenant Henry Feller walked into the semi-private room—four patient capacity—and stood at the foot of the bed, glowering, with his hands on his hips. Dodger looked up finally and tossed the magazine casually onto the table/medicine stand/cabinet next to the bed.

"You're back a lot quicker than I thought you would be—that is to say, never. Anything wrong?"

"You miserable bastard..."

Dodger moved to say something, but snapped his mouth closed before anything smart-ass escaped. Instead he chose only to ask "What?"

"I said, you miserable bastard. You might have at least told me that everyone at home was *dead*, fer Christ sake, you son of a bitch."

Dodger blinked. "Henry, I didn't know—honest to shit I didn't."

"You lived there, goddamn it. How the hell could you not know?"

"Henry, I didn't live there. Hell, I moved away just before Christmas in...'14...yeah in '14, right after my Father died. That was a year after my Mom. I moved to Sioux Falls. I've never been back to Mitchell—there's nothing there, my family's all moved away or dead—no reason for me to go there any more."

"You never told me."

"Goddammit, Henry, you never asked. You never bothered to ask."

Henry's response surprised both of them. Before saying anything further, Henry grabbed at the metal frame of Dodger's bed and vomited on the floor, then slipped sideways and fell heavily beside the bed, unconscious.

Nurse Mary Evelyn Feeny was the first to arrive, followed by Nurse Ruthie Hannaford, when Major Anderson's shouting had brought most of the ward staff to the room. Lieutenant Feller was passed out at the foot of Major Anderson's bed. He was lying in a puddle of vomit, which by the looks and smell contained most of his breakfast, lunch, and what was undoubtedly a large quantity of now illicit liquid beverage—booze. Ruthie and Mary Evelyn managed to get him cleaned up and settled in the bed next to Dodger. Then Mary Evelyn took his vital signs and was shocked by what she read.

His temperature was approaching 103, his blood pressure was only 110 over 55, and he was having obvious trouble breathing. A listen through a stethoscope told her he had one lung sounding like it was ready to collapse, and Major Anderson offered it was probably another attack brought on by the gas he had taken in. She would hear the whole story later, from Ruthie, who had coaxed it out of The Dodger. Nurse Feeny's first concern was to getting his temperature down. With Ruthie's help and the muscles of two large male attendants, they got him stripped and into an ice bath where he could rest while she and Ruthie rigged a breathing tent and fired up a small steam generator. When she took his temperature twenty minutes later, his internal was down to 101.7. As the attendants were getting him out of the ice bath, she saw the "pits and puckers," what the veterans called their scars left from bullet wounds. He had two, one in front on the right side and a larger one in his back.

CHAPTER FIFTY-NINE

Friday, October 10, 1919
Hartford Veterans Hospital
Hartford, Connecticut

ormer First Lieutenant Henry Feller was sitting at the folding card
table he and former Major Dodger Anderson had purchased and—in
defiance of hospital regulations, set up between their beds in Ward 2-E. The
ward was a semi-private, two-patient-capacity room billed for some reason
to Wilhelm Investment Banking, as per former First Lieutenant Feller's
instructions, it being former First Lieutenant Feller's thinking if you pay for
it, the bureaucratic bastards can't give you that much shit about it. *This*
would lessen somewhat the inevitable harassment by the VA powers-that-be;
i.e., Missus Dora Thatcher-Dunne.

In the month in which he had once more been a patient in the
Hartford VA, Henry had developed a finely tuned sense of those
things which would piss off the bureaucrats, and he found glee—and
therapeutics—in employing them whenever he could. It was the least he
could do, while most of the staff considered it as either high comedy—
because he *was* one creative sonofabitch when it came to screwing with
the administrators—or the work of a genuine pain in the ass—because
he had evidently forgotten shit flows downhill. Every time he screwed
with the administrators, they simply passed it down to lesser staff which
usually meant the Nurses and orderlies.

It was not the greatest of the changes in him Mary Evelyn Feeney
noticed since his re-admittance. When he had been a patient the first
time, Henry had had an odd, that is to say quirky, sense of humor,
very much akin to Doctor Dolbey, once again the attending physician.
But there was no longer a hint of humor. Now the shenanigans were
malicious not puerile. Whatever had happened in the short time
between his discharge and his sudden reappearance was bad enough to
have stifled his often spontaneous attempts to act the prankish little boy
and turn him mean. It was as though he had two sides of his life, and

the first time she had seen the side she could like. This one she wasn't sure. Now he was surly even to Doctor Dolbey, who had saved his life once again by instantly recognizing the symptoms of another disease, dormant since Africa.

"I don't believe it has a name, but at least it's not Blackwater Fever—his urine hasn't turned black, has it?"

"No, Doctor."

"Good. That's why they call it Blackwater Fever you know—his water turns black, probably from the clotted blood. In any case, if he had it, I'm afraid there's not much we could do for him—it's fatal about 99 percent of the time. Rather nasty, what?" Dolbey pulled the bottle of pills out of his jacket pocket and handed it to Mary Evelyn. "Two each, every six hours for the first two days, then one every six for a week. That's a good lass."

"Doctor, may I ask you something?"

"Right-o."

"What are these? You seem to give them out quite regularly, and I know they're not from the pharmacy."

"Right you are, my good girl. They are a combination of quinine and its basis cinchona—actually the bark of the cinchona, which I personally think has rather more guanidine than quinine to it. I'm not boring you, am I? I have a tendency to go on a bit—rather reminds me of one of my former associates, old Meinhartzhagen. He was an ornithologist, a birder, and he'd go on and on about his bloody feathered friends… endlessly."

"Yes, Doctor."

"Is that a 'Yes, I am boring you,' or just an acknowledgement I still exist?"

"No, Doctor Dolbey, you are not boring me. I'm interested, but I was wondering why you have your own supply."

"Because, my good girl, *officially* this medication doesn't exist, especially since it was developed by a Hun Doctor, in a Hun Colony. Can't allow the Hun to have anything like brains or humanity or compassion, don't you know. Not officially." Dolbey looked closely at Mary Evelyn, whose face broadcast a combination of disbelief and wonderment. "At a place called the Amani Biological Institute in German East Africa, the good Doctor Albrecht Zimmerman developed this medication for the German East Army, the *Schutztruppen,* after our blockade cut off the regular supply of quinine. Actually, it's rather more effective than the original. I got to know Zimmerman after we took Amani in '16. Good man, that."

Dolbey strode away to continue his rounds of the ward.

CHAPTER SIXTY

Monday, October 20, 1919
Hartford Veterans Hospital
Hartford, Connecticut

*D*odger Anderson *finished reading the intra-hospital communication—known as a "pinky" because of the color of the triplicated copy sent to the patients—and tossed it onto the small bedside table.*

"Well, Henry, it's official. I'm as good as I'm going to get, and the powers that she are releasing me into—or should I say onto—the world. As of Monday next, I am out of this glorious facility, free to do whatever I wish—run a marathon, climb Mount Washington, whatever."

Henry Feller tossed the magazine he was reading onto the floor between their beds, saying, "You're too old to run a marathon—nobody'd wait around for you to hop across the finish line. And Mount Washington is too cold and windy—a man could freeze his bollocks off climbing up there. So I guess that leaves whatever."

"Henry, you are the absolute heart of understanding. What would I do without you to commiserate with?"

"Oh, without me you'd probably be a nasty, bitter son of a bitch all pissed off about having lost a leg."

"Thanks."

"Don't mention it. So whatever?"

"I was thinking about getting hold of Eddie Rickenbacker and having him help me develop a steam-powered wheel-chair. You know—kind of like the Stanley Steamer. Eddie could race it and I'd let them photograph me."

"No—seriously whatever?"

"Whatever what?"

"Whatever are you going to do? I mean, other than try mightily to get into the pants of the young and willing Nurse Ruthie?"

"Why you rotten bastard..."

"I am too, which is beside the point. So whatever are you going to do?"

"Mount Washington's too cold and windy to climb, huh?

"Believe me…"

"Haven't the foggiest. Be a dancing instructor maybe?"

"Naaa, that would never work. Ruthie would never let you get close to other women… regardless of the fat and ugly part. What did you used to do? You didn't run a grain elevator like your dad, did you?"

"Hell no—you're looking at a true upper-mid-western LaFollette Progressive. I wouldn't stoop to being a tool of an evil capitalist like John Sargent Pillsbury."

"So which evil capitalist were you the tool of?"

"The Sioux Falls Steam Printing Company."

"Doing what?"

"I was the plant manager."

"No shit?"

"Hey, it was an evil capitalistic job, but somebody had to do it."

"Were you any good at it?"

"I did it for four years and they didn't fire me, so I suppose you could say I was adequate at it."

"So then why don't you go back to it?"

"Well…other than the fact they hired some young, snot-nosed shit to take my place, and it requires the ability to walk around the plant all day and climb up onto and over things—big things—like printing presses and paper unspoolers and such. Having one leg makes it a little difficult."

"What's the next step up from plant manager?"

"Well, I suppose it would be Plant Superintendent or somesuch. Why?"

"Where would that come into the hierarchy of it.?"

"Way higher up. Why?"

"But it wouldn't require climbing around on the machines? Right?"

"I don't suppose it would. Why?"

"So you could do that? Without the climbing around?"

361

"Yeah, I suppose. Why?"

"And you're pretty sure you could run the production end of it? Make sure everything got printed and looked the way it was supposed to and all?"

"Goddamn it, Henry—you gonna tell me what the hell you're getting at..."

"Well, could you?"

"Goddamn it, Henry, yes. Yes, I suppose I could."

"You got a lawyer?"

"Yes, as a matter of fact I do."

Henry sat up in his bed and reached for the call button summoning the duty Nurse. As it so happened, the duty Nurse was Ruthie Hannaford. When she stuck her head in the doorway of 2-E, Henry looked up at her and asked her to fetch a telephone.

"I don't know if that's allowed, Henry," she said.

"Ruthie," Henry ordered, "don't give us any shit, just bring a telephone—or someone with the authority to bring one. This is too important to fart around with."

Ruth Hannaford's eyes widened and for a moment it appeared as though she were about to tell Henry off—at least that's the way Dodger read the look on her face. But she stalked away without saying anything and returned in a few moments with Mary Evelyn Feeny who was the Senior Nurse on duty.

Mary Evelyn asked, "What's the purpose of your request?"

"I want to call my lawyer, and my banker, and I don't want every swinging dick in the place to listen in on my conversation."

"How would you like your mouth washed out?"

"Don't play games. Just bring us a goddamned telephone. If I have to take a cab to New York to talk to my lawyer and banker, I'll have them figure out a way to back-charge it to Missus Dora Thatcher-Dunne, the Kaiser of this charnel house, and I'll let you explain howcome.

Henry and Mary Evelyn Feeny glowered at one another until Mary Evelyn took the telephone from behind the folds of her uniform skirt and set it on the bedside table. Henry swung off the bed and plugged the cord into the wall receptacle. He lifted the receiver from the hook and dialed a number from memory. Then, cursing under his breath, he quickly dialed a single digit and asked the switchboard for an outside line to the long distance operator; telling the young lady the memorized number. He waited for the connection.

"Stefen Wilhelm, please," he said to whoever answered at the other end. Then following a further, short, wait, "Slim—Henry Feller here. Is that property we talked about still up for sale? Good. Make an offer. Go ten percent under the ask, but take it at the ask if we have to. Get hold of Aaron Weintraub over at Stein, Stein, Stein, Stein and the rest of the Jews, and tell him I need a standard contract. No, not on the buy—this is for management. Superintendent."

Henry was interrupted here by Dodger's holding out his hand. Henry put his palm over the mouthpiece of the telephone after quickly saying, "Wait a minute..."

"If that's who it sounds like it is," Dodger said, "give me the phone for a minute."

Reluctantly, Henry handed the receiver to Dodger.

"I assume this is Wilhelm Investments," Dodger said into the receiver. "And you must be Stefen Wilhelm...My pleasure, I don't think we've ever spoken before. Stefen, is Fat Fred at his desk? Good—put him on and listen in if you wish. It will make things go a lot smoother. Fatso? Dodger. How the hell is you? Look, your Brother and my idiot savant friend, Henry Feller, are concocting some sort of business arrangement to stick a screw to me. What the hell are they talking about? A publishing house? How quaint. Oh, a full plant? Printing, linos, bindery, the whole shootin' match, eh? Well, that explains why he sounded like he only knew half of what he was talking about. I assume he's going to buy it. Ask Stefen if a fifty-fifty partnership is agreeable. Good—make it happen. Look, I get out of this hell hole in a week, so we'll have to expedite the paper work. Is a first-of-the-month takeover possible? Well, find out, and I'll try to be back from either my honeymoon or a first class drunk by then." Dodger laughed at whatever Fred Wilhelm said. "I don't know, I haven't officially asked her. But she's standing right here. Hang on." Dodger put his hand over the receiver and looked up at Ruth Hannaford. "Hey, Ruthie, will you marry me?"

Taking his hand off the receiver Dodger spoke into it again. "Freddy? I think she said yes just before she ran the hell out of here. What the hell. Put Stefen back on. I guess he'll want to talk to Henry, now that we've kept them from screwing us. Take care. You too. Here he is."

Dodger handed the receiver back to Henry and lay back on his bed with a terribly smug smile on his face.

An hour later, after Ruth Hannaford had been coaxed back into 2-E and it had been amply explained to her former Major Anderson was in fact serious as hell about asking her to marry him, she had tearfully accepted—as Henry was pretty sure all along she would. And then she had cried on Mary Evelyn Feeny and had accepted a very chaste kiss on the cheek from Dodger and a peck on the forehead from Henry, who was going to be Dodger's best man. Then Mary Evelyn and Ruthie had gone back to their duties on the floor.

Henry, lying on his bed with his head propped up on one elbow, finally said, "I didn't know you knew the Wilhelms."

"Obviously."

"So, for how long?"

"Henry," Dodger said, shaking his head in resignation, "who the hell do you think loaned my father the money to buy a grain elevator? I mean, Jesus God, he was a former Norksy sod-buster—a failed sod-buster, I might add."

"Hell, Dodge, I thought he got the money from the railroad."

"No, Henry—you *assumed* he got the money from the railroad. Not, as I recall, you ever asked. What the hell was the name of that First Sergeant of yours?"

"James—Luther James. Why?"

"You remember what his favorite line was?"

"Yeah—'Assume makes an ass of you and me.'"

"That's your trouble, Henry. You are smarter than thirty-eight kinds of dog shit, but you *assume* since you're so goddamned smart, whatever you *assume* must be so. That's how come you didn't know I moved away from Mitchell, and how come you didn't know your folks were dead, and how come you didn't know Otis Jividen was dead, and everything else that's ever taken you by surprise. Jesus, Henry, you are one of the damned smartest people I know, but sometimes you are just plain goddamned stupid."

Thanks, Dodge."

"Don't get all cocky. I'm still the best friend—maybe the only friend you've got in the world, and I'm the first one to admit you have saved my ass repeatedly: all the time we were growing up and twice in one goddamned day for really and truly. And I am forever grateful and in your debt. But it don't mean you ain't from time to time the stupidest son of a bitch I ever met. Common sense stupid, not book stupid. Whatever happened to James, anyway?"

"He was the first one killed at Essey."

"Oh."

CHAPTER SIXTY-ONE

Friday, November 14, 1919
Hartford VA Hospital
Hartford, Connecticut

Henry Feller was sitting at the table between the two beds in the now private room, playing solitaire. Other than the cards, the table held a couple of magazines, a bottle which obviously contained some kind of proscribed adult beverage, and a glass made cloudy by the fingerprints and smudges of use. Henry neither tried to conceal the bottle or look contrite when Mary Evelyn Feeney made her rounds.

She thrust her head and shoulders into the doorway. "You're not allowed to have that, you know. It's against the rules of the hospital—and against the law, too," she said in her most authoritative tone.

After he had carefully placed a queen of clubs on a king of hearts, he put the cards down and poured an inch of the liquid from the bottle into the glass. "Anyone who tries to take it away from me is going to get their ass kicked. That includes that hymn-singing old biddy Anna Adams Gordon. And you don't even want to know where I'd put her friggin' hymnal."

"You're drunk."

"Nope. Wish I was, but I'm not. I can't seem to drink enough to get drunk lately."

"You are drunk."

"Bullshit."

"Watch your mouth."

"Why? You gonna report me to ol' whatshername, our esteemed administrator?"

"No, I'll bust that bottle over your thick head." Mary Evelyn's eyes shot sparks.

"Not goddamned likely."

"Don't take the Lord's name in vain."

"Why not? He takes *mine* in vain all the time."

"How would you like it if I washed your mouth out with soap?"

"How would you like it if I kicked your prissy Irish ass?"

"Do you talk like that in front of your Mother? I bet *she'd* wash your mouth out."

"Not any more."

"Oh, I suppose you'd kick her ass if she tried?"

"Not any more."

"What do you mean, then?"

"Just what I said. She doesn't wash my mouth out with soap any more, or give me a peck on the cheek any more, or tell me what a helluva fine writer I am anymore, or tell me how handsome I look in my uniform anymore…'Cause she's *dead*—supposedly from pining for me, until the Spanish Flu took her. So she doesn't do anything anymore except lie there in her coffin and molder." Henry poured himself another half glass of liquor, spilling some on the table. He downed the liquid in one gulp before he continued. "She's dead. My Father's dead. *Both* of my sisters are dead. *All* of my Grandparents are dead. The only one left is my younger Brother, and he wasn't at all understanding about my not showing up or writing for the last five or six years. He thinks I'm an absolute shit, which, come to think of it, is the same way I think about him for being such an absolute shit about it." Henry poured another drink with similar results. "Son of a bitch," he said.

"Don't talk like that."

"Why? Will God chastise me severely? Hell's bells, lady, I already feel like that poor sonofabitch Job. I can only give thanks that He didn't arrange to have some Heinie sumbitch blow *my* leg off and cripple *my* arm. But then again, it might be part of some greater plan to do it to my best friend so I can suffer by watching him for the next umpteen years."

"I understand the way you feel about your family—I really do."

Henry was about to come back with an answer befitting his feelings on the subject, but the look on Mary Evelyn's face stopped him. "You have no idea," he said flatly.

"I lost my husband in the war."

For the twelve-thousand-eight hundredth time, Henry's mouth ran away with his sense. "Well, keep looking. I'm sure you'll find him eventually..."

Whatever he was about to say next was stopped in mid-utterance when Mary Evelyn Feeney slapped him, open-handed, as hard as she could, across the face. The unexpected blow almost toppled him backward off his chair. He managed to catch himself by grabbing for the covers on his bed. Mary Evelyn glowered at him.

There were tears in her eyes. "You drunken bastard! Don't you *ever* say anything like that again," she spat.

Henry glared back at the Nurse. "I'll see your husband and raise you one entire family *and* the only woman in the world I ever really loved—enough to consider *never ever* coming back to the United States because she would have never left German East. Because, after all, she was Wahehe, and her tribal home was there. In this country, polite society would have called her a *'negress,'* and south of Pierre, South Dakota, she would have just been a *'nigger.'* But to the great fortune of polite society, she was killed one day while getting water from a village well. Killed by some skulking Limey sonofabitch several miles away."

Henry reached for the bottle on the table, only to have his hand stopped in mid-reach. He shook off Mary Evelyn's hand. Then took the bottle and poured another half glass, defying at Mary Evelyn all the while.

"Either raise or fold—it's your bet," he said.

Mary Evelyn Feeny stormed out of the room. She was busy brushing a tear from her cheek and walking hurriedly along the corridor with her head down when she ran abruptly into Doctor Dolbey, nearly knocking the both of them sprawling.

"What in Heaven," he said as he caught himself on a door frame.

Mary Evelyn regained her balance, quickly apologized, then blurted, "That exasperating sonofabitch..."

"Are you speaking of our esteemed administratrix, or one of the patients?"

"Feller."

"Ah, let me guess—he's been at the bottle again."

"No, Doctor, he's still at the bottle. I don't think he's stopped since his fever went away."

"Well, he's had a bit of a rough go."

"Doctor, we've *all* had 'a bit of a rough go'."

"I don't think you catch my drift. He hasn't lost just a friend or a parent or a loved one. He's lost them all. And because of the timing, he's found out about most of it all at once. How long did it take you to recover from finding out your husband had been killed?"

"I don't know—a month? Two?"

Doctor Dolbey shook his head. "No, my good girl. You may not realize it, but you haven't recovered from it yet. Oh, you may have put aside the immediate traumatic shock of the notification, but every time I observe you with a patient, I see you caring for your dead husband, as though it would bring him back."

"And what's wrong with that?"

"Nothing, nothing at all. It's admirable, in fact. It's what makes you such a damn fine Nurse—provided you eventually realize he is not coming back, regardless of how well you care for any number of men like him. And, of course, provided once you do realize the truth, it doesn't change the way you care for your future patients."

"Doctor, that's silly."

Dolbey shrugged. "We'll see. Right now, we are going to the cafeteria and have a soothing cup of tea—I'll make my own, thank you very much—and try to recover from our close brush with injury just now."

"Doctor, I don't have time…"

"Doctor's orders. Follow me."

In the cafeteria, Doctor Dolbey asked for and received a metal pot of hot water, which he placed on a borrowed hot pad on their table. From the depths of his smock pockets he pulled a tea ball, a paper envelope, and a silver teaspoon. After pouring hot water into a ceramic cup, he carefully measured loose tea from the envelope into the tea ball. Then he poured the water from the cup back into the pot, placed the teaball in the now heated cup, and poured into the cup enough hot water to cover the ball. That done, he glanced at his wristwatch to start his mental timer. He did all of this as Mary Evelyn sat across from him in rapt fascination.

"Do you remember exactly what you did immediately after your received the notification your husband had been killed?" he asked.

"I think they told me I swooned—passed out on the porch. The Chaplain's wife was patting my cheek and holding a cold towel on my forehead when I came back around."

"And then what?"

"And then I cried and threw things for about two weeks."

"And that was for just your husband?"

"Yes, of course."

"Well, my good girl, just imagine what it would have been like if they had told you that your whole family, as well as your husband, were all dead and gone. Would that have been significantly worse, do you think?"

"Of course."

"And how do you think you would have reacted to that?"

"I have no idea…" Mary Evelyn stopped, suddenly realizing she had just echoed Henry's accusation. "Oh dear…"

Doctor Dolbey lifted the tea ball out of the cup and allowed it to drip some before placing it on a saucer. He pushed the cup of freshly brewed tea to Mary Evelyn. "Drink that. You'll find it very soothing." He then repeated the entire ritual to brew himself a cup.

Mary Evelyn sipped her tea. It was unlike any tea she had tasted, nearly smoky in flavor. "What is this?" she asked.

"Oh, it's African. We call it red bush. I believe the Germans called it roybus—not spelled anything like it's pronounced, though. Here," he said sliding the sugar bowl to her, "try it with just a little sugar—brings out the flavor a bit more."

"It's very good, Doctor. But tell me, you seem very taken with African things."

"Oh yes, that I am. It's a very remarkable place. A beautiful place, especially up in the highlands where the weather is mild."

"Do you plan to go back?"

"No."

"Really? Why not, if you think so highly of it?"

"Because, my good girl, it is also the most dangerous and savage place I've ever been. And I have every intention of living a long and dull life and finally succumbing to pneumonia at an advanced age in cold, damp, and dreary England." Dolbey sipped his tea and winked at Mary Evelyn. "Why do you ask?"

"Because I was wondering what would make someone drop everything he knew and cared about and stay in—what did you call it?—the most dangerous and savage place."

"It would have to be something frightfully compelling."

"Yes, it would—frightfully."

They both sipped their tea. Dolbey had been absolutely right. The tea not only tasted good, but it also soothed Mary Evelyn's bruised sensibilities. She thought back through her conversations with Henry Feller and the changes she had seen in him, and she began to understand what had affected him so profoundly. She was deep in thought when she noticed, belatedly, that Dolbey was watching her closely, and she blushed slightly when she realized he was staring at her.

"Yes, Doctor?"

"How much do you know about Major Anderson—what is it you call him? Dodger?—Wherever did that come from?"

"He told Ruthie Henry gave him the name when they first met. I think it's from a book."

"Ah, no doubt the 'Artful Dodger' from Dickens. I say, how odd. Feller named him, you say?"

"No, Ruthie says. That's what Dodger told her."

"So they've known one another a long time, then?"

"Since childhood. They grew up together—least ways in the same town."

"Feller saved Anderson's, life you know."

"Yes, Ruthie told me."

"That's how he got gassed."

"I think so."

"That wasn't a question, dear girl. That was a statement of fact."

"Oh?"

"Feller used his own gas mask to keep Dodger alive after they were both wounded. He got gassed when he couldn't hold his breath long enough."

"I didn't know that part."

"Hmmm." Dolbey rose suddenly and ordered, "Wait here. There's something I have to retrieve from my office. Won't take but a moment." He strode out of the cafeteria and then back within a few minutes, carrying under one arm a stack of what were obviously books, tied up and wrapped. Setting them on the table, he slid them to Mary Evelyn.

"I don't think you should speak to Feller, Missus Feeny, until after you've read all of those. They are a quick read—shouldn't take more than four or five days. I'll assign one of the ward gorillas, as you so correctly call them, to take care of Mister Feller until you're finished." Dolbey held up his hand to silence Mary Evelyn's protest. "Doctor's orders."

Mary Evelyn carried the books home in a linen bag on her twice daily streetcar ride—Market, transfer at Trumbull, transfer again at Asylum, get off at the corner of Ann and walk three buildings down the block to her apartment house. She put the books on the entrance hall table, hung up her coat and hat, and fed the small yellow cat she had taken in right after she took the apartment. She put a kettle of water on the stove to boil, then shrugged out of her uniform, which she folded carefully and put on a chair next to her bed, setting carefully on top her starched white cap with its Mass General RN graduation pin attached.

After putting on her nightgown and housecoat, she took a box of tea from the cupboard and waited for the water to boil. Regardless of Doctor Dolbey's very proper English tea ritual, she spooned tea directly into her cup and poured in boiling water and stirred the brew until the tea was dark enough to suit her. However, she decided to do one of the things the Doctor recommended and used her spoon to hold back the tea leaves as she poured the brew into a second cup, to which she added a cube of sugar. She took her tea to her Morris chair, switched on her reading lamp, and retrieved the bundle of books from the hall table.

She untied the string binding and began to unwrap the package, sure that she would find books on African medicine or herbal remedies or something like that.

What she found were five volumes. The first, the one on the bottom, was much thicker and heavier than the others. She took the book from the top of the stack. Its cover was faded beyond reading and the corners were beginning to fray. She opened it to the title page.

INTO THE FORBIDDEN CITY
FROM THE JOURNALS OF
HENRY A. FELLER

It was nearly midnight when she put down the book. She had forgotten to eat, and it was now too late. She was too tired to start cooking anything. In the morning she could go down to the little coffee shop on the corner and have something for breakfast. Turning off the light, she climbed wearily into bed, letting the cat curl up to warm her feet. During the night she awoke suddenly, sure she had heard the little Chinese girl screaming over the bodies of her dead parents outside the wall of the arsenal. At the same instant of waking she knew that for the first time in over a year, she had not reached out automatically to touch Wally and to be once more devastated to discover his warmth not beside her in the bed.

By Monday morning she had finished all of the books. The largest was the easiest—mostly photographs of the Philippines. She even recognized a couple of the men in the photos. Fred Funston of course— since he had been the main subject of one of the other books—and President Roosevelt, but she thought it odd that Henry evidently didn't think much of the former President. That was obvious in his writing— he was not overly afraid to show his opinions. She had found Kermit Roosevelt both interesting and troubling, and she couldn't decide which aspect was the most important. Mostly she felt sorry for him. Aquinaldo, on the other hand, came across as charismatic—in a vicious sort of way—and not overly bright. But it was Henry who stood out— shown—as the writer. Mary Evelyn thought about him a great deal as she was reading his books, and now understood why Doctor Dolbey had wanted her to read them. The author was simply not the same man as the patient in 2-E. The writer was witty and compassionate, with the same quirky sense of humor she had first seen in him on his first admittance. The patient now in 2-E was bitter—and well on his way to becoming an uncontrollable drunk.

When she signed in at the hospital, she went immediately to Dolbey's office and returned the books, thankfully.

"Well, then, I suppose this means—seeing as you spent your entire weekend reading—that you wish to be placed back in the ward?"

"Yes, Doctor."

"Very well, then. I'll call off the gorillas." Dolbey smiled. "Good timing that. You missed the fun on Saturday night. I had put Rolf Larson to watching our problem child; Rolf's the largest of the gorillas, as you well know. He and Feller struck it off, straight away. Seems they're from the same part of the interior and have some common acquaintances. By the time I got there, they were both well on the road to oblivion, and Larson was singing some of the filthiest songs even I have ever heard. Fortunately, once I let him finish—particularly nasty words set to an old Welsh song, as I recall—he was drunk enough to be docile, and so I managed to get them both to bed without bloodshed." Dolbey chuckled.

CHAPTER SIXTY-TWO

Monday, November 17, 1919
Hartford VA Hospital
Hartford, Connecticut

"*W*hat was her name?"

"What was whose name?" Henry looked up from his game of solitaire after carefully putting a jack of spades on a queen of diamonds.

"The woman you were ready to forsake your family and country and career for." Mary Evelyn Feeny was leaning on the door frame of 2-E, holding a tray with Henry's mid-day meal and a small cup of what he called his daily-daily, one of Doctor Dolbey's little unauthorized pills.

Henry scooped the cards off the table. Without saying anything, he set his whiskey bottle on the floor beside his bed and gestured for Missus Feeny to put the tray on the card table. He was surprised when she did so without comment and then took a seat in the other chair.

"Zanta," he said, finally. "Her name was Zanta, Zanta Rajabu. It means 'beautiful girl' in Swahili. Her brother, Jabari, was my best friend, or one of them at any rate. He was an *Askari*, a German soldier. Jabari and Zanta joined the *Schutztruppen,* the German Imperial army in German East Africa, to replace their older brother, Omsha, when he was killed."

"She was a soldier?"

"No, she was a soldier's sister. A lot of the *Askaris* had family with them in the column. They kept the army civilized—set up the camps, cooked the meals, washed the uniforms, that sort of thing."

"Oh, they were—what do you call them?—porters?"

"No, the porters were called *ruga-ruga*. They did the heavy carrying. Sixty-pound bundles—ammunition and such, medical supplies, only military stuff. The families carried all the personal gear. Like I said, they kept the army civilized."

"How did you get to know Zanta?"

"Got to know her brother first. He was Paul Von Lettow-Vorbeck's orderly, as had been his brother, the one who was killed. I'd seen her around, and then he introduced us—Jabari that is, not Paul." Henry went off on a tangent. "You know who Paul Von Lettow-Vorbeck was?"

Mary Evelyn shook her head.

"*Oberst-Leutenant,* later *Generalmajor* Paul Emil Von Lettow-Vorbeck, was the commanding officer of the Imperial German forces in German East Africa. He was the only German officer who never surrendered at the end of the War. At the time—I think it was December of '18—the *Schutztruppen* were in Rhodesia when the German government, through the British army, had to order him to lay down his arms. So he marched his army into one of the towns there—I could find it on a map, if I had a map—and the Brits sent him and his officers back to Germany—those that wanted to go. And the *Askaris* were sent back to German East, which I think is now being called Tanganyika. Paul is the only certifiable German hero to come out of the war. They had a victory parade for him in Berlin when he got home. Where the hell were we?"

"You were telling me about Zanta and her brother."

"Yeah…Well, just about the time we retreated from Morogoro down toward Lindi, I took sick—probably the first bout of what this was," Henry said, making a downward pointing gesture implying the here and now. "I did just about the same thing, only then it was in the middle of a dirt track in the bundu."

"What's the bundu?"

"That's one of the names for the bush, or veldt, or whatever. Absolutely shitty country. The only things that grow there are nasty plants, nastier reptiles and vermin, and even nastier animals."

Mary Evelyn nodded, and Henry did not fail to notice she didn't try to berate him for his language. It almost sounded as though she were interested.

"Anyway, when I woke up something like three weeks later, Zanta was next to me on the sleeping mat, keeping me warm on one side—with Jabari on the other side. They had carried me along with the column all those days so I wouldn't get left behind and eaten, like some of the other poor bastards had."

Mary Evelyn's eyes grew wide with what Henry interpreted as disbelief.

"Yes, if an *Askari* was too sick to march, he got left behind, unless there was some kind of transport—carts or trucks or whatever—which there hardly ever were after Amani was captured. That's the scientific institute where they made all sorts of stuff for the army. Or unless he had his family with him. Paul didn't like to do it, but he had to. He couldn't slow the column. The Brits were on our ass all the way. Every time they got close enough, they'd throw a few shells our way. I think it's called harassing fire. It was, and it did. But, as I was saying, those who got left behind, unless they had family to keep the carnivores at bay were pretty well under a death sentence. The hyenas and jackals were the worst. But the big cats—lions and leopards, especially the lions—were pretty bad too."

The way he said it, so matter-of-fact, made Mary Evelyn shudder involuntarily. "Are you planning to write about it?"

"Not really. All of my journals were lost when I had to make a rather hasty departure. The last time I saw my journals, they were in the hands of a not-too-steady *ruga-ruga* who was trying to help Jabari as well. I don't know if they made it back to Jabari's village or not. Not to mention the fact I don't know exactly where the hell that is in the first place, other than up in the hills northeast of Iringa."

Henry shrugged, then shook his head, and shrugged again.

CHAPTER SIXTY-THREE

Friday, December 19, 1919
Hartford VA Hospital
Hartford, Connecticut

*I*t was Henry's first time out of the hospital, on the condition he had to take a keeper with him. His "keeper du jour" was Nurse Mary Evelyn Feeny. They walked to the streetcar stop, Henry setting a pace he felt he could handle. They took the cars from the corner near the hospital to the train station. After confirming his "keeper" wouldn't mind a little side jaunt, he bought two two-way tickets to Springfield, Massachusetts, which amounted to about an hour's ride. On the way, he spoke of a lot of small things, but he never really told Mary Evelyn why he wanted to go to Springfield so badly.

After a few questions put to a "red-cap" at the Springfield station, they again took the streetcars to a corner near a large fenced-in government facility—it had to be a government facility, judging by its architecture: brick, bureaucratic fortress. The gateposts bore bronze plaques identifying it as The Springfield Arsenal; the guard shacks signified the facility as being wary of letting just anybody in. However, when Henry flashed his identity card, certifying he indeed was, or had been, a commissioned officer of the Army of the United States, he was handed a visitor's pass—with one for his "keeper" as well—the guard Sergeant got a chuckle out of that one. And after signing the guest book, they were allowed to wander in and about. On their self-conducted tour, Henry grew far more animated than Mary Evelyn had seen him in several months. It was obvious to her whatever it was he was talking about, he found what the government did here absolutely fascinating. She had to admit she understood maybe only ten percent of it: windage, minutes of angle and wind-doping, breath-control and trigger-control, and several other terms she could only guess at. On the walk between buildings, he told her about taking a team of complete novices and winning the state rifle matches but then getting soundly beaten when they went on to the national competition.

"We found out what small fish we really were when we got to the national rifle matches at Camp Perry, Ohio. I mean, they cleaned our clock. I think we came in somewheres around thirty-seventh of the forty-some teams. It was a massacre." Henry laughed. It was the first time she had heard him laugh in months.

Her bemused look caused him to stop and look at her. Then as they walked further into the arsenal, she explained when he had been first brought to the hospital, his sense of humor had been one of the things—perhaps the main thing—allowing her to overlook many of his other little—and big—foibles. But then, when he had come back after going home, he had changed. He no longer had that streak of boyish humor she had found so appealing.

"That's because I haven't found much funny lately. Even with Dodger. And hell, we always used to joke around with one another. I figure it's probably the War. Nothing we've ever faced before was like that."

"Is it because you got a double dose of it?"

"How do you mean? Oh, Africa?"

"Yes, Africa."

Henry shrugged. He pulled the collar of his overcoat up around his ears and ducked his chin to protect it from the cold wind kicking through the buildings. "Probably—God knows, they were both unpleasant enough. Except for the killing—that was pretty much the same."

They walked a few steps before Henry stopped and pointed to a tall slender tower rising above the building in front of them. "That must be the old shot-tower. I've read about it, but I just couldn't get a good mental picture of it. They'd melt lead at the top and pour it through a sieve, and let it drop down into a water bath. By the time it got to the bottom, the lead was cool enough to not flatten when it hit the water, and it was perfectly round. The size of the ball was determined by the sieve. I think originally they made 75 caliber balls, but mostly 69s. That was for the first sixty or so years, until they started using Minie bullets. You don't know what the hell I'm talking about, do you?"

Mary Evelyn shook her head.

"For the first fifty years or so of our history, this place made most of the firearms for the Army—this and Harper's Ferry and later Rock Island. Still draws a blank, doesn't it?" Henry sounded resigned to preach to the unknowing and uncaring.

Mary Evelyn was nearly embarrassed by her ignorance—Springfield was, after all, in the western half of her home state, and she should have at least heard about it in school, especially if it were really as important as Henry seemed to think. But, then, he wrote books about history, and she didn't. If she ever wished to keep up with him, she realized she had a great deal to learn. And she immediately wondered why she should even consider that important.

Inside one of the production buildings, Henry approached one of the supervisors, and while Mary Evelyn hung back and tried to remain as inconspicuous as possible, Henry held an animated conversation at length, finally nodding happily and pumping the man's hand. He gathered-up Mary Evelyn and led her back outdoors.

"That's what I wanted to come here for," he beamed. "Found out they are making the special National Match Rifles again, and how to go about putting in an order for one through the Director of Civilian Marksmanship."

"You mean you bought a gun?"

"No, I mean I learned how to order one."

"And what do you intend to do with it?"

"I intend to use it to shoot in the National Matches at Camp Perry, Ohio, next summer. Why?"

"Isn't that where you said your team was so badly beaten?"

"Yep, but I don't intend to shoot with a team. I intend to shoot as an individual."

"You can do that?"

"No—I'll have to sneak in, in disguise. Probably as a Chinaman, maybe as a *Ladrone…* Of course I can shoot as an individual; I've been a life member of the National Rifle Association since my thirteen birthday."

Henry looked at Mary Evelyn whose cheeks were now flushed red. He wasn't sure if she were angry—which she seemed to be a good deal of the time lately—or just embarrassed at being caught in her ignorance again.

"Damn, I wish my Mother was still alive," he said suddenly.

"Why is that?"

"So she could teach you something about guns and shooting."

"What?"

"She was a hell of a shot. She bought her own guns out of her pin money. I cut my teeth on that little Lightning 32-40 of hers. And she was the best wing-shot I ever met. She could wup me hollow with a shotgun ten out of ten."

Henry walked along toward the guard shack at the front gate, suddenly quiet. He produced his identity card and turned in their visitor badges to the guard Sergeant, talking to the man, who then pointed down the block to the right and motioned some other turns. Walking down the block to the streetcar stop with his hand on her elbow, he finally managed to say, "Since my Mother can't, I'd be happy to show you how to shoot—if you're interested."

"I don't know. I've never shot a gun in my life. Not even my Father's or Brother's."

"I figured as much, just by the way you were asking."

"Do you really intend to go to this Camp Perry next year?"

"Yes."

"And you're that good? I mean …"

"Yes. The year we won the state National Guard championship, I came in a close second as an individual, and I haven't gotten any worse. That was before I went to Africa the first time and managed to save Kermit Roosevelt's young ass on at least one occasion. So, in answer to your question, yes, I'm good enough to compete at Camp Perry. Whether I'm good enough to do any good there remains to be answered."

"Oh."

"Well, at least they don't shoot the losers. Or at least they didn't the last time I was there," Henry laughed.

"You have a nice laugh."

"So I've been told," he laughed again.

When they climbed aboard the Pearl Street trolley, Henry asked the motorman whether the car stopped at Chestnut and was told to pull the bell cord when they wanted to get off. But in any case it was four stops, and then they could hop the Chestnut Street car and take it down to Maple. Henry thanked the motorman and they took seats where they could watch the street signs. When the car stopped at Chestnut, they hurried off and dashed over to the Maple Street car that was fortuitously waiting as it took on passengers. Mary Evelyn was not at all sure what Henry was about as they climbed aboard the second car. It was so crowded they had to stand, swaying as the car rolled along and sending blue-white sparks into the cold late afternoon air from its power connector pole.

They hopped off the car at Park Street, and Henry guided her by the right to the center of the block and then down a half-flight of steps and into a warm and cozy little restaurant. There they were greeted by a larger than portly waiter who beamed at them and ushered them to a table set, precariously, as Mary Evelyn considered, under a boar's head mounted on the wall near what had once been a bar but was now a display area for salads.

"*Guten abend, Mein Herr und Genadige Frau.*"—Good evening, Mister and Good Missus.

"*Guten abend*," –Good evening—Henry answered, adding, "Since the *Fräulein*—an *unmarried* lady—doesn't speak German, that I know of, perhaps it would be better if we spoke in English."

"Of course. How may I serve you?"

"Well, I was hoping for some *Wiener Schnitzel*—veal chops—and maybe a nice *apfel schtrudel mit schlagobers*—apple turnover with fresh whipped cream dollops—with coffee."

"Very good, Sir. Would you like some of our special tea?"

"I don't think so."

"It's very good, Sir. It's our special *Mai* tea." The waiter's eyebrow rose knowingly.

"Well in that case, I think we'll try some. *Danke*."—Thank you.

"*Bist nichts.*"—It's nothing.

Within moments the waiter was back with a teapot and two cups. Henry thanked him again and carefully poured a very pale liquid into each cup. "Try it. If you don't like it, I'll drink it," he said as he slid one cup to Mary Evelyn.

She looked dubiously at the nearly colorless liquid. When she lifted the cup she could feel that it was not even warm, and the first sip told her the contents were not tea. "What is this?" she asked.

"I'd say it was probably 1915 or '16—it takes about four years to be drinkable at all, and there hasn't been a really good year since 1910."

"But what is it? Specifically."

"It's *Mai Wein*. German white wine. Probably Moselle, but possibly Riesling. Hard to tell without the bottle."

"God, you're incorrigible. It's against the law."

"A lot of things are against the law. Shooting one of your own allies in cold blood is against the law, but if it meant saving my ass, I'd do it… again." Henry gave Mary Evelyn a long look. When she finally turned her eyes away, he shrugged and took another large sip of his Mai Tea.

The waiter appeared with two huge platters of *Wiener Schnitzel*, with warm potato salad and red cabbage on the side. After he set the platters on the table, he hovered. Henry looked up at him after forking the first large portion into his mouth. It was the first non-hospital food he had eaten in weeks, and the very smell of it had started him salivating.

"Ach. Das is sehr gut, sehr gut,"—Oh, this is very, very good—he told the waiter, then remembering not to speak in German, he finished with, "My compliments to the chef."

Mary Evelyn was much more tentative as she sampled the German food for the first time. But by the third forkful, she had to agree with Henry the meal was, indeed, delicious. She even found the "tea" blended nicely with the food—and managed to smile shyly when Henry caught her sipping at her cup.

The waiter, pleased his customers were happy, still hovered. Finally he could not contain his curiosity any further. "If I might ask *Mein Herr?* You obviously speak German very well, but the accent—the accent is nothing I am familiar with?"

"Most recently I spoke in German East"

"*Ach, Herr Gott!* You were with *General* Von Lettow-Vorbeck?"

"Yes, as a matter of fact, until 1917. I was a correspondent."

"You knew the *Generalmajor?*"

"Yes. Actually, I knew him before the war. We first met in China."

"My wife's Brother was with the *General.*"

"Oh really? What was his name?"

"Kemper. *Leutnant* Karl Kemper."

"I met him. At Manza Bay, he was in charge of some of the salvage operations on the *Kronborg.*" Henry could see by the look on the man's face that he had no idea whatever what Henry was talking about. "Did *Leutnant* Kempner survive the war?" Henry asked to change the subject.

"Yes, thank God. He's back in Frankfurt, now."

"I'm very glad to hear that. He was—is—a good man. Do you correspond?"

"Yes."

"Please tell him then Heinrich Feller wishes him the very best. But now we must be going, we have a train to catch. How much is the meal?"

"For a friend of *Generalmajor* Von Lettow-Vorbeck, it is my pleasure to serve you."

"Don't be silly," Henry said, tossing a Five-dollar note onto the table.

As they walked through the door and started up the steps, the man called out after them "'*Wiedersehen!*"

"'*Wiedersehen*," Henry called back, adding "*Frohe Weihnachten!*"— Happy Christmas.

They walked in silence to the corner and caught the streetcar going back up Maple. After several transfers and a fifteen-minute wait on very hard benches in the crowded passenger area, they boarded the train for the ride back to Hartford. The coach car was far more crowded than Henry thought it would be, and they were forced to sit next to one another facing a middle-aged couple carrying several large shopping bags filled with small boxes—Christmas shoppers. They were nearly at the Connecticut state line before Mary Evelyn finally spoke.

"Did you really know that man's brother-in-law? Or were you just being nice, and taking the chance he hadn't been killed in some horrible way?"

Henry had to think for a moment who Mary Evelyn meant, then suddenly realizing her intent, said, "No, really, I did meet him, just that once. But the circumstances were such it is easy to remember. Most of what I've done in my life has been caused by sets of strange circumstances and pure accidents. The events that got me thrown out of Mindanao, were also the way I met Arelio and his family, and the Brother just happened to be, or had been, one of Aquinaldo's lieutenants, who had just happened to have been captured by Fred Funston, who just happened to be on the same boat when we went to the Philippines in the first place. And it was in the Philippines where I just happened to be attached to Arthur MacArthur's division and met his son, Douglas, who just happened to end up as my division commander in France and is now the Commandant of the Military Academy. It's all coincidence—fortuitous, but coincidence nonetheless."

Mary Evelyn said nothing, and when Henry looked at her, she was sleeping, with her head resting on his shoulder. She napped until the conductor came down the aisle and called out "Hartford". When she awoke she blushed for falling asleep while Henry was talking.

When she tried to apologize, he held up his hand, saying with a laugh, "German food does that to you."

"Do you really mind if we stop by my place for a minute?" she asked. "I wasn't expecting to be gone all day, and I'd like to feed my cat. It's not very far from the hospital."

"Not a problem."

They caught another streetcar at the entrance of the Hartford station and with a couple of transfers ended up at the door of Mary Evelyn's apartment. Mary Evelyn unlocked the door, then, opening it a crack so the cat could not escape, reached in and switched on the lights. She ushered Henry in and offered him a seat in her Morris chair. He didn't bother to take off his overcoat, simply unbuttoning it before he sprawled into the chair.

Mary Evelyn took her coat off and tossed it casually on the bed before hunting around in her cupboards for a snack suitable for a cat. The room was so warm and cozy, Henry very nearly asleep sitting in the chair. He was suddenly brought back to full-wakefulness when a yellow ball of fur leaped onto his lap then walked up his front to peer closely into his face. Henry reached up and stroked the cat's back fur and was rewarded by a head-butt and a very loud purr. When Henry looked up, Mary Evelyn was watching.

"He must like you," she said. "He never did that before."

"What's his name?"

"Oh, he doesn't have a name. I just call him 'cat'."

"Well, I'm going to call him 'Sam.' I had a cat named Sam that looked just like him, way back when, when I was a kid. So 'Sam' it is."

Mary Evelyn finally settling on a simple bowl of milk. Normally the cat—or, as she now supposed, Sam the cat, would rub around her ankles until she actually put the bowl on the floor. When she realized the cat was not doing its usual routine, she looked over toward the Morris chair. Henry Feller was asleep, with the cat curled up on his chest, also asleep. Mary Evelyn picked the cat up and set it down along side the milk. She had to shake Henry's shoulder to awaken him. He came awake with a start, his eyes for a moment showing flashes of bewilderment, fear, and a touch of what might even be read as panic.

"I have to get you back to the hospital," she said as she shrugged into her coat.

They said hardly a word to each other on the trolley ride. Then Henry walked along and held the door open for her as they entered. Henry then waited as she checked them in. He followed her up to his room, waiting for her as she stopped at the Nurses' station and glanced through a stack of memos.

"I suppose I'll see you in the morning, right?"

"I come on duty at 8:30. I'll bring you breakfast and your pills. Thanks for the meal."

"Hey, thanks for getting me out of this…here."

"And for being your 'keeper'?"

"Ah. You heard that."

"That's what you said to the Sergeant at the gate of the Arsenal."

"I was joking."

"I know. I'll see you in the morning."

"Yeah. We'll have to do it again…sometime."

"I'd like that."

CHAPTER SIXTY-FOUR

Friday, February 6, 1920
Hartford VA Hospital
Hartford, Connecticut

His release from the clutches of the administration of the facility, and thereby its administratrix, came on a Thursday, to be effective the following Friday, for no particular reason other than it would make Missus Dora Thatcher-Dunne less work in clearing him from the books. She and he both breathed massive sighs of relief to be shy of one another.

Dodger Anderson and his new wife, the former Ruthie Hannaford, were still off somewhere honeymooning, with occasional flitting stops back in Hartford to check on the publishing plant, undergoing a complete maintenance overhaul before they started publishing whatever the hell it was they thought they were going to publish—that remained just the least bit sketchy in their plan of business.

So it was left up to Mary Evelyn and Doctor Dolbey to help Henry vacate his room. At the entrance to the building, a Hupmobile taxi was waiting, its exhaust making an acrid white cloud in the frigid air.

"I took the liberty of ordering up a ride for you, Henry" Doctor Dolbey said, as he helped Henry toss his duffle bag and suitcase into the Hup's small trunk. "Besides, old sod, you can afford it. And I hate long farewells, so I will simply tell you to stay in touch—knowing full-well that you won't. Just try to remember you are an absolute hot house of tropical diseases. Should you come down with anything else, don't try to call me. Just go to a competent hospital. They will call me. Other than that, have a long and pleasant life." Dolbey turned and walked back into the hospital, leaving Ev and Henry standing on the curb next to the waiting Hup.

"Do you have a place to stay? I never thought to ask," Mary Evelyn said.

"Yeah, as a matter of fact Dodger found me an apartment. I figure I'll camp there until the plant is up and running. Then, we'll see."

"Well, I guess it's goodbye then. Like the Doctor said, take care of yourself."

"Ah, you wouldn't mind if I called you or anything, would you? I mean, we could maybe go have some *apfel schtrudel mit schlagobers* or something—maybe corned-beef and cabbage next month?"

"That would be nice, if I'm not on duty or anything."

"I'll give you a call then."

"If you remember to."

Their goodbye was interrupted by a gruff basso voice. "Hey, Lootenant, don't run off—I got some of your sh...stuff here." Rolf Larson was helping shove a furniture dolly along the sidewalk as he called out to Henry. When he came up even with the taxi, he quickly walked around the forward end of the dolly and put his shoulder against the load to help bring it to a stop. The load was a large steamer trunk, with a smaller foot locker perched on top. Both bore the stenciled identifying markings for 1LT FELLER, H.A. O347748.

"Where the hell did you get those?" Henry asked.

"The Army sent 'em down from Camp Edwards. They was in storage. You mean old lady two-names never told you they was here?"

"Larson, why would she do that? There might have been something in them I could have used sometime in the last four or five months."

"Well anyway, here they are, Lootenant. I'll help load them into the back of your cab." Without further ceremony, Larson and the other man—who Henry recognized as another of the ward gorillas—manhandled the trunk and footlocker into the backseat of the Hup. That done, Larson jerked his thumb at the other man. "Polikowsky, take the dolly back and wait on me in the boiler room." Larson ordered. Polikowsky took hold of the rope that served as a tug line on one end of the dolly and trundled back down the sidewalk. Half way to the side entrance he stopped and called back, "What if ol'whatshername wants to know where you are?"

Larson, a look of exasperation on his face called, "Jesus, Polikowsky, just tell her you don't know where I am, just that I'd meet you in the damned boiler room."

The helper nodded and proceeded on, the dolly clattering after him.

"Goddamn dumb-ass Polack—er, sorry, Ma'am," Larson mumbled. He was pretty sure Mary Evelyn Feeny and he felt the same way about the administrator, but he tried to keep his mouth in line when he was around the Nurses, not that they didn't know all the words, but it was a sort of us-against-her attempt at a small form of solidarity. He held out his paw to Lootenant Feller. "It's been a pleasure to know you, Lootenant. In spite of everything. You take care of yourself. I wish I could have served under you."

"Thanks, Rolf. I appreciate it. Like I told you before, though, why don't you quit this hellhole, go back to Minnesota, go to college, and spend the rest of your life turning out little squareheads?"

"Ya know, Lootenant, I might just do that." Larson pumped Henry's hand again and then held the taxi door for him.

The cab pulled away from the curb into traffic and turned out of sight at the next corner. Larson and Mary Evelyn stood watching it disappear. Without saying anything, Larson took a handkerchief out of his Pea-coat pocket and handed it to Mary Evelyn, who used it to dab her eyes and then blow her nose daintily. When she tried to give the handkerchief back, Larson waved her off.

"Keep it. The cold air does that to you—always makes my nose run. I've got another one anyway, miss."

When her shift ended at six-thirty, Mary Evelyn followed her usual ritual of trolley transfers to her apartment. She hung her coat on a hanger and stowed it in the small closet. As she was preparing the teakettle to boil water—deciding later whether to make tea or coffee—there was a knock on her door. In all the time she had lived in this building, she had never had a visitor, other than the very brief visit by Henry Feller. So she was quite leery about opening the door.

"Who is it?" she called.

"New neighbor," a male voice answered, muffled by the door. "I was wondering if you had a can opener I could borrow so I can fix something to eat. I seem to have forgotten to buy one."

Mary Evelyn slid the safety latch into its recess before opening the door a crack, just far enough to see who was standing in the hallway. She gasped.

Henry Feller was holding a can of tuna for her to see. He was in his shirtsleeves, without a tie or jacket. Two doors down and across the hall another apartment door stood ajar. "If you don't have a can opener," he said, "Sam's going to miss out on a real treat."

Mary Evelyn opened the door and ushered Henry into her apartment. By her expression, he could tell she was not amused, even when she said, "I suppose you think this is one of your little jokes."

"By which you mean what?"

"Moving in here."

"I didn't move in *here*. I moved in down the hall. And if it's anybody's *little joke*, it's that asshole Dodger's."

"Don't use that kind of language. He's your best friend."

"So? My best friend may happen to be an asshole."

"I asked you not to use that language."

"OK, so Dodger *isn't* an asshole."

"Argh, you are incorrigible." Mary Evelyn went to her kitchen cupboard and fished around in a drawer. "Here," she said, handing Henry a can opener.

He put the can of tuna on the counter and then began to turn the opener around the lid. He was immediately joined by a yellow ball of fur. When he had opened the can enough to bend back the lid, he stepped back and watched Sam begin to feed.

"Don't let him eat all of that—it'll make him sick."

"Spoil-sport."

"You're not the one who'll have to clean it up."

"So, tell me—what are you in such a piss-off over?" Henry watched the cat feeding.

"What?"

`"I had a faint notion you might actually be happy to see me...that is, before I walked in here and evidently caught you in the middle of a first-class piss-off."

"I suppose you think it's funny that you can just show up and move in. You and Dodger…"

"I don't suppose you'd believe me if I told you I didn't realize that Dodger had rented me a place in your building until I arrived here?"

"No, I would not."

"OK, don't. But that's what happened."

"You expect me to believe that?"

"No, but ask yourself this—Dodger and Ruthie have been away for how long?"

"A month or more."

"Did Ruthie ever come here?"

"No."

"Dodger?"

"Of course not."

"Did either of them know where you lived?"

"Not that I know of."

"Then how in the hell could they have set up this little joke? I asked Dodger to find me a place to stay until the plant got up and running. It took me several days to get a message to him to call me, and then I believe he made all the arrangements by telephone. Or the Wilhelm Brothers did. I didn't find out until the cab dropped me at the front door earlier, and even then I wasn't exactly certain. Most of the buildings in this neighborhood look alike, you know. And I didn't recall where exactly I had been *two months* or so ago, considering I was half asleep. Mostly I remember Sam. And that, as they say, is the whole truth."

"Well…OH Shit!" Mary Evelyn spun suddenly and dashed into the far corner of the kitchen, grabbing a dish rag on the way past the sink. Sam was retching. Simultaneously, Sam was avoiding being cornered, so that when he finally spewed up most of the tuna he had gobbled, he managed to miss Mary Evelyn's cloth and left his puddle partially behind the gas stove.

CHAPTER SIXTY-FIVE

Wednesday, June 8, 1921
Offices of Anderson & Feller
Hartford, Connecticut

*H*enry Feller and Dodger Anderson sat across the desk from one another. *Both had their heels on the edge of the desk top. It had taken several weeks and a great deal of expense to have the desk shipped to Hartford, Connecticut, from Yankton, South Dakota, following several more weeks of dickering with the present managers of the Burlington Railroad over buying the desk in the first place. Henry's persuasiveness, his several hundred shares of Burlington stock coupled with Dodger's even greater stock bundle had finally gained them the privilege of having the gigantic mahogany monstrosity hauled East over several railroads and then manhandled upstairs to their office, where it took up most of the floor space. When he first saw it, Henry felt like crying.*

The desk had been crafted by Henry's father, Emil, originally as an anniversary gift to Henry's mother. When it was discovered the piece was too large to fit in their home, Emil had completed it and given it to Henry's grandfather, Kevin, for his use in the Yankton office of the Burlington—the 'Q'—railroad. Now, the marquetry was dinged and the surface showed years of hard use, with deep scratches and gouges. But the compass rose was mostly still there, as was the linden leaf. Several hundred more dollars and an excellent local cabinet maker had restored the huge thing so Henry and Dodger could now abuse it on their own hook, by resting their heels on it.

In the year of operation now under their belts, Anderson & Feller Publishing had managed to work all of the kinks out of the equipment. Dodger had indeed known what he was doing when it came down to it. They had spent more money selling off obsolete equipment and installing new. They were now on par with most of the large printing houses and could produce everything from small pamphlets to full quarto volumes from scratch.

If they only had anything to produce. If they even had the promise of anything to produce.

In a year they had re-printed Henry's books after buying the rights back from Ryan's. Other than that, unless Henry could travel back to Africa and somehow manage to find one particular *Askari*, if that *Askari* was still alive, and see if that *Askari* had indeed held onto Henry's journals, and if he had, then Henry could sit down and write another book. It might or might not sell because it was about a time and place of which one person in a million might possibly know something.

So the founders of Anderson and Feller Publishers rested their three heels on the edge of Kevin Mahoney's desk, built nearly forty years before, and they tried to figure out a way to make enough money to stay in business.

"I've been thinking," Dodger began.

"I'm truly glad. It proves you're nowhere near as brain dead I thought you were."

"Goddamn it, Henry—seriously."

"Only if it has to do with making bundles of money do I take whatever you say seriously. You know that."

"What do you remember most about the people we grew up with back home?"

"Seriously?"

"Yeah, seriously."

"They were all old, they all had beards—except the women, of course...well mostly..."

"And?"

"What is this? A game of 'Twenty Questions'?"

"What tied them all together?"

"What do you mean?"

"Jesus, Henry, sometimes you are so damn dense. Who published your first article?"

"The G.A.R."

"And it was...is?"

"A veterans club—Civil War veterans. Most of my kin belonged."

"And what are we?"

"Well, hell yes, we're veterans too."

Dodger casually tossed a folded brochure across the desk to Henry. "You ever hear of this bunch?"

Henry skimmed the text. "The American Legion? Never heard of them."

"They are *our* veteran organization. They make pretenses of being mostly a 'Patriotic' organization, but they are organizing—or trying to—everyone that was in the Great War."

"And?"

"And their membership is up over a million members at last count... and climbing."

"So?"

"So how many National Guard and National Army Divisions were there?"

"Hell, I don't know. I got there late, remember. Ask me how many field companies were in the *Schutztruppen*. But by the look on your silly-ass face, you already looked it up and are about to impress me, right?"

"Twenty-sixth through the Forty-second National Guard. Seventy-sixth through One-hundred and first for the N.A.—National Army, the draftees. Plus Eight for the Regular Army; plus the equivalent of another for the Marine Corps. And all the ships at sea..." Dodger grinned smugly.

"I repeat—so?"

"How many men were in the Rainbow with us? Not to mention how many mothers and fathers of the men who didn't come back?

Henry shook his head. He had no idea.

Dodger got that I'm-stuck-trying-to-teach-a-lump-of-clay look and shook his head. "Henry, you dumb shit, I don't suppose you ever thought about the reason we had our way with the Heinies so easy was we outnumbered them by, like, three to one."

"Never gave it much, thought, that is to say, I never gave it any thought."

"Our divisions had between thirty and thirty-five thousand men— that's as many as a French or British Army Corps. Hell, our infantry brigades were bigger than some German divisions."

"So what the hell are you getting at?"

"What I'm getting at, Henry, you who are dumber sometimes than a box of rocks, is there are a *helluva* lot of veterans just like us, who would like to have something at hand to show to their children and grandchildren when the little urchins ask 'What did you do in the Great War, Grandpa?'"

"Hmmm."

"Well put. How about this?—'Cause as I recall, you've had some experience putting one together, right? How about a nice photographically supplemented large folio kind of book that takes the umpity-umpth division, or the whatever—pick one at random—following then from day one at training camp in the wilds of upper East Swillbog Noo Yawk, through the Armistice? I think it would sell. I mean like Mark Twain used to sell his books, by prepaid subscription. That way we'd know how many to print and already paid for, and anything else we sell is gravy."

Dodger tossed two other envelopes across the desk. One was the brochure for a steamship cruise to the American Cemeteries in France, departing New York in May, 1924. The other contained the membership forms for the American Legion.

"Besides, Henry—it might be fun."

CHAPTER SIXTY-SIX

Thursday, September 22, 1921
Old State House
Hartford, Connecticut

Their appointment was at 1:15 in the afternoon in a small office on the Old State House building's main floor—though considering the number of steps they had to climb, Henry thought it should have been called the second floor. Dodger and Ruthie met them in front of the Connecticut Mutual Life building across the street, and they had all—along with Doctor Dolbey and Rolf Larson, who were going to act as witnesses, according to the law of Connecticut—trouped as a group across Main Street, up and into the great red-brick and white-colonnaded Federal edifice, which the little brass plaque said had been built in 1796.

They had decided to go this route because, first, everyone they knew or cared to know in Hartford was already here, and there was no way in hell Mary Evelyn's parents or other family would trek to Connecticut to see their kin marrying a *Protestant* and outside a Catholic Church to boot. Of course Henry had no one he cared to know about it—oh, he'd eventually write Junior and tell him, and it would confirm Junior's belief in him as a first-class asshole.

Though he wasn't at all certain they needed one, Henry checked with Dodger as they walked down the hallway to make sure Dodge had brought the ring along. Henry had purchased it on his last trip through New York, sneaking out of the hotel while Mary Evelyn napped in her room after the long, long train ride from Toledo. There they had caught the nearest train connecting with the New York Central in Cleveland. He had tried to contact Hostetler and Harris, but had no luck at all. Ryan's was under new ownership and Hostetler had departed for points unknown—somewhere in the Midwest, the secretary thought. Harris was not in at the *Times* and Henry, knowing he had only that evening before catching the train for Hartford, didn't bother to leave a number.

It wasn't that important anyway. He figured they knew he was alive, if they wanted to contact him, they would.

His life seemed suddenly to be in reverse gear, as though he were trying to catch up on the years he had been "away." Mary Evelyn had surprised him repeatedly, today was the ultimate culmination of the proof of that. She had actually agreed to go to Camp Perry with him and had even appeared to be interested in what was going on there, regardless of the fact he had bombed out of the Wimbledon Match after three shots. He had finished in the top ten in the individual Service Rifle match, however, and was surprised as hell by the fact, considering he hadn't fired in competition in over ten years—closer to fifteen.

When he had told Mary Evelyn her agreeing to go along had come as a surprise, she had patiently explained to him—as though he were a little slow, he thought at the time. She said since they were already engaged to be married, and since they were both mature adults—reasonably—and since they would be staying in separate rooms for the whole trip, and since she knew how much it meant to him to shoot at Camp Perry—to at least the tune of the cost of his new Springfield-made, star-gauged, National Match 1903 rifle, that he had been playing with ever since it had arrived—it was the least she could do in trying to find out why exactly he thought it was so important.

Her razor-sharp, irrefutable illogic, caused his life to roll backwards another few months to the day she had asked him to marry her—sort of—which was also the day he had told her he was moving out of her life again. That had been at the end of April when everything began to look like Anderson & Feller was going to turn into something other than a pipe dream. The complete maintenance overhaul had finally satisfied Dodger's expectations, and the machinery was given a test run, which amounted to resetting Henry's second book, the China book, on the largest of the Merganthalers—three of the really big linotypes, two of the slightly smaller, and two others that were considered small by Dodger. This printing duplicated the font style and size of the original Ryan edition.

Then the endless stream of salesmen—bindery supplies (Henry was astonished at how many bits and pieces went into making a hard-bound book), ink (colors and black), paper (in American and European sizes, weight, texture, shelf-life, rag content), on and on and on. Fourteen-hour days dragged by, and then he dragged himself back to his apartment late at night ending up face-down on the unmade mattress until the alarm clock jangled him into a semblance of activity at six the next morning to face it all over again.

Without Dodger, the whole affair would have been a joke. The sumbitch really did know the printing end of the business. But the commute from the west side of Hartford to the plant and back was wearing Henry out. When the keys were finally turned over to Anderson & Feller, Henry had gone exploring and discovered the executive offices on the third floor—at least that's what they planned to call them and where they intended to have them, with printing and binding on the first floor and in some of the basement, and with editorial spaces on the second. The third floor executive space was actually a suite of six rooms, an outer reception room leading to inner reception rooms, leading into two large offices separated by a large conference room. Henry measured the office he and Dodger had flipped a coin for, discovering his twenty-two by twelve utility apartment would fit nicely in the corner. Therefore, he decided to move his few things into his office and live there until he could find something decent within walking or short-hop riding distance.

When he told Mary Evelyn his plan, she got quiet at first, but then sullen, then very mad. "That's one of the stupidest things I've ever heard of" was the kindest thing she had to say about it once he had pried it out of her she was in fact pissed off by his decision. "You have no place to cook, for instance, no place to keep your precious beer cold… "

"The toilets are nicer," he offered. "There's one attached to each office."

"Where will you sleep?"

"I've got a mattress. I even have a blanket."

"What will we do about Sam?"

"Well, he is *your* cat."

"Right, that's why he's sitting on *your* shoulder."

"So I'll take him along."

"Where would he live? You can't let him run loose in a printing plant—he'd just get killed."

"So I won't take him along."

"He'll yowl after you all the time, then, like he does now. He mopes whenever you leave."

"It sounds as though it's about as much you as it is Sam who doesn't want me to leave."

"Don't be silly. You can do anything you damn-well please. You always have."

"That sounds like you're pissed off I'm leaving, but you were all pissed-off when you thought I'd moved in to this building just to be near you."

"I was worried what the neighbors would think."

"What neighbors? You wouldn't recognize any of the neighbors from this floor if they all lined up and bit you on the ass."

"Watch your mouth."

"My mouth speaks the truth—as the Dakotas used to say. I don't recall you ever meeting any of the other neighbors."

"And you have?"

"Sure—I met the Irish guy at the end of the hall the day I moved in, there's a nice old Jewish couple next to me, and the lady in the next room is from somewhere south of London." Henry tried desperately not to look smug—and was glad he failed. It just heightened Mary Evelyn's piss-off.

"Hey, lady, I'm pushing forty years old. I've managed to live by myself for many of those years, mostly in places where the people, flora, and fauna were all trying to do me in. I'll be all right for the few weeks it'll take to find someplace closer to the plant."

"What if you get sick?"

"I'll call Doc Dolbey."

"If you're lucky… if you don't just collapse and die, like you almost did the last two times."

"The last three times—I collapsed and almost died in German East too. "

"That's right, you did. You're nearly forty?"

"Next year."

"I wouldn't have thought you were that old. You act so childish some of the time."

"Thanks a lot. '*That old.*' And how old are you to be passing judgment on me?"

"Well then, go ahead and do it. Live like a hog. Eat in cheap diners. Drink your beer warm. Just walk away from someplace where you can get a hot meal. Ask me if I care."

"Do you?"

"Do I what?"

"Care."

"Of course not. If you want to live someplace where you don't even have a stove or an icebox, then be my guest."

"I think you do."

Mary Evelyn's eyes began to tear. In spite of herself, she reached out and touched Henry's cheek, though she intended for him to think she was reaching for Sam, who was still perched contentedly on Henry's shoulder.

"That's what I thought," he said.

They had kissed one time then—a novelty for Henry. He remained in the Westside apartment until he found a nice double first-floor about three blocks from the plant the week before they left for Camp Perry. The movers would be coming tomorrow morning to haul their worldly goods across town. They had even decided to buy a car, a Winton, which Henry said he knew how to drive, and he was once more surprised when Ev said she could too. Eventually, provided the business went well, they would look for a house within driving distance of the plant.

The Friday before had been Mary Ev's last day at the VA hospital, and she had enjoyed it immensely, both because she got to have a long talk with Doctor Dolbey, and then have a much shorter, even sweeter one with the administratrix, old lady two-names. When she had finished, the administrator was rapidly flashing from blanched white to apoplectic red and was unable to say anything when Mary walked out of her office and slammed the door hard enough to crack the frame. On her way out, Doctor Dolbey had handed her two small bottles, one filled with his unauthorized little cinchona pills for Henry, just in case, and the other containing something made from yohimbe, yet another of his African herbals.

"If you ever feel adventuresome, Mary Evelyn, try one. If not, throw them away. But just remember many, many African women use them— it makes their really intolerable lives just a little more tolerable."

Henry thought the ceremony was a bit slower when compared with the last civil ceremony marriage he had attended. But again, without the religious folderol, it was over in a matter of minutes, and Henry Feller and Mary Evelyn Feeny were pronounced husband and wife by the state of Connecticut. Mary Ev and Ruthie Anderson, of course, both burst into tears when Dodger pulled the ring out of his pocket and Henry slipped it onto her finger, though Henry thought Ruthie was probably a little more impressed with the Tiffany box than the gesture. And Henry was even a good boy when it came to prying. He refused to look at the date lines on the marriage license so he still didn't know Ev's exact age. Even though she had told him that's where he could find out for sure, if it were *that* important.

CHAPTER SIXTY-SEVEN

Thursday, September 2, 1926
Congregational Cemetery
Mitchell, South Dakota

*R*ather than take the train, the Fellers had chosen to drive all the way
from Connecticut. To be honest, Henry was not looking forward to
the long, long drive back. Not with four-year-old Bobby being an absolute
pain in the ass, two-year-old Skeeter being in the middle of the "terrible twos"
and infant Otis still nursing. Six new tires and a radiator hose later, he was
grudgingly sorry he had not listened to Mary Evelyn's advice and simply
taken the train to Sioux Falls and hired a car. God knows, they could afford
it, so he was almost ready to believe her claim he was simply too cheap to go
the most comfortable way.

Mary Evelyn was additionally miffed he had told her to stay with the
kids in the Dodge, while he attended to the present business at hand.
That's what he had called it, and his wife had, quite rightly, reminded
him, but more sharply than necessary, it was just his way of refusing to
call a spade a spade. For he had come to say goodbye—and had chosen
to take the long way around to do it so he might imprint every swell and
hollow of the lay of land and every ridge and hillock into his mind's eye
forever—to his family and to the place where he had grown up, to the
place he loved as dearly as any he had been to on the face of the earth,
but which now held too many hurts, as his Grandfather Kevin used to
say.

The Feller section was near the top of the low rise in the center of
the cemetery. Junior had done well by the folks, and Henry was willing
to admit as much, even telling Junior so to his face. It would be the first
time he had spoken or written to his Brother in nearly seven years. The
stone was large, but not massive—in other words, not ostentatious. It
simply had "Feller" etched on a piece of reddish marble. Under the family
name were two smaller plaques, one for Emil and one for Kathleen, with
the days of their lives enumerated. There were fresh flowers in a glass

container at the corner of the stone, and yellow roses planted—Mother had always liked yellow roses—in front, where the never-ending prairie wind rustled the petals.

Henry knelt by the stone and idly plucked a few weeds from around the rose bushes. "Mom, Pa—I figure this is the last time I'll ever be here, so I guess this is good-bye." Henry leaned forward and put his head on his arm resting on the top of the stone. "I'm sorry—I really am so sorry for all the things I should have done. I'm so sorry." He thought of the bit of the catechism Zanta had tried to teach him: *Lord, my God, for all those things I should have done that I did not do, I am sorry and I ask your forgiveness; and for all those things that I did do that I should not have done I am also truly sorry and ask your forgiveness.*

He was sobbing when he felt Mary Evelyn's hand on his shoulder. She was holding Otis on her hip. "The boys are finally asleep," she said quietly.

Henry stood and wiped his cheeks on the sleeve of his shirt.

"Is it always so windy?" Mary Evelyn asked.

"Always. This is the prairie. After a while you don't even notice it."

Henry stood erect and slowly turned in a full circle, taking in the view from the top of the high ground, mentally photographing the land that he had walked and ridden across all those years pressed between the leaves of his memory. He put his arm around his wife's shoulder. "Let's be heading back, now. I'm finished here."

CHAPTER SIXTY-EIGHT

Saturday, August 6, 1927
Rainbow Hill
Owings Mills, Maryland

A steady stream of taxis and private automobiles wound slowly, bumper *to bumper, up the driveway to the entrance of what Henry Feller called the MacArthur 'fishing shack', the palatial, thirty-two room house that had been a wedding present from Philadelphia financier Edward Stotesbury to the then West Point Commandant, Brigadier General Douglas MacArthur and his bride, Louise Cromwell Brooks, Mister Stotesbury's stepdaughter.*

Henry vaguely remembered Louise Brooks from his single evening with her in Chaumont, France. It had been the same evening when he, along with Generals MacArthur and March, had gotten three sheets to the wind and swapped war stories about their times together in the Philippines and China, times when they all had been considerably younger and dumber.

The occasion on this particular evening, now flitting rapidly away as the Feller taxi sat in the line of automobiles, was the tenth reunion of the officer corps of the Rainbow Division, one day shy of the date of the Division's activation at Camp Mills, New York. Henry was about to suggest they dismount and walk the rest of the way to the front entrance, in spite of former Major Dodger Anderson's likelihood of needing assistance getting about on his new artificial leg, when the taxi lurched into motion once again and carried them another fifty feet closer to their ultimate goal.

Ruthie Anderson and Mary Evelyn Feller were both staring in wonder out of the side windows of the taxi, a new LaSalle, at the mansion and at the line of autos turning into the drive and forcing the regular traffic on the road to thread its way around the jam—without the blowing of too many horns or the rendering of the Unitarian digital hand signal, mostly. Henry had heard about the MacArthur house from his usual source about anything having to do with money, Slim Wilhelm.

Slim had gotten quite a laugh out of it, at Henry's expense. They had been having a luncheon on one of Henry's detested visits to New York, three, maybe four years ago. They had gone to a little hole-in-the-wall place Slim touted because of its association with the writer William Porter, known to the world as O'Henry. Henry couldn't have found the place again if he'd had to, but the place served a decent chunk of charred beefsteak. Over their meal Slim had asked Henry, in passing, whether he had seen MacArthur since his marriage. Henry had to admit he hadn't even known Douglas had gotten hitched, and one thing led to another and Slim had said Douglas had married a divorced woman named Louise Brooks. Which sparked Henry's memory connection and he recalled as how he had met her in France. Then he had said Douglas must be doing pretty well by himself to be able to afford a wife on an army officer's pay, and Slim had about choked.

When Slim regained control of his voice, he managed to say, "Oh, yes, you might say he's doing all right. You have no idea who she is, do you?"

"Does it sound like I do?"

"Point taken, but seriously, you don't know who Louise Brooks is? Actually Louise Cromwell Brooks?"

"No, Slim, goddamn it, I confess—I do not know, nor do I much care, who the hell whatshername is."

Slim shook his head, laughing. "She's Edward Stotesbury's stepdaughter."

"So?"

"So? You've never heard of him either, I suppose?"

"Guilty as charged—and equally indifferent."

"Henry, Henry, Henry. Edward Stotesbury just happens to be the richest man in the United States. Henry Ford and John D. Rockefeller go to him on bended knee when they need a quick loan. Jesus, Henry, Edward Stotesbury gave your old army buddy a little fishing shack of thirty-odd rooms on about twenty acres as a wedding present for taking his horny daughter out of circulation. They were married at his other fishing shack down in Florida, in a place called Coral Gables, where you have to have two-comma money…"

"Now *that* I remember."

"Don't interrupt. A place where you've got to have two-comma money just to be allowed to breathe the air—which, by the way, smells like a swamp."

"And you'd know about that, right?"

"As a matter of fact I would, thank you very much. We have a place down there. About two blocks from the Stotesbury place. And it still smells like a swamp. There are some things money cannot change."

And that is where Henry had found out about Douglas and his daddy-in-law's estate, and parenthetically, had picked up the term "fishing shack" meaning anything with more than ten rooms. So, by Henry's way of thinking, that particular trip to detested New York City had paid off, though, glancing out the side window of the LaSalle over his wife's shoulder, he had to admit Rainbow Hill was one hell of a fishing shack.

Dodger had been grumpier than usual, especially after the foursome had spent a day in New York so the ladies could shop for new outfits— as though they both didn't already have enough couture clothing to fill an entire room. And on top of that, both women had decided to get new bobs, even shorter than the bobs they usually sported. Henry thought it was Ruthie's hair that had set Dodger off more than the absurdly high prices of the dresses, cloche hats and chain-mail evening bags. Dodger had always loved Ruthie's long hair and had gotten roaring drunk when she had first bobbed her hair just a year after they were married. Mary Evelyn, a couple of years older, and considerably wiser, had followed Ruthie's lead, but Mary Evelyn had taken it in stages, ultimately ending up with hair just as short.

Ruthie was always the wilder one of the pair, and her taste, though influenced by Mary Evelyn, reflected the difference in their ages. Ruthie was an out-and-out flapper. Ev was stylish, without being outlandish— whatever she did or wore, she did to make herself look good as a woman. The trouble was being stylish was damned expensive. The pastel beige silk crepe she now wore was about two inches longer than the lime green one Ruthie wore. Both flattered the female hip-line and cleavage, not something Henry minded because the silk moved with a very pleasant and erotic flounce as Mary Evelyn walked. But Jesus it was expensive. At least Ev's taste in head gear was more to his liking than the paint-bucket cloche Ruthie sported. Ev had chosen a simple head scarf with a hang-down on one side that came nearly to her shoulder but in front of her ear. It was also silk, but of a color that went well with the dress—at about the same price.

When they finally arrived at the base of the steps leading to the grand entrance of the MacArthur's fishing shack, the cabby jumped out and ran around to open the doors for his passengers, reminding Henry very much of the little Jewish driver he had had in France.

"Park around here somewhere, and keep your eye on the entrance— I don't figure we'll be here all that long," Henry told him, getting a full eye-roll from Dodger, who knew how expensive a cab was. In answer, Henry shrugged. "Where the hell else are we going to get a ride back to the depot?"

They fell into line up the steps to the portico. At the top, dressed in a very elegant cut-away evening ensemble stood MacArthur, greeting each and every guest as they topped the steps. When he saw Henry and Dodger, Douglas strode to meet them, dragging his wife along, rather unwillingly.

"Feller, Old Man. And the Artful Dodger. How absolutely splendid it is you could come. And these must be your ladies? Absolutely ravishing. May I present my wife, Louise. Darling, these are two of the finest of my young officers, both of whom shed their blood for their country. Feller here was the commander of my headquarters platoon and the Artful Dodger, Major Anderson, was the Executive Officer of the Ammunition Train. It is absolutely splendid to see both of you."

Douglas gushed on for several more minutes, while his wife gave absolutely no indication she in any way remembered meeting Henry— which was fine by him, since, as he recalled, he had considered her a mere bit of fluff, an available lightweight, when they had met briefly.

After Douglas's rosy greeting, they wandered into the innards of Rainbow Hill, to be duly impressed by its opulence: fourteen foot ceilings, with twelve-foot-high French doors topped by Moroccan arches leading out to patios with spectacular views of the grounds. This evening the estate was lit by hundreds of luminaries defining the walkways through the formal gardens, including a tree with a wooden panel dangling from it that told one and all it was a Japanese Ming, presented to the General by Hirohito, the Emperor of Japan.

"No one ever said Douglas wasn't ostentatious," Henry whispered to Ev.

Toward nine o'clock, the nearly three-hundred guests, all former officers of the 42d Rainbow Division—of whom Dodger and Henry knew a dozen by sight and another couple of dozen by name—began to wander toward the great hall set up as a formal dining room. A wet bar—contrary to the lemonade only Volstead Act law of the land—beckoned at one end, and when Henry handed Ev a glass of white wine, she looked at him with "that look" and surreptitiously held up three fingers, meaning he was allowed only three drinks of illegal booze—or face the consequences. Now knowing his limitation, Henry ordered up a nice single mash Scotch whiskey and was about to offer a toast to Dodger when he saw a couple he recognized coming into the room, a general officer sporting his new and stylish mess-dress uniform, complete with lapels and a double row of medals, and his lady, a svelte, raven-haired woman, who turned and saw Henry at about the same instant he recognized her. Henry's toast froze in mid-word, his face went white, and all he could manage to say was "Holy Shit." Immediately Ev's, Ruthie's and Dodger's attention was drawn to the couple, the distaff side of whom they saw rapidly dragging her husband across the intervening space toward them, all the while nearly shouting, "Oh My God! Henry, Enrico, Henry."

In what seemed like two or three huge bounds, Maria Teresa Lamanti threw herself onto Henry, wrapped her arms around him, and planted a large, loud, wet *beso grande* on his cheek, all the while pressing her now mature, but still marvelously significant frontal orbs into his dinner jacket. "It's been so long. Oh, Henry. You were supposed to write."

Nearly a quarter of a century before, Henry had saved the life of Maria Teresa's younger brother, Arelio, during an attack on the American garrison at Iligan on the island of Mindanao. Things had gone rapidly from a placid introduction to the Lamanti family to several torrid, lust-filled months of cohabitation while Henry, with the assistance of Maria Teresa's older brother, Roberto, gathered the facts and wrote the rough draft of Henry's book about Fred Funston and the capture of Señor Emilio Aquinaldo, leader of the Philippine Insurrection. When his work of the book was finished, Henry had passed the key to Maria Teresa's apartment on to Douglas MacArthur, who had done the same service for the General Officer now standing close by when Douglas had come down with malaria.

Henry shrugged helplessly. Ev was standing near at hand, her face passive—that meant she was either amused or Henry would find himself living the rest of his life in a particularly vicious Irish-Catholic form of hell-on-earth. He was trying desperately to remember if he had ever told his wife about Tamanti, his Filipino, nymphomaniac opera singer.

He was saved—perhaps—by Maria Teresa realizing this was neither the time nor place to renew quarter-century-old passions. She had in fact matured. She was no longer the teenage ingénue. Granted, she was still one hell of a stunning woman, but the rapidly burning fires had been banked and were now laid on for sustained warmth, not instantaneous searing. She turned to Ev, who she seemed to intuit was Henry's present concern.

"Enrico and I knew one another in Manila. There he wrote one of his books, the one about Aquinaldo and Funston, about what my brother Roberto told him. And he saved Arelio's, my younger brother's, life. Enrico is a hero for our family."

That was damned nice of her to put it in that order. Maybe, just maybe, Ev will believe about a third of it.

"How is Arelio?" Henry asked.

"Oh, he is very, very well. He is the managing editor of *El Mundo*, it's a daily now. He took your advice and went to Leyte to the American school there and then to the University of Manila. Yes, he is very well. He has a very nice family—three boys and two girls. And 'Berto, he is also as well as can be expected. He is the manager of a plant for *Mineral de Panay*. They make all sorts of ceramics and whatever. And Henry," Maria said, turning to the vaguely familiar, portly man she had dragged across the room, "this is my husband. I think you might remember him. He was only a lieutenant when you left Manila. You do remember Charlie Rose, don't you?"

"Of course I do." Henry shook Charlie Rose's hand warmly. "It has been a very long time, Charlie."

"It most certainly has. I think it was the Manila Army and Navy Club in what? Aught three or aught four? It was my first tour in the Philippines. Come to think of it, it was Douglas's first tour there too, but you were the old timer. You'd been there since what?"

"Ninety-eight. I actually knew Douglas's father for a couple of years before I ever met Douglas. Might I ask, or should I just assume you were once part of the Rainbow?"

"Oh yes. At the start. I was the first Operations Officer. Douglas beckoned and I, salivating mightily, answered his call. I was transferred up to Corps in December of '17, a month after we got to France."

"Ah, that explains it then. I joined the Rainbow in January of '18."

"You didn't come in with the Guard, then. Like Major Anderson, here?" Rose gestured toward Dodger, then turned to him and offered his hand. "Belatedly, by about a decade, I'm sorry to hear of your bad luck, Dodger. I hope everything else is all right with you."

"Yes, Sir," Dodger answered. "Couldn't be better, considering. General, may I present my wife. Ruthie, this is General Charles Rose."

Ruthie gave a little curtsey and took Rose's offered hand, smiling and saying the expected pleasantries to the general and his lady.

"When I left Manila," Henry said to Ev and the Andersons, "Missus Rose here was the toast of the town. She is an opera singer, or was at that time—one of the reasons why all the young *Americano* officers flocked to the Manila Opera House."

"And I presume all the young *Americano* journalists too," Ev added

"And the not-so-young journalists, as I recall. I believe it was O'Keefe who first lured me there. You remember O'Keefe, General?"

"Photographer fellow? Did a hitch in one of the Volunteer regiments?"

"That's him."

Before the conversation could return to Tamanti's career, or lack of, to haunt Henry, a very black waiter opened the large double doors that separated the reception room from the dining room. Behind him standing at rigid attention was a uniformed enlisted man, an impeccably turned-out Sergeant wearing one of the new Army Dress Blue uniforms, with starched white shirt and black tie. The Army had done away with the standing collared tunic the year before, going to a flat lapel jacket, much like a civilian suit coat, that was worn with a khaki dress shirt and four-in-hand tie and a leather belt with open brass buckle. On seeing the new style at Camp Perry, Henry's very first impression—having spent many long hours in overheated, chaffed misery, while wearing a tunic—was the enlisted men were now a bunch of lucky bastards. Now the Sergeant, obviously a Filipino, announced in very good English, with hardly a trace of accent, "Dinner is served." *Hummph, Douglas must have brought him back from the Philippines.* Then Henry had an odd, marginally pleasant idea flit through his mind. *I wonder if the Sergeant is related to Tamanti.* Followed immediately by *I wonder if Louise Cromwell Brooks MacArthur knows about Tamanti?*

Several hundred guests all trooped dutifully into the dining room and wandered around until they found their names caligraphed on small cards perched atop of their place settings. Then followed a few minutes of shuffling as various couples and foursomes traded around to seating more to their liking rather than governed by the rank—or lack of it—held ten years before. So it was that Dodger and Ruthie swapped their designated places with a drygoods broker, a former lieutenant from Iowa, and his wife, taking seats across from Henry and Ev. General Rose and Tamanti disappeared into the throng, though Henry saw them later, sitting near the head table, seven or eight places down from Douglas. They never spoke to one another again that evening.

Nor did they find the opportunity to talk to Douglas again either, which was the real purpose of coming to the reunion. Dodger thought he was going to talk Douglas into an Army publishing contract for all of the textbooks and pamphlets the Army used at its various training schools and the war college. It would have been a nice chunk of change if it had worked out.

When they managed to make their departure, their cabby was waiting for them dutifully, smoking a cigarette in a circle of other smoking, waiting, cab drivers. The trip back to Baltimore was uneventful and quiet. The cab dropped them at the front entrance of their hotel, a few blocks from the waterfront. Henry was careful not to let Dodger see the bill.

Late that night, as they lay in bed approaching sleep, Ev suddenly asked, "Was she good in bed?"

"Who? Louise MacArthur?"

"No, your Filipino opera singer, wife of the tubby general."

"I think *feral* would be the best word to describe it."

"Oh. And how long did that last?"

"Not very—and I've still got scars to prove it. I passed her on to Douglas, who apparently passed her on to Charlie Rose."

"That's awful."

"She seems to have managed to come out on top."

"Do you mean that literally, or figuratively?"

"Whatever, she is now a very diplomatic but still sultry general's lady, so who am I to pass judgment?"

"And the fires still burn?"

"No. It was pleasant enough while it lasted, but I just didn't want to die that young. Besides, I would bet you dollars to donuts the Roses have a cook and a housekeeper."

"Oh?"

"Otherwise they'd starve. And Charlie doesn't look like he's missed many meals in the last few years. And *that* didn't come from Maria Teresa's cooking, 'cause she could burn water."

"Humph."

"Why? She make you nervous?"

Ev poked him in the ribs.

"You shouldn't be—you came complete with a yellow cat and major appliances. What more could I ask for?"

CHAPTER SIXTY-NINE

Wednesday, April 6, 1927
Anderson & Feller, Publishing
Hartford, Connecticut

*H*enry Feller was sitting at a corner of "The Desk," as it was now called *by everyone associated, no matter how remotely, to Anderson & Feller, including the Ferocious Feller boys and the Anderson Girls. He was wishing Dodger and Ruthie had taken a vacation at some other time. Spread open on The Desk before him were the galley proofs of the latest Anderson & Feller book in the popular series* American Divisions in the Great War. *This one was all about the 79th Division, the National Army Division filled with draftees from Maryland, D.C., and eastern Pennsylvania. In their 43 days on the Western Front, they had taken nearly seven thousand casualties. Henry now meant to make certain all the "I's" were dotted and all the "T's" crossed and all the numbers and such correct—and do it in time to make his own publication deadline of the first of the month next, that being a little over two weeks away.*

So he was not overly happy when Mary Evelyn buzzed him on the office intercom and told him there was someone in the outer office to see him, someone who wouldn't give his name. Henry hoped he had clicked the intercom off before muttering "Shit!" but then decided it wouldn't really matter if some paper salesman knew he was pissed-off.

Mary Evelyn had evidently decided his not refusing to see whoever Mister Anonymous was meant she could bring him in. She ushered the man into the office and quietly closed the door behind her. Ten seconds later, Henry saw the little light on the intercom blink on without the buzz, which meant—bless her female snooping heart—Mary Evelyn was listening in on whatever was said.

The man was as tall as Henry and slim with an impeccably trimmed spade beard. *No salesman, this.* He was dressed in a very conservative and equally impeccably tailored suit. Henry was willing to bet that if he looked at the label he would find a Bond Street, London, address. The man assumed the position of "at ease" as he waited for Henry to come out from behind The Desk to offer his hand. His grip was surprisingly strong.

"I say, we finally get to meet face to face," he said, smiling.

"Am I supposed to know who you are?"

"Ah. Let me test your memory." There was a school-boy twinkle in his eye when he began to recite: "I thought I saw an aeroplane upon the Athi Plain, I looked again and saw it was a Kavirondo Crane." His eyes glinted mischievously.

"I always thought you had written that. I guess this proves I was right. What are you doing in the States? Plotting the overthrow of Silent Cal?"

"Actually, Old Boy, I'm here visiting a mutual friend—who, by the by, is the one who told me where I might find you."

"And who might that be?"

"Why, Dolbey, of course. Got here just in time, too. He's due to leave at the end of the month. Finally going back to Leeds—he's taken a position at the hospital there, epidemiology, as it were. I suspect he'll get rather more business in his specialty there, than here."

"No doubt. So what brings you here?"

"Actually, Old Boy, I'm looking for a North American publisher." He pulled a folded sheaf of papers out of his coat pocket and handed them to Henry. "I've had my legal people do a preliminary contract. Look it over and let me know if the terms are to your liking. My card and telephone number in New York are attached to the last page." Without further preamble, the man shook Henry's hand and walked out of the office, shutting the door behind him.

Within a few seconds, Mary Evelyn made her presence known. "Would you mind telling me who that was," she said as Henry walked around the desk and picked up his telephone to dial the number for Weintraub and Stein. He clasped his hand over the mouthpiece while holding the receiver to his ear.

"That, my dear, was Colonel Richard Meinhertzhagen. And I think we are about to become the North American publishers of bird books."

CHAPTER SEVENTY

Monday, June 10, 1929
Anderson & Feller, Publishing
Hartford, Connecticut

*R*uthie Anderson, who often doubled as one of two executive secretaries to the officers of the company shared her office position with Mary Evelyn Feller. Their sons, the three infamous "Ferocious Fellers" and Ruthie's three daughters, known collectively as the Anderson Girls, who were nearly the same age—within days and months—often roamed around the offices and, when escorted, the printing plant. It was less a lark for them than a way to stave off the boredom of being around their parents.

Henry and Dodger looked up from whatever it was they were doing when Ruthie announced the Wilhelm Brothers—both of them—were in the outer office and wanted to see Henry and Dodger. Dodger waved his hand and Ruthie turned back into the outer office and beckoned. They were well beyond the point of being overly formal.

Stefen Wilhelm, senior partner of Wilhelm Capital Investment Corporation, was the godfather of Henry's three sons, as was Freddy, junior partner, same investment company, to Dodger's kids. Oddly, it never crossed either Henry's or Dodger's mind to ask the Wilhelms if they had any problems with the arrangement, because in all the years he had known them, Henry had never come right out and asked Stefen whether or not he had a particular religious preference. It was one of those things he just simply didn't know. And considering the circumstances, he now felt it was too late to ask and did it really matter? There were times when he was damned near certain the Wilhelms were Jewish, other times when he figured they were old line German Lutheran, others when they might be Catholic, and again others when, at least by their conversation, they might be agnostics of the finest stripe. They didn't seem to mind being made part of the christening ceremony, but then again, Henry knew for a fact that Stefen had also been in on a Catholic baptism, and at least one *bris*. Go figure.

Stefen and Freddy, tossed their hats onto the sideboard next to the coffee pot, and plopped into two leather upholstered Morris chairs set at the one end of The Desk. Emil's creation had jokingly been referred to in the last couple of years—since the launching of the *USS Saratoga*—as "the *USS Dodger*, the secret American aircraft carrier."

Henry walked over to the sideboard and opened one of the doors. "You guys want a snort or coffee or what?" he asked.

"Since you offered," Freddy said, "I'll take some of that highly illegal Scottish swamp water you always seemed to have a plentiful supply of."

Stefen snorted and held up two fingers to signify he was of the same mind. "How the hell do you manage to always have that stuff?"

Henry poured four glasses half full of O'Neils Islay #1 and passed them around. "You may have noticed on your way up here to the edge of civilization, there is this big-ass body of water to the south and east. Up here in the stix we call it Longggg Geyeland Sound. And way the hell over east of here it butts up against this place called Scotland—well, actually, an island off of Scotland, called Islay, which is a very apt name for an island, especially as how the Scots are sort of dim. Well, anyway, that's where they make this highly illegal beverage, but because they are dim, it takes them twenty-four years to get it done—unlike my shirttail kin in Kentucky who used to do it in twelve, that is, before Miss Nation and the rest of the low-life prohibitionist harpies said I couldn't have it any more because it was *EVIL*."

Stefen Wilhelm rolled his hand over in a circular gesture. "Will you get the hell to the point?"

Henry blinked. "I bring it back in a steamer trunk, a keg at a time, whenever I make yet another sad pilgrimage to the cemeteries of Flanders."

"Don't they inspect your luggage?"

"How long have we had the blessings of Prohibition?"

"About ten years."

"Stefen, my lad, it don't take no bureaucrat no ten years to become ingrained and corrupt. They can read a passenger manifest. They see what I've paid for my first class passage. They are not above taking a small remuneration to, how shall we say, smooth the way for my easy passage through their Byzantine labyrinth. And they know I'm a businessman and not some tommy-gun-toting Chicago hood who'll bump off their family if they do what they are supposed to do."

"You bribe them."

"Goddamn right I do."

Freddy Wilhelm harrumphed.

"I've got money, they want it, so I help them by giving them some of it. I've got my Scotch, and they've got their jobs tomorrow—which is the sole purpose of every bureaucrat. And their wives have a little something as a reward. Let Miss Ella Boole's pure but dry peasants do without."

It was Stefen's turn to laugh. "Well, at least you must not consider us to be among Ole Ella's unwashed masses." He lifted his glass and said *Prosit* before taking a healthy sip.

Henry waited for Stefen and Freddy to fortify themselves before asking, "How many pounds of flesh is it going to cost the Dodger and me to find out what has managed to bring you two into the wilds of Connecticut?"

Stefen put his glass down on the desk. "We're on a trip to visit all of our long-time clients to make sure we have long-time clients in the near future." The Wilhelm Capital Investment Corporation had been handling—successfully, if not spectacularly—the Feller and Anderson money, as well as that of all the other branches of the families, since Stefen and Freddy's grandfather Otto had first set foot in the country before the Civil War.

"That was muddled—in fact, it was some of the best muddling of the language I've heard lately. So, to exercise my editorial prerogative, what the *hell* are you trying to say?"

"Cutting to the chase, we've been hearing and seeing things lately— nothing specific, and not all of it in this country. In fact, most of it comes from Europe, from our grand and glorious allies, the Brits and the Frogs," Stefen said.

Stefen looked to be on the edge of agitated, something Henry would have considered leap-pipe-cinch impossible before today. And Freddy appeared to be in agreement with everything his Brother said. The

Wilhelms' *angst* immediately made Dodger and Henry nervous. They put down their whiskey glasses and leaned forward with their elbows on the desktop.

"How so? No bullshit—just say what you came to say."

"They are still pissed off about the Dawes Commission[12]. The Frogs especially."

"Christ, that was five years ago."

"So? That's one year longer than the war lasted, and they figure it was just the beginning of our coming to the aid of the hideous Hun."

Slim Wilhelm sipped his whiskey and then slumped back into his chair. From his eyes, Henry could read he was struggling to keep from putting his heels up on the edge of the desk…and something else. Henry gestured for him to have out with it.

"Most of your problem, my friend," Slim said, "is your relative well-being has insulated you from the daily grind. I hate to say it, Henry, but sometimes you are incredibly…*naïve*…about the real world, especially the real business world. Granted, you and Dodger have made a bundle publishing to a niche demand. But it has kept you from watching all of the kinds of things other businessmen have to follow on a daily basis just to stay afloat."

Henry gestured again for him to continue. Slim and Dodger—and, of course, Mary Evelyn and Ruthie—were the only humans he listened to when it came to listing what he admitted were his manifold faults.

Slim asked, "Have you heard by any chance, the line that came out of the White House last year, when Silent Cal heard Herbert Hoover was a cinch for the nomination?"

Henry looked to Dodger, who shrugged—evidently Dodger didn't know where Slim was leading either. Henry shook his head.

"Well anyway," Slim continued, "when Silent Cal heard Hoover had the nomination in his pocket, he suggested we change the motto on the dollar bill from 'In God We Trust' to 'I Hope That My Redeemer Liveth'." Slim took another sip of his Scotch. "The Smoot-Hawley Tariff Bill is going to come out of committee in the next couple of weeks. I don't see where it's going to get anything but rapid passage. Hoover, who is nothing more than a younger, Quaker, version of Lafollette, won't veto it. And when the French and the other Europeans see what the increases tally, they'll raise their tariffs until American businesses can't or won't bother to sell anything in Europe. And we're already sniping with the Japanese in the Pacific—they want oil, we don't want the competition."

"Well," Dodger said, "we don't sell a whole lot of our publishing to Europe."

"No, you're subscription publishers. I know all that. Just try to remember to sell something, whoever it is you're trying to sell to has to have money to buy it. And because the wondrous Fed—the supposed Federal Reserve Banking System, our Governmental Watchdogs par excellence—have managed to decrease the available money supply by about a third. And you do use banks—easier than taking the money out of your pocket." Slim waved away any rebuttal from Dodger.

"I know, I know. Talked to your family lately?" Slim looked from Henry to Dodger and back. He was well aware Henry hardly ever— meaning never—wrote or spoke to his surviving brother, but he wasn't sure how close a contact Dodger had maintained to the other Andersons, in South Dakota, and various other places. Finding nothing to go by in their looks, he continued, "The First Bank of Mitchell failed last year. Two others—the First Street Bank and, I think, the Railroad Bank—in Sioux Falls both failed this spring. For your information, Henry, Junior, who is also a Wilhelm Brothers client, was pre-warned and was not too badly injured when the Mitchell Bank imploded, but a lot of farmers lost everything." Slim took another sip of his Scotch.

"The business indexes, the things we watch to see how the market is doing, went into decline last fall—before old Hoobert Heever[13] was elected. I suppose some of it is because the average businessman knows Smoot-Hawley will put the screws to business. But a lot more of it is due to the drop in the supply of money available to do business."

"How the hell did the Feds manage to screw things up that much?" Dodger asked.

"Mostly by not doing what they are supposed to do—shore up banks and keep them from failing. Of course, all the banks that have failed are little hometown banks, unworthy of the notice of the newspapers. Tell me, do you seriously think anyone in New York gives a real shit whether some little street-corner bank in Lower East Bum-wad, Dakota, goes under? Get serious."

"So what are we supposed to do about it?" asked Henry.

"Get out of the market. Sell. Now. We don't think there's any time to lose. The bottom is going to fall out, probably about the time Smoot-Hawley becomes law. And anyone still in is going to lose their ass." Stefen looked at Henry. "In a big way, a really big way." He didn't blink. "Sell your stock. Sell *all* your stocks. Take the money and put it in a safe place. *Do not just put it in a bank.* In all probability, the government will close the banks to stop the run and you won't be able to get to your money, if it's still there. If you have a safe, put it there."

"And if you're wrong?"

"If we're wrong you can fire us and reinvest at any time you want, and then you'll lose your ass on your own, but it's *our* obligation to tell you what we think is going to happen."

"Another thing," Fred said, "don't just unload it all at once. You are major holders in some of the companies, and the sudden sale might trigger the sell-off. Watch what is happening in the Senate and Congress and act accordingly, but watch. You should know enough about business timing by now that I don't have to tell you how to plan it. At least you own your own company," Fred added. "No outstanding debts, no shareholders to piss and moan."

"Other than our wives?"

Freddy looked at Dodger. The Missus Feller and Anderson were equal partners in the publishing house.

"Any we should think about keeping?" Dodger then asked.

"You mean what's likely to be there afterward? The railroads, maybe. US Steel. Bell. But there's no guarantee. They might *all* have to restructure. No, I'd say get rid of it all. Wait for the bottom and then get back in on the ground floor of the rebuilding. That way, you could come out way ahead. But it will take *years*, so be patient."

CHAPTER SEVENTY-ONE

Wednesday, September 7, 1932
Offices of Anderson & Feller
Hartford, Connecticut

As it turned out, long after Henry had forgotten the conversation had ever taken place, the later date Douglas MacArthur had mentioned to Henry in the hospital at Chaumont, France, in 1918, turned out to be 1932, a mere fourteen years. It was on a hot Wednesday afternoon in September that two packages arrived by express at the offices of Feller and Anderson Military Publishers from the firm of Bailey, Banks & Biddle, Philadelphia, Pennsylvania. The first package held four identical, oblong boxes covered with blue leather and gold embossed printing. Inside the first box was one of the new Silver Star Medals recently authorized to replace the Citation Star, which was worn on the campaign service ribbon. The reverse of the medal was engraved with "Major D.B. Anderson 117*th* Amn Trn." The next two boxes contained the newly authorized Purple Heart Medal, one again engraved as the Silver Star had been, the other engraved "Lt Henry A. Feller HHD 84*th* Infy Bde." The last was a Distinguished Service Cross, the second highest award granted by the Army of the United States. It too was engraved with Henry's particulars. The second package—really a flat, padded envelope—contained the citations and extra service ribbons for the awards, and a short note from General Douglas MacArthur, "The witness portion of the approval process was waived at the behest of the General Officer commanding. It took a little longer than I thought it would, but here are your well-deserved awards." The note was signed, "God Speed to my old comrades in arms. Lt-General Douglas MacArthur, Chief of Staff, United States Army."

Dodger and Henry looked at one another. Simultaneously they murmured "Well, I'll be damned."

CHAPTER SEVENTY-TWO

Thursday, June 18, 1942
Offices of Anderson and Feller
Hartford Connecticut

Henry Feller, *chairman of the board of Anderson and Feller Publishing—
a position he traded off every other year with Dodger Anderson,
presently president of Anderson and Feller, because of a stipulation in
Connecticut Corporate law that didn't allow the holding of a corporate
position for life—waved his sons into the office he and his partner had shared
for the past twenty years. Then Henry motioned for them to take seats in the
familiar, leather-upholstered Morris chairs in front of the huge desk taking
up most of the office space.*

Bobby, now just twenty years old and in his sophomore year at
Dartmouth, took the seat nearest the window. Eighteen-year-old
Kevin—called Skeeter—took the one farthest from the door, leaving
the middle and most worn chair for sixteen-year-old Otis—called Gus.

Henry walked to the cabinet at one corner of the room and took out
a crystal decanter of O'Neil and four tumblers. He poured an inch of
liquor into each of the glasses and then passed one to each of his sons,
well aware of the strange looks they gave him. He looked at each one in
turn, then sat down and took a long swallow from his glass.

"Not a word of this to your mother," he told them. "This is going to
be a man-to-man talk, and I am willing to treat you all as adult males,
but I don't want to have to explain everything I'm about to say to your
mother…again…since I've already had to assure her I wasn't about to
do—as she so aptly put it—anything too stupid for an old fart like me to
contemplate." Henry looked over his spectacles at his sons and waited
as each nodded their acceptance of conditions.

"Yesterday," he continued, "your mother called me on the carpet.
Somewhere she had heard I had talked to General MacArthur's ADC—
aide de camp—nice young man, a Colonel who managed to get out of
the Philippines with the General and has been running errands for him

ever since. We spent some time telling one another war stories. He was particularly interested in the times I spent with the General, such as they were. But somewhere in the translation, your mother got the notion I was contemplating trying to get back into the Army. And she was not happy about it. It took me the better part of the day to convince her I wasn't about to put my old, fat, slow ass in the line of fire again, Douglas MacArthur or no." Henry took another healthy swig of his whiskey. She said many unkind things. Unfortunately, most of them were—are—true. One of the things she pointedly emphasized was all three of you are bound to try something noble and patriotic." Henry again looked over the top of his glasses at each of his sons in turn. "Just by the looks on your faces, I see she was right." Henry held up his hand before any of them could interrupt.

"Gus," Henry said, looking directly at Otis, his youngest, "don't even think about running off to enlist. You are just too damn young. This war is going to last far longer than any of us wish to think about—years—so your time will come. Until it does, do yourself a favor and do a little planning. Figure out what you want to do or what you're good at, then go from there, with my blessing.

"Skeeter, you and Bobby are old enough. I or your mother can't stop you. But think about this—you have not only the five choices of service, but also whether you are bright enough to go as an officer or enlisted swine. And don't give me that all-knowing condescension—your great-grandfathers were both enlisted men and non-commissioned officers, and fine ones at that. I was an officer, but I ran around with enough 'other-ranks' before I became one I saw the differences, not only in our army but in several others as well.

"Bobby, you have the easiest choice of all, if you're patient. Get your degree or get into an accelerated program and get it early, and you *will* be an officer. Skeeter has the problem of being impatient. But if he can finish some schooling, he can go as an officer also. That is about the only advice I am at liberty to give.

"Your mother, by the way, is already resigned to the fact you are all going to go into the service at one time or in one form or another. And so am I. I would consider myself a piss-poor parent if I hadn't instilled at least that much patriotism in you. I don't have to like it, but I do accept it."

Bobby Feller set his empty glass on the desk top. "Mom really must have been worried about you kicking back into your old habits."

The statement drew an unfathomable look from his father. Finally Henry said simply, "It was not pleasant. What your mother and I ask is you forget about something else we've heard of—that you are all planning to serve together." Henry paused, watching them carefully to catch their reaction. It was obvious to them just where their parents had heard of their plans—the damned blabber-mouthed Anderson girls.

"Considering the closest thing you boys have ever come to in the way of violence and danger has been the occasional automobile accident..." Henry said, looking directly at Bobby, who had recently done in a perfectly good 1939 Packard 280 on a slippery curve on the way home from Dartmouth, "so serving together, while it sounds 'neat,' really amounts to a means to have all of you together in the wrong place at the wrong time. In other words, your mother and I would get not just one, but three, telegrams telling us the government regrets to inform us our son—Robert, or Kevin, or Otis, or some combination—has, or have been killed in action. One would be bad enough. Three would probably kill her—and wouldn't do me any good either. So plan to serve in different branches or different services. I don't care which. And I'm willing to take my chances—really, your chances—that God will find it in Him to let one, two, or all three of you come through this war, alive and well."

CHAPTER SEVENTY-THREE

Thursday, August 3, 1944
Anderson & Feller, Publishing
Hartford, Connecticut

T he phone on Henry Feller's desk rang twice before he managed to cross the office and pick up the receiver. As expected, it was his wife on the other end of the private line.

"You'd better come home," was all she said.

Twenty minutes later, having broken most of the traffic laws of the state of Connecticut and the 35-mile-per-hour wartime speed limit as well, Henry pushed open the front door of their house on Simsbury Road, and found Mary Evelyn still sitting next to her end of the private telephone. Her face was ashen. As he walked across the room, to her, she held out a yellow Western Union telegram envelope.

"I was afraid to open it."

Henry took the message from her hand and slit the top fold with the letter opener.

WESTERN UNION TELEGRAPH COMPANY
2 AUG 44
WAR DEPARTMENT
WASHINGTON, D.C.
THE SECRETARY OF WAR DEEPLY REGRETS TO INFORM YOU THAT YOUR SON, CAPT ROBERT DAVID FELLER, ARMY OF THE UNITED STATES WAS KILLED IN ACTION 17 JULY 1944, NEAR ST JEAN DE HAYE, NORMANDY, FRANCE.
SIGNED
HENRY L. STIMSON

"Bobby..." was all Henry could manage to say as he slumped onto the sofa and wrapped his arms around his wife's shoulders. It was nearly a minute before she began to sob, her face buried in the collar of his jacket.

CHAPTER SEVENTY-FOUR

Tuesday, March 20, 1945
Anderson & Feller, Publishing
Hartford, Connecticut

"*C*ome home, right now—there's been another telegram."
The phone went dead in his hand as he reached for his overcoat on his way out of the office. "Please, dear God, no." Mary Evelyn's voice on the other end of the phone had been as close to sheer panic as he had ever heard.

This time she met him at the door. He ripped the end off of the envelope without preamble. Having read the contents, Henry staggered to the loveseat in the front hall and sat heavily. He beckoned for Mary Evelyn to sit beside him.

WESTERN UNION TELEGRAPH COMPANY
19 MARCH 45
DEPARTMENT OF THE NAVY
WASHINGTON, D.C.
THE SECRETARY OF THE NAVY REGRETS TO INFORM YOU THAT YOUR SON CAPT KEVIN T. FELLER, USMCR, WAS SERIOUSLY WOUNDED ON THE ISLAND OF IWO JIMA, 4 MARCH 45 AND IS PRESENTLY ABOARD THE US NAVY HOSPITAL SHIP REPOSE BOUND FOR THE US NAVAL HOSPITAL, SANTA BARBARA, CALIFORNIA. YOU WILL BE INFORMED AT A LATER DATE AS TO THE EXPECTED DATE OF HIS ARRIVAL AT THAT FACILITY.
SIGNED
JAMES FORRESTAL

CHAPTER SEVENTY-FIVE

Friday, September 28, 1945
United States Naval Hospital
Santa Barbara, California

*C*aptain Kevin Feller, USMCR, was sitting up in his bed and reading. It was the second time he had read Douglas Southall Freeman's biography of Robert E. Lee. The first time had been as a source for one of his papers during his senior spring at Providence. He found now he disagreed with some of Freeman's positions even more strongly than he had as a callow, but whole, youth. A ghost twinge from his former left leg caused him to let the book flop onto his chest and at the same time made him wonder when the sonofabitch was going to stop hurting. It had been over six months since he had come to on the hospital ship where a Navy surgeon had broken the news to him he was 1) damn lucky to be alive, and 2) they hadn't been able to save his leg. The only other thing he remembered, chillingly, was the realization the Jap mortar round was going to hit goddamned close. He couldn't remember if he had had time to yell to his men to get down or not. There had been an extremely loud roar, and then he'd come to on the hospital ship, sans leg. As of late the twinges no longer caused him to break out in cold sweats, and they seemed to be coming at longer intervals, so maybe they were going to go away eventually.

When he went back to reading his book, he caught the flicker of movement out of the corner of his eye. His body automatically tensed, and his eyes did a quick scan, plotting the best path to cover and the position of his weapons. *Well, you damned fool, at least you didn't dive under the bed, or fall onto the floor and flop around like an overturned beetle. Wonder how long that part of it will last. Jesus, I was only on Iwo for two weeks, which was quite long enough, thank you very much. I was the last Captain left standing—no pun intended—in the 27th . And of the 242 men who came ashore on the landing, I think I had two NCOs and maybe a dozen of the original riflemen left. Everybody else was fresh meat. I can't even remember their names, but I see their faces every goddamned night.*

All of these thoughts were churning around inside Captain Feller's head as he looked toward the door to his room, the place where he had first noticed the motion. Standing there, actually leaning there, with his shoulder against the door jam and his other hand leaning on his cane, was one of the last people Captain Kevin Feller, USMCR, ever expected, or wished to see—his father-in-law, Dodger Anderson. He was dolled up in a well-cut, double-breasted, dark gray pin-striped business suit, and he was holding a grey fedora in his off hand.

"You look better than I figured you would," Dodger said as he pushed himself away from the door and limped to the chair next to the bed, lowering himself with a grunt and tossing the hat onto the table. "They haven't changed military hospitals in twenty-five years. I think this is the same table your Dad and I had in our room in Hartford."

"I suppose Ruthie told you where I was."

"Oh, yeah. 'Course, considering this is the nearest hospital to the receiving station at the Naval base, I could have probably figured it out for myself."

"Have any trouble getting past the gorillas at the gate?"

"Skeeter, I'm a former field grade type officer, and a certified hero to boot," Dodger said, pointing to the lapel of his suitcoat with his thumb. There were two pins sharing the buttonhole, one a purple and white roundel, the other an American Legion membership badge. Dodger had been correct in assuming the ward gorillas would defer to a man with a limp and a cane—and the lapel button of the Purple Heart medal.

"When you figure they're going to let you out?"

"Probably not until early next year—they said they were having a hard time finding a whale to carve my new leg from."

"You wouldn't make a good Ahab—not obsessed enough. Matter of fact, you wouldn't make a good Fred Allen either. You can't seem to conceal the bitterness." Dodger Anderson looked without blinking. "That why you told Ruthie you wanted a divorce?"

Skeeter glared at his father-in-law. "That's none of your business."

"Bullshit. She's my daughter. She hauled her ass out here to Sodom on the Pacific to marry you, she worked in a goddamn bomber plant instead of coming home after you got shipped out, she worried herself sick every time they showed a dead or hurt Marine on the newsreels. And when you did manage to run out of luck, you repaid her by refusing to see her when she came here, and then you sent her a fucking post card asking if she would like a divorce." Dodger Anderson was as angry as Skeeter could ever remember seeing him. "Now, asshole, I'm going to tell you what you are going to do for yourself."

When Skeeter opened his mouth to reply, Dodger gave him a withering look. "Just shut the fuck up and listen. I'm also going to blow holes in all of your arguments. Like the first one you were thinking of using, the one that says you are no longer a whole man because you lost a piece of yourself. That's bullshit, and you know it. Unless you know something I don't including all the Navy Doctors I talked to on the way in here?

"And the part about being guilty by being alive won't work either. You're alive because of one thing—the luck of the draw. It could have just as well been six inches one way or another, and then some other poor sonofabitch would be lying here wondering how come he's alive and the Captain got it.

"You don't even know how lucky you are. Medicine has come so goddamned far in the last twenty years you can live through a wound that would have killed me or your father just by way of ignorance. They'll have an artificial leg on you so fast it'll make your head spin, and it will bend and move and let you do a hell of a lot more than just gimp around on a wooden—and I might add—very uncomfortable stump extension."

"And then what?" Skeeter managed to slip in while Dodger was taking a breath.

"How the hell would I know? It's your life, not mine. Jesus Christ, you have a college degree, and you are a decorated veteran. You have one big thing your old man and I never had after the last war—you've got the GI Bill. Shit, you've always got your nose in some goddamned book anyway, why don't you go back and get a Masters or a PhD?"

"I suppose that's possible..."

"Of course, it's possible. Hell, you're a frigging Marine. You're supposed to be able to do anything, aren't you?"

"Yeah," Skeeter replied bitterly, "everything but keep my men alive."

"Can that shit. That's part of the job. If you don't believe me, ask your old man. I don't suppose he ever told you he started out with a fifty-man platoon, but when we were done for the day, he was down and the eight men left were being led by an acting corporal. Yeah, just ask him about keeping his men alive—should be good for a chuckle." Dodger glared at Skeeter who looked away.

"Of course, he did manage to save my ass. That allowed me to live a cripple for the rest of my days—isn't that how it goes? Maybe you think it would be better if we had died instead of inconveniently staying alive to be cripples? I sure as hell don't. I've been one happy sonofabitch every morning I wake up."

CHAPTER SEVENTY-SIX

Thursday, August 8, 1946
600 Simsbury Road
Bloomfield, Connecticut

The taxi was a 1939 Chevrolet. It was very much the worse for wear after an entire World War of extended use without the benefit of spare parts or new tires. Still, it managed to make it all the way out to the Simsbury road address—Albany to Bloomfield to Simsbury, actually—from the train depot without losing any major parts, which Gus considered a minor miracle. The cabby pulled up to the front door and helped Gus pull his two sea bags out of the trunk. Gus fished into the pocket of his white "kidney crunchers"—his summer dress bell-bottom trousers—pulled out part of the wad of his final pay, and paid his for his cab ride with a generous tip. This was acknowledged by the cabby with a tip of his hat and a "Gee, thanks, sailor."

Gus squared his hat, hoisted one of the sea bags onto his shoulder, grabbed the tie of the other, and dragged it up the steps to the front door.

Before he could ring the bell, the door opened and his father said, "Saw you get out of the cab, you managed to get everything taken care of before I could find my shoes. Here, let me give you a hand with that." Henry took one of the sea bags and hefted it. It was heavy. They carried their loads inside and upstairs to Gus's room, where the bags were dumped unceremoniously at the foot of the bed.

"Where's Mom?"

"She's over at Ruthie's. They're doing girl things with Little Ruth—she's due in about three weeks—and they're getting ready to bring the next generation of 'Ferocious Fellers' into the world."

"What's cooking for this evening?"

Henry shrugged. "We'll have to see what your mother wants to do, but I don't think it'll be anything special or extravagant. Probably eat at someplace close and then show you off to Dodger and Ruthie. Why? You got other plans?"

"Nope, I'm just glad to be home. Not that it's like I was stationed on the other side of the world or anything. Sometimes it really bothered me, to tell the truth. It didn't even feel like being in the service."

Gus Feller—until this morning when his discharge had been finalized, Sonarman First Class Feller, Otis A.—had, since leaving the Naval Recruit Training Depot, Great Lakes, Illinois, the day after his eighteenth birthday in 1943, been assigned to the destroyer escort *USS Amick* (DE-168). Gus proved an outstanding sonarman and worked his way up to 3rd Class and then 2nd Class, and finally in January, 1945, to 1st Class. The promotion came through at the same time as his transfer to the destroyer *USS Ericsson* (DD-440), the flotilla leader for the *Amick*, her sister DE, *USS Atherton* (DE-169), and the frigate *USS Moberly* (PF-63). The anti-submarine flotilla was berthed at Narragansett, Rhode Island, not quite a hundred miles from 600 Simsbury Road.

Gus even had been allowed to have his personal vehicle, a 1939 Pontiac, so he was often home on leave and often sometimes when his watch was given liberty. He wasn't technically supposed to do that, but what the hell—even if he had obeyed the speed limit, it was less than a three-hour drive home. Unfortunately, Gus chose to use the same routes all the time. The first time, the Connecticut trooper had waved him on as soon as he saw Gus's uniform. The second time, the same trooper in the same spot had given him a stern warning about watching his speed. The third time, it had cost him nearly a month's pay. After that, he had put the Pontiac in the garage and had taken the train back to Rhode Island.

Later, Henry Feller was sitting on the sofa in the living room when Gus came downstairs. The white bell-bottoms were replaced by a pair of khaki slacks and a light cotton shirt. The only remaining issue items were the Navy oxfords. When Gus saw Henry glance at the shoes, he grinned. "None of my old shoes fit any more, and yes, I tried them all. I'll have to go buy some tomorrow."

Henry rose and walked to the liquor cabinet. He grasped a bottle of bourbon by the neck and held it up, cocking his head to ask if Gus wanted some.

"No thanks, Pop. I'm swearing off the stuff for a while."

The statement caused Henry's eyebrows to rise. He poured himself two fingers in a tumbler and gestured with his free hand for Gus to explain.

"I got to the point where I was liking it too much. And then I had a pretty good-ole Chief tell me why I was boozing too much, and I decided he was right spot on. I haven't touched anything since."

"So," Henry asked, "what was he right spot on about? If I may ask?"

"No, I don't mind. In fact, it's made me think about it quite a bit, and I've made a couple decisions. But anyway, Chief Sims said I was trying to drown guilt, and guilt is like shit—it always floats to the surface."

"So what were you feeling guilty about?"

"On the evening of the day before VE Day, there was an old collier, the *SS Black Point*, hauling a load of coal up Long Island Sound to Boston for the power plants. She was old and slow and had never been out of the Sound during the whole war. A little after nine o'clock, she was hit by two torpedoes—killed twelve merchies outright—and she capsized in 95 feet of water just off Point Judith. It only took her 15 minutes to go down, and the other thirty-five or so merchies on her were lucky to get off.

"Another merchantman, the *SS Kamen*, rescued the rest of the crew and radioed the position in to us. We were on standby anyway and had steam up, so we were on the way out of harbor within fifteen minutes. The DD-440, my ship, was leading, and I picked up the sub on the bottom in less than 20 fathoms, almost as soon as we cleared the nets..."

"Nets?"

"Antisubmarine nets. They were strung across the mouth of the bay. The U-Boat had no where to run and no place to hide. And the skipper was really p-oed about the sub sinking the old coal ship. So all four of our ships went into formation and spent the rest of the night criss-crossing the area. We must've rolled over a hundred cans, but every time the noise died down I could still hear her down there. We stayed on her all night, and the next day Lakehurst sent two blimps up to help. Finally, a whole bunch of stuff come bobbing up to the surface, a chart table, planking, clothing, oil, loaves of bread, and the Captain's hat. We got a confirmed kill."

"So, where does the guilt come in?"

"Pop, the war was over. There's a five hour difference between Eastern War Daylight Time and Zulu time—Navy talk for Greenwich Mean Time. Germany had surrendered, unconditionally, about five hours before we sailed out of Narragansett. In fact, we even learned afterward Admiral Dönitz had tried to radio all the German boats the war was over and to return to base. But evidently the *U-853* didn't get the word. That's the real problem. We learned all about our last kill after the war was over. The German embassy sent a roster and one of our divers identified the hull number. Pop, I killed 55 men that didn't have to die. Just by doing my job. And add to that the dozen merchies that bought it on *Black Point*. Sixty-seven men. But the worst part is I know *all* of their names, all the way from *OberLeutnant* Helmut Frömsdorf, to the lowliest new *Unterseebootman*, Axel Dolph, and I've seen photographs of a lot of them—the German embassy was *very* thorough."

"And?"

"I've decided pretty much since I had a large hand in killing sixty-odd innocent men, I should, now that I'm out of the service, try to do something about maybe saving some innocent lives. That's as far as I've thought it through, Pop."

"So? What's next?"

"I don't know—back to school, I guess. Pre-med, mayby pre-theo. I haven't decided beyond that point, but the GI Bill ought to get me into pret'-near wherever I want to go. Bobby always liked Dartmouth." Gus shrugged. "Let's see if I can handle the academic stuff, and then I can pick and choose from there."

Henry looked at his youngest. It was the first mention of Bobby, and the pain was still there, just below the surface. "Well, let me know what you need."

"I shouldn't need much. I've still got most of Bobby's insurance money left. There was no place to spend it on a destroyer escort."

Henry cocked his head. He knew Robert had taken out the usual and customary GI Insurance before going overseas, but he'd thought the lack of the benefit was just another indication of the glacial bureaucratic process. So this was the first he realized perhaps Robert had made arrangements other than those he had assumed. "Oh?" He now asked.

"Bobby made me and Skeeter the beneficiaries of his GI insurance. We each got five thousand dollars." Gus stopped and looked closely at his father. "You didn't know that, did you." It was a statement not a question.

Henry shook his head. He wondered how many other things he did not know had been shared by his sons.

"We all did the same thing, at first. I think Skeeter changed his over to Ruthie when they got married, but I'm not certain. Anyway, you remember how we all got together in Chicago just before Bobby shipped out? That's when we all decided we would make each other the beneficiaries of our GII. We figured you and Mom didn't need the money, anyway, and we all sort of pledged not to spend it on anything usual and customary—just go out and have a helluva good time in memory of whichever one of us had got it. We were all pretty drunk at the time, and it seemed like a real good idea when Bobby proposed it. Anyways, that's how it happened. I still have about four grand in the bank, so college shouldn't be any problem. You gonna tell Mom?"

"Probably—eventually. But you might want to know the other half of it. Actually, the other third of it."

"How's that?"

"Slim Wilhelm, your mother, and I set up trust funds for each of you when you were born. Come to think of it, I think Dodger and Ruthie did the same for the girls. So, now you and Skeeter get to divvy-up Bobby's third between you. God, that sounds so callous, but it's the truth. When Bobby got killed, his trust fund portion went to the survivors. I don't even know how much it amounts to—you'll have to ask Slim. He handles all of that kind of thing. But I would make it high on your list of things to do. It means you won't be dependent on 'twenty for fifty-two.'[14]"

Henry set his now empty glass on the end table and picked up the telephone. "I'd better call your mother and tell her you're home. We might as well go over there, and you can make your nice-nices to your Aunt Ruth and Ruthie, and then we can get something to eat."

CHAPTER SEVENTY-SEVEN

Monday, April 20, 1953
1562 Coventry Lane
Coral Gables, Florida

T*he jangling of the telephone woke Sam the cat—number seven in a long line of yellow tom cats reaching back to 1890. Sam VII then woke Henry Feller from his midday nap by leaping from his chest. Henry hurried to pick up the phone before it could disturb Ev, forgetting once again his wife of thirty-one years could not be disturbed by a ringing telephone. Mary Evelyn had succumbed to ovarian cancer in January, and other than Manuel and Dorita Gonzalez, Henry was alone in the house and would be for the foreseeable future.*

The voice on the other end of the phone was Stefen Wilhelm, and Henry gave silent thanks. Slim knew Henry well enough to not continually spew condolences, the verbal equivalent of ripping a scab off of a nearly healed wound. A double wound, by Henry's way of thinking. Ev's diagnosis and downhill spiral coincided with Henry's losing battle to get Douglas MacArthur the Republican nomination for president. Ev's illness was kept a secret to all but a small circle of intimates. Still, dealing with it made Henry much shorter in fuse than usual. He would tolerate very little in the way of typically dirty campaign politics from either side. He considered Adlai E. Stevenson of Illinois, an empty egg-headed Socialist and dismissed the attempts of the Democratic Party to contact Douglas. He stated often and loudly he thought the Democrats had in all but fact delivered the country into the hands of Joe Stalin without so much as a by-your-leave.

His reaction was even worse when he was contacted by Kevin McCann, one of Dwight Eisenhower's former staff officers, who asked if Henry had ever heard of a teenage Filipino-Scottish mistress named Isabel Rosario Cooper. Supposedly MacArthur brought her to Washington from Manila after he was sworn in as Army Chief of Staff. He had established her in an apartment in Georgetown, and then in a hotel on 15th Street N.W., while MacArthur himself lived with his mother at Fort Myer near Washington. McCann made the mistake of implying to Henry if Douglas made a serious run at the nomination, it was more than likely Douglas's morality would be opened to the light of day and the viewing of the general public—vis-à-vis, his first wife[15], and her relation to General Pershing, and others, and his stashing of the sixteen-year-old Filipino mistress.

Henry had gone into instant boil. Barely keeping his voice and temper in check, he had told McCann to check with General George Catlett Marshall, who had been Truman's—that is a Democrat's—Secretary of State, as well as having been Eisenhower's and, for that matter, McCann's commanding officer. "Ask him about his advice to Dwight when your general wanted to divorce Mamie and take up with his chaufferette—I believe he referred to her as that big-titted Limey bitch. You do that. Then you take a real long considered think about whether you want to get into the morality issue at all." And that's pretty much where the issue died. As did Douglas's bid for the nomination.

The truth was, Douglas had simply made too many enemies during his career, both inside and outside the military. The biggest trouble with Douglas, after all, was his genius and his ego were both monumental, and no one could tell which one was at work at any given time. He remained transparently opaque—or was it opaquely transparent, or perhaps both at once. The powers that were within the Republican Party decided a little mediocrity was easier to deal with. Douglas never got beyond the grin and wave stage toward the nomination. And in the end, Henry lost both the political battle and his wife, and the man who had once been the best clerk Douglas MacArthur had ever had was now the President of the United States.

"Hank, you old fart, how's things going?" Stefen asked without preamble.

"They could be better. Why? You got some widows and orphans to evict?"

"Naaa, nothing that interesting. You know or remember a guy named *Herr Doktor* Kaufman?"

"Head of the Bundesbanc?"

"That's him."

"Heard of him, never met him. Why? You want to evict him?"

"No, nothing that pleasant. He's got a little deal working you might be interested in."

"What sort of little deal?"

"Involves Africa."

"Been there—still have the scars and the Doctor bills to prove it. And?"

"Involves Paul Von Lettow."

"That's Paul Von Lettow-Vorbeck, Stefen. Christ, you've got enough German in you to make the distinction. Please."

"Right—anyway, if you'd care to listen, Adenaur is sending *Generalmajor* Von Lettow-Vorbeck—is that better?—back to formerly German East Africa to try and locate his surviving soldiers."

'Askaris...'

"Whatever. Henry, shut up and listen. Adenaur wants to pay them off. Evidently they were never paid at the end of the First War. They didn't surrender, you know, they just stacked their equipment in wherever."

"Rhodesia."

"Whereever. When the German government told them to stop fighting...and I guess they just walked home from there."

"That sounds about right. Paul said the officers were all sent—transported—to Mombasa and shipped back to Hamburg. That's where he found out he was a hero, and a *Generalmajor*."

"You ever think of publishing something about your time from War One over there?" Stefen asked.

"Well, other than I don't know where the hell my notes are—I haven't seen them for thirty-five years. In fact, I'm not sure they weren't used to wipe the very black and very soiled asses of most of the Wahehe tribe. Other than that I would consider it."

"Would you like to go pick them up?"

"What?"

"Henry, honest to Christ I think you're getting senile. Wouldn't you like to go and at least see if they are still in existence and not covered with the shit of nations? Or at least the—what the hell did you call them?"

"The Wahehe. But Slim, why don't you stop beating around the goddamn bush and tell me about this little adventure you seem to know so much about yet are so goddamned reticent to talk of."

"OK, since you insist."

A half hour later, Henry asked into the receiver, "All right, Slim, you've convinced me. So when do I leave?"

"The *Bremen* sails from Naples on May 10th."

"Why the hell would I take a boat? I can fly to Nairobi and take the train or catch a connecting flight to Dar—be there in three days, tops."

"Because your friend is taking the boat, Henry. The General and his companion, a guy from the Bundesbanc. I've got his name here someplace if I can find it."

"Christ, I haven't been on a boat in damned near twenty years."

"You got something better to do? Think of it as a vacation. You do know what a vacation is, don't you? Anyway, you can fly to Naples and catch the boat there, is that better? I'll have Alva get the tickets and make the reservations—all right by you?" Alva Fleischer was, and had been, Stefen Wilhelm's secretary-cum-executive-assistant-cum right-hand for nearly twenty-five years.

"Well, at least I won't end up in a French youth hostel, sniffing the great unwashed and listening to college types beat on bongo drums and read bad poetry," Henry snorted.

"I'll tell Alva. I'm sure she'll be delighted to hear she has your trust."

"Same to you, Slim. Stay in touch."

CHAPTER SEVENTY-EIGHT

Monday, June 15, 1953
Lobby of the *Deutsches Bundesbanc*
Dar es Salaam, Tanganyika

A t the end of the two-week waiting period, the Deutsches Bundesbanc *provided space in the lobby of their edifice, as had been ordered by the Chancellor of the Federal Republic of Germany, for the purpose of gathering all those Afrikaners claiming prior service in the armed forces of the then German Empire during the 1914-18 War. By rough count, some three hundred oldsters—many led by younger men obviously their sons and grandsons or some other male relative—had appeared to make their claim against the government of the Federal Republic.*

Herr Dieter Sietman, the representative of the President of the *Bundesbanc,* sat behind a large, highly polished desk made of some exotic local wood. To his right sat the local Bank Managing Director, to his left *Generalmajor* Von Lettow-Vorbeck and the *Amerikaner* Henry Feller. Before them, a sea of very black faces stood impassively.

The process was one Henry, Dieter, and Paul had thought out on the *Bremen.* As each man presented himself, he gave his name and rank and the number of the *Schutztruppen Feld Kompainie* he had been a member of. Many of the applicants held out the Imperial Eagles or the shoulder tabs from their uniform jackets, emblems still holding the company numbers kept shiny over the years with tender and loving care. If the applicant could not remember, or had no physical evidence to offer, he was asked a number of questions about his service. Then he was handed a broomstick—a *Gewehr* 98 Mauser rifle being deemed imprudent in the lobby of the *Bundesbanc*—and *Obersti* Von Lettow-Vorbeck barked out the manual of arms in German.

The thirty-ninth or fortieth man to present himself limp-marched slowly to the front of the desk, assumed the position of attention and was about to give his name and rank when he was interrupted by Henry Feller.

"I'll vouch for this man." Henry had seen the very black face, and the deformed nose with the straight-across scar; the bright eyes yellowed by years of fighting off God alone knew how many bouts of tropical diseases. He saw also the tall, handsome young man who had been helping hold his elder erect. "He is *Ombascha* Jabari Rajabu."

"No." Paul Von Lettow-Vorbeck said. "He was Schausch Jabari Rajabu, a totally worthless man who would never follow orders…or take advice from a friend." Paul looked to Henry, "He came back to duty after the wound healed somewhat and rejoined us until the end."

Dieter Sietman of the *Bundesbanc*, turned to Paul. "I assume this means both of you know this man to have been an *Askari*"

"*Ja*," *Generalmajor* Von Lettow-Vorbeck said simply.

"And this is the Jabari I have heard you speak of so often?"

"*Ja*."

Henry pushed his chair back from the desk and stood. Striding around the desk, he and Jabari looked at each other wordlessly for nearly a minute, before either of them could manage to speak.

"It has been many years, my Brother, my old Friend," Jabari said in Swahili.

"It has been a lifetime, my Brother, my old Friend," Henry answered, also in Swahili, though if you had asked him, he would not have known it. "The *Obersti* says you did not follow my advice, old Friend."

"I did after a fashion, my old Friend. I could not leave my duty. I am, after all, Wahehe."

"What of the rest? Did you follow my advice there?"

"Oh yes, my old Friend. When the war was over, I followed your advice to the letter."

"And?"

"There were many enthusiastic maidens, and many, many *kitoto*— babies—and many many goats and cattle, my old Friend. And you?"

"There was one very willing maiden and three *kitoto*, all sons, and enough money to be comfortable and to visit old Friends in my old age."

"And how are your sons?"

"One is very well, very successful—a college professor. The other is a Christian minister."

"And the third?"

"Alas, we lost the third. He was killed in the War."

"I am so sorry, My Brother."

"So am I, my old Friend."

Jabari put his hand on Henry's shoulder, gently leading him to where the tall young man who had assisted him stood waiting. When Henry and Jabari approached, he raised his hand, palm outward. "*Shikamoo, Bwana*—hello, Sir"

"*Marahabaa!*—I acknowledge your respect," said Henry, offering his hand for a western handshake.

"This is my grandson, Omsha, whom we call Mosi, it is a proud name and my brother lives in him, old Friend. Does he not look like her?"

Mosi Rajabu was a well set up young man in his twenties. His nose was straight set between piercing black eyes. His thin lips were turned up at the corners in a slight grin as Henry kept his hand in his own. His skin was a deep rich brown, shaded on the darker side of baking chocolate, with tinges that might be called ebony. His teeth, what could be seen of them, were white and even. His Swahili bore the traces of an accent learned in the English schools.

"Yes he does, old Friend, yes he does. Does he know of her?"

"Some. I have not told him all."

"Then I shall, old Friend, then I shall."

CHAPTER SEVENTY-NINE

Wednesday, June 17, 1953
Oyster Bay
Tanganyika

enry Feller sat in the padded rattan lounge, resting his feet on an overstuffed ottoman and taking in the breathtaking view of the spectacular beach and the Indian Ocean beyond. He had been brought from Dar es Salaam to Oyster Bay, to Mosi Rajabu's home. He held a glass of chilled and sweetened rooibos tea on his chest, occasionally sipping the aromatic liquid. Jabari had gone into the house on some errand, and Mosi had gone to the master bedroom to change into something more comfortable than the linen suit he wore as a badge of importance.

Mosi was with the Ministry of Commerce. He had been put through the English preparatory schools and then had gone off to England to earn a degree in economics at Edinburgh. When there was time, he said, and his career was settled and assured, he would like to go back and do his post-graduate studies at Cambridge. Or perhaps one of the American schools—Wharton perhaps? It was a request within a statement within a wish. Henry was aware it would be a very large feather in the cap of any junior commerce minister to "influence" a wealthy American by wining and dining him in the more affluent suburbs. Africa was not all that different from New York or Chicago—and a hell of a lot more civilized than Moscow or Paris, or Washington.

Jabari emerged from one of the doors carrying a largish canvas case with web straps encircling it, buckled to contain whatever it held. Waving his head, Jabari motioned for Henry to move his feet from the ottoman so he could set the case down. That done, he immediately began unbuckling the straps, as Henry sat upright on the lounge and put his tea on a coaster on the triangle-topped table, within reach of his right hand.

Rajabu unfolded the canvas and there Henry saw a stack of five large notebooks. Jabari took the top one and handed it over to his Friend.

There was a flash of recognition as Henry opened the front and read the hand writing, his hand writing: *"Journal of Henry A. Feller 1913."*

"I never thought these would survive," he said, his voice filled with emotion.

"But I was told to keep them safe for the day you returned for them. It was a charge of honor."

Henry pondered. "But when I gave them to that *ruga-ruga*, you were barely conscious. I told him to take you back to your village and gave him my haversack with these in it." Henry thought hard, struggling to relive the happenings of nearly four decades before. "I told the *ruga-ruga* some instantly concocted tale to frighten him into doing what I told him, but—God as my witness—I don't recall telling him to have either you or himself watch over these as a...what did you call it? A charge of honor, which I assume is on the same order of a sacred trust. That's why I never bothered to see if you were alive or any of that. Jesus, if I'd have known, I would have been back over here looking for you." Henry's rambling ended abruptly when he looked into Rajabu's face.

His Friend was waiting patiently to speak. "No, no, no, My Brother. You don't understand. It was not *you* that charged me with this task."

"Oh?"

"I do not know if you are prepared to be told all of it. I do not know if you will be willing to believe it."

"My old Friend, the other night I had to assume Mosi would be able to believe, if fate had not intervened, he would have been my nephew. He seemed to handle that. Anything you have to tell me I will believe, My Brother. Granted, I may not like it, but I will believe it."

"The Colonel told me to keep them safe."

"Oh, the *Obersti*—you took them back to the *Schutztruppen?*"

"No, no, no. Not the *Obersti*—the other Colonel, Colonel Meinhartzhagen."

"How the hell did he know you had them?"

"One of my cousins in my village was one of his men—that is, in his pay. He had been following your travels from before the time you met Pietr Pretorius down in the Rufiji Delta." Henry began to interrupt, but Jabari held up his hand to silence him. "Another of his men—I believe he was one of the cooks for the *Königsberg*—was watching you. The Colonel knew much about you."

"And how much did *you* tell him?"

"Not much. There was no need. He knew far more about you than me." Jabari blinked.

Henry shrugged. Knowing Meinhartzhagen—which evidently wasn't anywhere near as well as he thought he did—nothing about the feisty little Brit surprised him. "It sounds as though he actually came to your village."

"Dressed like an Arab. How did he put it?" Jabari thought for a moment. "Ah, *a la* Pretorius. I of course was shocked. But he said he was only coming to see if my wound was healing. I have never found out how he knew about that, for my cousin swore he did not tell him—so there must have been someone else in the village also in his service—and to make apologies for the evil intent of the South African."

"He knew about that?" Henry blurted.

Jabari shrugged. The fact that the Colonel made the apology proved the point. "He said he had made sure you were sent safely out of the country. That's when he told me to look after your journals because they were probably the only honest thing that would ever be written about— "Our little corner of the war"—Yes, that's what he called it: "Our little corner of the war." Then he asked me to go back to the *Schutztruppen*."

"So you were one of his spies?" Henry said flatly.

"No, My Brother, I refused to go on his terms. I told him I was going anyway, because I am Wahehe, but I would not be his spy. I was sure he had others, in any case."

"And he accepted those terms?"

"Yes. We made contact again after the war. He was the one who made certain Mosi went to the right schools and was sent to the proper university. He once wrote Mosi was a surrogate son for him, to take the place of the son he lost in the war. It made him very sad, old Friend."

"I know, old Friend. It makes us all very sad—Richard, Paul, and I...all losing sons and being unable to help an old Friend bear the grief." Henry fell silent. *I think I've just decided to get hold of Slim Wilhelm when*

I get home. I think he's still on the board of the Wharton School. If he isn't, he knows who is. I think Bobby would like that.

CHAPTER EIGHTY

Saturday, August 15, 1953
German Lloyd Liner *SS Danzig*
The Indian Ocean

enry Feller closed the last of his journals. *They were all there. Nothing
had been lost save time. Jabari had done exactly as he had been asked
to do. He had kept the journals safe and ready to deliver back into Henry's
hands. His eldest son first, and then his grandson had been charged with
carrying on the commission should Jabari die before the author could retrieve
his books. All five journals had obviously been well cared for, dusted often
and not allowed to rot or mildew. It must have been a prodigious task.*

Lying on his berth in his cabin, Henry read through the words he
had written a lifetime before, and each word brought back the events
and the emotions. And the people. The journals were a set of volumes
filled with the dead—black and white, English, German, Wahehe,
Kikuyu, farmer, soldier, bureaucrat, scientist. They were all there as
they had been.

On the fourth day out from Dar es Salaam, he finished the last
journal. He had been reading steadily since the ship departed, sailing
out through the same channel taken by the *Königsberg* nearly forty years
before. For the next days, he had food delivered to his cabin, sending his
apologies to the Captain and the rest of the Lloyd staff.

Henry set the journals on the sideboard and opened one of the
small closets built into various nooks and otherwise wasted spaces in
the cabin. He carried the extracted case to the desk and popped open
the latch. After some thought, he decided to use the typewriter without
removing it from the bottom of the carrying case, unfastening only the
top and setting it aside. The little rubber pegs on the bottom of the case
would hold the affair steady on the desktop and keep it from sliding
around while he worked. From the top left-hand drawer of the desk he
took out two sheets and a piece of carbon paper, making a neat sandwich
to roll into the typewriter. Mentally counting letters and spaces, he

moved the carriage half of his count plus one space, set the Capital Lock and began to type:

HAYA SAFARI:
An African Adventure
From the Journals of Henry A. Feller

He pulled the sheet of paper from the typewriter and looked it over. It looked right, so he rolled a new page onto the platen and after typing an "i" at the middle of the top, three single spaces down, he punched the spacebar eight times, indenting, and set the tab stop. And then he typed from memory—he could go back and check it later, but considering it was one of his favorites, he was pretty sure he was spot on.

> **Old men forget; yet all shall be forgot,**
> **But he'll remember, with advantages,**
> **What feats he did that day.**
> **Then shall our names,**
> **Familiar in his mouth as household words…**
> **Be in their flowing cups freshly rememb'red.**
> **This story shall the good man teach his son…**
> **And Crispin Crispian shall ne'er go by,**
> **From this day to the ending of the world,**
> **But we in it shall be remembered…**

EPILOGUE

Friday, September 22, 1958
Congregational Cemetery
Mitchell, South Dakota

*K*athleen Lindstrup, thirty-three years old, mother of two—a son and a daughter—whose husband Darryl ran Lindstrup Tractor Supply, was busily pruning away a lot of the third season growth on the great yellow rose bush. It was the third one she could remember planting over the years, and it was nearing the end of its life. She was already thinking about what she was going to replace it with. Of course it would still be a yellow rose of some sort—that was family tradition—and since her father had died when she was thirteen, the tending of the family plot had been her job. Twenty years. Longer by half than the years she and Dare had been married, a month after she turned twenty-one and two days after he had been discharged from the Army Air Force following three years of being, as he called it, "a weather clerk sitting on or in a snow-drift in Alaska." He often joked about his service, though he told her it had been mostly numbingly boring.*

There had been just the one stone when she was a little girl, the big reddish marble stone was now in the middle of the plot, where her grandmother and grandfather were buried, the people she had never met and, therefore, had no memory of. To the right was her mother and father's—a slightly smaller grey stone nearly hidden by prairie asters.

As she was pruning, Kathleen heard tires crunch on the gravel drive and turned to see a large and new, greenish-blue Cadillac Coupe de Ville roll to a stop at the edge of the walk leading to the little fenced-in area where she knelt. She didn't recognize the car. Nobody in Mitchell had a car like that. Nobody in Mitchell could *afford* a car like that. And even if they could, they *wouldn't* because it would be like thumbing their noses at their neighbors. Evidently the visitor was from out-of-town, and had enough wherewithal to buy into the "You Auto Buy Now" advertising campaign that was trying to undo the slow car sales across the country.

A quick lean to the side and she could see the Florida license plate, and she smiled, congratulating herself on her astute logic.

The man who climbed slowly out of the Cadillac was elderly and had the bad coloring of someone who was seriously ill and knew it. He moved slowly around the front of the car and, with the aid of a cane, began a shuffling, small-stepped walk down the pathway, taking care where he gingerly placed his feet for each step. When he came to the fence, he stopped and looked in toward the stones, as if to assure himself he was in the right place.

Kathleen wasn't sure he had seen her kneeling by the fence, so she made as much noise as she could in rising. She didn't want to give him a heart attack. "Can I help you find someone?" she asked.

He turned to her and smiled. The young lady he saw was medium height, maybe five foot six or seven, with a slim body, barely covered, by his way of thinking, by the Capri pants and light blouse she wore. Her hair was naturally blond and hung straight below her shoulders, in conflict with the current fad of short, curled, hair. And her eyes were startlingly blue. He wondered if she had ever seen a picture of his mother, because she was a dead ringer for her. "No, this is the right place—just that it's changed considerably since the last time I was here. There was only Mom and Pa's stone then. I assume the other one is Junior's, but then again, 'to assume makes an ass of you and me,'" he chuckled.

"You must be my Uncle Henry, the writer," the woman said.

"And you are?"

"I'm Kathleen Lindstrup. That is, I was Kathleen Feller."

"That was my mother's name."

"Yes, I know. I was named after her. Emil was my father."

"My brother."

"Yes."

"And did he tell you about my being the black sheep of the family— that I was the biggest bastard he ever met?"

"No, the only 'biggest' he ever mentioned in regard to you was you were the biggest thing to ever come out of Mitchell, South Dakota."

451

"Humpf—you aren't just saying that to get on my good side, are you?" The words sounded harsh but were belied by the smile on the man's face.

"No, I wouldn't do that. If I wanted to get on your good side, I'd just quote portions of your books. Dad had them all, you know. He practically had them memorized. And he practically had us memorize them. I told him he ought to send them to you to have you sign them, but he was too damn stubborn—said it ran in the family. I know you didn't part on the best of terms."

"That, my newly found niece, is possibly the understatement of the century—well, anyway, the half-century. What I just said—the part about being the biggest bastard—is pret' near a direct quote, and as I recall, the only usable one in most polite company."

"Well then, could I make up for his stubbornness and ask you to sign them for me?"

"You could do that."

"And would you?"

Henry thought for a minute. It was impossible to tell what he was thinking by his blank facial expression. Finally, he said, "I'd be delighted."

"Good. You can follow me home and I'll make you a cup of coffee. With any luck, my husband will be there and you can meet him and the kids."

"That would be nice. It's always an occasion to meet family you didn't know you had. And by the way, it looks like you have been taking very good care of the plot. You must care about them a great deal."

"Yes, I do."

Kathleen started to walk toward the gate when Henry called after her, "I don't see a car or anything. How did you get here?"

"Oh, we just live down the road. I walk."

"Well, we can't have that. Climb in. I'll drive you home."

"Thank you, that would be nice. I've never ridden in a car like that."

"You'll get used to it." Henry held the door of the Coupe de Ville open for his niece.

The Federal Republic of Germany finally managed to pass a bill through the *Bundestag* to pay the veterans of *Generalmajor* Paul Emil Von Lettow-Vorbeck's *Schutztruppen*. In 1961, the *Bundebanc* once again sent a representative to the former Colony, this time to Kigomo on the shore of Lake Tanganyika. The survivors of the 1914-18 war gathered there, many for the second time in ten years, and were paid—with interest—what they were owed.

Jabari Rajabu was not among them. Jabari died at Mosi's home in 1959. One of his proudest possessions was a Swahili Language copy of *Haya Safari, An African Adventure,* signed by the author and dedicated to him and to his sister, Zanta. It is kept proudly encased over the mantle above his grandson's fireplace.

Following the awarding of his Master of Arts degree in International Business from the Wharton School, Mosi Rajabu returned to Tanganyika and eventually became the Minister of Economics for the Confederated Republic of Tanzania. He retired to his farm in the Pare Hills in 1991.

Generalmajor Paul Emil Von Lettow-Vorbeck returned to Germany. In declining health, he reopened his long-standing correspondence with novelist Isak Dinesen—Karen Blixen—best known for her 1938 novel *Out of Africa.* They had met on the ship to Mombasa in 1914. They met twice more in his life: in 1940, just a week before the German invasion of Denmark, and again in 1958, when he was living in Hamburg near his daughter, *Gräfin* Ruth von Rantzau. Isak Dinesen sent him flowers on his ninetieth birthday. Paul Emil Von Lettow-Vorbeck died March 9, 1964, at the age of ninety-four. He preceded his long-time friend Henry Feller in death by only four months.

Henry August Feller died of congestive heart failure in Coral Gables, Florida, on July 12, 1964. He is buried in the section of Woodlawn Park Cemetery in Miami set aside for the veterans of World War I. Funeral services were conducted by his son, The Most Reverend Otis Feller, D.D., Retired, who now resides in Jacksonville, Florida. Henry Feller's other surviving son, Doctor Kevin Thomas Feller, Ph.D., is professor emeritus of history at Shimer College in Waukegan, Illinois. Henry Feller's grandson, Colonel Robert Henry Feller, USMC, Retired, holds the David Welsh Chair in Military History at the University of Minnesota.

Oh yes—the two china-head dolls that were sent west by Grandmother Kathleen Mahoney to her granddaughter and namesake, Kathleen Feller (nee) Mahoney, were finally donated to the Enchanted World Doll Museum in Mitchell, South Dakota, by the estate of the late Kathleen Lindstrup in 1983.

Now... *this* part of the story is over.

[1] What the Red Army soldiers called themselves. The term comes from the odd green color of the Red Army uniform. Additionally, cucumbers were and are a favorite but very disposable food.

[2] The political branch of the Red Army. The Waffen SS and such portions of the regular German Army who would obey were under standing orders from Hitler and Himmler to summarily execute any commissar taken captive.

[3] The Soviets called it a hospital, but it was a prison. By the time of the fall of the Soviet Union, it was the KGB's second most important building.

[4] The English Raj equivalent of the German *Machs schnell* and the French and American use in Indochina of *Di Di Mau* or *Di Di Maulen*.

[5] The *SMS Maria von Stettin*, according to Charles Miller's *Battle for the Bundu*, (1974) was next seen in the harbor of Batavia, Java, several weeks later, not appearing any the worse for wear.

[6] VC = Recipient of the Victoria Cross, the highest British award for Valor. GCB = Knight Grand Commander of the Order of Bath, the British senior order of knighthood. GCMG = Knight Grand Cross of the Order of St Michael and Saint George, the sixth highest order in the British service. Honored individuals have usually rendered important service in relation to the Commonwealth or foreign nations. Humorously known as "God calls me God."

[7] Chaumont was the site of the American First Army Headquarters.

[8] The four National Guard Regiments forming the 83rd and 84th Infantry Brigades of the 42nd Rainbow Division were all originally combat-tested in the Civil War: the 165th had been the 69th New York (Irish); the 166th had been the 4th Ohio; the 167th had been the 4th Alabama; and the 168th, a consolidation of several Iowa regiments.

[9] The name given to the fore-and-aft overseas cap by the doughboys—'doughs' for short—the apocryphal story of its naming came out of the 167th Infantry after the Red Cross Farm battle, when Major General Menoher, the Rainbow commander asked one of the privates of the 167th if he knew the name of his brigade (the 84th) commander. "General MacArthur, Sir," was the reply. And what kind of general was he, Menoher asked, expecting the Alabamian to say 'A Brigadier General.' Instead, after careful consideration, the recalcitrant Rebel blurted out "Well, I'll tell y'all, by God, he's a piss cutter!"

[10] Forty and Eight, the painted instructions on the outside of French freight cars. *Quarante hommes et huit cheval*; literally 40 men or 8 horses. It was a name taken up by veterans following the Great War, The Forty & Eight Society which was a portion of the Veterans of Foreign Wars/ American Legion for the rest of the Twentieth Centnury.

[11] *Rocks and Shoals* was the popular name for the *Rules Governing the Naval Service* the equivalent of the Army's *Code of Military Justice* and *The Articles of War*.

[12] Charles C. Dawes, a banker, had been in charge of procurement for the Wilson Administration during World War I, and was put in charge of an international commission by President Calvin Coolidge (Silent Cal) in 1923-24 charged with solving the problem of hyperinflation of the Deutschemark in the Weimar Republic. France and Britain had demanded reparations in the billions of dollars and goods (railroad cars, merchant ships, and machine tools, for example, all without payment of any sort, which demands were to be satisfied by the Weimar's Republic's printing increasing billions of papers bills, unbacked by hard money. The result: England and France began to actually purchase goods from Germany in 1923, those goods were paid for with the nearly-worthless paper; thus, hyperinflation, to the point wherein it was more economical to burn money than to try to buy firewood with it (ushering in the era of the 1 Million DM postage stamp). By April 1924, the Dawes Commission had proposed that the reparations of the Versailles Treaty be lowered, and that the Deutschemark be pegged to the US gold-standard dollar, that half of the future reparations come from taxes, and that the United States lend Germany money to get back on its economic feet. The Dawes Plan earned Dawes and Sir Josiah Stamp Nobel Peace Prizes, and the everlasting enmity of the French.

[13] In a classic early broadcasting gaff, national radio commentator Harry Von Zell, introducing the new President of the United States, declared "Ladies and Gentlemen, The President of the United States of America, HOOVBERT HEEVER" over nationwide radio.

[14] A part of the post-World War Two legislation package, along with the GI Bill, to help discharged veterans return to civilian life. The program offered those veterans who did not have a job to return to immediately, twenty dollars a week for fifty-two weeks.

[15] Douglas MacArthur and his first wife, heiress Henriette Louise Cromwell Brooks, the step daughter of Edward Stotesbury were divorced in 1929. Louise's Brother Jimmy Cromwell Jr., was no less a socialite, in his twenties he married Delphine Dodge, daughter of Horace E and Anna Dodge of automotive fame. After that marriage went down the tube, he married Doris Duke in 1935, but that only lasted a couple of years. Delphine in the meanwhile took up with an Irish boxer—and drank herself to death in 1943. Louise ended up married to the actor Lionel Atwill, best known for his role as the police inspector in *Frankenstein*. He was blackballed by the Hays Commission after being implicated in an orgy and rape scandal in 1943 for which he received five-years probation.